# PURSUED

## *A Maggie McKenzie Mystery*

# PURSUED

*A Maggie McKenzie Mystery*

## A NOVEL

# LYNN GARDNER

Covenant Communications, Inc.

Cover image: *Young Woman Holding Camera, Front View* by David De Lossy © Photodisc / *Alamy, and Photographer Silhouette on Foggy Field* © Tomas Bercic.

Cover design copyrighted 2009 by Covenant Communications, Inc.

Published by Covenant Communications, Inc.
American Fork, Utah

Printed in U.S.A.
First Printing: June 2009

16 15 14 13 12 11 10 09    10 9 8 7 6 5 4 3 2 1

ISBN-13 978-1-59811-550-5
ISBN-10 1-59811-550-2

*My thanks to Nikki, who diligently read every draft of this book, all six of them, and to Rachel, Traci, and Rebecca for their red pencil abilities. And special thanks to my husband, who patiently tolerates being ignored while I'm writing.*

# ONE

London
Wednesday, 4:00 P.M.

The tall man in the Armani suit left St. Martin-in-the-Fields Church while the afternoon concert was still in progress, pausing on the top step to survey Trafalgar Square below before he put his cell phone to his ear. "Yes?"

"The goods arrived an hour ago. The inventory is complete."

His reply was clipped and quick. "Transport everything immediately to the tunnel. Make sure you're not stopped on the way."

"Sure, boss. I know the drill. Any word from Section Two?"

"Watch the news," he retorted, casually descending the steps. "You'll know as soon as the rest of the world. Report when the commodities are safely stored." He ended the call, slid the phone into his suit pocket, and entered the Café in the Crypt below St. Martin's Church with a satisfied smile. One more detail in the design had fallen into place without complication.

* * *

Jakarta, Indonesia
Wednesday, 11:00 P.M. (4:00 P.M. London time)

"Is the bomb ready?" the man in the black skullcap asked quietly.

"Yes, sir. I've armed it myself," the ex-soldier replied. "I loved watching these in Afghanistan. It's awesome how they totally annihilate everything in range."

"Let's get this plane in the air. We have twenty minutes to target. The boss wants to see the explosion on the five o'clock news in London."

"Afraid all he'll see is the aftermath, sir. Who's going to film it if they don't know it's coming?"

The man in the skullcap smiled. "The boss has arranged for a news crew to film the village on the edge of town from the top of the hill. They'll be right in place to capture the whole thing for the evening news."

"Hope that film crew isn't too close. These aren't called Daisy Cutters for nothing. They cut the daisies, all right, and level everything else within a nine-hundred-foot radius."

\* \* \*

Los Angeles International Airport (LAX)
Wednesday, 8:00 A.M. (4:00 P.M. London time)

Maggie McKenzie settled into a quiet corner of the airport awaiting the boarding call for her flight to London. As she pulled out her new digital camera to view the last few shots, she noted the crowd gathering under a TV monitor down the terminal. Her cell phone rang before she could muster enough curiosity to investigate what the excitement was about.

"Hi, Alyssa."

"Maggie, you forgot something important."

"What?"

"Me! I want to go with you!"

Maggie laughed. "We've been through this a dozen times. I don't know how long this assignment will take, and you can't miss the start of classes." Though they were identical twins, Maggie felt older than and very protective of her sister.

"I'd rather be with you." Suddenly Alyssa gasped. "Maggie, can you see a TV monitor from where you are? You'll never believe what's happening at LAX . . ."

Maggie dropped her camera into her over-sized bag and sprinted for the TV. "Alyssa, what's going on?" she asked as she ran. She pictured Alyssa's sapphire eyes wide with excitement and her shoulder-length auburn hair swirling as she paced in front of the TV.

Alyssa's phone was breaking up. ". . . film crew . . . Mel Gibson's arrival from Australia . . . terminal four . . ." Maggie could only hear a few words before static obliterated the rest. She hung up and joined the crowd at the TV monitor to see the actor and his family besieged by reporters and microphones as airport security rushed the scene.

Suddenly the report turned into an LAX-only broadcast. The fuzzy picture of a man appeared on the screen. Apparently several men had been detained for carrying dangerous items in their luggage. Another member of their party had slipped away unnoticed and was now wanted for questioning.

"The man we are seeking wore a gray sport coat, black turtleneck, and had a dark, neat beard. If you see him, please notify security immediately. He was last seen in terminal four." The pictures were too fuzzy to identify the man, but Maggie finished watching the broadcast as it repeated itself, then she headed back to the waiting area near her gate.

Maggie had only gone a couple of steps when she encountered a family in crisis in the middle of the terminal walkway. A crying child clung to her mother, who was trying to handle her frightened daughter, a small baby, and their luggage.

"Are we going to be on the airplane with that bad man?" the girl asked tearfully.

"Oh, no," her mother assured her unhappy daughter. "He was hurrying to catch another flight. He didn't mean to knock you over. It was an accident, Tara."

That didn't console the child. "He scared me. He yelled at me," she said, still sobbing.

"He was just in a big hurry and he didn't see you," her mother assured her. Maggie stepped closer to the harried woman kneeling in the midst of terminal passenger traffic. "Can I help?"

"Thanks, we'll be okay," the young woman said. "Tara was just knocked on the floor by someone racing to catch a flight. I'm sure he didn't see her, but he yelled at her and it scared her."

Maggie knelt beside them. "Tara, I'm a photographer. Would you like to see the pictures I took this morning? I have a mama deer and her baby and a mother cat and her kittens."

Tara let go of her mother's neck and looked at Maggie. "Do you really have a picture of a baby deer?" She sniffed, wiping her nose on her sleeve.

"I do." Maggie nodded and pulled her camera from her bag. "And I'd love to have a picture of you, too." She glanced at Tara's mother. "Would it be okay if I took her picture?"

The young mother stood and shifted the baby into her other arm. "Yes." She smiled. "Thank you for distracting her."

Maggie framed the child's tear-streaked face in her viewer, snapped the picture, and backed away to click a full shot of the child. "Can I get a picture with your pretty suitcase?"

Tara posed, holding her miniature pink wheeled carry-on. As Maggie snapped the picture, a man ran into the shot and into Maggie, nearly knocking the camera from her hands. He grabbed her to keep them from both hitting the floor, then instead of apologizing, he tossed a curse at her and raced on through the terminal with two security guards in close pursuit.

It took Maggie a minute to realize the man wore a gray jacket and black turtleneck shirt. And he had a short, well-trimmed black beard. She gasped. The man from the broadcast.

\* \* \*

London
Wednesday, 4:10 P.M.

When his phone buzzed, the tall man in the expensive Italian suit glanced across the table in the underground Café in the Crypt. "Pardon me," he murmured to his table companion, turning slightly away. "Yes?" he said quietly into the phone.

"They blew it. Everyone's been arrested except Ulric. They're chasing him through the airport, but so far he's evaded them. What now?"

The man smiled apologetically at the gentleman sipping tea across the table. "Will you excuse me, please? My secretary has a question." He rose and stepped outside to reply. "Deliver the commodities and stay with them until you hear from me."

"Then what?"

"Don't call me again unless it's an emergency. Phase two of the maneuver is ready. Those personnel were expendable, with the exception of Ulric. We need what he's carrying, and we needed it yesterday."

He pocketed the phone, brushed an imaginary piece of lint from his sleeve, and returned to the table. "So many details to be taken care of," he smiled as he sat down and reached for his cup.

"Is your secretary able to keep things in order, then?" the older man asked politely.

"Absolutely, but when it comes to the intricate business of government, she's always very careful to get the details perfect. She doesn't want to make any mistakes." He glanced at his watch. "Sorry, old chap. I have to run or I'll miss my five o'clock appointment. See you Saturday at the club."

\* \* \*

Madrid, Spain
Wednesday, 5:15 P.M. (4:15 P.M. London time)

"Miguel, get that Daisy Cutter loaded on the plane. If we're late, heads will roll, and yours will be the first to hit the dirt."

"Si, señor. I wish to live to see the aftermath of this weapon. Nothing will remain when it detonates."

"Get a move on, man. We have to make the evening news in London so the boss will know we followed his orders precisely."

"Señor, one thing puzzles me. Why did you call the news channel?"

"So they can film this awesome baby when it does its job and shows the world we mean business. Hurry up."

\* \* \*

LAX
Wednesday, 8:15 A.M. (4:15 P.M. London time)

Maggie and little Tara followed Tara's mother and the baby to the chairs near the boarding gate.

"I'm Jennie," Tara's mother said, settling into a chair with the baby and depositing their bags at her feet. "Thanks so much for helping." She smiled gratefully. "At least the baby wasn't crying at the same time. I hope that man didn't hurt you when he bumped into you. It would have been a shame if he'd knocked your camera to the floor."

"I'm Maggie. No, he didn't hurt me, and yes, it would have been a disaster if my camera had been broken."

"Will you read me a story?" Tara asked, looking up at Maggie with pleading eyes. "I brought my favorite book." Maggie sat next to Jennie with Tara on her lap and read the little book cover to cover—twice.

"Thank you so much, Maggie," Jennie said. "I hate having to check in two to three hours early for international flights. It feels like forever, especially with an active four-year-old and a baby. We were doing fine for a while, but by the time you met us, I was at the end of my rope. I don't know how I would have handled them both without your help."

Maggie smiled. "It's been my pleasure. The wait is frustrating for me too. I'm glad this search for the guy in the turtleneck isn't going to postpone our departure."

"Can I see the pictures now? The ones with the deers and kittens?" Tara asked.

"Of course." Maggie called up the pictures on her camera. She quickly scanned forward to the picture of the doe and fawn she'd snapped at dawn as she'd walked on the trail above Alyssa's family's estate on the outskirts of San Buenaventura. "I took this just at sunrise when the deer had come down to the spring to drink. Look how big the little deer's eyes are, and see her spindly little legs."

Tara nodded. "I've only seen deer in the zoo. But Melanie has a black cat that just had six black kittens. Can I see the picture of your cat and her kittens?"

Maggie found the picture of the tabby cat and her five tawny-colored babies. "This is my sister Alyssa's cat."

Before she could say more, she heard someone say, "I think that redheaded woman was taking pictures when he came through here. Maybe she got one of him."

Maggie looked up to see a man pointing at her and two airport security guards hurrying toward her. She moved Tara from her lap onto the seat next to her and stood.

"Ma'am, I understand you may have a picture of the man who ran through the terminal a few minutes ago. Is your camera digital, and if so, could we see the photos you were taking recently?" the uniformed guard asked politely.

"Of course," Maggie said. She turned the viewer back to her last photo of Tara. "I was taking a picture of Tara, and he ran right into the shot." She handed the camera to the guard.

He showed it to the other officer. "It's much better than the one on the security camera." Turning back to Maggie, he said, "We'll have to take your camera, ma'am. We need this picture. This man is a person of interest in a terrorist investigation. He's been spotted leaving the airport, and we could use your photo to help apprehend the guy."

"Sorry. You can't have the camera, but if you can get me to a computer, I'll download it for you. I'm a journalist on assignment, and I have to have my camera." Just then Maggie heard the boarding call for her flight to London. "And I'm leaving on that flight that's boarding right now."

"I'm afraid that won't be possible. We'll need you and the camera to remain until we get that photo."

Maggie panicked. She couldn't miss this flight, and she absolutely wouldn't go without her camera. Examining her options, she hit on a simple but slightly expensive solution. She sighed. "Okay. Here's the memory stick." She popped the stick out of the camera and handed it to the guard.

She dug a business card from her bag and gave him that, too. "Here's my card if you need to get in touch with me later. I work for the San Buenaventura newspaper, just up the coast. You can reach me through the paper if you have any questions before I get back. However, that shouldn't be necessary. This is what you wanted—you've got your picture. I'm out fifty dollars and some nice shots—but I'm sure it's worth it."

The guard hesitated, but Maggie didn't give him time to think of another reason she shouldn't get on the airplane. She shouldered her bag and headed for the line forming at the gate. Jennie was struggling to gather up her two children and their paraphernalia, and as Maggie glanced back over her shoulder to see if the guards really were going to let her go, she realized Jennie needed help.

Hurrying back, she asked, "Are you going to England? Is this your flight?"

When Jennie nodded, tickets in her mouth, Maggie grabbed the diaper bag and held out her hand to Tara. "It seems we get to fly on the same airplane, Tara. Will you hold my hand and we'll go get in line? Do you have everything?"

Tara nodded and pointed at her little pink carry-on. "It's all in here, even my teddy bear."

Maggie helped Jennie to the head of the line where families with small children were boarding first. "Can you handle it from here?" Maggie asked the stressed young mother.

"Yes, thanks. I'm always afraid Tara will wander away while I'm concentrating on diaper bags and purses and carry-ons. She's curious as a puppy—she stops to look at everything and gets lost if I don't have hold of her, but I don't have enough hands!" She smiled. "Thanks again for keeping her busy earlier."

"I'll find you when we get to Montreal and help you during our layover," Maggie promised and waved at Tara as they disappeared into the jetway to the airplane. She stood waiting in line for her section to board, unaware of the man who kept moving closer to her. Only when the hair on the back of her neck stood up did she pivot slowly and look straight up into the coal-black eyes of a man standing inches behind her.

He wore a brown leather jacket, plaid shirt and jeans, and was clean shaven—nothing out of the ordinary, really. Yet his intense stare made her uncomfortable, and she instinctively clutched her bag tighter. A chill shivered through her, and she quickly turned around, hoping he wouldn't be sitting near her. There was something very creepy about this man with dark, angry eyes and a jagged scar down one side of his face. And she wished someone would tell him to cut down on the after-shave. But that someone wasn't going to be her.

# TWO

Private runway outside Washington, D.C.
Wednesday, 11:15 A.M. (4:15 P.M. London time)

A battered jeep sped across the tarmac to the aircraft currently being loaded by two burly men who looked like longshoremen.

"Finished?" the driver asked as he jumped out of the jeep.

"Ready to go!" one of the burly men answered. "This baby's gonna make someone sit up and take notice. There's not much that delivers the shock and awe of this monster."

"Good. That's what we want. When they see what's left of the target, they'll jump to do our bidding. Now let's get this thing in the air. The boss has zero tolerance for inefficiency."

* * *

LAX
Wednesday, 8:45 A.M. (4:45 P.M. London time)

Maggie arranged her carry-on under the seat in front of her so she could access her laptop without getting into the overhead compartment. She needed to work during the flight to prepare for her assignment, but in the meantime she slipped a fresh memory card into her camera. She loved the newest-generation technology that contained tons of memory, eliminating the requirement for multiple clips to accommodate all the pictures she took on assignment.

As the plane taxied onto the runway, Maggie breathed a sigh of relief that the search for the man in the airport hadn't prevented them from

leaving on time. She retrieved the manila envelope her editor, Lionel
Lawson, had given her last night as she left the office. In her haste to
pack and arrive at the airport on time, she hadn't bothered to look at it
yet. She assumed she knew the contents, more or less. To her surprise,
she discovered an old envelope tucked inside. The British postmark
intrigued her, but Lionel's note contained a bigger shock.

> *The private investigator I hired obtained this letter from the*
> *midwife who delivered your biological brother. Don't know*
> *if this old address will be any help, but while you're pursuing*
> *your primary assignment, see if you can locate this family.*
> *Apparently they adopted the boy at birth.*

Maggie sat motionless, staring at the name and address on the
twenty-six-year-old envelope. A brother. Another of Lily's children
whom her husband, Cleat, had lied about, telling Lily the baby had died
at birth. Had Lionel revealed this new information to Lily and Alyssa
yet, or was he waiting for Maggie to see what she could find in England?

Until last Christmas, Maggie didn't know she had been adopted and
had an identical twin sister, Alyssa. On Maggie's first day at her new job
with the *San Buenaventura Press,* she had discovered her birth mother,
Lily. Lily managed the newspaper offices where Lionel Lawson was
editor-in-chief. To complicate matters further, her new boss, Lionel
Lawson, was the adoptive father of Alyssa. Maggie shook her head.
What a tangled web.

She thought of Alyssa and what she called the "princess syndrome"—
pampered, pretty, precocious, and sometimes petulant when she didn't
get her way. But during the last six months Alyssa had shed the air of
discouragement and depression that had resonated from her when
Maggie and Flynn found her in Louisiana. For seven years she'd been
mentally beaten down by her biological father, who had kidnapped her
on her sixteenth birthday.

Maggie wondered if Dr. Flynn Ford had kept his promise to help
Alyssa through the "reentering" process after her kidnapping. Since
Maggie was out of town on assignment so often, Alyssa could easily
have been meeting with Dr. Ford to learn how to extinguish the
anger and resentment victims frequently exhibit after their ordeal.

Alyssa certainly had ample cause to be engulfed by those debilitating emotions. But Maggie would never know if that was happening, because Flynn had vowed to stay out of her life until December to let her decide if she really loved him, while at the same time deciding his true feelings for her—and her religion.

\* \* \*

London
Wednesday, 4:45 P.M.

The tall man folded himself into the taxi and gave an address in the government district of London. "Could you hurry, please? I have an important appointment at five o'clock. I'll double your fare if you get me there in time."

The cabbie became serious about his driving, and his passenger leaned back and checked his phone messages. Only one needed an immediate answer.

"Yes, Sylvia?" he said, noting with satisfaction he had chosen the right driver. Barring a traffic snarl, he could easily make it to his office before five o'clock.

"The cabinet minister's secretary called, sir. He'd like to meet you on Saturday for a business lunch. Shall I tell him you can be there?"

"Yes, but check my calendar for the time. I'm meeting Sir Wilford at the club in the afternoon. Leave me enough time to get from lunch to the club."

"Yes, sir."

"Anything else, Sylvia?"

"No, sir. It's been a peaceful afternoon."

"Thank you, Sylvia. I'm returning to the office now. If there's nothing else, you can go home."

"Thank you, sir. I appreciate that."

He rang off, pocketed the cell phone, and smiled. *That will be the last peaceful afternoon you'll have for a long time, Sylvia,* he thought. *You'd better enjoy it.*

\* \* \*

Sydney, Australia
Thursday, 3:50 P.M. (Wednesday, 4:50 P.M. London time)

"Aw, Boss, do we really have to blow up the Harbor Bridge? Can't we make your statement with Ayres Rock or something? My dad worked on this bridge seventy-five years ago. It's almost like a member of the family."

Immediately Orville was sorry he'd spoken. The bigger man whirled on him with murder in his eye. "Get that loaded on the dolly and to the plane before I tie you to the bomb and send you down with it."

The cowering man didn't reply, just helped load the Daisy Cutter as he silently pledged to get out of town as soon as this job was over and lose himself in some other part of the world where he'd never have to face this madman again. *Too bad about the bridge, and probably the Opera House, too,* he thought. That was a real shame to destroy something so beautiful and vital to the city.

Orville felt truly sorry he'd gotten involved in this caper. Some things just weren't worth all that money. If there was some way he could stop this bomb—and still live—he'd do it. This wasn't what he'd bargained for when he signed on to take his brother's place. He hadn't known what the target was until this morning, and he wanted no part of destroying those historical landmarks.

If Hank, Orville's no-good brother, hadn't broken his leg, he would be doing this. But if Orville could screw up the drop, and still get away, it might be worth the try. Maybe.

\* \* \*

London
Wednesday, 4:55 P.M.

The man in the gray Armani suit generously tipped the cabbie, then nodded to his secretary as she exited the building and hurried to catch the bus down the street. He glanced at his watch, then entered the gray stone building and took the elevator to his seventh-floor office.

He switched on the television and settled back in the burgundy leather chair to watch the world's reaction to his latest handiwork—his greatest accomplishment yet.

\* \* \*

Sydney, Australia
Thursday, 3:58 A.M. (Wednesday, 4:58 P.M. London time)

"Two minutes to drop," the Boss said, checking his watch. "Get it ready."

Orville knew this was his last chance to save his beloved Harbor Bridge, as well as the lives of all those on the bridge or anywhere near it. He wasn't a bad man, unlike his brother, who was rotten through and through. He'd just ended up in the wrong place at the wrong time. But maybe he could make amends for his brother—if he could just live through it.

He armed the bomb under the close scrutiny of the Boss, and then backed away. That's all Orville knew him by—the Boss. He didn't think his brother knew the Boss's name either. Just as well. Orville wished he didn't know what the Boss looked like—knowing things like that could ensure a man's death, and Orville wasn't ready to die. Not if he could help it.

The Boss, satisfied all was ready, headed forward to the cockpit to watch the target approach. Orville quickly defused the bomb and donned a parachute. When the bomb bay doors opened and the bomb dropped through, Orville went out right behind it. All he needed was a couple of hours' head start, and he'd be free—and safe.

\* \* \*

London
Wednesday, 5:05 P.M.

"We interrupt this newscast to bring you horrifying pictures from Indonesia of an unbelievable explosion on the outskirts of Jakarta. Flames are devouring everything left standing by what onlookers said was the most terrifying bomb blast they'd ever seen or heard. A news crew, filming nearby, caught the explosions on tape as they occurred."

The man in the Armani suit smiled with satisfaction.

The news reporter paused. "Wait, we have a report coming in from Spain. Another huge explosion has leveled several city blocks in a suburb of Madrid. Here are pictures from that incredible scene." The fiery pictures said it all. Death and destruction everywhere.

The news reporter looked stricken. "Unbelievable. We have still another explosion, this time in the United States, just outside the capital city of Washington, D.C. As yet, we have no word from any group claiming responsibility for these calamities. Here are pictures from the latest massive explosion that wiped out an entire suburb just a few miles from the White House."

Again the man in the Armani suit smiled. He settled back and crossed his legs, awaiting the final report—the one from Sydney that would confirm to the world that he meant business—and that nowhere in the world was safe. But when that report came, he sat straight up in his chair, then leaped to his feet and stared at the television in disbelief. He reached for his cell phone, his blue eyes turning ice cold. Someone would pay dearly for this.

"This just in from Sydney, Australia," the newscaster reported. "The famous Harbor Bridge, one of the identifying landmarks of this beautiful city on the bay, has just sustained superficial damage from an object dropped by an airplane. Authorities are speculating it may have been one of the targets of the unknown terrorists who have spread destruction across the world tonight. Divers have been called to find the object, hoping that it will shed some light on tonight's catastrophic events."

* * *

Flight 187, en route to Montreal
Wednesday, 10:30 A.M.

Maggie pored over her itinerary before checking her travel guide to Great Britain. She wanted to make sure she hit the highlights, but she also wanted to find some fascinating off-the-beaten-track spots to write about. And now she had to work in a visit to an additional town she'd never heard of.

The man in the seat next to her interrupted her thoughts. "You're concentrating awfully hard on something."

Maggie looked up from her guidebook. "I beg your pardon?"

"I said, you're concentrating very hard on that book. Is your trip business or pleasure?"

Maggie closed the book and laughed. "Both. I'm the travel editor for a small coastal newspaper, and we're getting ready to launch a new glossy travel magazine for the Sunday edition. My very pleasurable assignment is to bring a fresh perspective to Great Britain's typical hotspots, plus highlight a few other interesting places frequent travelers might not have discovered."

"Some people have all the luck," the man said enviously. "So what's on your schedule?"

Maggie turned in her seat, leaning against the window to take a good look at her neighbor—rusty brown eyes, curly auburn hair, and a sprinkling of freckles across his nose, but his most notable asset was his infectious smile. Warm and sincere, it made Maggie feel like he was truly interested in her instead of just idly passing the time during a boring flight.

"Actually, I've just done some quick revisions of my original plans. My boss tossed in an additional assignment, but I think I can hit most of my list and still work in this new destination. I thought I'd begin on the southern coast near Brighton and work my way over to Bath, then up to the Cotswolds, Stratford-upon-Avon, and back toward London. If I then base out of London, I can do most of the sights there and even manage a couple of day trips, possibly up to Oxford and over to Dover. Is there someplace you'd recommend that I might have not thought of?"

"I assume you're taking in the great cathedrals of England—Winchester, Salisbury, Canterbury, Coventry, St. Paul's. They shouldn't be missed. And if they are on your itinerary, a lesser known one that is a must-see is Wells Cathedral. If you're going to Bath, you'll be in the vicinity. It's definitely worth the stop."

"Thanks." Maggie jotted it down in the front of the book. "Anything else I shouldn't miss?

"You're not going to Wales?" he asked, raising an eyebrow.

"Actually, I didn't think I'd have the time," Maggie admitted ruefully. "This is my first trip to England, and I'm really just going by the recommendations in the guidebooks, though I've always been entranced by Wales and its legends."

"When you're at Bath, you're only about twenty miles from Wales. If you're serious about wanting my suggestions, I'd be happy to give you some of my favorite spots."

"Please do. By the way, I'm Maggie."

He flashed a smile. "Todd. Okay, let me take a closer look at your agenda, and I'll see if some of my favorite haunts are the same or nearby."

Engrossed in her conversation with Todd, Maggie failed to see the man who'd slipped into the empty seat behind them, listening intently to the conversation.

* * *

London
Wednesday, 6:00 P.M.

His phone call finished, instructions for the demise of all involved in the aborted explosion in Sydney having been relayed, the tall man in the gray suit fixed himself a drink, then turned back to the news. He glanced at his watch. Time the world knew what was about to happen.

Not wanting to miss a word of the broadcast, he aimed the remote control at the television set, turning up the volume.

"Minutes ago, a letter was delivered to Number Ten Downing Street, and simultaneously to leaders in Washington, Paris, Tokyo, and other capitals across the world. News agencies received a copy of this letter with instructions to read it at six o'clock. In keeping with those instructions, the message is as follows:

"'You have seen what we can do to your cities and countries. This is just a small taste of what is in store if you do not comply with our instructions. Within seventy-two hours, you will release all prisoners of al Qaeda from your prisons and deliver one billion dollars to the Swiss and Cayman bank accounts we specify. If these demands are not met precisely as instructed, Paris will be the next target. With each hour that passes without your complete compliance, another major city in the world will be destroyed. These will not be like the first targets, which were simply to get your attention. These will be city centers, capitol buildings, financial districts, your beloved national treasures. London will go an hour after Paris, and New York an hour after that. Los Angeles will be next, then Tokyo. Other cities in other countries will follow. I hope you have more intelligence than to let that happen. The countdown begins now.'"

The newscaster sat staring at the letter after he finished reading the contents on the air. He looked up into the camera, a stunned expression on his face.

The man in the Armani suit stood, smiled in satisfaction at the broadcast, finished his drink, and left the office. He would be at his country estate several miles out of London with a severely sprained ankle when they called him with the news. His injury would, unfortunately, prevent him from returning to London. That would give him time to check on the next phase of the plan.

\* \* \*

Flight 187, approaching Montreal
Wednesday, 12:10 p.m.

Todd drifted off to sleep, lulled by the classical symphonies in his earphones while Maggie reordered her agenda, making her first destination Arundel, a city south of London and very near Brighton. Todd had said the castle was worth a stop—and that just happened to be where the letter her boss had given her had been mailed from twenty-six years ago.

Maggie was amazed the investigator had been able to trace this information about the baby after so many years. Her brother would be about two years older than Maggie and Alyssa. Would there be a family resemblance? The twins had eyes of sapphire blue and hair the deep red color of a roan pony. She'd always wondered why she was the only one in the McKenzie family with red hair. Now she knew. What a shock it had been to discover—at age twenty-four—that she'd been adopted!

# THREE

Chicago, Illinois
Wednesday, 12:10 P.M. (6:10 P.M. London time)

Flynn Ford focused his intense, dark eyes away from the television report that had hit him like a fist in the stomach, and back to the number he was calling in Los Angeles.

"Alyssa, this is Dr. Ford. Did you say Maggie was going to London this week?"

"Hi, Dr. Ford. Yes, I talked to her before she got on the plane a few hours ago. Why?"

"Have you seen the news?" Flynn asked, trying to smooth back his unmanageable, thick dark hair. Combined with his tall, lean physique, it made him look more like a woodsy outdoorsman than an office-bound psychologist.

"You mean the excitement at LAX this morning?" she asked. "Actually, they're still looking for one of—"

"Alyssa," Flynn interrupted. "Where was Maggie going when she got to England? Did she leave an itinerary with you?"

Alyssa suddenly realized that this was not a social call. "Dr. Ford, you sound worried. What's the matter?"

"Apparently you haven't heard the most recent news: some terrorist organization has bombed several cities across the world and is promising to blow up more if their demands aren't met." He paused. "London is on that list."

"Oh, no! That's terrible! But I don't think even my dad has Maggie's itinerary. I'll give you her cell phone number," Alyssa said. "She got a new phone for international coverage. I know you weren't going to talk to her until Christmas, but . . ."

"Her life is more important than my self-imposed moratorium on seeing her. What's her number?" Flynn Ford scribbled the number as Alyssa gave it to him. "If you talk to her, ask her to stay away from London, but please don't mention that I called you."

"I don't understand."

"I'll explain later. For now let's just say I want her number in case things get crazy over there and I need to speak to her. Remember, don't tell her I called and asked about her. Those are doctor's orders. Speaking of doctor's orders, your next appointment with me is a week from tomorrow, right?"

"That's right, though I may need to postpone it." Alyssa said without an explanation. "Oh, by the way—happy thirty-third birthday tomorrow."

"How did you know?" Flynn asked in surprise.

"I cornered your secretary on my last visit." Alyssa laughed. "Do you want me to bring a cake to my next appointment?"

"Thanks for offering, but that's not necessary, Alyssa. Hopefully I'll see you next week." Flynn hung up and immediately called to book his ticket on the next flight to London.

* * *

Montreal, Canada
Wednesday afternoon (Wednesday evening in London)

When Maggie disembarked the flight from Los Angeles to catch her connecting flight to England, the world was in chaos. She was sick at the thought of all the destruction that had occurred and disgusted at the terrorists' demands. Though she knew she'd be flying into a targeted area, she not only felt a strange lack of fear, but an unsettling sense of excitement. But uncertain whether her editor would want her to continue on to London, she called the *San Buenaventura Press.*

"Hi, Lily. This is Maggie. Is the big boss in?"

"Oh, Maggie! I've been so worried about you. Where are you?"

"We just landed in Montreal. I have a layover before the flight to London takes off. That's why I called. In view of the current situation, does Mr. Lawson want me to continue?"

"As your mother, I'd like to tell you to turn around and come right home. I can't stand the thought of having found you only to lose you again. Unfortunately," Lily said with a sigh, "Lion gets to make those decisions, not me. Did you get the additional assignment he gave you?"

"Yes, Lily. I wondered if he'd told you about it. How do you feel about the possibility of having a grown son you thought was dead all these years?"

Lily paused before answering. "I don't dare even think about it. I won't get my hopes up until you've actually found the Rathford family and met him face-to-face."

"I understand. I'd planned to go to Brighton first, but amazingly, Arundel is just a few miles from there, so I've decided to make that my first stop. My curiosity will keep me from doing anything else until I know if he really is alive."

"Thank you, Maggie. Please stay connected so I'll know what's happening. Would it be too much trouble for you to call in every night?" Lily asked.

"I promise I'll let you know immediately when I find something," Maggie assured Lily. "If you don't hear from me, it's because I don't have any news to tell you."

"I'll connect you with Lion. Hold on a minute, dear."

Maggie held her breath while she waited for her editor to come on the line. As her birth mother, Lily would naturally want her out of danger. And Rose McKenzie, her adoptive mother, the only mother she'd ever known until seven months ago, would be having absolute fits worrying about her only daughter. Maggie decided to keep her and other family members updated by e-mail to avoid the inevitable scoldings she'd get over the phone.

But Maggie's excitement about the opportunities for her in England overrode any concerns she might have for her own safety. She not only had an opportunity to find a brother everyone thought was dead, but she also had a slight chance for some firsthand investigative reporting, the kind of work she had hoped for when she studied criminal investigation in college.

"McKenzie! You're not thinking of deserting your post, are you?" Lionel Lawson roared into the phone.

Maggie held her cell phone away from her ear. "No, sir. I'm excited to be on my way to London right now. The airlines are still up and running, though every flight will have a military presence. I just wanted to make sure that nothing had changed and that my assignment is still the same."

"Don't go getting yourself in over your head, but if the opportunity arises for a story . . . Well, you know what to do. I'll expect you to be in the thick of things if you have the chance."

Maggie smiled. "Yes, sir. You know I will be, if the opportunity presents itself."

"Good. Keep in touch." Lawson hung up.

*Or if the opportunity to be in the thick of things doesn't arise on its own,* Maggie thought, *maybe I can find a way to help it along.*

Then reality set in. No way, she realized, would she even get close to the big story. But maybe she could round up some special interest stuff from the local English people as she worked on her other assignments.

* * *

London Heathrow Airport
Thursday, 9:00 A.M.

During the flight, Maggie had located Tara and Jennie's seats, and when they landed in London, she squeezed through the crowded aisle to help the overburdened mother and her children deplane. Maggie carried the diaper bag and held Tara's hand to keep her from getting lost. She didn't notice the man with the dark, angry eyes and the ugly scar down his cheek checking the addresses on Jennie's luggage as it came around on the carousel. Jennie's sister was waiting outside of customs, so Maggie turned over her charges, waved good-bye, and hurried to pick up her rental car, expecting she would never see them again.

The new international crisis screamed from CNN reporters on television monitors in the airport terminal and special-edition newspapers on newsstands. Every country's head was sequestered with government leaders and in close contact with the other presidents, premiers, prime ministers, and chancellors across the globe. Many countries had a standing policy not to negotiate with terrorists. Would the threat of all those destroyed cities change that policy?

Maggie watched the TV broadcast while her paperwork was being prepared, the somber reality of the situation sinking in more fully now that she was here. London was on the terrorists' list. What monstrously evil men could even think of such a thing? How could they callously destroy not just an entire city full of people, but the historical treasures that were here? Surely the governments would come to some agreement with the terrorist factions or capture the leaders and solve the crisis before that happened.

As she signed the contract for the car and waited for the keys, the telecast reported that a man had been found dead in one of the restrooms at LAX several hours earlier. He had no identification on him, but was dressed in clothes resembling those of the escaped man that airport security had been seeking—the man associated with terrorists. The reporter stated that although police were reasonably sure they had found the right man, they were still asking viewers to stay alert. The picture Maggie had given airport security flashed across the screen, asking viewers to call if they had any additional information.

Maggie experienced a moment of disquiet. What if they didn't have the right man? Could the man on the run have killed the man in the restroom, changed clothes with him, and somehow assumed his identity? Perhaps he had even hopped on the murdered man's flight. Then she shook her head. There was no way he could have doctored an ID so quickly. It had to be the right man. When the clerk handed her the keys and directed her to the shuttle that would take her to the parking lot where she would retrieve her car, she forgot about the man in the gray turtleneck. Her adventure was about to begin.

\* \* \*

Ravenwood Estate, two hours west of London
Thursday, 9:30 A.M.

The ringing of the tall, slender man's cell phone disturbed the peaceful quiet of his finely appointed library.

"*Yes,*" he snapped.

"She made it through customs," the man with the scar reported. "She still has it in her bag."

The man smiled at the news. "Good. I assume you can retrieve it before she leaves London." He reached for his cup of tea and raised it to his lips.

"I'll get it in the parking lot while she's loading her luggage into her rental car."

"Excellent." He gently placed the antique china cup back in its saucer. "Then proceed directly to the conference room. Start disseminating the information immediately so they'll have time to get the goods into place. It will take some time to transport everything, as it will have to be done in small, inconspicuous amounts."

"Yes, sir. I should make it out there in four or five hours. By the way, if you want a little insurance, in case our young lady gets smart, she was chummy with a woman and her two kids. Their London address is 12 Abbey Lane."

The man scribbled the address down on his linen napkin. "Thanks. I like to have insurance. I'll join you this evening, but start the planning session as soon as you arrive. The others will be waiting for you." He disconnected, placed the phone on the tray beside his cup of tea, and consulted his silver pocket watch. Since he was already two hours out of London, he wouldn't have to leave for another hour or so.

* * *

London
Thursday, 9:40 A.M.

Ulrich watched as Maggie, along with four other people, waited to be picked up and delivered to their cars. Maggie appeared to be interviewing the people around her, and soon a small crowd had gathered, anxious to be interviewed.

Ulric fumed. There was no way he could get close enough to the girl to snatch her bag. Even if he tried something like that, those two young men talking to her looked like they could outrun him. He'd have to bide his time and wait for another opportunity. He cursed under his breath. He didn't have time for this kind of delay. The minutes were ticking away. Things had to be in place before the seventy-two-hour deadline. He glanced at his watch to see exactly how much time they had to get it all ready. He shook his head. Not nearly enough.

* * *

Flynn Ford landed in London just a few hours after Maggie on a nonstop flight from Chicago. So many passengers had canceled their reservations that it hadn't been any trouble to get a seat. A phone call to Lily had gotten him Maggie's agenda, plus Lily's eternal gratitude for his plan to quietly tail Maggie and keep an eye on her, unbeknownst to Maggie.

He shook his head. This insane action would only be taken by a man deeply in love, and he knew it. He wished he could act more openly to protect Maggie, but he'd promised her they'd spend a year apart so he could explore her religion and so she could be more certain she really loved him. If he stayed out of sight, he could keep that vow.

Flynn didn't fully understand why he had concocted this impetuous scheme to follow Maggie. He thought it was out of character for him to even contemplate something like this. He was a successful psychologist with a comfortable practice in Chicago, as well as many patients in Los Angeles, whom he flew out each weekend to treat, Alyssa being one of them. But he realized that where Maggie was concerned, he had a history of doing things that were out of character. After all, he'd taken a spontaneous weeklong road trip last December in order to keep an eye on her.

As he headed to Arundel, he didn't give a thought to not being able to locate Maggie. Lily had given him the address of the Rathford family from the old envelope, which had contained a payment to the midwife for the delivery of Lily and Cleat's baby boy. That was all Flynn knew, but he thought Maggie would create enough of an impression with her beautiful blue eyes and shoulder-length red hair that he should be able to catch her sooner or later.

The sooner the better, though. Flynn didn't like the urgency he was feeling to find Maggie. He didn't receive spiritual promptings often, but this certainly had all the markings of one. He felt absolutely driven to find the girl who had taught him that he could love again. He couldn't lose Maggie. He simply couldn't.

# FOUR

After the first few miles, Maggie became accustomed to the novelty of driving on the wrong side of the road, though she was very happy to leave the madness of the M-25 freeway. It reminded her of the insane driving conditions on the 405 in Los Angeles. As she drove south toward Arundel, she wondered what Lily's son would be like, if she could find him. She really couldn't call him a brother, not yet anyway. She already had five McKenzie brothers at home on the ranch in Idaho whom she dearly loved.

And what if his inclinations leaned more to Cleat Wiggins's personality and characteristics than Lily's? Maggie shuddered. She wanted to give Lily peace of mind, to put at rest her questions about the birth of her first child, but she didn't want anything to do with someone as evil as Cleat Wiggins, a man she could never call her father. Her mouth simply could not say that revered word in connection with Cleat.

Maggie also hoped to put her own fears at rest. Once again she pondered the question that had plagued her since she'd discovered her less-than-desirable natural paternal bloodline. Which had the most powerful influence, heredity or environment? Was Cleat's apparent psychosis inheritable in the same way some people seemed to have a predisposition to some forms of cancer because of their body's chemical makeup? Was there some brain circuit that hadn't connected properly that caused sociopathic behavioral problems? Or had Cleat's character been molded more by the people and events of his surroundings? From what she'd read, expert opinions varied on the impact of genetics on many psychological conditions, and the jury was still out on the verdict.

Long before Maggie reached Arundel, she could see the castle on the hill. She parked in the busy village center, grabbed her oversized bag, which doubled as a purse and catchall, and jumped out of the car. She hurried along the cobblestone street, following signs to the information center, where she asked for directions to Hilltop House on Chanticleer Lane.

"Who were you lookin' to find, miss?" the woman behind the counter asked.

"Mr. and Mrs. Llewellyn Rathford," Maggie said.

"Sorry, miss. They no longer live there." The woman shook her head. "Misfortune befell the family about ten years ago, and soon after, they moved."

"Do you know where?" Maggie asked, fearing her pursuit of the truth was over before it had really begun.

"Hmm. I think the vicar at Saint Nicholas would remember." The woman glanced at her watch. "He should be in the sanctuary about now. If you just follow this street up to the top and turn left at the castle, soon you'll come to St. Nicholas on the right." She gave Maggie a colored brochure on the village and pointed out the route on the little map. "Are ye relatives from America, then?"

Maggie looked up sharply at the woman. "Why did you ask that? Is there a family resemblance?"

The woman bobbed her head. "Oh, yes. The same flaming hair and blue eyes. In fact, you're the spitting image of young Damon Rathford— but much prettier of course. Yes, he was a handsome youth, but his mean disposition overshadowed his good looks, and you didn't notice his fine features. Now take you, you have a lovely light shining from your blue eyes and a goodly countenance. From the opposite sides of the bed, I'd say. Good luck, missy."

Reeling from the woman's comments, Maggie left the shop. *Mean disposition.* The words echoed in her head, sending a shiver of trepidation rippling through her. *Please, no,* she thought.

As she resumed her climb up the steep street, the castle battlements loomed above the picturesque village, their rounded Norman turrets creating images of pageantry and feudal lords in Maggie's head. Home to the dukes of Norfolk for over 850 years, the brochure said.

The street was busy with people going to market and stopping for tea. There were also some who were undoubtedly tourists. She turned around once, having the strange thought that she was being followed, but with so many on the narrow street, how could she tell? Who would be following her—and for what reason?

Half a block down the street, she found the Parish and Priory Church of Saint Nicholas of Arundel, which, according to the huge sign in front, had been rebuilt in 1380. The beautiful old church had arched windows with elaborate tracery separating the stained glass.

Ancient tombstones filled the courtyard, some tilting precariously, some ivy covered, and some so old they were totally illegible. Maggie didn't stop to see if the name Rathford appeared on any of them. The doors to the church stood open wide, and she ventured inside.

Fading frescoes adorned one of the chapel walls. Gold gleamed from the elaborate altar at the front of the chapel, and the ornately carved marble of the canopied preacher's pulpit next to it was stunningly beautiful. Maggie pulled the camera from her bag and captured the beauty for her article.

An elderly woman busied herself at the bulletin board in the back of the chapel and nodded absently at Maggie as she wandered, looking for the vicar. Unable to locate him, Maggie approached the woman. "Is Father Richards in today? At least, I think it's Father Richards I'm looking for. His name is on the sign out front."

The woman stepped toward her and cupped her ear. "What?"

"Father Richards, the vicar? May I talk to him?" Maggie repeated loudly.

The woman pointed to a heavy wooden door with iron hinges of ancient design. "There's where he hides out." She returned to her bulletin board.

As Maggie approached the door, it swung open wide. "Were you looking for me?" the tall, gray-haired man asked.

"That depends," Maggie said with a smile. "I'm looking for the vicar of Saint Nicholas Church. If that's you, I'm very happy to meet you."

The vicar extended his hand, and Maggie offered hers. "I'm Maggie McKenzie. I'm looking for information on—"

"The Rathfords," Father Richards finished for her as he held her hand in a firm grip.

Maggie stared at him in astonishment. "How did you know that?"

"Why else would an American woman, who bears more than a striking resemblance to one of our former families, come seeking a poor parish vicar?"

Maggie tried to extract her hand from the vicar's firm grip. "You're very perceptive. I'm looking most specifically for their son Damon.

"Why are you looking for Damon?" Father Richards asked.

"I should think it would be obvious, since you've noted the family resemblance." Maggie finally gave up, leaving her hand clasped tightly in the vicar's.

Father Richards drew Maggie into his office, nodding his head at the woman watching them. "Not that she could hear anything we said unless we were standing next to her, but we don't need to disturb worshipers who frequent the chapel." He studied Maggie intently for a moment, then released her hand and waved her to a tapestry-covered chair in front of his massive walnut desk.

He settled into his black leather chair and leaned forward, elbows on his desk. "You've heard the phrase 'angels and demons'?"

Maggie nodded, noting the troubled look in the vicar's deep-set, gray eyes.

"If you and Damon were to meet, it would be like bringing angels," he pointed at Maggie, "and demons together." He paused, waiting for her reaction, but Maggie didn't know how to react. His words left her speechless. Had the woman from the information center been right? This wasn't what she'd expected—or wanted—to hear.

"Go on," she murmured.

"What do you want to know?" he asked.

Suppressing her apprehension, Maggie plunged ahead. "First of all, I'd like to know why you said that about Damon."

"Because it's true. He had such a mean streak, the kids used to call him Demon instead of Damon. He persecuted younger children, tortured animals, and played cruel pranks on everyone. One day he went too far—though it was deemed an accident, a child died."

"Is that why his parents moved?"

Father Richards nodded silently.

"Do you know where they are now?" Maggie asked, hoping fervently that this man not only had the information she needed, but would be willing to reveal it.

With narrowed eyes, the vicar stared at her for what seemed a very long time before asking, "Why do you want to know?"

Maggie took a deep breath. "I think he may be my brother."

"And?"

"His birth mother, Lily, would like proof he didn't die in childbirth."

Father Richards castled his fingers and leaned back in his chair. "Leave it alone, Miss McKenzie. No good can come of it."

"Don't you think she should know whether or not the son she thought died years ago is living?"

"No." Father Richards shook his head emphatically. "She's better off not knowing anything about him. Leave it be. Let him remain dead to her."

"That seems rather heartless," Maggie said quietly. "Can you imagine how this woman feels, not knowing if she has other children somewhere that she doesn't know about?"

Father Richards leaned forward and stared at Maggie. "Why wouldn't she know, if she gave birth to them?"

"My mother's first two babies were born at home. Her then-husband administered drugs during childbirth, supposedly to help her, and when she woke, he told her each time that the babies had died and he had buried them. She believed him. On her third pregnancy, she insisted on going to the hospital so they could save her child if there were problems. Under general anesthetic, she gave birth to twins, but while she was in recovery, her husband met a man whose wife had just given birth to a baby who died. He sold one of the twins to this man so his wife would have a baby to take home. I was that twin. Lily's husband made sure she never knew she'd delivered two little girls. Until seven months ago, I didn't know I was a twin. I think she should know the truth about whether her wicked husband sold any of her other babies, or if they truly died at birth."

"Go home. Let her believe the baby died. If this is your brother, you don't want to meet him, and his mother doesn't need to know what he's like. It would be a nightmare for her. And although Damon's brother is better behaved, he left home to seek his fortune, and I believe was never heard from again."

Maggie sat dumbfounded at this information. "Brother?"

"You said yourself there were two babies born and sold before you. It seems they were sold to the same family—Damon has an older brother named Llewellyn. The two boys look just alike. Neither of them were the little angel that you undoubtedly were as a youngster, though, as I said, Llewellyn is more civilized. He seemed to have repented of his dirty tricks and predilection for fire by his midteens. Damon never seemed to outgrow his dangerous pranks."

"These boys can't be that bad," Maggie objected.

Father Richards interrupted her. "I will not aid you in your quest, because it will only bring you grief. That's why Damon's parents had to move. They were driven out of town by his pranks. He seemed to take great delight in dealing pain to people, whether physically or psychologically."

Maggie shivered. *Just like his father,* she thought.

Father Richards stood. "I'm sorry to be the bearer of such bad news, but I can't in clear conscience send you into the arms of your brother—if he is indeed your brother, though the family resemblance is too great to be a coincidence."

"Thank you, Father. I appreciate your honesty and your good intentions." Maggie stood and hooked her bag over her shoulder.

Father Richards spread his hands on the desk in front of him and leaned toward Maggie, fixing her with a piercing gaze. "But you intend to pursue this anyway, regardless of my admonitions."

Maggie nodded. "I didn't come all this way just to turn around and go home having the same questions unanswered that I arrived with. My birth mother deserves better than that."

"Your birth mother must be a very good woman." Father Richards rounded the corner of his desk and opened the door, signaling the end of their interview.

"She is," Maggie said as she approached the door.

"And the birth father?" Father Richards asked.

"It sounds like Damon is a chip off the old block. My father kidnapped his daughter—my twin—when she was sixteen years old and treated her like a slave for seven years until we located her. He murdered several people to keep from being caught. I'm not sure they even know how many yet."

Father Richards put his hands on Maggie's shoulders and looked down into her deep blue eyes. "Stay away from Damon Rathford. He will bring you and your mother only grief and heartache at best. At worst . . ." The vicar looked over Maggie's shoulder and stopped speaking.

Maggie turned and saw the old woman watching them. Father Richards nodded silently at Maggie in farewell and retreated into his office, shutting the door quietly behind him. Maggie stood where he had left her, quite undecided about where to go next.

The woman continued staring as Maggie slowly walked toward the door. As Maggie passed close by where she stood, the old woman crossed herself.

Maggie stopped. "Do I frighten you?" she asked loudly near the woman's ear.

The old woman nodded.

"Why?" Maggie asked.

"You're one of them."

"One of who?"

"Those Demon Rathfords."

"You mean Damon," Maggie corrected.

The old woman shook her head. "No. Demon. And you look just like him."

"Do you know where I can find his parents?" Maggie asked.

The woman stared into Maggie's eyes for a moment without speaking. The fear she'd exhibited seemed to have dissipated somewhat, and she shook her head. "No, you aren't like him. You have kindness in your eyes." She reached out and touched Maggie's arm, then leaned forward and whispered in a conspiratorial tone, "His parents moved to Avebury. I don't know what became of him."

"You mean Amesbury?" Maggie asked, thinking she'd misunderstood the woman's accent. She'd seen Amesbury on the map just above Salisbury, but she had never heard of Avebury.

"No. Avebury. His parents were good people, but not good parents. They couldn't handle him."

"Do you know where in Avebury they live?" Maggie asked, not having any idea whether this was a small town or large city, though she thought she would have heard of it had it been of significant size.

"Just Avebury." The old woman looked around the foyer as if she were afraid she had been overheard sharing this information. "And I'd watch out for that awful man lurking outside. He has evil eyes." She snatched her purse and shopping bag from under the table and hurried away.

# FIVE

"Wait," Maggie called to the old woman. "What man?" She ran to the door as the woman disappeared into the cemetery. She stood in the doorway and looked around for the man the old woman had warned her about but saw only a family crowding up the narrow walk. Maggie slipped out of the church as they filed in. The father stayed behind with a young boy, pointing out family graves and telling stories.

Maggie photographed the old headstones and the church and made mental notes on the stories the father told his son. Although she gleaned interesting information for her article and got some great pictures, she still felt a sense of disquiet. She occasionally looked around, feeling jittery, her nerves on edge.

Had the old woman really seen someone? Maggie shook her head, deciding it had probably been the vicar's news that left her feeling so disturbed. But his words had been more than disturbing, she thought—they had been truly frightening.

If the vicar, who had an obligation of sorts to think the best of people, had said those things about Damon Rathford, what was Damon really like? How she wished Alyssa were here. Or Flynn. The search for Alyssa had been less frightening with Flynn at her side. She felt a pang in her chest at the thought of him. How could she possibly wait until December to know if he still loved her? If he didn't, it would break her heart.

As the man and his son entered the church to join their family, Maggie hurried across the street to photograph the beautiful Catholic church with its tall spires and huge stained-glass window. She was immediately joined by a tour group, which filled the entrance, rendering any attempt at obtaining publishing-quality photographs of the building quite impossible.

As she left the Catholic church and snapped pictures of the castle at the end of the street, Maggie was jostled by some girls passing on the sidewalk, talking about lunch. Suddenly realizing she hadn't eaten since her meal on the plane, she followed the trio of teenage girls into the bakery and sandwich shop. The chattering girls were soon joined by three young men.

Maggie thoroughly enjoyed her sandwich until she overheard one of the girls say, "Did you get a look at that creepy guy hanging around outside? Reminds me of pictures I've seen of Jack the Ripper. He had the most horrid expression and such angry eyes—and that scar was positively frightening."

Maggie didn't hear another word after that, nor could she eat another bite. Angry eyes? Scar? The old woman at the church had said someone with evil eyes was lurking outside. She thought of the man who had been standing behind her in the LA airport and remembered the ugly scar cutting across his face. Could it be the same man? She shook her head. It was preposterous—why would he be following her? And yet she couldn't believe it was merely coincidence, either. Maybe she hadn't been paranoid when she'd felt she was being watched.

Leaving half of her sandwich uneaten, she asked if she could leave by the back door and then quickly slipped out into the narrow alley behind the store. She entered the curio shop next to it by their back door, and hurried to the front of the shop. When she looked across the street and down two stores, she saw the man that both the girl and the old woman had described. It *was* the man from the airport.

Was he following her? Maggie wasn't about to play cat and mouse with this man—he looked way out of her league. She needed to leave town as quickly and unobtrusively as possible and continue her search for the Rathfords. She nodded and smiled at the woman who ran the curio shop, backtracked to the alley, and ran as fast as she could to the end of the block and the parking lot.

Although she was reluctant to leave without photographing the inside of the castle and the rest of this quaint, ancient village, Maggie left Arundel quickly, having spent scarcely an hour there. She didn't stop until she was several miles down the road. She stayed on the little country roads until she was sure she'd eluded the man with the scar, then pulled over and stopped at the top of a little hill with a scenic overlook. From here she could see the road to Arundel; she would also have some warning if the man had chosen the right road out of town and was pursuing her. She was hopeful she'd lost him for good. She knew that up to now she'd probably been very easy to follow, but he couldn't know where she was going next.

Maggie pulled out the travel guide and located Avebury, consulted the map, and plotted her course. She figured it to be approximately one hundred kilometers west to Salisbury, then another forty kilometers north to Avebury.

Surprisingly, the guidebook cited Avebury as a tourist destination with ancient upright stones much like its more famous counterpart, Stonehenge. What were the Rathfords doing in a tiny village that, according to the book, appeared to have no other support than tourism? Maggie wondered. She glanced at her watch and made a quick decision not to arrive at Avebury after dark. As she reached to start the car, her cell phone rang. Without even checking her caller ID, she knew it was Alyssa calling.

"Maggie, what's happening? I expected a phone call by now."

"And what am I supposed to be calling you about?" Maggie asked, smiling at her sister's scolding tone.

"That you've located the Rathfords and our older brother."

"Sorry. No news yet. I just left Arundel, where they lived at one time, and I'm on my way to Avebury, where they supposedly moved. I have no idea if they still live there or not—or actually, if they ever did. An old woman in a church whispered the secret of where they'd gone."

Alyssa laughed. "That sounds so mysterious. I want to be there with you so much!"

"Frankly, I wish you were," said Maggie, meaning every word of it. "But you've got some catching up to do after your seven-year hiatus on learning, so getting enrolled in your college prep classes is your first priority."

"I have a surprise!" Alyssa exclaimed. "I did that already. I thought if I went in early, I could preregister, then come and join you and get back home in time for classes to start. Mom says I can come if we can arrange to meet somewhere."

More than surprised, Maggie exclaimed, "I can't believe Lily would agree to let you come. Are you sure she said it was okay—since all this terrorist activity has occurred?"

Alyssa faltered. "She said yes when I asked her yesterday. I didn't tell you then, because I thought it would be a fun surprise. Besides, I bought my tickets before I heard about the bomb threats. But Mom can't stop me if I want to come. I am an adult, after all. I'll be with you, so we can take care of each other. Maggie, I want to be there when you find our brother. Please say yes," Alyssa pleaded.

Maggie mulled over her dilemma. Did she want Alyssa to know about their brothers if they were like Cleat Wiggins? Maybe it wasn't a good idea to dig too deeply into family secrets. *If only we knew what they were like today,* she thought.

"When do you leave?" Maggie asked quietly.

"Tonight on the redeye. I'll be there tomorrow morning and join you wherever you are. What do you think?" Alyssa held her breath, awaiting Maggie's answer.

"I'm excited about the idea, but I'm not sure this is a good place to be coming right now. It's a zoo in London. Some people are already evacuating just in case the government can't come to some sort of agreement with the terrorists."

"What about you?" Alyssa rejoined. "Don't you think this might affect your travel?"

"Actually, I plan to be on the far side of the country when the deadline approaches," Maggie said, "but I'm completely certain the heads of government will figure out something. They can't just let all these beautiful cities be destroyed by a bunch of terrorists. I'm sure every agency is working 24–7 to find the terrorists and prevent the attack."

"Then you'd better pray that happens," Alyssa said. "Your God seems to listen to you. And put in a good word for me, so I can find you when I get there. I've never done anything like this before, and I'm scared stiff, but I want to come so bad I'll face anything to be with you. It might be crazy, but I feel like I have to."

"Okay, if there's no talking you out of this . . . and part of me doesn't want to anyway. Call me when you land tomorrow, and I'll figure out how to connect with you. I've read that the train system here is marvelous, so we shouldn't have too much trouble. And by the way, Alyssa, God will listen to you, too. You can pray anytime you want, and He'll hear you."

"Thanks, Maggie. Well, I better finish packing. I'm supposed to land at nine o'clock in the morning. Don't get too far away!" Alyssa said. "See you tomorrow."

Knowing she wouldn't be alone in her quest cheered Maggie somewhat, even as a huge black cloud moved across the sun. It started to sprinkle, then pour. Soon the downpour became a deluge, and at the traffic circle, Maggie couldn't see any of the road signs. She ended up on a small unpaved country road with streams of water running down the hill, nearly obliterating the road. At the first driveway, she pulled off the road to wait out the storm and reformulate her plans.

* * *

Totally immersed in her *Guide to Great Britain,* Maggie nearly jumped out of her skin when someone knocked on her window. The rain had all but stopped, and a pleasant-looking English lady with an umbrella to protect her from the remaining drizzle smiled through the rain-spotted glass. Maggie rolled down the window.

"Are you all right, young lady? Do you need help?"

Maggie laughed sheepishly. "Yes, I'm fine, thank you. Just a little lost. I was headed for Salisbury, but in the downpour I missed my road at the roundabout and ended up here. I thought I'd better just stay put until the rain stopped and I could situate myself."

"As for your location, this is the village of Bury. And I'm Liz Barlow."

Maggie stepped out of her car and offered her hand to Mrs. Barlow, then gasped at the previously obstructed sight behind the English woman—a perfectly preserved thatched roof on a brick and stone manor house. At the end of the driveway, a huge barn sported the same type of roof. At the peak of the roof, fancy crossed stitching held the thatching in place.

Mrs. Barlow laughed. "You like my roof. Have you never seen one before?"

Maggie shook her head. "No, in fact, I've never been to England before. This is my first day—I haven't even been in your country twelve hours. May I take some pictures?"

"Of course." The petite blond woman, dressed in a soft pink cashmere sweater and classic English tweed skirt, recited the history of her home, built in 1544, while Maggie worked magic with her camera, capturing the house, the beautiful English gardens, and the barns.

When Maggie told the woman of her assignment for the newspaper, Mrs. Barlow suggested that Maggie spend the night in Alton at the bed-and-breakfast of a friend. That way she could visit the Jane Austen home in nearby Chawton and write about the famous author.

Mrs. Barlow used Maggie's cell phone to make a reservation right on the spot and then gave her directions to Alton. Maggie thanked her gracious hostess and backed out of the driveway, feeling better than she had in hours. The doom-and-gloom feeling caused by the man with the scar and Father Richards's warning had been dispelled by this elegant, gracious English woman.

* * *

Ravenwood Estate
Thursday, 1:00 P.M.

"Ulric, where the devil are you?"

"Sorry, Mr. Constantine," Ulric said into the phone. "I couldn't get close to her at the airport, so I followed her to Arundel and she gave me the slip. But I overheard an old lady tell her to go to Avebury, so I'm on my way there now."

"You idiot! You're supposed to be disseminating the information on that USB flash drive right now. It needs to be decoded, and you're still hours from here."

"Sorry, Mr. Constantine," Ulric grumbled. "She's never been alone for a minute except in her car."

"Then you should have driven her off the road, dispensed with her, and reclaimed the flash drive. It's vital. No more pussyfooting around. You don't have time to be nice—just kill her and get here with the information. We can't fall behind schedule. This has been timed right down to the second, and you won't screw it up for me. Do you hear?"

"Yes, sir, Mr. Constantine."

Ulric knew he'd fouled up. He'd never heard Constantine lose his cool. The man had ice in his veins. He'd always insisted on keeping the body count down so as not to draw undue attention to the organization, but Ulric was more than happy to make this exception. He didn't like to be given the slip by a mere girl. She'd pay dearly.

\* \* \*

Arundel
Thursday, 1:00 P.M.

Flynn entered the information center in Arundel and asked the woman at the counter if she could direct him to Hilltop House on Chanticleer Lane.

"Why, you're the second person today who's asked after that address," the woman behind the desk said with surprise.

"The first must have been a beautiful young woman with blue eyes and a mane of wild red hair," Flynn said, smiling at the woman.

She nodded. "Yes, sir, you're right. It was."

"And what did you tell the young lady?"

The lady shook her head. "The family that lived at that address moved away about ten years ago."

"Did you tell her where they went?" Flynn asked, a sudden sinking feeling in his stomach.

"No, sir, I could not, but I directed her to the vicar at Saint Nicholas. He should know."

"Thank you," Flynn said, "and where do I find the vicar at Saint Nicholas?"

"Top of the street, turn left at the castle."

"I thank you, madam." Flynn fairly flew out of the center and up the steep street to find the parish church of Saint Nicholas.

The vicar was just leaving when Flynn arrived, out of breath. "You're in a bit of a hurry, my good man," the vicar observed as Flynn held up his hand for him to wait.

"I'm trying to catch up with Maggie McKenzie, an American with blue eyes and red hair. I believe she visited with you earlier today," Flynn panted, handing the vicar his card.

The vicar examined the card and frowned. "Yes, Dr. Ford. What do you want with her?"

"I believe she's in danger. I'm trying to catch her to accompany and protect her." That was the truth. Flynn just planned to do all this without Maggie's knowledge.

"She is most definitely in danger. I tried to warn her about pursuing this foolish quest of hers, but she wouldn't listen to me."

"What were you warning her about?" Flynn asked.

"She wanted to find her brothers. These young men are not what you call peaceful, law-abiding citizens—one of them, at least. I warned her not to continue her search, but I understand she talked to one of my parishioners who told her where she might find the boys. I'm sure she's on her way to Avebury at this moment. By the way, this same parishioner told me she had seen a man following Miss McKenzie. She described him as looking sinister, with a scarred face and very angry eyes. Is this who you are trying to protect her from?"

Flynn nodded slowly. This must be the reason he had felt prompted to come to England. "Yes, I'm sure of it. How long ago was she here?"

"She can't have been gone more than a couple of hours. Maybe three," the vicar estimated.

"Thank you, sir. What's the fastest way to Avebury from here?"

"Drop down to the A-27, take that to Salisbury, then up to Marlborough and over to Avebury. Good luck to you. I hope you find her before she gets herself into trouble she can't handle."

Flynn raced back down the hill to his car. He hoped so too. He grabbed his road map to see where he was going, and before starting the car, he uttered a silent prayer for guidance. He could not lose Maggie. She was the most important thing in his life, and he needed to tell her that.

# SIX

Rural England
Thursday, 2:00 P.M.

The lush, green rolling hills of rural England enchanted Maggie. They were totally unlike the sagebrush-covered mountains on her family's ranch in Idaho or the long miles of barren desert between Utah and the coast of California, which she often traveled. Though these rural English roads were extremely narrow with only occasional places wide enough to pass a car, Maggie much preferred them to the four-lane freeways she'd been on earlier that day where cars and trucks whizzed by on either side and she'd missed seeing the beautiful English countryside.

Maggie also appreciated the fact that in the rural areas, she could stop to take pictures of little villages with moss-covered thatched roofs, some sporting large birds made from thatch with long tails that perched on the peak of the roof. Maggie drove in and out of rain showers for a couple of hours, talking into her tape recorder about what she was seeing in the countryside, working on her articles as she drove.

She found herself in the town of Petworth with a ravenous appetite. Her half sandwich earlier in Arundel hadn't satisfied her hunger. As she pulled into the town square, the sun shone on a sparkling white stucco pub with a large green sign and gold lettering proclaiming "The Star."

Liz Barlow had recommended eating at pubs, saying that locals ate there because they usually served the best food, so Maggie pulled into the one vacant spot near the building. She grabbed her oversized bag containing her camera, notebook, tape recorder, and all the accoutrements of a good reporter, and headed for the front door, not having any idea what to expect when she set foot inside this totally unknown territory.

A cheery atmosphere welcomed her, and a happy hostess seated her at a table by the window and left a menu. Maggie studied the clientele. A woman in her seventies with a colorful kerchief tied around her head shared a table with what appeared to be her daughter and granddaughter. At another table, a couple of young married women fed babies in booster seats and chatted animatedly.

In an adjoining room, a group of older men surrounded a polished wooden table and sipped ales. Two were dressed in business suits, three in open-collared shirts and dress slacks. It looked like they were discussing something with passion and ardor. This scene was not at all what Maggie had expected to find in a British pub. She unobtrusively snapped a few pictures for her article before noticing the CNN broadcast on the television in the back of the room. The picture she had taken of the man escaping in the airport flashed across the screen. Everyone, it seemed, was set on apprehending this man. Maggie only hoped they did. His face made her shudder, even on television.

When the waitress approached and began describing the different items on the menu, she suddenly dropped her pad and pencil. Her hand flew to her mouth as her eyes widened, first in disbelief, then in fear. She stumbled backward, nearly falling over the table behind her.

Maggie jumped to her feet. "Are you okay?"

The girl's arms shot out in front of her in defense. "Don't ya touch me, mum. Keep yer distance."

"What's the matter?" Maggie was mystified at this suddenly irrational behavior from the formerly cheerful waitress.

"I've had enough trouble with the likes of yer family, and I don't intend to have anything further to do with ya."

"I'm an American," Maggie protested. "I just arrived in England today. What are you talking about? Why are you afraid of me?" But even as she asked, Maggie had a sinking feeling that she knew exactly what this young woman feared.

The frightened waitress shoved a chair between them. She shook her head. "Ya look so much like him, ya could be his twin."

"I do have a twin sister, but she's in California, and she's never been to England," Maggie said calmly. "Who do I look like?"

"Demon." Her voice quivered as she spoke his name. "Do ya know him? He's aptly named, for he is, in very deed, a demon."

"No, I don't know him," Maggie said truthfully, slowly sinking back into her seat. She needed to talk to this young woman, and to accomplish that, she had to overcome the outright fear the girl had for her. "Can you take my order, and while they prepare it, could you sit and talk to me about this Demon who looks like me?" Maggie picked up her menu and quickly chose the cawl, which was described as a Welsh beef stew with bacon and potatoes in a thick, spicy broth.

The girl, visibly shaken, hurried to the kitchen to place the order but wasn't quite as quick in returning. When, with shaking hands, she placed a glass of water on the table, water splashed on Maggie's jacket. The girl drew back in fear as if expecting to be struck.

Maggie brushed the drops away, smiled at the girl, and pointed to the seat opposite her. "Please sit down for a minute and explain who you thought I looked like, and why you are so afraid."

Obviously still reluctant to get too close, the girl edged around the table and slid onto the chair, remaining perched on the seat's edge as if ready to fly away at the slightest provocation.

"Ya have the same blue eyes and red hair as Demon Rathford, but I can see now that ye aren't just like him. He'd have struck me clean across the room if I'd spilled even a drop of water on him."

"Who is this person you call Demon?" Maggie asked.

"He's just that—a demon—a madman," the girl said with a shudder. "He and his older brother lived here some time ago."

"Demon had a brother?" Maggie asked.

"I didn't know the older brother well. All I knew was that he loved to blow things up. Fire crackers, soda bottles, anything that exploded. He moved before Demon started coming in here. Some people around here think he got sent away because he was a bad influence on Demon. Others believe he ran off to avoid the authorities."

"Does 'Demon' still live here in Petworth?" Maggie asked.

"No, mum, the family used to live a few miles from here in Arundel, but he visited every pub in the area, even after his folks was driven out of town."

"Can you tell me what happened?" Maggie asked quietly.

"I can only tell ya that a lot of firecrackers in one place is as dangerous as dynamite. I got to get back to work now, mum." Apparently relieved for an excuse to seat the new customers at a table across the room, the girl scurried about delivering their drinks and taking their orders. When she brought Maggie's order, she gave Maggie time for only one question.

"You mentioned they moved away," Maggie said. "Do you know where they went?"

The waitress shook her head. "I don't know for sure. I think it was north. But I wouldn't go looking for this family, mum. It's just looking for trouble, if you don't mind my saying."

Even the delicious, hot stew couldn't dispel the cold chill that seeped through Maggie. What kind of brothers did she have? One with pyromaniac tendencies whom no one seemed to know what happened to, and another that everyone called a demon.

But, she rationalized, these were very small towns. Every resident in the village would know about everything that happened. With each telling of a story, it would be enlarged and added upon, so by time the last neighbor heard it, the tale would have been magnified and probably expanded beyond recognition. She determined that she would do her best to take the gossip with a grain of salt until she could uncover the truth.

Still, Maggie couldn't dispel the disquiet she felt remembering the fear in the girl's eyes and voice. The vicar and old woman in Arundel had been just as discouraging. Maybe it wasn't a good idea to pursue the matter further. Maybe she really should just forget the family quest and concentrate on her assignment for the paper. She smiled ruefully. That wasn't an option for Mary Margaret McKenzie. Maggie wasn't a quitter.

Somberly, and filled with qualms about continuing this increasingly frightening pursuit for the truth about Lily's children, Maggie turned the rental car north between the tall hedgerows that lined the rolling green fields. As she drove, she murmured a prayer for guidance and protection. She was surely in need of both.

The miles and time flew by as Maggie recorded her impressions of the landscape and small towns to fill her travel articles, stopping occasionally to take pictures. An older couple with two monstrous dogs in the back seat of their car followed her as she drove through the country-side. They seemed to stop everywhere she did, taking pictures right behind her.

Finally, at one little town with a beautiful church, the elderly English woman approached and confided, "When we saw what you were taking pictures of, we decided you have a natural eye for beauty, so we're copying all your shots. I hope you don't mind. We never would have thought of the angle you've taken of some things. Thank you so much."

Maggie laughed. "You're very welcome. Tell me something. Do you always travel with those huge dogs?"

The woman smiled and nodded. "They belong to our son and his family, but we borrow them when we travel. We were robbed once. Two old people traveling alone, you know, are often the target of pick-pockets and thieves. But since we've begun taking Duke and Duchess with us, we've never had a minute's trouble."

"I can certainly see why," Maggie said. "Enjoy your vacation."

Following the directions Liz Barlow had given her, Maggie soon found the town of Alton and pulled into the driveway of a large, two-story brick home with ivy growing up the walls—the Manor Bed-and-Breakfast.

Vera, the stocky housekeeper and cook, showed her up the stairs to a pleasant, airy room with a book-covered mantel over a small gas fireplace. There were two twin beds with white coverlets and blue pillows.

Maggie apparently was the sole guest in the house, and Vera invited her to come back down to the old-fashioned kitchen/family room. She thanked Vera for the kind offer, but she preferred peace and quiet to the constant running dialogue of this friendly gray-haired woman. Maggie wondered if this was Vera's normal behavior or if she was just lonely tonight and wanted company and genial conversation.

Maggie immediately went to work crafting her articles for the new Sunday supplement to the paper. She downloaded the pictures from her camera and wrote a couple of articles, including material from her travel books and the narrative she'd taped as she drove.

The information on the brochure she'd picked up at the visitors' center in Arundel was very helpful, and Maggie decided she would just have to return there to see everything she had missed when she'd had to flee from the man with the jagged scar and angry eyes. Why had he followed her? No matter. Whatever the man's motives, she had eluded him and felt fairly certain he wouldn't be able to find her now.

When Maggie finished her articles, she ventured downstairs to ask Vera if the house had an Internet connection. Vera gave her permission to use it for a few minutes, and Maggie sent her work and a personal note to Lily.

As she turned to go back upstairs to her room, the BBC television special playing in the next room caught her attention. It was a special report on the terrorist situation. Vera invited her to stay and listen, and Maggie stood in the doorway while Vera settled into the chintz sofa to watch the broadcast.

"World leaders are divided on the solution to the current terrorist situation. France and Spain voted today to meet the demands of the terrorists and release the prisoners they hold. The British Commonwealth, the United States, Germany, Russia, and Israel are among those who hold adamantly to the belief that terrorists should not be bargained with nor should their demands be acceded to. As the world holds its collective breath, the nations' leaders are working around the clock on the problem. On a further note, sources accepted as spokesmen for Osama bin Laden deny that these threats have anything to do with their al Qaeda organization. Authorities believe these terror threats may have been made by one of the many cells that remain on the fringe of the main group."

"Where will it all lead?" Vera sighed. "The world is surely coming to an end with all this wickedness about."

"Yes," Maggie agreed. "I guess all we can do is pray for our leaders to be able to stop this madness. And on that note, I'm going to bed. It's been a very long day, and I didn't sleep well on the plane last night. Good night, Vera, and thanks for everything."

"I'll just lock up now. Sleep tight, missy." Vera padded in her big fleece slippers to the front door as Maggie disappeared up the stairs.

As she prepared for bed, Maggie mulled over the events of the day and her conversations in Arundel. She was struck by how three different people had all commented on how close her resemblance was to Damon, and yet how different her countenance was from his. No one had mentioned Llewellyn's appearance at all. What did their oldest brother look like?

There was no air-conditioning in the house, but she could feel a gentle cross breeze if she left the window open and her door ajar. Since she and Vera were alone in the house, and she'd seen Vera lock the downstairs doors, Maggie felt quite safe in leaving her door open, something she would never think of doing in other circumstances.

* * *

Ulric had stopped at every pub along the road after leaving Arundel, hoping to spot the girl's rental car in the parking lot. When he reached Petworth, he had laughed out loud. Success. He would grab her bag as she left the pub. However, four burly farm boys got out of their cars just as she came out of the building. They hadn't entered the pub till she'd driven away, and Ulrich had been stuck following her. Again.

Ulric wasn't queasy about killing people. He'd done it so many times he'd lost track, but he was very careful not to get caught. He didn't want to spend his life in prison, or worse yet, not have a life to spend. So he was anxious to take care of this elusive lass at the first isolated opportunity along the road.

Unfortunately, the opportunity had slipped by him a second time that day, because of that dratted old couple and their monster dogs. He had a thing about big dogs like Indiana Jones had about snakes. So he had bided his time and followed at a discreet distance until the redhead pulled into the driveway of the bed-and-breakfast. He had smiled then, his dark, sinister eyes gleaming. There was only one other car in the driveway.

As soon as the lights went out, he'd let himself into the girl's car. If the bag was there, he'd be off in a flash. If it wasn't, he'd let himself into the house and take it from her while she was sleeping. Just maybe she'd never wake up. She had been a major pain today, and Mr. Constantine was not happy. Yes. He would administer eternal sleep to her tonight—right after he retrieved the flash drive he'd dropped in her bag at the airport in Los Angeles.

* * *

Petersfield
Thursday, 9:55 P.M.

Flynn's frustration had reached an all-time high. He hoped he was being guided to find Maggie, but he hadn't overtaken her on the road and hadn't found her at any of the hotel dining rooms or nicer pubs where he'd stopped. Didn't she have to eat? Or sleep? He sighed. He must not be on the right road.

His only clue to her whereabouts was the little town of Avebury. Maybe she'd driven directly there hoping to find her brother's family instead of stopping along the way. He checked his map one more time, then headed west from Petworth to Winchester and up to Avebury, praying he could find Maggie before that man who'd been seen following her caused her any trouble.

Did he dare call her? That was probably the smartest thing to do. When he found a place to pull over, he'd swallow his pride and call. His stomach was tied in knots with worry. He couldn't spend the rest of the night in his present state. She needed to know she was in danger—if she didn't already—and if he wasn't too late.

* * *

Alton
Thursday, 10:00 P.M.

Maggie curled up in the little overstuffed chair in her bedroom and read her scriptures for fifteen minutes, said her prayers, then checked her cell phone for messages and turned it off. Alyssa wouldn't remember the time difference, and Maggie didn't want to be disturbed. Tomorrow was soon enough to reconnect with her twin. She was glad Alyssa was coming—she needed some moral support in this increasingly discouraging pursuit of their brothers.

* * *

Ulric shined his light into the young woman's car, looking for the oversized bag she always carried on her shoulder. Since she was driving a little station wagon, he could see all the way into the back. Not there. Too bad for her.

He turned toward the house, planning to enter through the French doors on the ground floor. Suddenly he heard footsteps crunching toward the driveway. He ducked behind the shrubbery and carefully peered out.

A young man with a backpack walked up the steps, unlocked the door, and disappeared inside. Ulric watched through the window as the twenty-something fellow went into the kitchen, made a short phone call, and raided the refrigerator. When he'd finished eating, he went silently upstairs. No television, no music, no noise.

Ulric decided he would make his move now. Before the young man settled down for the night, he'd unlock the door so the kid's movements upstairs might mask any noise he inadvertently made. Then when all was quiet, he'd creep up to the girl's room and get the bag.

He slipped his knife between the doors, found the bolt, and with the sharp point, forced the bolt back and pushed the door open. He smiled in satisfaction. These old locks could be opened by a child, and he'd seen no sign of any kind of security system. Not even a dog.

He waited ten minutes. All the lights were out. There were no noises in the house. He opened the door a crack and slipped through.

# SEVEN

Ulric carefully stepped on the sides of the stairs, avoiding the middle where they were most likely to creak. He was almost at the top, ready to step onto the landing, when something caught him on the back of the head. Hard. It was the last thing he remembered.

His knife clattered noisily to the hardwood floor, waking Maggie. She leapt out of bed and ran to the open door. Bright lights flooded the upstairs hall, banishing darkness from every corner and revealing a man sprawled in the middle of the floor, bleeding from a wound in the back of his head. A young man bent over him.

Maggie gasped as she stared at the man on the floor. She knew that face, even with the angry, dark eyes closed and without seeing the scar on his cheek.

Two images collided in her mind. *Why didn't I realize this before?* The man with the scar wasn't just some creepy stalker. This was the bearded man who had collided with her at LAX. Clearly he'd altered his appearance from the picture being broadcast of himself enough to elude the authorities. Maggie couldn't believe she hadn't made the connection until now, though she could see she was up against a pro. And he wasn't the only one he'd fooled. He must have already had a passport that matched the modified look, right down to the clean-shaven face.

There was no doubt in her mind that the scar-faced man and the alleged terrorist were one and the same. But what did he want with her? As she stared at the man on the floor, she could only conclude that he had been seeking revenge for the fact that she'd given his photo to the security guards. After all, her picture of his face had been on every CNN broadcast in the world.

Downstairs, someone knocked on the door. Both Maggie and the young man leaning over the body glanced toward the entryway. From somewhere under the stairs, Vera's sleepy voice called, "Just a minute." She padded to the front door, wrapping a robe around her as she went.

"Detective Inspector James," the man at the door said to Vera and stepped into the front hall. "You rang for the police. Said there was someone lurking in the bushes. We checked, but didn't see anyone."

"That's because he's up here, Inspector," the young man called. "When I walked up the driveway, I saw someone duck into the bushes. I'd read about the burglaries in the area, and I thought he might be looking the place over to break in. So I went inside, called you, then waited with the cricket bat in case he got in before you arrived."

The inspector bounded up the stairs and bent over the unconscious man. "Doesn't look like anyone we've been chasing in connection with the break-ins, but the bloke does look a bit familiar." He stood and looked at the two young people on the landing. "Do either of you know this man?"

"I do," Maggie said hesitantly. "He probably looks familiar because you've seen his picture on television. He's the man who escaped at Los Angeles Airport when they arrested the rest of the terrorist group flying in from Australia."

"What's he doing here?" the detective asked.

Maggie shuddered. "I can only think he was planning to take revenge because it was my picture that made his face famous. The security camera pictures were fuzzy, but I inadvertently snapped his picture when I was photographing a little girl. I gave the picture to the airport security people, and they've been showing it ever since."

"Your name, miss, and what you're doing in England?" the detective asked.

"Maggie McKenzie. I'm the travel editor for an American newspaper, and I'm doing a Sunday edition on England. You know, all the places Americans want to know about. I was just on my way to Avebury."

"And you?" The detective turned to the young man.

"Rolf Owen, a friend of the family. I'm returning to Marlborough to attend university. I have a key to the house, and I make myself at home when I'm passing through."

"'Tis true, Inspector." Vera puffed up the stairs. "He stays in Steven's room when he comes. Like a member of the family, he is."

A second policeman hurried up the wide staircase. "I've checked everything twice, sir. There doesn't seem to be anybody else about."

Maggie shook her head. "No, there wouldn't be. I'm sure he was alone."

"Call the ambulance, Sergeant, and let's get this man out of here." The inspector cuffed the unconscious man's hands behind his back, but left him lying as he had fallen. The wound on the back of his head was no longer bleeding, and he was showing signs of regaining consciousness.

"Come on down," Vera said, taking Maggie's hand. "I'll fix a nice cup of tea to settle your nerves. Come, Rolf. I'll put the kettle on for everyone."

Maggie allowed Vera to lead her to the stairs and was just about to follow her down when she became conscious of her pajamas. "Oh, I need to go get dressed."

Rolf laughed. "You're more modest in your sleep attire than most people are on the street these days. Don't bother. You can have a hot cup, then go back to bed and get a good night's sleep."

Maggie had to admit her pajamas were modest by any standards. Pants to the ankles and a baggy tee top with a kitten curled in a basket on the front. She followed everyone to the kitchen, and Vera put the kettle on to boil.

"Would it be too much trouble if I had some hot chocolate instead of tea? That would be more soothing than anything else I can think of." *Except having Flynn at my side,* she thought.

"Cocoa it is," Vera said.

Maggie sat at the table next to Rolf, whom she noted for the first time was a very good-looking young man with a shock of black hair falling over his forehead. His eyes were deep set and serious and so black she could almost see herself mirrored in them.

"Your accent is slightly different from those I've heard so far. You're definitely not English. And I don't think Scottish or Irish, either. Welsh, maybe?" she guessed.

Rolf smiled broadly and acknowledged, "Welsh it is."

"Thank you for saving my life," Maggie said sincerely. "You did, you know."

Rolf nodded. "I'm glad I came when I did. I hadn't planned to stop by tonight. I was going to continue to Marlborough so I could finish my preparation for classes, but I changed my mind at the last minute, and here I am."

"An angel unaware," Vera piped up from the stove.

"An angel what?" Rolf asked.

"Someone doing angels' work, unaware they're helping," Vera explained, setting cups and saucers on the table for them, as well as for the two policemen, though they hadn't joined them in the kitchen yet.

"You were definitely my guardian angel tonight, Rolf. Is there some way I can repay you?" Maggie asked.

Vera answered before Rolf could say anything. "Most assuredly, Miss McKenzie," she said, pouring hot water over the cocoa in Maggie's cup. "Ya can give Rolf a lift to Marlborough. It's right on your way to Avebury."

Maggie looked at Rolf. He nodded. "If you were of a mind to do it, it would be very helpful to me."

Maggie quickly reached for her cup and sipped while she thought about that. She felt she did owe it to him, and he was a close friend of the family who owned the inn, but what else did she really know about him? He could be a serial killer in disguise. *Well, probably not that, considering his actions earlier.* But considering she had just been followed by a sinister man halfway around the world, now hardly seemed the time to throw caution to the wind.

She decided it was best to totally frank with Vera and Rolf. "I'd love to, but I know nothing about you, Rolf. I never give rides to strangers. It's just something a girl shouldn't do. On the other hand, you seem very nice and I'd like to help out. May I think about it tonight? I'll give you my answer first thing in the morning."

Rolf nodded. "I understand, Miss McKenzie."

But Vera huffed and overpoured Rolf's tea. "Seems ta me you'd be grateful for the company of such a brave young man, bein' in a strange country and all."

Maggie didn't know how to respond. Luckily, she was saved from having to make any response at all by Detective Inspector James's appearance at the table.

"The media will probably be all over you two shortly. Capturing an international terrorist wanted in half the countries of the world is a reporter's dream. Right, Miss McKenzie?"

Maggie hadn't even thought of that. "Of . . . of course," she stammered. She realized she should be upstairs writing the story and e-mailing it to Lily for her paper. "And if you'll excuse me, I think that's exactly what I'll do. I've been so stunned by what happened, I hadn't even thought of writing the story. My editor would never forgive me if I dropped the ball on this. If you don't have any further questions for me, Inspector, I think I'll go take care of that little matter."

"I'll talk to Mr. Owen here first, and Vera, then if I have further questions, you can come down and answer them. In the meantime, the press is having a frenzy at the station. I'm sure it won't be long before they're here."

"My goodness, Inspector, then I'd better get me dressed, hadn't I?" Vera said, padding quickly toward her room, her slippers flopping noisily across the floor.

Maggie hurried upstairs and typed the story of her encounter in the airport with the terrorist whose picture she'd snapped accidentally, and who had then bumped into her, nearly knocking her down. She wrote of giving up her memory stick to airport security so they could have the clearer picture she'd shot. With that information in the article, maybe Lionel Lawson would spring for a new memory stick and she wouldn't have to absorb the cost. She could always hope.

She told of being followed and eluding the man, only to have him find her and apparently attempt to gain his revenge for plastering his picture over every CNN broadcast in the world. Maggie described Rolf's actions, which had saved her life. Then she grabbed her camera and her laptop and connection and ran downstairs. She managed to coax Rolf into having his picture taken for the article and included a picture of the housekeeper and Detective Inspector James as a bonus. Vera allowed her to use the Internet connection again to send the story.

The inspector was right about the media arriving en masse, and Maggie escaped upstairs before they could get her picture. She didn't need to become an instant celebrity. That wouldn't help her with the articles she planned to write, she was sure. No amount of coaxing by Vera would get her out of her room. Finally the hubbub died down, and Maggie was able to fall into an exhausted sleep. But not until she had first thanked her Father in Heaven for sending Rolf and petitioned for guidance on whether or not to take him with her to Marlborough.

Ravenwood Estate
Thursday, 11:00 P.M.

Constantine furiously slammed his fist on the table, knocking over the small statue of Rodin's *The Thinker* and the glass that had stood beside it. They crashed to the floor, smashing into a thousand pieces. He'd just caught the late news reporting Ulric's capture.

"The bumbler!" he shouted to no one in particular as he jumped to his feet. "The stupid, bungling bumbler!"

Constantine paced the length and breadth of his library, his mind racing. How was he going to find the blasted girl and retrieve the flash drive now? He didn't even know what she looked like. How ridiculous of her to decline to be photographed tonight. He stopped short. Was there a reason she had refused to have her picture taken? Had she found the flash drive in her bag? Would she know what to do with it if she had discovered it?

These thoughts worried Constantine. They worried him very much. He needed that information—it was vital to the success of this venture. He didn't like changing plans at the last moment, especially after they had already been announced to the world.

How could he get his hands on that infernal young woman? Then he remembered Ulric's last call, the one about the insurance. Ulric had given him the address of a woman and her children that the girl had befriended. If something happened to them, would that bring her out into the open?

It would, unless she already knew about the memory stick and had plans of her own for it. Constantine reached for his cell phone to put things in motion.

# EIGHT

Alton
Friday, 5:45 A.M.

Maggie woke with a start and sat up in bed, completely disoriented. Her dreams had been troubled by raging fires and explosions that had rocked the world off its axis. Were they a portent of things to come or just a reflection of recent events?

She glanced at the clock. Five forty-five. She needed to be on her way to Avebury to see what she could discover about the Rathford family, particularly their adopted sons. And she needed to do it before Alyssa arrived in England. If the news was too bad, Maggie wanted to hear it on her own and not in company with her twin. Alyssa had suffered enough trauma already in the hands of Cleat Wiggins.

Maggie peeked out into the hall, heard no one moving, and slipped into the bathroom. She was showered, dressed, and ready for the day by six fifteen. As she exited her room, her bag over her shoulder, Rolf emerged from a second guest bathroom, dressed and holding his backpack in his hand.

"I'm sorry Vera put you in such a spot last night about giving me a ride today. You don't have to do it, you know," Rolf said quietly. "I understand your position."

Maggie laughed. "She did seem pretty peeved when I didn't jump at the chance. But it's okay. I asked about you, and I've decided you're a good security risk."

Rolf raised his eyebrows. "And to whom did you go for this appraisal?"

Maggie started down the stairs. "The very highest authority. The one I always go to for guidance. So if you're ready for an early start today, I'm ready," she said over her shoulder.

"Not until you've eaten my English breakfast," Vera chimed in from the kitchen. "Sit yourselves down in the dining room. I have the table set already."

Maggie looked at Rolf with a question in her eyes.

"She heard you getting ready," he said with a smile. "She prides herself on giving good service, so you're getting a much earlier breakfast than she would normally serve—and you'll be very happy you are. She's an excellent cook."

They sat at the large round table covered with a white linen cloth and flowers in the center. Orange juice had already been poured. Unbuttered toast rested in a caddy surrounded by several types of jam. Then Vera came in with two plates in her hand.

"This is a typical English breakfast, and since you've only been in country for twenty-four hours, I thought ya might like to try it. It's Rolf's favorite, so when he's here I always fix it."

Maggie stared at the colorful breakfast served on milk-white English china. One egg, over easy; one slice of bacon, barely done; fried mushrooms; and one small tomato, halved and fried only to heat it through and covered with Parmesan cheese.

They ate in silence for a few minutes until Vera appeared again with some fresh fruit. This was more breakfast than Maggie normally ate, since she'd left the ranch, but it was delicious, and she expressed that to Vera.

The cook nodded her thanks, then as Maggie put her napkin on the table and prepared to leave the dining room, Vera asked, "Where ya off to in such a hurry this fine morning? You're not even going to linger for some coffee or tea? I make the best."

"I'm sure you do, but I must get on my way," Maggie said. "Thank you for your kind hospitality. This is such a beautiful home."

"Did you know this house was built in 1810?" Rolf asked, sliding his chair back and standing as Maggie did. "It's contemporary with Jane Austen's home in Chawton. Have you been there?"

Maggie shook her head. "No, I thought about going so I could feature it in an article for my paper, but I've changed my mind. I'm anxious to get to Avebury and finish my business. Maybe I can visit another time, when I've taken care of these other things."

Rolf grabbed his backpack and reached for Maggie's bag to carry it for her, but she thanked him and declined. It contained all of her worldly possessions, including a change of clothes so she didn't have to lug her suitcase in every night. She liked to have the bag at her fingertips at all times.

Vera stood at the door wiping her hands on her apron and thanked Maggie for staying and for giving Rolf a ride.

Maggie smiled. "I'll be happy to have someone who knows the roads and can keep me from getting lost on the roundabouts. Thank you, Vera, for a delicious breakfast and a very comfortable stay."

Not one for long good-byes, Maggie headed for the door with Rolf right behind her. When Maggie started the car, Rolf clicked his seat belt and turned to her. "Do you want the scenic route or to go directly to Avebury?"

Maggie didn't even have to think about it. "The direct route, please. I have some business I need to get out of the way before I can think about pleasure touring or even my assignment. Point the way, please."

Rolf nodded. "The shortest ways are frequently the back roads, so if you don't mind the narrow little lanes, turn left out of here and we'll go through the countryside until we come to a main thorough-fare."

"Actually, I prefer the country roads. Otherwise, I never get to see anything but the car in front of me when we're flying down the freeway at sixty miles an hour." Maggie glanced at Rolf. "Tell me about yourself and your family. Where were you born? Where are you going to school? What are you studying?"

Rolf laughed. "Do Americans always ask so many questions?"

"Only when they want to know something." Maggie glanced at him and flashed a smile. "I think it's only fair to know who I'm traveling with, don't you? I'll be glad to tell you more about myself when you're through."

"Fair enough. I was born in Wales. My father was a coal miner, but he wanted something better for me, so he and my mother worked and scrimped and saved so I could go to college and have a better, easier life than they had. They instilled in me a love of books and reading and learning. I have what you Americans would call an undergraduate degree in teaching, but I'm working on an advanced degree in literature, and I have my eye on opening a bookstore. The English government has a loan program for Welsh businesses, and I think I can get enough to buy the store. That way my mom can work in the bookstore instead of at the pub, while I teach. Eventually I hope to have a whole string of stores, then—" Rolf stopped and turned to Maggie. "I'm sorry. I didn't mean to rabbit. I just get excited about my dream. I forget that no one else finds it as interesting as I do."

"Rabbit?" Maggie asked.

"Go on about something, talk, ramble on forever," Rolf explained.

Maggie laughed at the expression. "Actually, I find it fascinating," she said, squeezing by a small truck on the narrow lane. "I've always been in love with books, and I try to learn everything I can. That's one reason I became a journalist. I wanted to share my passion with others, and through my research and articles, I can do that."

Rolf pointed left at the intersection they were approaching. "We'll go through Froyle. It's shorter."

After a moment of silence, Maggie asked, "Rolf, do you believe in God?"

Puzzled, he nodded his head. "Yes. I believe we are guided by a higher power."

"Well, Mr. Rolf Owen, I believe that you were guided to me by that higher power last night—and you arrived just in the nick of time. Thank you again for following your instincts, as you called it, and coming, even though you hadn't planned on it."

"I assure you it was my pleasure. Now I'll begin earning my ride. See the white two-story building just ahead? It's called the Hen and Chicken Inn. It's a pub and inn that's been here for over four hundred years."

Seeing the little pub reminded Maggie about The Star and the waitress's report of her brother. "Rolf, why would someone frequent the pubs? No, that's not exactly what I mean. What goes on in the pubs besides eating and drinking?"

"The village pubs are the center of village life. People come to visit, to gossip, to tell good news or bad. They play darts, cards, chess, or just sit and listen to the hum and the buzz. They come to find jobs, to hire people, to feel the life and energy of the village."

"Why would someone visit a lot of different ones?" Maggie was trying to understand why the girl at The Star had remembered Damon so vividly.

"When you travel, you stop to dine and drink, or, as I said, find a job if you're interested in the area."

This still didn't answer Maggie's questions, but it would have to do for the present.

"What is it?" Rolf asked.

Maggie was puzzled. "What is what?"

"Your eyes are no longer smiling. You're worried about something?"

Maggie shook her head. "Not really. I'm just a little apprehensive about what I'll find in Avebury."

Rolf waited for her to elaborate, but when she didn't, he asked, "And what business takes you to Avebury that has you so worried?"

Maggie hesitated. "It's a very long story and might be boring for you."

Rolf smiled. "I'll take that chance."

Maggie recited the main details of her life, starting with her growing up years at the McKenzie family ranch in Idaho. Then she told Rolf about her new job at the newspaper in California that had led her to discover she had a look-alike who'd been kidnapped. She explained that she had sought out the girl, who quickly became so important in her life that she could hardly think of anything else. The girl turned out to be her twin sister, separated from her at birth. Now, Maggie explained, she was pursuing other siblings who may have been adopted at birth and brought to England as babies.

Rolf leaned forward. "And you believe one of them might be in Avebury?"

Maggie nodded. "The last known address we had for him was in Arundel. But apparently Damon, the person we believe might be our brother, has a . . ." Maggie paused. How to describe it? "A cruel streak," she continued. "He liked to play vicious pranks on others, and a child was killed during one of them. At least that's what the vicar at St. Nicholas told me. And a waitress at a pub in Petworth confirmed Damon's reputation. His parents were forced to move from the village. A woman at the church told me they'd moved to Avebury, but that was some years ago, so I'm not sure I have much hope of finding them."

Rain began falling in torrents, and Maggie could barely see the road in front of her. She centered all her attention on the road and left the conversation hanging.

"Would you like me go with you to Avebury to meet this man?" Rolf finally asked, breaking the silence in the car. "I'd be glad to. I don't have to be in Marlborough until tomorrow. I just couldn't pass up the opportunity of a free ride today."

Maggie thought about it while she concentrated on the rain-slick road. "Are you sure it wouldn't be an imposition?"

"Not at all," Rolf assured her. "I've been to Avebury many times, and my knowledge of the area might help. Often the home is named, and if you don't know where it's located, it will be hard to find. They don't use the numbering and street system like London and the larger cities."

"Thank you," Maggie said, experiencing a refreshing feeling of relief. "I'd be glad for your company and your expertise."

The next two hours passed quickly and pleasantly while Rolf told Maggie about his life in Wales and how he had had the opportunity to leave his small coal-mining town and attend university when so few others were able to. He'd worked the mines for a couple of years before his family had saved enough money for him to leave his village and begin his higher education, so he was older than most of his classmates. Rolf's descriptions opened a whole new world to Maggie. She longed to photograph his home in Blaenavon and the colorful people and way of life he described.

"Tell me about your university," Maggie said, enjoying the lilt and rhythm of Rolf's Welsh accent.

"I'm tutoring students this summer to help with my advanced degree expenses. The money my parents scrape together doesn't quite cover everything, so I do whatever I can to pay the rest of the costs. I don't tell them I'm working two or three jobs and seeking grants to help. It would be too discouraging for them, as they are doing all that's physically possible and sacrificing more than I wish they had to."

They fell into a comfortable silence for a few minutes while Rolf gazed out the window at the rivulets of water streaming across the glass.

Then he asked, "If this man you're pursuing is such an unpleasant character, why do you want to find him?"

Maggie thought about that. "When I set out on this quest, I had no idea what kind of person he was. It just seemed a good idea to search out what appeared to be an older brother and get acquainted. Then I could go home and tell our biological mother that her scoundrel of a husband had sold another one of her children besides me, and that he was alive and well. I think Lily has a right to know if any of her other children survived. I learned that there's probably another older brother adopted by the same family, too."

Rolf frowned. "Are you sure you want to continue now that you know what kind of person your brother Damon is? And what about the older brother—what do you know of him?"

"That's just it," Maggie said with a sigh. "I don't really know anything except hearsay. It seems that the older brother reformed in his teenage years, but no one knows anything about him now. And maybe Damon was a wicked child who repented and is now perfectly charming."

Rolf stared at Maggie, whose eyes were deep pools of apprehension. "But you don't believe that. You are frightened by him."

Maggie didn't reply. Rolf had voiced the truth.

# NINE

Avebury
Friday, 8:00 A.M.

Rolf directed Maggie to the tiny village of Avebury. They parked in the National Trust parking lot and walked the long narrow lane toward the village, passing many of the huge, upright stones—right out in the open.

"Rolf, what exactly is the National Trust?" Maggie asked. "I'm assuming it's like our national park system that cares for and manages places of national interest. Is that correct?"

"Righto. I believe many of your national treasures are huge places like your Grand Canyon and Yellowstone Park. Ours are more often historic homes or sites."

"Tell me about this place," Maggie said. "I've never heard of it before."

"This is one of the largest henges in Britain," Rolf explained. "Have you seen Stonehenge?"

Maggie shook her head. "Only on TV documentaries." The journalist in Maggie couldn't resist capturing these prehistoric monoliths, even as her head buzzed with questions for whoever would talk to her about the Rathford family. She took two dozen pictures in the three or four minutes it took them to cover the lane from the parking lot to the village where the entrance to the Avebury stones was located.

"These are all mostly unworked stone," Rolf pointed out. "Stonehenge's stones were formed. And these are much more spread out. They believe these stones were placed between 2600 and 2100 BC. Do you want to walk the circle?"

"No. Not today." Maggie shook her head, sending ripples of auburn hair across her shoulders. "I just want to get this over with as quickly as possible."

They headed for the thatch-roofed Red Lion Inn, a picturesque, two-story pub that offered rooms to let—just about the only establishment on the short street that Maggie could identify, besides a tiny post office and gift shop. She snapped pictures of the obviously ancient pub before heading inside, hopeful she'd have quick answers to her questions.

The minute they walked through the door, the loud, robust conversation ceased. Everyone turned to stare at Maggie.

She took a deep breath and approached the bar. "Do you know if Damon Rathford still lives around here?" she asked the barmaid, not caring if the patrons who were straining to hear the conversation succeeded.

The girl looked around the room. "Anyone want to answer that question for the pretty lady?"

Maggie didn't like the sneer on the girl's face, the tone in her voice, or the murmur that began behind her in the room and grew until it was so loud that even if someone had answered the question, she couldn't have heard them.

Maggie whirled around and faced the group of a dozen or more men. "I'm from America," she said loudly, trying to project her voice above the noise, "and I'm looking for Damon Rathford. I think we may be related."

"That's an understatement, missy!" someone yelled. "Ye're the spittin' image of the demon."

"Does he still live around here?" Maggie repeated.

"Not if we can help it, he don't," another replied. "We don't want to lose any more of our barns."

"Do his parents still live here?" Maggie pressed, hoping to glean some information from this jeering group.

"Not since about five years ago," the maid behind the bar said. "When their demon son was kicked out of town for trying to burn the place down, they moved."

Maggie turned back to the unpleasant girl. "Do you know where they went?"

"Why do you want to find the likes of him?" the girl asked. She leaned across the polished dark wood bar and stabbed her finger toward Maggie. "If you're related, you must be like the rest of the family. Are you a fire-loving demon, too?"

Maggie recoiled as if she had been struck. Rolf caught her as she stumbled backward.

"Folks 'round here don't like that sort of people, so if I were you, I'd just keep on moving. You never know what sort of bad luck might find you if you stick around." The barmaid laughed loudly, as if she had said something very funny.

Maggie eyed the group, then stepped toward the nearest table and leaned down to the one old man who hadn't raised his eyes since she walked in the door. "Can you tell me where they might have moved?"

The man slowly raised his head, and his eyes grew wide as he looked at Maggie. He didn't say a word, just stared into her deep blue eyes for a very long moment. "Leave it alone, mum," he said so quietly she almost didn't hear him. "Leave it alone," he mumbled again. "Ye're no match for him. He's evil. Methinks ye're not." With that he slowly got to his feet and shuffled out the door.

Maggie turned to the patrons who had quieted to hear the interchange. "Will someone please tell me where I can find Damon's parents?"

This time her request was met with stony silence. Rolf took her by the elbow and led her from the pub. "You'll not get an answer from them while they're together. Let's see if we can catch the old man. If he's alone, he might tell us something."

But as they turned to leave, Maggie caught sight of the television, which flashed a picture that made her stop dead in her tracks. It was Jennie, Tara, and the baby. Maggie stared a moment to make sure of what she saw, then ran to the bar. "Could you please turn that up?" she asked the girl behind the counter.

The announcer was repeating the message: "Will the young woman who was seen helping these Americans on the flight from Los Angeles yesterday please check in to the nearest police station? Last night, Jennie Albright and her two children were taken forcibly from her sister's home, where they had come for a month-long visit. Local police believe that the young woman who helped Mrs. Albright with her children as she boarded and deplaned may be able to offer some clue as to why they were abducted or where they might be at this time."

"Rolf! That's me they're talking about! I was the one who helped Jennie and Tara. What could possibly have happened to them? Where's the nearest police station? I've got to go talk to the police."

"What about your brother? What about the Rathford family?" Rolf asked.

"They'll have to wait. I've got to find out what happened to Jennie and Tara." Maggie fairly flew back to the car with Rolf right behind her.

* * *

Avebury
Friday, 8:00 A.M.

Flynn tried again to reach Maggie on her cell phone. Still no answer. She must not have turned it on yet this morning. No matter. He would wait right here in Avebury until she showed up. She'd probably time her arrival for when the National Trust site opened. He was sure she'd want to photograph it.

Flynn finished his breakfast and began checking out of the bed-and-breakfast where he'd spent a restless night worrying about Maggie's safety. It was then that he saw the story on the morning news about the American photographer who had inadvertently snapped a picture of the escapee wanted for questioning as a terrorist at LAX. The reporters stated that recent events revealed that the wanted man, whom authorities had presumed dead after finding a body in an LA airport restroom, had assumed a false identity and pursued the photographer all the way to England. The escapee had been captured last night as he crept up the stairs to take revenge on the young woman for plastering his picture all over the world. In order to protect her privacy, the American photographer's name wasn't mentioned, nor was her photo shown.

Could that photographer have been Maggie? She could have taken the picture CNN had been running for the last twenty-four hours. That must have been why that man had been trailing her. Flynn felt sure it must be Maggie. Thank heaven the man had been captured. Flynn shook his head and smiled as he paid his bill. Just like Maggie to duck out to avoid publicity. She wanted to be behind the camera, not in front of it.

But Maggie would still come here to find the Rathford family—and Flynn would be waiting. As he picked up his bag and walked to the door, another news bulletin caught his attention. The police were seeking an unknown young woman who had helped a mother and two children at the airport in Los Angeles; the mother and children had suddenly disappeared upon arriving in England.

Flynn caught his breath. That would be so like Maggie to step up and help anyone needing any kind of aid. But why did the police want to talk to her—if it actually was Maggie they were seeking? She wasn't the only Good Samaritan in the world, but she definitely was one of them.

He dropped his bag in the trunk of his car and drove the short two blocks to the Red Lion Inn, the center of all activity in Avebury. He would wait for Maggie there.

\* \* \*

Ravenwood Estate
Friday, 8:15 A.M.

"Thank you, Inspector. The bulletin should bring her in as soon as she sees it. I'd appreciate it if you could let me know immediately so I may come personally and conduct the interview. I realize it is highly irregular for a member of the government to get involved in police work like this, but I fear for our national reputation as well as our tourist industry. The public will be appalled, knowing an innocent young mother and her children could be snatched from the safety of a British home. We must get to the bottom of this without delay."

Constantine hung up, a satisfied smirk on his perfectly tanned face. His blue eyes were not smiling, however. They would have struck fear into the heart of anyone who saw their icy glint. This had all gone wrong. Ulric had been one of his most trusted employees. That was why he had been given the job of delivering the plans from Australia.

It must be the young woman's fault. She must have cursed Ulric. Why else would he suddenly have been unable to follow through on the simplest of jobs? Any street urchin in London could have snatched her bag in a flash. He'd seen Ulric cut someone's throat without a second thought. What had prevented him this time?

Constantine couldn't wait to meet the girl face-to-face. Then he'd see about a curse.

* * *

Avebury
Friday, 8:15 A.M.

Maggie unlocked the car and climbed in, but as she stuck the key in the ignition, she saw a little note stuck under the windshield wiper and a young boy scampering off into the bushes. She got out, retrieved the note, and opened it. It contained one word. *Lacock.*

She got back in the car and gave it to Rolf. "What or where is Lacock?"

Rolf smiled. "It's a beautifully preserved medieval village a few kilometers from here. It's a favorite of filmmakers. Part of *Harry Potter* was shot in the Abbey there, as well as *Pride and Prejudice, Emma, Moll Flanders,* and the *Mayor of Casterbridge.* The whole village is under the auspices of the National Trust. Nothing can be changed without permission."

"I assume this note is here to help me find the Rathfords. But why would the family have moved to a place like that?" Maggie asked, puzzled.

"Why would they move to a place like Avebury, which is also a National Trust property?" Rolf countered.

Maggie looked up sharply. "Could this be at pattern? Maybe Damon's father is employed by the National Trust. When they have to leave an area, he just applies for a transfer and off they go to another idyllic spot until their troublesome son gets them expelled."

Rolf nodded. "That sounds logical."

"Will they have a police station there?" Maggie asked.

"I'm not sure—possibly just a constable. If we pass through a city that has a station before we reach Lacock, we can stop there first."

"Then let's investigate Lacock," Maggie said, starting the car.

They drove in silence for a few minutes before Maggie glanced at Rolf. "What kind of activity could Damon be involved in? It sounds like he sets things on fire, which is certainly bad, but people are reacting like he's a fiend of the worst kind. I thought it was Llewellyn who was intrigued by fire, not Damon. What does Damon do that causes such uproar?"

"People in these little villages are a superstitious lot. If they don't understand something, they ascribe it to some supernatural phenomenon. Think about the crop circles. They say men from outer space made them. If they don't understand it, then it must be Satan or witches or little green men or gnomes or elves or fairies. Nothing has natural cause and effect. Everything is discussed, dissected, bandied about, enlarged, exaggerated, and attributed to anything but human nature. And the people here have a long memory. They don't forgive and forget."

Rolf's explanation made Maggie feel a little better, and she thought about his words for the next few kilometers to Lacock, with Rolf pointing the direction at each turn in the road. Maggie remained lost in thought, driving by rote, not noting the countryside she passed through or the historic districts that would ordinarily have delighted the journalist in her.

* * *

Avebury
Friday, 8:20 A.M.

Flynn paced the block in front of the Red Lion Inn in Avebury, puzzled that Maggie hadn't appeared or answered her cell phone yet. Since he'd learned of the capture of the suspected terrorist, he had breathed a little easier, but once again his fears had begun running wild. Why hadn't she turned on her phone? Surely she kept her charger handy, so it couldn't be a dead battery.

He approached the door of the Red Lion Inn. Time to go inside and ask a few questions. But as he put his hand on the doorknob, a small boy ran up to him.

"Are you waiting for someone, mister?" he asked quietly.

"Yes, I am. Why do you ask?" The boy didn't look like a beggar. He was well-dressed in clean clothes and had shoes on his feet.

"Grandfather would like to speak to you, if you have time," the boy said, pointing to an old man sitting on a picnic bench to the side of the pub.

Flynn followed the boy toward the old man, but suddenly, the old man got up and moved swiftly to the rear of the building. Flynn stopped. The boy took his hand and pulled him along.

"I don't think he wants anyone to see him speaking to you," he confided in a low voice.

When Flynn and the boy rounded the corner of the inn, the old man stood almost hidden in the shadows of a huge ancient tree.

"You look like an American. Are you waiting for a young American woman?" the old man asked softly.

Flynn nodded, hope flooding through him. "Yes, she has auburn hair and very blue eyes. Have you seen her?"

"She was here this morning, asking about a family who was driven from the village a few years ago."

"Where is she now?" Flynn asked, his heart racing.

"I guided her to Lacock. Perhaps that was a mistake. She may be in danger if she finds the family. You must catch her before she does."

"What kind of danger?" Flynn asked.

"I cannot say—the son in the family she seeks may not be stable. What's more, I'm told that when she and the young man accompanying her saw the bulletin on the telly about the kidnapping of a woman and her children, they raced from the inn. Your friend is a good young woman with kind eyes. I hope you find her quickly."

The old man turned and disappeared through the heavy shrubs with the boy close on his heels. Flynn stood still, stunned at the news. Not only had he missed Maggie, but she was apparently in danger of another kind. And who was the man with her?

Flynn dialed Maggie's phone number one more time. Voice mail again.

# TEN

Lacock
Friday, 8:40 A.M.

When she turned onto High Street and parked by the Old Market Cross in front of the school, Maggie finally became aware of her unusual surroundings. She felt as if she had suddenly been transported back in time.

"This is amazing," she said, getting out of the car and gazing up the wide street lined on both sides with two-story, ochre-colored brick homes and stores. "Is there a building here less than four hundred years old?"

"Probably not. Like I said, the whole town is under the auspices of the National Trust. Nothing can be changed, and nothing new can be built."

There were no sidewalks, but places of business had placed huge tubs of petunias and geraniums or shrubbery in front of their establishments to delineate the walkways from the parking areas.

Maggie looked around. "I didn't see a sign for the police station anywhere. Do you have any idea where it might be?"

"I'll go inquire at the pub." Rolf smiled at Maggie. "You stay here so you don't incite the patrons." He strode off down the street to a three-story redbrick hotel flying a yellow flag with a red lion emblazoned on it.

While she waited, Maggie peered in the alcoved window of the combination village store and post office, where sweets in jars, country preserves, and English wines were arranged on display. She decided she would take a moment to find something to bring back to Lily and started to enter the store when the shop girl met her with a broom in her hands. Maggie stepped back quickly, fully expecting the girl to start swinging the broom at her.

"Oh, sorry, mum. I wasn't watching where I was sweeping." She smiled and looked up at Maggie, but suddenly the smile faded from her face and her mouth fell open. She stared at Maggie for so long without moving that Maggie was afraid the girl had suffered a stroke.

"Are you okay, miss?" Maggie asked quietly, standing motionless by the door frame, not wanting to frighten the girl who still held the broom in her hands.

"If I believed in reincarnation," the girl breathed the words slowly, "I'd swear on my grandmother's grave that you were Demon, come back to haunt me."

"What? Is Damon dead?" Maggie almost whispered the question.

As if in a fog, the girl slowly shook her head, her eyes never leaving Maggie's. "He ought to be, but he has nine lives, like the black cats he loves."

"Does he still live in Lacock?" Maggie asked quietly.

Again the girl shook her head. "The town voted for them to leave. No one wanted that madness to spread further than it already had."

"What madness?"

"No one knew exactly what—it was all a big secret. All the local lads he involved swore an oath to never tell about the group. Then after the Comstock barn burned, folks here had had about enough and forced the family to leave."

"Where did they go?"

Before she could answer, a gaggle of teenage girls noisily exited their car in front of the store and brought the shop girl back to her senses. She blinked, cast a frightened glance at Maggie, and hurried back into the store, shutting the door solidly behind her.

"So much for that," Maggie said aloud.

"So much for what?" Rolf asked, coming up behind her. "Who are you talking to?"

"Myself, now," Maggie said, still gazing at the door that had slammed in front of her. "But I was talking to a girl who thought I was the reincarnation of Damon. When I asked where the family had moved, it was if she awoke from a trance and ran away." Maggie turned to Rolf. "What did you find out?"

"Probably about as much as you did," Rolf shrugged. "The Rathford family did live here with one son who was in his early twenties at the time. They were asked to leave some three years ago. No one knows for sure where they went. When I asked if Mr. Rathford was employed by the National Trust, my informant shut down and busied himself with a bona fide customer. End of interview."

"The age sounds about right. He should be just a couple of years older than Alyssa and me. And what did you find out about the police station?" Maggie asked.

"There's a large one at Melksham, just down the road, which would put us right on the way to either Bath or Wells, which are both big National Trust areas."

"Are you game to continue, or are you ready to return to Marlborough and your tutoring?" Maggie asked, getting into the car.

Rolf got in, buckled his seat belt, and smiled at Maggie. "I have until tomorrow morning at eleven. My time is yours as long as I can make my appointment."

Maggie checked the time. Eight forty-five. With their early start, they'd covered a lot of ground this morning. She studied the map and silently prayed for guidance. Where should she look? She knew Bath was a large city and that it would take a lot of time to search there.

"Tell me about Wells," Maggie said. "I need a little guidance on where to search next. I'm not feeling like Bath is the answer, since the last three places the Rathfords lived have been small villages. Wells looks like another mostly rural setting. Is it?"

Rolf nodded. "Yes. And using the criteria of smaller and more rural, that's probably a good guess. But if you get detained at the police station, you may never get to Wells and solve the Rathford mystery."

Maggie looked at him. "What do you mean?"

"I've been thinking about it. I have a lot of questions as to why they would put out such a bulletin. You said you met the woman in the airport, helped her with her children, sat at different places on the plane, and then simply handed her off to her sister in the baggage area. What could you possibly know about her that could help determine why she was kidnapped?"

Maggie went limp and slumped against the seat. Rolf had a point. "Tell me what you're thinking," she said.

"My father always told me that I read too many books, which gave birth to a vivid imagination," Rolf said slowly. "But just to be safe, why don't you ring in to the police instead of going to the station? Ask them how you can help them, and tell them all you know over the phone. Then, if there is something rotten in Denmark, you won't be stopped from your assignment or your pursuit of your family. They can't trace your cell phone like they could a landline."

Maggie looked at Rolf with new eyes. "I did think the bulletin was odd, but I would never have thought of an ulterior motive. With the police involved, I figured it was totally legit and that I needed to do what I could to help."

Rolf smiled a little sadly. "I'm sure this happens in your country at times; however, here there is frequently corruption in high places. This smells a little funny to me."

"You're exactly right," Maggie exclaimed. "I was so anxious to help Jennie and Tara that I didn't think beyond that."

"If you want to speak to the police, you can dial 100 for operator assistance for the nearest police station, or 999 for emergency service."

"But if I don't want them to know my location, I could call operator assistance and ask for Scotland Yard in London," Maggie said. "They certainly have all the information on this broadcast, and they wouldn't be able to pinpoint my location to the nearest station."

"Good thinking," Rolf said.

Maggie left a message for Alyssa on her cell phone, then called Scotland Yard in London. There was little she could tell them—she didn't even know Jennie's last name. Their acquaintance had been brief, and they had not exchanged personal information. She had simply helped the woman with her little girl and a piece of luggage. She quickly hung up and turned off her cell phone when she'd completed her short report. She suspected that leaving it on might make it possible to trace her location, and if Rolf's instincts were correct, that wouldn't be a good idea. Now Maggie was anxious to get on with her quest.

\* \* \*

London
Friday, 8:50 A.M.

Alyssa clicked on her cell phone as soon as she deplaned at Heathrow. She planned to call Maggie and see where they were to meet. She wasn't surprised to find a voice mail waiting; Maggie was always on top of things.

"Alyssa, have someone direct you to the Victoria Station, and then catch the train to Bath. I'll meet you there at eleven thirty. I'm heading for Wells to do some research, but I'll leave for Bath in plenty of time to meet your train. Call me if you have a change of plans."

Alyssa dropped her cell phone in her pocket and clutched her suitcase tighter. *I can do this,* she kept saying to herself. *All I have to do is find someone to tell me how. I* can *do this.*

As she turned to find a porter or any official-looking person to help her find the right station out of Heathrow, her cell phone rang. She glanced at the caller ID. Dr. Flynn Ford.

"Hi, Dr. Ford. You just caught me. I'm trying to find someone to direct me to Victoria Station so I can catch the train to Bath."

"Bath . . . England?"

"Don't be mad. I didn't tell you, because I knew you'd just try to talk me out of going."

"I'm not mad, just surprised. What are you going to do in Bath?" Flynn asked hopefully.

"I'm meeting Maggie. She left a voice message—said she'd meet me in Bath at eleven thirty. She's going to Wells now, wherever that is. The English do have a thing about water, don't they?"

"Water? What do you mean?" Flynn asked.

"You know, Bath, Wells, both having to do with water." Alyssa laughed. "I'm so excited I can hardly stand it! Who'd have thought seven months ago I would actually be flying halfway across the world all by myself!"

"You've come a long way, Alyssa. You deserve all the happiness you can grab," Flynn said sincerely.

"Oh, by the way, what did you call me about?" Alyssa asked, almost as an afterthought.

"Just wanting to know how Maggie was coming on her pursuit of your long-lost brothers," Flynn said casually.

"I'll let you know later. She didn't tell me anything more than where she'd meet me. Do you want me to call you when I catch up with her?"

"Yes, please do. I'm anxious to know what you find out. Thanks, Alyssa. Have a great time," he replied. Alyssa told him good-bye, then hung up the phone to continue her search for the right station.

* * *

Flynn disconnected and breathed a sigh of relief. Finally. He headed back to his car, located Bath on the map, and then looked for Wells. Not that far.

*Please, guide me to Maggie before something happens to her*, he prayed.

* * *

Ravenwood Estate
Friday, 8:50 A.M.

"Mr. Constantine, sir, we've just had a call from that young woman who befriended the Albright woman and her kids."

"Good. Where is she? I'll helicopter right there."

"Well, sir, she didn't come in to a station. She said she saw the broadcast and figured it was her they were talking about, but she said she knew absolutely nothing that would help the police find out why the woman and her kids had been kidnapped. She answered our questions, but I had to agree there was no good reason for her to interrupt her holiday for a trip to the station."

"You did trace the call, didn't you?" Constantine demanded.

"We tried, sir, but she called from a cell phone, and as soon as she hung up, she must have turned off the phone, so we weren't able to get a fix on her location."

Constantine paced the floor of his library but found it too confining for his immense anger at this frustrating news. He stepped through the

French doors onto the terrace overlooking the grounds and with extreme effort gained control of his temper and his tone.

"What exactly did the woman say?" Constantine asked.

"That she had simply assisted Jennie Albright with her little girl because the woman had her hands full with a baby and the child and their luggage. So she entertained the child, assisted them on the plane, and when they landed, she found them and helped carry the luggage and the child off the plane. She didn't know anything about them at all, not where they were from or where they were going or even their last name. She only knew that a sister met them; she turned the child and the diaper bag over to the sister and said good-bye."

"What other questions did you ask her? Did you get her name?" Constantine demanded.

"No, sir. I'm sorry. I asked for her name, and she said it didn't matter, because she had no information that would help us. Is there anything else I can do for you, sir?"

Constantine gritted his teeth to keep from shouting into the phone, "Yes, go shoot yourself in the foot, you idiot!" Instead, he said quietly, "Thank you, Inspector. Please let me know if you learn anything else about the young woman or if she calls in again. I'd like this solved as quickly as possible so that we can get Mrs. Albright and her children returned safely. The longer this goes on, the more tarnished our national image will become, and the more pressure will be exerted on Scotland Yard."

"Yes, sir, I understand. I'll stay in touch."

The man known as Mr. Constantine disconnected and stared out across his vast gardens to the woods beyond. Then he dialed a familiar number. "Edward, I have a suggestion which may get you a bonus. A newscast this morning mentioned that some American reporter had inadvertently taken a picture of that escaped terrorist in LA. The picture ended up all over American networks and CNN. Find out the name of that reporter and get a picture."

He disconnected, turned back into the library, and rang for his butler. "I'd like to do some shooting. Will you have the stable boy saddle my horse and set up the clay pigeons? And I won't be here for dinner tonight. In fact, why don't you take the rest of the day off and go see your grandchildren? I think I keep you far too busy for their liking."

The butler dipped his head in a quick bow, muttered, "Thank you, sir," and hurried off to the stables, glancing back over his shoulder at his composed but clearly angry master. When Mr. Constantine had that look in his eye, sane men scattered.

After giving the stable boy his instructions, the butler returned to the house and told his wife they were going to town for dinner. Neither of them thought it wise to stay around this evening.

# ELEVEN

Lacock
Friday, 8:50 A.M.

"How long will it take us to get to Wells?" Maggie asked Rolf. "Do we have to go through Bath? I'm not sure I want to drive in that big city on the wrong side of the road. I like these little rural lanes."

"It'll take about forty-five minutes," Rolf said. "And you can avoid Bath, but when we go back to meet Alyssa, we should spend some time there. It's an ancient city, and it's uniquely beautiful."

"I hope we have time for that. Fasten your seat belt. We're on our way." Maggie turned onto the road, then drove without conversing for a few minutes, mulling over the events of the morning.

"Tell me more about yourself, Maggie," Rolf said, interrupting the silence. "Interests, dreams, that sort of thing."

Maggie laughed. "Could you be more specific, please?

"Do you have a boyfriend?"

Maggie glanced at Rolf. "That's a question I don't know if I can answer."

"Why?" Rolf said. "Either you do or you don't."

"You might think so, but my situation is complicated."

"Ahh. Complicated. This could be interesting."

Maggie shrugged. "I guess you can judge for yourself." She had already told Rolf about her search for Alyssa. Now she added Dr. Flynn Ford to the story, reporting his part in the search, and the fact that he was a psychologist studying Stockholm Syndrome.

"I've read about that. People who have been kidnapped sometimes form a bond or attachment to their captors and frequently turn on someone attempting to rescue them. Isn't that right?" Rolf asked.

"Yes. Before I met Dr. Ford, his wife and child had been kidnapped—and she'd apparently succumbed to Stockholm Syndrome. When the FBI found them and tried to rescue them, she came out shooting at her rescuers. She was killed in the volley of shots, as was her little girl. Flynn couldn't get over their deaths, couldn't put it behind him. He started a serious study of the syndrome, interviewing victims everywhere, trying to understand how and why it happens."

Maggie caught her breath, remembering Flynn's anguish as he told her the story. He'd had to stop the car and get out in the cold and rain to regain control of his feelings. "Flynn and I had a few days of pretty intense emotions while we were trying to reach Alyssa. She'd indicated she was in great danger, and we were trying to reach her before her captor killed her. When we finally located Alyssa, we all flew to my home on the ranch in Idaho for Christmas. We wanted somewhere safe from the media circus to allow Alyssa to acclimate back into a normal situation. By this time I had fallen in love with Flynn, and he had told me he loved me. But then he slipped away in the middle of the night on Christmas Eve without saying good-bye." Maggie stopped, experiencing again the pain she'd felt reading his note the next morning.

"That's all? He just left?" Rolf's voice was full of disbelief. "You haven't heard from him since then?"

Maggie tried to shake off the melancholy that always gripped her when she thought of that morning. "He did leave a note, telling me he wanted to give me time and space to decide if I really loved him, or if I had just been caught up in the intensity of our shared experiences. He also said he needed time to investigate my church to find out if it was something that appealed to him." Maggie was quiet for another long minute. "I'd told him I couldn't marry anyone not of my faith."

Rolf let out a slow whistle. "So I take it you're still wondering where he stands."

Maggie nodded. "He called me on Christmas night to explain things. We're supposed to meet on Christmas Day in Salt Lake City." She amended quickly, "If we still feel the same as we did last Christmas."

"And you still feel the same?" Rolf asked.

Maggie flashed Rolf a rueful smile. "Unfortunately, yes. There hasn't been a day in the last seven months that I haven't thought of him, wondered what he was doing, how he felt about me."

"What if he decides not to embrace your faith?" Rolf asked, deep concern filling his voice. "What will you do?"

Maggie hesitated before answering. "I guess I'll just get on with my life without him. My faith means too much to me to marry someone who doesn't believe as I do." She tried to smile at Rolf. "So, does that answer your question?"

Rolf nodded. "I can see why you didn't know quite how to answer it. Thank you for telling me that. I wish you all the best."

"Thank you, Rolf," she said, then glanced at the gas meter. "Whoa. We're almost running on empty here. I haven't been paying any attention."

Maggie spotted a petrol station just ahead. She pulled up to the pump, and Rolf jumped out to refuel while Maggie went inside to pay. As she waited for Rolf to finish, she listened to the television newscaster giving the hourly countdown to the deadline from the terrorists: only thirty-three hours until Paris would be destroyed if the terrorists' demands weren't met. The next segment showed the pictures of Jennie Albright, Tara, and the baby, asking for anyone with information to please come forward.

Maggie was stabbed to the quick. Could she have done more? Could the police have wheedled some information from her that she wasn't even aware she had? Maybe she should go to the nearest police station and turn herself in.

But a little something in the back of her mind told her that no, it would do Jennie no good, and certainly not Maggie, either.

"Maggie?" Rolf touched her arm. "Maggie, I'm through. We can go now."

"Oh, I'm sorry. I was just a little lost in thought."

Rolf looked apologetic. "I've just had a phone call from a student who lives outside of Bath. He has an exam tomorrow and wanted to know if I could meet him somewhere today and give him some extra help. When I told him we were near the city, he was elated. Would you mind dropping me off at Bradford-on-Avon? It's the next little town, and from there you can bypass Bath and go on to Wells." Rolf sighed. "I'm sorry, Maggie. I did so want to be with you when you found your brother, but I can't turn this student down. He's struggling, and he must pass this exam."

"Rolf, I totally understand. I do appreciate your help and the moral support you've given me. Come on. Let's get you to Bradford."

The drive to Bradford took only ten minutes, and when Maggie stopped to drop off Rolf, he asked for her cell phone number. "Just in case there's a point where we can connect again, I'd like to stay in touch, if you don't mind." He handed her a little piece of paper on which he'd scribbled his number.

"Thanks, Rolf. And thanks again for all you've done for me, especially for saving my life." Maggie sincerely meant that. She knew she would most likely not be alive today if Rolf had not been inspired to change his plans and stay at the Manor.

"Anytime, Maggie." He slammed the door and waved as she drove off toward Wells.

Maggie glanced at her watch. Ten minutes after nine. She'd need to keep track of time so she could be back in Bath to meet Alyssa. Since this was the first time her twin had attempted such an adventure, Maggie couldn't leave her stranded at the station.

The miles flew by as Maggie, finally alone in the car, pondered again on the broadcast that had asked for her help. Was the request that she come forward just a shot in the dark from the police, hoping she had learned something from Jennie that would help them locate her?

Maggie shook her head. That would definitely be shot in the dark. But what else could it have been? Was there some connection between the terrorist she had photographed and Jennie's kidnapping? No, that was silly. But there was something amiss here. Maggie just couldn't put her finger on it.

Wells
Friday, 9:40 A.M.

Suddenly Maggie found herself in Wells. Her heart beat faster as she parked in public parking and followed the signs to the city center on foot. At the far end of the ancient, curved thoroughfare, the spires of the cathedral stretched above the fourteenth-century storefronts that lined the picturesque cobblestone street. Her first stop would be the local National Trust office, which was probably located near the cathedral.

Flower baskets overflowing with pink and white blossoms hung all along the sidewalk. At the end of the street, she discovered the National Trust office nestled between a castlelike turret and an ancient three-story rock building. As she stepped inside the antediluvian brick structure festooned with baskets and pots of flowers, she gasped, then nearly turned and ran.

Cleat Wiggins.

# TWELVE

Maggie grabbed the door and steadied herself. It couldn't be. Cleat was dead. She'd watched him die. But here he was—dressed up, slimmed down, and cleanly shaven. Maggie took a deep breath and blinked. She could see now that it wasn't Cleat, but the likeness was staggering.

When the older man looked up, he appeared as shocked at the sight of Maggie as she had been when she first saw him. They stared at each other for what seemed minutes, but in fact, could only have been a few seconds before Maggie received the second surprise of the morning.

"What have we here?" a pleasant masculine voice from behind her said, bringing her back to her senses. "If you were a man, I'd say you were my long-lost identical twin. I suppose, you still could be, but, of course, we'd be fraternal twins."

Maggie turned her head slightly, and an electric current flashed through her as she looked at what was the most remarkable resemblance to herself and Alyssa.

As she recovered her wits at the sight of the young man, she said in what she hoped was a casual, confident tone, "You must be Damon Rathford." She didn't want to sound as shaken as she felt.

The young man nodded slowly and strode across the shop with such purpose Maggie almost fled. He touched her face, stroked her hair, and laughed. "You're for real. You're not made up to look like me. Your eyes and hair color are so like mine, it's unbelievable!"

"Yes, I'm for real." She studied him for a moment, then turned back to the older man. "I would guess you're Cleat Wiggins's brother."

The man stood uncertain, as if frozen with indecision, not offering his hand, any explanation, or introduction.

"Yes, he is," answered Damon. "Except the family name is Rathford, not Wiggins. Cleat changed his name when he disgraced the family and fled to America. And now that you know who we are, my pretty little look-alike, who are you?"

"I'm Maggie McKenzie, and it would appear that we're related." Uncomfortable at such close proximity, Maggie stepped away from Damon's magnetic presence and toward the elder Rathford. "Cleat Wiggins was my biological father."

"Was?" Damon asked, raising an eyebrow.

"He's dead," Maggie said softly.

"And now you've come to claim his portion of the family fortune." Damon's voice suddenly became ice-cold and his eyes even colder.

"I know nothing of a family fortune," Maggie said, drawing herself up to her full five feet eight inches. "Cleat was dirt-poor his entire life and apparently spent what money he could scrape up on drugs. No, I didn't come to talk about money. I don't want it or need it, if there is, in fact, any such thing as a Rathford family fortune. I came to talk to you, Mr. Rathford." Maggie turned to the older man and stepped toward him. "Could we speak privately for a minute?"

"Anything you have to say, you can say in front of me," Damon said. "If Cleat Wiggins was your father, that makes you my little sister, since he sired me as well." Damon stared at her. "Is that what you wanted to speak to my father about?"

Maggie nodded. "I wasn't sure you knew you were adopted."

"Of course I know. What else do you want?" Damon demanded.

Maggie did her best to smile at the still-scowling Damon. "I just want to tell you that there are actually more of us. I have a twin sister, Alyssa. An identical twin." Maggie laughed at the picture that appeared in her mind. "We would certainly turn heads if the three of us appeared anywhere together."

Damon's dour expression turned to astonishment and then amusement. He spun toward the other man. "Well, well, Father. It appears your brother Cleat was more prolific than we thought." Damon turned back to Maggie, smiled broadly, then grabbed her hands and swung her around in the small gift shop. "There are actually four of us, little sister.

You have not just one brother, but two! We are a whole room full of look-alikes!"

Maggie waited for his exuberance to wane and then released herself from his grasp. She looked up at Damon, who was at least six inches taller than she was. "Where is the other brother?" Then she corrected herself. "*Our* other brother."

"Our firstborn sibling considers himself too good to cavort with the likes of us," Damon said rather bitterly. "He became a great soldier, took himself to Wales, set up a 'respectable business,' established a solid name and reputation in politics and government, and distanced himself from this little branch of his family. We rarely see him, except occasionally when his picture appears in the paper."

A customer entered the shop, and Damon turned to the door to greet the newcomer. He was the epitome of polite graciousness, asking quietly what he might do to help the young lady. In spite of Damon's earlier coldness, Maggie had difficulty believing this was the same man people had been calling "Demon" everywhere she went. Maggie turned to Mr. Rathford, who averted his eyes rather than meet her gaze. While Damon charmed his young customer, Maggie approached the elder Rathford.

"Did you make two trips to America, or were you living there when Lily and Cleat's boys were born?" she asked quietly.

Seemingly drained of all energy by the interchange between his son and Maggie, Mr. Rathford merely inclined his head in invitation and turned slowly toward the office. Maggie followed right on his heels. He closed the door and sank into the chair behind the desk, motioning toward the other chair in the small room.

"My wife and I were childless for many years," he began quietly. "Then Cleat wrote that his wife was having a baby and that they had no money to raise the child. If we wanted to come and get it, we could raise the baby as our own. At first he said his wife didn't want the baby yet was afraid of having an abortion, but when we arrived in America, he wouldn't let us meet Lily. He finally admitted he hadn't told her about us, and that he planned to tell her the baby died. I believe he administered drugs so she wouldn't remember anything of the birth."

Maggie nodded. That part of the story she already knew.

Mr. Rathford continued. "I should have realized that my less-than-honorable brother wouldn't do anything purely out of the goodness of his heart. He wanted money—a lot of money—when we arrived to take the baby." He rested his elbows on the arms of the chair and hung his head in his hands. "I knew the adoption wasn't entirely aboveboard, but I couldn't just turn around and come home, leaving my wife with empty arms when we were finally so close to getting a child after so many years."

This also had a familiar ring to Maggie. She had heard her adoptive mother, Ruth McKenzie, speak of her anguish after losing two little girls and having no baby to take home from the hospital to cradle and love.

Slowly, Mr. Rathford resumed his narration without looking up at Maggie. "We returned here with Llewellyn. My wife had never been happier. The child was adorable—even beguiled *me* with his happy little smile and sweet disposition." He sighed and paused for so long Maggie feared he had gone to sleep with his head in his hands.

Then he continued, even more quietly than before. Maggie had to lean forward to hear him. "My brother contacted me again about four years later. His wife was pregnant. Did we want this child, too? After all, it was my own flesh and blood, he reminded me, and I could raise the children as they should be raised, in a proper English home, with the education and good manners that would be required to make them genteel and cultured. I could raise them to uphold the honor of the Rathford name."

Mr. Rathford finally raised his head and faced Maggie. "He knew that would get my attention. Heritage has always been important to the Rathfords." He sat up a little straighter. "Father constantly stressed our historic genealogical lines—our roots extend beyond William the Conqueror and Charlemagne."

"But that wasn't important to Cleat?" Maggie asked, not wanting Mr. Rathford to stop his narration, and hoping the customer would keep Damon busy long enough for her to hear all of Mr. Rathford's story. She feared once he returned, she might not get anything more from this quiet man.

"Cleat cared about nothing except himself. Whatever he could do to get gain with the least amount of effort seemed to be his aim in life. He disgraced the family name when he was caught in a theft ring that he himself had organized in his late teens. Father regarded that as far worse than having succumbed to the temptation offered by someone else. In a rage, Father disinherited him, threw him from the house, and forbade him to ever use our name again."

"But you kept in touch with him after he went to America?" Maggie asked quietly.

"He wrote to me when he needed funds. I secretly sent money every year or so, especially after he was married. It was bad enough to have my younger brother hungry when I had plenty, but I couldn't stand the thought of his wife suffering because of him."

Mr. Rathford leaned forward. "I have a question, Miss McKenzie, if I may ask something quite personal. You mentioned a twin sister, an identical twin."

"Yes," Maggie said, surprised at the initiative Mr. Rathford was exhibiting for the first time in their conversation.

He cleared his throat. "I perceive that you are a sweet girl with a kind disposition. You seem—how can I say this—confident and at peace with your world. Is your twin of like temperament and character?"

Maggie had to think about his unexpected question for a minute before she could answer. "I don't have an easy answer to that, Mr. Rathford. Cleat sold me immediately after delivery to a man whose wife had just lost her baby during childbirth. They took me into their loving family and raised me as if I had been born to them. I didn't know I was adopted until seven months ago. Cleat didn't sell Alyssa; Lily took her and ran away from her abusive husband, but she didn't feel able to raise the child on her own. A wealthy man and his wife opened their home to them, adopted Alyssa, and kept Lily on as her nanny. Alyssa wasn't ever aware Lily was her birth mother." Maggie rose and paced the small space in front of Mr. Rathford's desk as she spoke.

"When Alyssa was sixteen years old, Cleat located Lily, abducted Alyssa, and held her hostage for seven years. He treated her like a slave, not allowing her to attend school or have friends. She's still recovering from that terrible ordeal. So Alyssa and I are different. But I believe you're asking if any difference in our temperamental makeup seems to be genetic, and at this point, I can't really say."

Mr. Rathford rubbed his hand over his eyes, and then looked up at Maggie. "I asked because I wondered if the family traits had continued with the two of you."

Maggie stopped in front of the desk and stared at him. "Family traits?"

Mr. Rathford hesitated, then proceeded slowly. "When we brought Damon home, Llewellyn seemed to change, to become another child completely."

"In what way?" Maggie asked.

Mr. Rathford didn't have an opportunity to answer, as Damon suddenly burst through the door like a whirling dervish. "There you are. Have you eaten breakfast, my pretty little sister? I'd like to wine and dine you and show you our beautiful cathedral."

He didn't wait for an answer but grabbed Maggie by the hand, whirled her into his arms, and kissed her forehead. "You'll love this place." He held her at arm's length and smiled down at her. "What a wonderful surprise you are."

"You are quite a surprise yourself," Maggie said, hoping he remained a good surprise.

"The Crown at Wells is the best hotel and pub in town. Come on. I want to hear all about you and your twin." Damon clutched her hand tightly in his, nearly dragging her from the store with his long-legged stride.

"First we'll have breakfast, and then I'll show you the centerpiece of this little city that is in truth, only a village." Damon talked as fast as he walked. Fortunately, they didn't have far to go, or she might have walked right out of her shoes trying to stay upright as he pulled her along beside him. "Where do you live, Maggie?"

"Southern California right now, but my parents have a ranch on the Utah-Idaho border where I was raised," she answered breathlessly.

Damon stopped in the middle of the cobblestone street and pointed at the three-story gabled building in front of them with English-style mullioned windows. "There it is. Beautiful, no?"

"Beautiful, yes," Maggie said and finally had the presence of mind to pull out her camera and take pictures. Damon waited, clearly amused, while Maggie photographed every angle of the historic square where they stood.

"Now that your tourist impulses are satisfied, we can eat." He ushered her into the cool, dark interior of the well-preserved old building and greeted the hostess with a pleasant familiarity that surprised Maggie. Where was the fear she'd encountered everywhere else? The Damon she'd met didn't seem to inspire it.

As they settled at their table overlooking the street, Damon bragged about this fourteenth-century coaching inn that had become a fancy, modern-day hotel. The waitress came at that moment, and Damon whisked both menus from her hand, preventing her from passing one to Maggie. "Let me order for you, Maggie. This is your first time in England, isn't it?"

"Yes, my very first. I'd be delighted if you'd order. The food I've had so far has been delicious. I just haven't been in the country long enough to get a fair sampling of all the cultural dishes I've wanted to try."

When Damon had ordered their meal, Maggie settled back in her chair and said, "Now, tell me about Wells. What makes it so special to you?"

Damon pointed to the street outside their window. "See that seemingly ordinary avenue ending in the open square?"

Maggie looked at the picturesque three-story buildings lining the street opposite the Crown hotel that mostly contained chic shops. The avenue led to the corner with the turreted gate. She nodded.

"This is Market Square, the site of markets and fairs since the 1100s. The tower you see next to the National Trust shop is Penniless Porch, so named because many penniless beggars sought alms from churchgoers who entered the cathedral grounds through that gate. Do you have anything to compare with that antiquity in America?"

"Nothing that has been inhabited continually all those centuries," Maggie admitted. "I'm amazed by all of this. No wonder you love it so much."

Apparently satisfied with her admiration of the town, Damon seemed to descend a step or two from his animated state, relaxing and leaning back in his chair. He looked at Maggie and examined her closely, staring so intently that she blushed and looked away.

"You're staring, Damon. That makes me uncomfortable."

"It's just so hard to believe you've existed all these years and that we've never known about each other. I felt like an only child most of my life. My brother didn't like me to be around him. He didn't like me tagging along behind him. Were you were raised as an only child, Maggie?"

"Far from it. I have five older brothers who you'd probably consider cowboys, and our home was filled with noise and fun. Individually they teased me unmercifully, but they were the first to jump to my defense if anyone ever said a harsh word to me."

"What about your twin sister?" Damon looked puzzled. "Weren't you raised together?"

Maggie repeated to Damon parts of what she had earlier told his father about Alyssa. "So you see, neither of us knew we had a sister until Christmas, seven months ago."

"Old Cleat really was a scoundrel, wasn't he?" Damon said. "I'm his namesake, you know. He was another Damon Rathford, like countless generations before us."

Maggie nodded, but avoided further comment, as she didn't want to reveal yet how much worse than a scoundrel Cleat had really been. She stared out the window so she wouldn't have to meet his gaze.

Damon leaned forward. "What are you hiding from me, Maggie?"

She glanced quickly back at Damon. "What do you mean?" she said, trying to sound puzzled and look innocent.

He frowned and shook his head. "Don't ever lie to me, and don't try to keep anything from me, little sister." He reached across the table and took Maggie's hand in his, stroking her palm. "I perceive you're harboring a secret, and I want to know what it is. Now."

# THIRTEEN

Wells
Friday, 9:50 A.M.

Flynn arrived in Wells just in time to see Maggie and Damon cross the street from the National Trust Office to the Crown hotel. He parked down the street far enough that Maggie wouldn't see him, then crossed to the sidewalk, where he had a clear view of the hotel entrance.

He quieted his wildly beating heart. Grown men weren't supposed to react this way, were they? All he wanted to do was take her in his arms and tell her he'd never let her go again. Alyssa had said that Maggie wasn't dating anyone. He hoped that meant she was just waiting for December to meet him and tell him she loved him. What a stupid thing he'd done, waiting like this, when they could have been together all this time. Then again, he had wanted her to be as sure of her feelings for him as he was of his feelings for her.

But Flynn Ford found himself in a dilemma. Should he do what he'd proposed to do in the first place and just watch Maggie from a distance in order to protect her, or should he follow his heart and reveal his presence?

Maybe he'd give it a day, let Maggie get to know her newfound brother—since even at a distance, Flynn could see the man's red hair and his resemblance to the twins. He tried not to feel pangs of jealousy that this other man could spend time with his Maggie and he couldn't.

His attention was abruptly diverted to the television screen through the open doorway of a store he was next to.

"Representatives of world leaders are closeted in an unknown loca-tion in the United States hammering out some sort of agreement or compromise to present to the terrorist organization that bombed four major cities in the world yesterday. And this report just in from Sydney, Australia. Divers have recovered the item that damaged the Harbor Bridge. It was an unarmed Daisy Cutter bomb, the same type used in Jakarta; Washington, D.C.; and Madrid. Australians are rejoicing that their famous bridge and Opera House on the bay escaped the destruction meant for them.

"The clock is still ticking on the deadline given by the terrorists. There are now thirty-two hours and ten minutes remaining to pay the billion dollars required to keep Paris from becoming the next city targeted by the terrorist organization."

Flynn was glad he didn't have the responsibility—and dilemma—that today's heads of state faced. They were caught between a rock and a hard place. If they gave in and dealt with the terrorists, it would cause an escalation of terrorism across the world. If they didn't, heaven help the poor people who lived in the targeted cities.

He couldn't imagine the chaos of trying to evacuate a city the size of London or New York. Nor did he even want to contemplate the vast treasures, historical and monetary, that would be lost forever if the terrorists carried out their threats. But he took some small comfort in knowing that everything that could possibly be done was being done to find and disable the explosives and prevent the terrorists from succeeding.

He walked to the far end of the street, casually checking out the window displays in each store, always keeping an eye on the entrance to the Crown. This would be tedious, he knew, but better than being in Chicago worrying about Maggie and not being able to do anything about it.

* * *

The Crown Hotel, Wells
Friday, 9:55 A.M.

"I'm not keeping secrets, but there are some things I promise you don't want to know, Damon," Maggie said, offering an apologetic smile. "I wish I too were innocent of the knowledge, so I don't want to burden *you* with it as well." She squeezed his hand and pulled hers free.

"After a statement like that, you must tell me. What is it that weighs so heavily on your mind? Come. Out with it," he commanded.

Maggie hesitated. Should she expose all the dirty laundry, or clean it up for Damon?

"The whole story, Maggie." His voice carried a note of warning. "I want to know it all, every sordid detail. He was my sire, too."

Carefully choosing her words, Maggie told of Cleat's cruel treatment of Alyssa for seven years, and his disposal of anyone who came too close to discovering the truth of the kidnapping.

Damon leaned across the table and asked quietly, "How many did he kill?"

Maggie shuddered. "At least six that we know of right now. There may have been more, and we may never know the whole story."

He leaned back in his chair, twisting the unique ring on his finger. The emblem emblazoned on it resembled the Pendragon crest of King Arthur, Maggie thought, and she was about to ask to examine it more closely when Damon asked, "How did he die?"

She closed her eyes. She didn't want to ever recall that memory again. It came unbidden often enough as it was, and she quickly drove it from her mind whenever it happened.

"Tell me, Maggie." His voice, almost a whisper, was coaxing, anxious for details. "I want to know about my father."

At that moment their meal appeared and spared Maggie reliving the gory scene for the time being. When the waitress left, she said quietly, "I can't speak of it over a meal, Damon. It will have to wait, or I'll have to skip eating altogether."

Damon didn't try to hide his disappointment; however, he silently waved at her to begin eating.

"This looks delicious," she said, attempting to get her mind on other things and put the unspeakable memories behind her, if only temporarily. She felt sure Damon wouldn't allow her to leave the subject alone for any longer than it took them to eat.

"I think you'll like it. You've discovered the best food is found in pubs, haven't you?" he asked.

"Yes," Maggie said. "When I first arrived in Arundel, they told me that, as a rule, the village pub would have the best in town. I think they were right."

Damon stopped with his fork halfway to his mouth and frowned. "You were in Arundel?"

"That's the address the midwife had for your parents. She'd saved the envelope in which they'd mailed her the money for your delivery. She didn't know why she'd saved it all this time. But if she hadn't, we might never have located you."

"We?" Damon said. "Your sister and you?"

"And our mother, Lily. Did you know that all these years she thought Alyssa was her only child? Cleat told her that you and Llewellyn died at birth and that he'd buried you. He never told her about me at all. Can you imagine her surprise when I walked into the newspaper office where she worked and told her I was her newest reporter? I had no idea why she looked so startled. She thought I was her kidnapped daughter who'd been missing for seven years."

"Do you like Lily?"

"Yes, very much. When you meet Alyssa, she can tell you more, having grown up with her."

"I'd like that. So, tell me more about being a reporter."

"For the last seven months I've actually been paid to do what I love most in all the world—take pictures and write about fascinating people, intriguing places, and entertaining events. I love doing it, and can't imagine that any other lifestyle could be as rewarding to me."

Damon raised his glass to drink, then said, "Tell me about Alyssa. Is she like you? And why didn't she come with you?"

"We look almost identical. Most people can't tell us apart unless they know us. She's beginning college prep classes this fall."

"Tell me, are you alike in any other way besides appearance?" He leaned toward Maggie with a knowing smile. "Is she as tenderhearted as you?"

"It's interesting that you and your father should ask those same questions when I've never considered them myself in the months I've known her. I guess we had such totally different beginnings that I didn't expect us to be alike. We do love many of the same things—we'll both reach for the same dress on a rack, and we share some of the same tastes in food. We discovered we had been wearing our hair in similar styles even though we had never seen each other before. We both love horses and have owned them and ridden since we were children. We've both always been drawn to taking care of hurt animals, though Alyssa wanted to save the whales and dolphins, and I took care of the critters found around the ranch. "

"In what ways are you different?" Damon put down his glass and concentrated wholly on Maggie's words.

"I was raised with a lot of responsibility—not a lot of money for frills, but enough for the necessities. Alyssa, from the time she was adopted as a toddler, was raised in a big home where she had everything she wanted. Then Cleat plucked her from those posh circumstances and plunged her into a life of servitude where she didn't have a penny to call her own and no one to love and appreciate her, or even talk to her."

Damon interrupted her. "You did have love and appreciation in your home?"

"Oh, yes," Maggie said with enthusiasm. "I felt I was the most loved child in the world. I had older brothers to spoil me, a father who delighted in telling me what a ray of sunshine I was to him, and a mother who just adored me, though they all made sure it never went to my head. I was never pampered when I was small like Alyssa said she was. I was simply surrounded by unconditional love."

Damon picked up his fork and proceeded to eat without further comment. He seemed to close down completely, as if the book that was Damon had slammed shut in Maggie's face. She knew immediately she'd said things she should not have vocalized. It hadn't occurred to her that Damon's own home may not have been so loving. She hadn't meant to brag about the affection she'd experienced in her home, and she feared she'd done exactly that.

"What's next on the agenda after we've finished eating?" she asked, hoping to pull him from the state of his silent withdrawal. "The cathedral? Someone told me it's more beautiful than either Salisbury or Winchester Cathedral."

Damon studied her for a long minute and then asked quietly, "Will Alyssa come now that you've found me?"

"Oh, Alyssa," Maggie exclaimed, looking at her watch. "She's on the train to Bath as we speak and should arrive around eleven thirty. I have to go back and pick her up at the train station. She'll be so delighted to meet you, Damon, and then maybe we can all go together to meet our other brother!"

"As far as you're concerned, there is only one brother, and you're looking at him." Damon's voice was flat and his tone final. "Forget Llewellyn."

Maggie leaned back in her chair. She lifted her glass of water and sipped slowly, watching his face, feeling the intensity of controlled energy ready to be unleashed—at her, she suspected—if she wasn't obedient to his demand.

She smiled pleasantly but chose her words cautiously. "You're used to getting your way. What happens when people don't obey your . . . wishes?" She paused before emphasizing the last word.

Damon leaned forward and, with ice in his voice, said quietly, "They regret it."

She continued to sip casually from her water goblet. "What did you mean when you said there was only one brother?"

Damon dabbed at his mouth and put his napkin on the table. "He won't see you," he said flatly. "He refuses contact even with Mother. He is without familial affection or connection." He sat quietly, brooding for a minute, watching Maggie as he picked up his goblet. "Do not attempt to find him." His tone told Maggie he would tolerate no disobedience in his instruction. He stared at her. "Will you promise you won't attempt to find him?"

"I can't think of a single reason not to make that promise—unless, of course, some silly stubborn streak in me rebelled at being commanded to do something that just as easily could have been politely requested." Maggie leaned forward, held up her water goblet, and clinked it against the glass Damon held. "To our individuality as well as our togetherness."

Damon stared at Maggie over the top of his glass for a minute. Finally he raised it in a salute and drained the contents.

"Do you want to show me anything right now, or would you rather wait for Alyssa to get here and take us both at the same time?" Maggie asked, hoping to get Damon to relax and resume his former friendly mood.

He nodded. "Let's wait. I assume you're planning to stay in town for a while?"

"Of course," Maggie said. "Would you recommend this hotel, or is it completely out of my price range?"

"This place is fine, but Maggie, you're welcome to come home—"

"Thank you, Damon," she interrupted, "but I think tonight I'll get a room for Alyssa and me. Tomorrow we may consider your kind offer, but tonight we have a lot to catch up on, and I do have a column to write and submit. What time should I leave for Bath?"

"Probably in thirty minutes, as traffic will be heavy in the city. Would you like me to drive you? If you want to check into the hotel here and rest a bit, or work, I'll go back to the gift shop, tell father what we're about, and then come back for you when it's time to go." Damon picked up the check and helped Maggie with her chair.

Maggie smiled. "Thank you. I don't mind the little country roads, but I'm not anxious to tackle heavy city traffic. I'll see you in half an hour. And thank you so much for the late breakfast. It was delicious."

They parted company in the lobby. Maggie watched Damon as he strode briskly across Market Square to the National Trust shop and disappeared inside. A shiver ran down her back as she turned to the registration desk to book a room for her and Alyssa.

Damon was an interesting study in contrasts. He was charming and delightful when he chose to be, but Maggie had already seen a darker, brooding side to this newly found brother. Just how much of what she had heard about him was true, and how much was unfounded rumor?

# FOURTEEN

Flynn watched Maggie's brother cross from the Crown to the National Trust office without Maggie. Maybe she planned to stay in the hotel. He'd need to find somewhere close where he could keep an eye on her. People were beginning to watch him, so he'd need some kind of excuse for hanging around on the street. He spied a stationery store down the block, went in, and bought a clipboard, legal pad, and bright red pen.

He crossed to the vintage clothing store on the corner where he bought a tweed hat, a jacket with leather patches on the elbows, and a plaid bow tie. With sunglasses and his new disguise, he felt sure that Maggie could walk right by him and not recognize him.

\* \* \*

Maggie's attractive room had two single beds and a couple of over-stuffed chairs that looked inviting; however, she didn't have time to relax. She'd parked in the city lot at the end of the street, which now necessitated walking back to get her car so she could park it closer to the hotel. This time she actually looked at the buildings on High Street and read the plaques attached to some of the more historic ones. And, of course, she took pictures.

She passed only an English man doing some kind of survey but hurried on by to retrieve her car and luggage with nothing more than a glance at the fellow. She parked at the rear of the Crown, lugged her suitcase up the winding staircase, and collapsed on the bed with her laptop. She quickly crafted a short introductory article on Wells, including the history of the surrounding countryside. She noted that Glastonbury, traditional site of Avalon and the King Arthur legends, lay a mere six miles from Wells—a must-see for her Sunday travel supplement.

She typed a note to Lily explaining she'd finally tracked down Cleat Wiggins's brother and had met him, as well as Lily's second-born son, Damon Rathford. She hesitated to say any more than that he had the same blue eyes and auburn hair as she and Alyssa. She thanked her for sending Alyssa to England and reported she and Damon would meet Alyssa's train at Bath within the hour and that they would return to Wells, where they had a room at the Crown.

As Maggie took her column downstairs to e-mail to Lily, she pondered her meeting with Damon and his father. What was it about Damon that both compelled—and repelled her? She was drawn to her brother and felt a very real attachment to her sibling, and yet he had almost frightened her with the anger she'd felt seething just beneath the surface. *Please guide me here, Father. I feel very confused.*

She had barely finished at the business center of the hotel when Damon entered the lobby to fetch her.

"I see you're ready and waiting," he said, smiling his approval.

"I just finished a short column for the paper and sent a note to Lily informing her I'd found you and that we were going to pick up Alyssa."

"What did you tell her about me?" Damon asked, staring down into Maggie's deep blue eyes that were so near the color of his own.

"Only that I'd met you and Mr. Rathford, and that there's a remarkable family resemblance."

Damon held the hotel door for her and guided her to his car. "What color are Lily's eyes and hair?"

Maggie waited to answer until they'd settled in the car. She didn't notice the English-looking gentleman tuck his clipboard under his arm and hurry to his car, nor did she see him pull out behind them.

"Cleat had the blue eyes, and when I saw him, his hair was grayer than anything else. Lily has dyed her hair, but I think she was blond. How about Llewellyn?"

Damon nodded his head. "He was born with the trademark red hair and blue eyes. He and I looked almost like twins, except for the four-year age gap. These days he's altered the color of his hair, so the likeness isn't as pronounced anymore.

"Now, I want to hear how our dear father died," Damon continued. "You have a captive audience for the next thirty minutes, at least, and I want to know everything you can tell me about him."

"Not about Lily, too?" Maggie asked, thinking his request a bit strange.

"Let's cover Cleat first before Alyssa gets here, since that could be uncomfortable. Alyssa can help fill in the blanks on Lily, since you said she lived with her as her nanny," Damon explained.

Maggie nodded, wondering where to begin.

Damon glanced at her. "I'm waiting."

"I'm just trying to figure out where to start. The first time I actually saw him in person was in my rearview mirror, sneaking up on me. I'd just rescued Alyssa, drugged and near death, from the back of his van. I narrowly escaped from that, only to discover he was driving away in his van on the tire I'd flattened to keep him from escaping. So I wheeled around and drove straight at him, planning to ram his truck if necessary to keep him from getting away."

Maggie paused, and Damon looked to see why she'd stopped speaking. "Did you?"

"Ram him? No. I hadn't had time to buckle my seat belt, and Alyssa was sprawled in the back seat totally unprotected. I couldn't take a chance on injuring her in the collision, so I veered to the side at the last minute." Then Maggie smiled. "I'll never forget the astonishment on his face when he saw me driving straight at him. I only wish I knew if he understood in that split second that it was really me, and not Alyssa who had come out of her drug-induced state and was trying to escape."

She shrugged. "Either way, he couldn't believe his eyes, and that gave me a lot of satisfaction. Fortunately the police arrived and took him into custody."

"So how did he die?" Damon asked, deftly avoiding a car that cut too sharply in front of them.

"The police handcuffed him with his hands behind him, and as they were taking him into the police station, he deliberately fell and hit the curb. He wrenched his shoulder and bloodied his head in the gravel, and he was making a huge deal of his injuries and pain, so they took him to the hospital, which just happened to be where Alyssa was being observed and treated. They recuffed his hands in front so it wouldn't hurt his shoulder, but he had faked his injuries. He made the police think he could hardly walk—until he got inside the hospital and saw Alyssa in the observation room."

Maggie shuddered and tried to block the rest of the scene, but it came, every detail vivid in her memory.

"Go on," Damon urged quietly.

"He broke free from the police escorts, ran straight to the observation window, raised his cuffed hands above his head, and smashed them into the window, shattering the glass. They yelled at him to freeze, but he ignored them and tried to vault through the window to reach Alyssa. Before he made it through the window, they shot him, and he fell," Maggie shivered uncontrollably at the memory, "across the jagged glass that remained in the window."

"The end of Papa," Damon noted wryly.

Maggie didn't speak. She turned and looked at the picturesque countryside, hoping to erase the graphic, violent memory, or at least to replace it momentarily with something more pleasant. She knew it would be months, or possibly years, before it didn't affect her like this.

"Tell me something, little sister," Damon said, a puzzled tone in his voice.

Maggie took a deep breath and prayed it wouldn't have anything more to do with Cleat. He was a subject she wanted to address as seldom as possible.

She looked up at him. "Yes?"

"If he was such a monster of a man, and if you hated him so much, why aren't you rejoicing in his demise? Why this revulsion at his death? You said you didn't know you were adopted, so it can't be that you're mourning the passing of your father."

Maggie shook her head. "No, and at that moment, I had no idea that beast was related to me at all. I am still totally disconnected from him psychologically. My parents are the people who raised me, loved me, and nurtured me. I can't use his name in the same sentence as the word *father*. I believe he was intent on killing Alyssa so she couldn't reveal the murders he'd committed and whatever else he was afraid she'd tell. He was truly an evil man. But I watched him die. It was a gruesome death."

Damon drove silently for a moment, then said quietly, "If the only address you had for me was in Arundel, how did you find me?"

Maggie was grateful for the change of subject. "Even though I'm working right now as a travel writer, I'm an investigative reporter," Maggie explained. "It's my job to know how to find people and track down stories and information. I studied criminal investigation in college, so investigative journalism wasn't such a big leap. To find you I stopped at the information office in Arundel and asked where I might find the address on the envelope the midwife had. The girl at the information desk said your family didn't live there anymore but recommended I check at St. Nicholas."

"And did you?" Damon asked.

"Yes. I met a sweet little old lady in the foyer who said your family had moved to Avebury. I'd never heard of it, but I found it on the map and headed there. You weren't there, but I received a clue you might be in Lacock, and about that time I began thinking your family must be associated with the National Trust, since those places were all administered by that organization. When I found that you were no longer in Lacock, I checked the National Trust to find other sites nearby where you might have been transferred. Voilà. I ended up in Wells. And there you were."

"You're amazing, Maggie. You fly all the way across the ocean with a twenty-six-year-old address, rent a car with the steering wheel on the opposite side than you're used to, make your way alone around the countryside, and find me on your—what? Second day in the country?"

"Yes," Maggie said. "But anyone could do it if they could read a road map. And I did have help—Rolf, a young man I was giving a lift to Marlborough." She laughed. "Do you know what has been my saving grace as I've traveled alone—without a navigator or map reader?"

Damon shook his head.

"I love your traffic roundabouts," Maggie said. "I can go round and round until I finally find the road I'm supposed to take. We need to have more of those in America. Once you miss your freeway exit there, it may be miles before the next one so you can turn around and go back."

They rode in silence for a few minutes while Damon wove his way in and out of heavy traffic in Bath. The architecture enchanted Maggie, and when they finally parked at the train station, she pulled her phone from her bag and dialed Alyssa's number to see if her train had arrived.

Without even saying hello, Alyssa answered and blurted, "You didn't tell me about your new friend Rolf! Were you planning on keeping him for yourself?"

For a minute, Maggie was speechless. Then she realized Rolf must have gone to the train station, knowing Maggie and Alyssa would be meeting there. "Of course not, silly. I already have man problems—I don't need any more. I thought Rolf was a very nice guy. How did you meet him?"

"He walked up to me and said, 'Alyssa, I presume.' I nearly fell over I was so shocked to hear my name. Then he explained about meeting you and finishing his tutoring and hurrying to meet my train so he could meet me and see if everything was okay." Alyssa finally took a breath. "Is it?"

Maggie laughed. "It's fine. Where are you?"

"At the station in Bath. I was just getting ready to call you and see if you'd arrived or were still on your way. We got to chatting and I forgot to call. Where are you?"

"We're outside the train station. Hang on a minute." Maggie handed Damon her phone. "They're here. Tell them where we are so they can meet us."

"They?" Damon repeated with a scowl.

"Rolf, the young man I told you about, met Alyssa at the train," Maggie explained.

Damon gave Maggie a disapproving glare and took the phone. He gave directions to Alyssa, and then directed another piercing look at Maggie as he returned her cell phone. "Get rid of him now. This is a private family reunion."

\* \* \*

Ravenwood Estate
Friday, 11:30 A.M.

When the telephone rang, Constantine muted the television broadcast he was watching. The constant conjecturing of news commentators irritated him to no end.

"Mr. Constantine, Edward here. The young woman you inquired about is Maggie McKenzie. She's the travel editor for the *San Buenaventura Press* in Ventura, a little beach town in Southern California. She's the one who snapped the picture of the terrorist in the Los Angeles airport. Security got the photo from her, and the rest is history."

"What's she doing in England?" Constantine asked, clicking off the television and wandering onto his terrace to watch the hawks circle in the clear blue sky.

"She's on assignment to do a travel section on England—pictures and articles to show middle-class Americans how best to see all the sights in their mother country."

"Edward, do Americans today have any idea that their forefathers rebelled against the king?" Constantine shook his head. "No matter. Were you able to get a picture of the person in question?" Constantine asked.

"I'm working on that. I told the receptionist at the newspaper I was a reporter for a London paper tracking down the American reporter who had escaped an assassination attempt by the terrorist. Apparently the office manager there is some relation to the girl, and she wasn't too keen on sending me a photo. She said if Maggie had declined to have her picture taken, she must have had a good reason, and she wouldn't release one either. I thought I could call the local library and pay the librarian to check the papers. If Miss McKenzie is a reporter with a byline, maybe there's a photo the librarian can fax me."

"That's why I pay you so much, Edward. You have a good head on your shoulders. Get the picture to me as soon as you have it in your hands."

"Yes, sir, Mr. Constantine. How's your ankle?"

"Thanks for asking, Edward. It's healing slowly. I'm sorry to miss all the conferences and meetings in London right now, but I'm not much good hobbling around on crutches. Sylvia is keeping me connected, and, of course, the cabinet secretary is in constant touch."

"I'm sure they'll be happy to have your wit and wisdom back in the government offices."

"Thank you, Edward. Remember, I need the picture as soon as you can get it to me. She may be a key to finding the Albright woman and her children."

"Yes, sir."

Constantine disconnected and slipped his cell phone in his jacket pocket. It was nice to have moles in high places. Edward Thompson's connection with Scotland Yard was invaluable to him, as were his contacts in military intelligence, and he knew that Edward's position and abilities, coupled with his reputation, would prove even more vital in the next few hours.

Of course, Edward's allegiance was to him, not the Yard or Queen and country. Constantine smiled. Maybe he was being a bit vain. Edward's allegiance was to the incredible amount of money he was paid—nothing more.

Constantine watched a spider weaving a web on a bush at the edge of his terrace. *Just like the web I'm weaving, Miss McKenzie, in which I will trap you like that miserable insect caught in the spider's web. Very soon now, you will be in my web.*

# FIFTEEN

Bath
Friday, 11:40 A.M.

Maggie calmly faced Damon. "Rolf has been very helpful to me. I will not be rude to him. Please be civil, and I'll explain to him that we need time to ourselves." She smiled up at his brooding face. "You'll be so entranced by Alyssa you won't even notice Rolf. She is a delight—and here she comes."

Damon turned stiffly toward the sound of excited voices. Alyssa ran the last few steps and threw her arms around Maggie. Then she turned to Damon, looked him up and down, and threw herself at him, embracing him with an impulsive hug.

"I am so glad Maggie found you!" She stepped back and looked at him again. "Just imagine! All these years we never knew anything about each other, and now, here we are!"

Maggie slipped quietly to Rolf's side while Alyssa captured Damon's attention. "He doesn't want you here. I'm staying at the Crown in Wells on Market Square. Are you going to Marlborough from here, or were you planning to come to Wells with us?"

Rolf, who was watching Damon closely, nodded. "I'm free this afternoon, but I'll come later tonight. By the way, tomorrow's tutoring session got canceled, so I was thinking we could do a weekend trip to Wales. I would love to show you Blaenavon."

"If the scheduling works out, we'd love that." Maggie turned toward Damon and hurried to make introductions. "Damon, this is Rolf Owen; he not only helped me find you, but he saved my life." She turned to Rolf. "I'm delighted to present my brother, Damon Rathford, the object of our search."

The men both nodded silently, reluctantly acknowledging the other, but the tension between them hung so thick Maggie could have sliced it with a knife.

"Damon, do we need to hurry back, or can we take thirty or forty minutes and get a glimpse of this historic city?" Maggie asked.

"If you'll excuse me," Rolf interrupted, "I need to be on my way. Alyssa, it was so nice to meet you. Maybe you and Maggie can join me in Wales for a bit of sightseeing before you return home. I'll be in touch later." With that quick good-bye, Rolf wheeled around and hurried back to the station.

Damon relaxed visibly and smiled at the two young women he now had all to himself. "By all means, let's show you one of England's golden jewels."

Damon put Alyssa's suitcase in his car and led the way up the ancient street, giving the two girls a quick history lesson on the city of Bath. "From ancient Roman times, the upper crust partook of the mineral springs here, coming from Londinium, as London was called then. Romans came here so often to 'take a bath' that the city eventually became known simply as Bath, shortened from its Roman name *Aquae Sulis.*"

"Have you ever indulged in the waters?" Maggie asked, curious about the lifestyle of this enigmatic man who seemed a constant contradiction of elegantly good manners and barely controlled outbursts.

"No, though if you'd like to try them, we can arrange that," Damon said.

Maggie laughed. "No, thanks. I grew up not far from Lava Hot Springs, so I've spent many hours in mineral pools."

As they walked, the midday sun cast a dramatic golden glow on the Georgian-style, honey-colored buildings. The spires of the abbey towered above them, piercing puffy white clouds and affording Maggie some beautiful photographs. Unbeknownst to Damon and Alyssa, she captured the two in an interesting closeup with the sun glinting off their matching auburn hair.

"Bath Abbey," Damon said. "The first King Henry of England was crowned here in 973, but I believe the earliest recorded church was built in about A.D. 350. Bath itself is over two thousand years old."

Alyssa hung on every word Damon said, and he seemed to bask in her adulation. During the drive back to Wells, Alyssa sat in the front passenger seat and spent the trip answering Damon's questions about Lily. When they arrived at the Crown in Wells, Alyssa asked Damon if she could meet his father.

"Of course," Damon said. "He'll be delighted to meet you. He's in the Trust office just across the street."

But when they reached the office, they found Mr. Rathford in great pain. "Thank heaven you returned, Damon. I'm having another attack— I must go home. Please take charge here." And without even a glance at the twins, he staggered to the back door and out to his car.

"Damon, I'm so sorry about your father," Maggie said. "Should he be driving? Do you need take him home?"

"No, it's his gallbladder. He's scheduled for surgery in two months, but with our socialized medicine, the waiting time can kill the patient. He'll be okay. Our home isn't far. But for now, I'm tied to the Trust office." Damon sounded truly disappointed.

"Not a problem," Maggie said. "First we'll get Alyssa settled into our hotel room, then I do need to work on my assignment. Since we're so close to Glastonbury, I'm dying to photograph it and do an article on the Arthurian legends. How about if we meet for dinner? What time will you be through?"

"Sixish," Damon said, waggling his hand to indicate a bit of uncertainty. "We can do a quick tour of the cathedral and the Vicar's Close, and then dine at the Crown about seven."

"Great. We'll see you here at six o'clock," Maggie said, and the girls headed across the street to the Crown.

\* \* \*

Ravenwood Estate
Friday, 12:00 P.M.

"Mr. Constantine, sir, Edward here. I think we may finally have a breakthrough."

"It's about time we had some good news," Constantine said stonily. It was getting harder and harder for him to appear civil to anyone. The minutes were ticking away too quickly, and Constantine knew that they still needed to get their hands on those plans before they could do too much more than begin moving the goods.

"That young man, Rolf Owen, the one who captured the escaped terrorist and saved the young American woman's life?"

"Yes, what about him?" Constantine sat up.

"I've had my men quietly looking for him. His picture was in the papers and on the telly, so his face was a familiar one. I just asked the boys on the beat to keep an eye peeled for him. I told them we needed to ask him a couple of questions about that night, but we didn't want an all points on him, because it might frighten him. I suspect he shies away from publicity."

"Get to it, man," Constantine commanded impatiently. "What about him?"

"He was just spotted at the train station in Bath—and he was with an attractive American girl. It might be that reporter you're seeking."

That brought Constantine right up out of his chair. "Where is he now?"

"I told my man to tail him without confronting him until I had further orders from you, sir. What do you want us to do?"

"Good work, Edward. I'll fly to Bath immediately. Have your man stay with him, giving you updates on the Owen man's location. When I arrive in Bath, I'll interview him personally. This deserves a bonus, as well as a promotion." Constantine headed for the door, feeling better than he had for two days.

"Thank you, sir."

"Just don't let that man out of sight. He may be the key to finding that reporter, who just might be an incredible help in locating the Albright woman and her children. That is number one on our agenda." Constantine disconnected, pocketed his cell phone, and hurried to the helicopter for his interview with the reporter who had given him so much trouble.

* * *

Wells
Friday, 1:00 P.M.

Alyssa unpacked her suitcase and hung her clothes in the tiny closet. "When are we going to see Rolf again, Maggie? He seemed really nice."

"He said he'd call my cell phone. How are you feeling after all that travel? Would you like to rest this afternoon, or do you want to go with me to Glastonbury?" Maggie asked, knowing how exhausting a long flight could be, coupled with jet lag.

"Mmm, if I had my druthers, I'd rather hang out here, relax, and get to know Rolf a little better. Not do much of anything," Alyssa said, flopping down into the overstuffed chair.

"Here's his phone number." Maggie handed Alyssa the little slip of paper with Rolf's number. "Call him and see where he is. He can't be far away."

"No, I couldn't do that. You call and ask for me, please," Alyssa pleaded.

Maggie laughed. "Okay. I'll get him on the phone, ask where he is, and find out what his plans are. If he's still in the area, I'll ask if he wants to spend the afternoon with you while I go to Glastonbury. Does that work?"

"Yes," Alyssa said. "That's better. It sounds more like a favor to you than me."

Maggie keyed in the number and brushed her hair while she waited for the phone to ring. "Hi, Rolf, this is Maggie. Are you on your way home to Wales?"

"No, as a matter of fact, I'm on a bus just arriving in Wells. Where are you?"

"We're in the Crown at Wells hotel. Damon had to take over the office this afternoon, and I'm going to Glastonbury to research an article. Alyssa just wants to hang out here. If you're not doing anything, would you like to keep her company?"

"I'd be delighted. Give me fifteen minutes and I'll meet her in the lobby of the hotel." He rang off, and Maggie told Alyssa, "You've got a date in fifteen minutes in the lobby. I'm going to go exploring and actually do some of the things I'm being paid to do."

Maggie grabbed her bag and headed for the door. "See you at six for our tour with Damon. Have fun this afternoon. Oh, if you have lunch with Rolf, see if you can be creative about buying his lunch. He doesn't have a lot of extra cash."

\* \* \*

Flynn had parked off the street and taken up his position as a survey taker when he saw the bus unload. He immediately recognized the dark-haired young man exiting the bus as Rolf Owen, the fellow who had saved Maggie's life last night. His picture was still staring out from newspapers and television broadcasts. Overnight, Rolf had become an instant celebrity.

Flynn had witnessed the reunion and immediate parting of the ways at the train station in Bath, and he'd also seen the man who had followed Rolf when he left Maggie, Alyssa, and Damon. He suspected the man was a plainclothes detective and wondered why the police were interested in tailing the young hero.

From his observation post on the sidewalk, Flynn watched Rolf walk quickly down the street toward the Crown; Flynn also observed the same fellow he'd seen in Bath still following Rolf. Maybe Rolf Owen had another side to him that the police didn't know about, a more sinister side. Maybe Maggie's benefactor wasn't the hero the papers made him out to be.

Flynn moved slowly down the street toward the Crown and saw Maggie emerge with her camera in hand, turn the corner, and disappear. Rolf apparently hadn't seen her, nor had the man following him. They continued to the Crown. Rolf went in, emerged a few minutes later with Alyssa, and they sat on the bench out front talking.

Flynn dialed Alyssa's cell phone. "Hi, Alyssa. This is Dr. Ford. Have you connected with Maggie yet?"

"Hi, Dr. Ford. Yes, she met me at the train station with Damon, our brother. You won't believe how much alike we all look. Maggie's gone to Glastonbury to do an article for the paper, and I'm just hanging out with Rolf Owen, the guy who saved her life last night."

"I saw that report on the news. I'm so glad Maggie is safe." Flynn watched as the man approached Rolf and Alyssa and spoke to them, showing them what surely must be a badge.

"Are you still there, Alyssa?" Flynn asked.

"Hold on a minute, Dr. Ford." Flynn watched as the man motioned for the two to go with him. They stood and started back up the sidewalk to where the man's car was parked.

"Dr. Ford, I have to go now. A policeman wants to talk to Rolf about the man he captured last night. He asked that I come, too."

"Alyssa, why would he want you to go with him?" Flynn asked. "You weren't even in the country last night."

Flynn watched Rolf whisper something to Alyssa.

"Dr. Ford, Rolf asked that you call Maggie and tell her 'something is rotten in Denmark.' He said she'll understand. Will you do that?" Alyssa sounded worried and puzzled.

"Of course. I'll call her right now." He disconnected and immediately keyed Maggie's cell phone number. This time she answered it.

"Maggie, this is Flynn. Where are you?"

"Flynn," Maggie stuttered. "I . . . I'm in England."

"I know that. You're in Wells, and you just walked behind the Crown Hotel, but where are you now? What are you doing?"

"Flynn, I don't understand."

"You don't have to. I'm on the street in front of the Crown, and I've just watched someone I suspect to be a police officer escort Rolf and Alyssa toward his car. I was on the phone with Alyssa at the time. Rolf said to tell you 'something is rotten in Denmark.' I assume that means something's wrong, but does that mean something more specific to you?"

"Oh, Flynn, what's happening?" Maggie cried. "Wait. Yes, yes it does. It means that the police want to talk to me about Jennie Albright and her children being kidnapped, and for some silly reason I think it has something to do with that terrorist who tried to kill me," Maggie said all in one breath. "Oh, Flynn, I'm so glad you're here."

"Where are you, Maggie? I'm coming around the corner of the hotel. Where are you from there?"

Maggie slammed the door of her car, ran back toward the hotel, and right into the arms of Flynn Ford. She clung to him with all the pent-up passion of seven month's absence. He tilted her chin up, looked into blue eyes shining with tears, and gently brushed a kiss across her lips. He didn't dare do more than that right now.

"How did you find me? What are you doing here?" Maggie stepped back. "What's wrong, Flynn? Something must have happened. It's not Christmas."

"No, Maggie girl, it's not Christmas." Flynn brushed a wisp of auburn hair from Maggie's cheek. "But when Alyssa told me you were flying to England and I heard the news reports of impending doom for London, I caught the first flight. I've been following your trail, rather unsuccessfully, since you left Arundel with a terrorist on your heels. You'll never know how worried I've been."

"Thank you," was all Maggie could say. She touched his face as if to make sure she wasn't dreaming. She took a deep breath. "Okay, now what are we going to do about Rolf and Alyssa?"

"Find out what the police want with them. Of course, I'm assuming that man was a real police officer. Let's leave your car here and take mine. I think that if we cut through this alley, we won't be too far from where they should be getting into his car right about now."

They hurried hand in hand through the alley and emerged on the tree-lined street just as they saw Rolf and Alyssa enter the back seat of a dark sedan.

"You wait here," Flynn said. "I'll get my car and come for you."

"Not on your life," Maggie said emphatically. "I'm not leaving your side."

"I'm sure the police think Alyssa is Maggie McKenzie, the reporter," Flynn patiently explained. "They probably don't know you have a twin yet. We can't let them see you. By the time they've discovered their mistake and Rolf and Alyssa find out what they really wanted of you, maybe we'll have made some sense of this."

"Gotcha," Maggie said. "Okay, I'll wait here, but please don't leave me again."

Flynn winced at that comment as he hurried down the street and across to his car. He doffed the hat, jacket, and bow tie and tossed them in the back seat, along with the clipboard. When the dark sedan pulled out of the parking lot, Flynn started his car and eased it into the street, then stopped at the entrance to the alley and leaned over to open the door. Maggie jumped in, and they followed the dark sedan at a comfortable distance out of town.

"Where is he taking them?" Maggie asked.

"Bath, maybe," Flynn guessed. "I saw this same police officer tailing Rolf there at the station."

"I don't understand what this is about, but whatever it is, I don't think we're going to like it."

# SIXTEEN

On the road to Bath
Friday, 1:15 P.M.

Flynn turned to Maggie. "When they broadcast that appeal for the young woman who had helped Jennie Albright with her children, what was your first thought?"

Maggie relaxed in her seat, closed her eyes, and went back in her mind to the Red Lion Inn, where she had first heard the newscast. "I wanted to run right to the police station and tell them all I knew."

"And what were you going to tell them?" Flynn persisted, carefully keeping a discreet distance between him and the car he was following.

"That's just it. When I thought about it, I didn't know a single thing about Jennie except her name, Tara's name, and that they were traveling to London. I didn't even know the baby's name. Jennie had her hands full with the baby, Tara, and the luggage. I entertained Tara and helped them board the plane. When we landed in Montreal, I helped again, and when we got to London, I took Tara and some of the luggage, and we met her sister in the baggage claim area. I gave Tara to her aunt, handed her the diaper bag I carried, and said good-bye. That was the last I even thought about them until I saw the broadcast."

"Tell me about your interaction with the terrorist at LAX," Flynn said. "How did you come to get his picture?"

Maggie recited the details of accidentally getting the terrorist's picture while photographing Tara. "He ran into me, nearly knocking us both over. He grabbed my arms, and I thought for a minute he was going to snatch my bag, but as soon as we were steady on our feet, he let go, cursed at me, and ran on through the terminal."

"That was the extent of your contact with him?" Flynn asked, puzzled.

"At first I thought it was," Maggie said. She told about the sinister-looking man behind her in line to board the flight. "He gave me the willies. And when I saw the man lying unconscious on the floor at the Manor Bed-and-Breakfast last night, I knew it was the same person."

"And you think he followed you out of revenge for taking his picture?"

"What else, Flynn? He'd never seen me before, and I'd never seen him."

"You didn't say how security got your photo."

Maggie recited those details. "I gave them my memory stick, and when my flight was called, I disappeared fast, before they decided they needed anything else from me."

Flynn frowned. "I can't help but think there must be something more you're not remembering, something important enough for a man whose face had become known to the public to openly trail you. Normally, he would have gone into hiding until he wasn't on the front pages and every newscast."

"But he did change his appearance. He shaved his beard. I saw him several times before I made the connection," Maggie said.

"Maggie, the man was a known terrorist—an expert at disguise, at trailing people without being seen, and at killing people and not getting caught. If he wanted revenge, why didn't he take it anywhere between the airport and the Manor last night? You should be dead, according to his reputation."

Maggie shivered. "I don't like the way you put that."

"I don't like it either, but those are the facts. This man was not an amateur. Why didn't he just shoot you from a distance and disappear?"

Maggie looked at Flynn, and her mouth dropped open. "Because he wanted something other than my life," she said slowly. She reached for her oversized bag and methodically removed everything in it, examining each item as she took it out. Her laptop, camera, tape recorder, notebook, cell phone, tiny sewing kit, small first-aid kit, Ziplock bag with toiletries, change of clothing, breakfast bar, passport, packet of tissues, small bottle of Tylenol, and a tube of hand cream.

"Is there no bottom in that thing?" Flynn asked in amazement as Maggie continued to pull items from the bag's depths.

"Yes, somewhere there is a bottom." Her fingers were searching in the corners now and along the seams. Finally they touched something she didn't recognize as belonging in her bag. She grasped it and held it up.

"What is it?" Flynn asked, trying to look at it and keep his eyes on the road at the same time.

"It looks like a portable USB flash drive for a computer. It's different than the kind I use, but I'm sure that's what it is."

Flynn whistled. "Wonder what we have on our hands?"

Without a word, Maggie retrieved her laptop computer from the floor and turned it on. While it booted it up, she replaced the contents of her bag.

Maggie inserted the little flash drive into her laptop, looked at the gobbledygook of letters and numbers on the screen, and sighed in frustration. "It's unreadable—maybe I just don't have the right software for this, but I have a feeling it's encrypted anyway. Now what are we going to do? We can't take this to the police, since we don't know who to trust."

Flynn thought for a minute "I have a friend in the FBI in Chicago. He could give me the name of a counterpart here in England we could safely work with."

"Then you'd better call him. We're halfway to Bath, and it might take a while to make the connection."

Flynn handed Maggie his cell phone. "Go to the directory and find Gary Sloane. Dial him and I'll talk."

Maggie waited until the line was ringing and then handed the phone to Flynn. "Sloane," a sleepy voice said. "This better be important, Flynn."

Flynn laughed. "Thanks for answering, Gary. I'm glad you picked up."

"I hope you have something pretty important to tell me," Sloane grumbled.

"Is it safe to talk?" Flynn asked.

Sloane got up and left the bedroom, closing the door quietly behind him. At least his wife didn't have to be wide awake at this ungodly hour. "So much for going back to sleep. Yes, you can talk."

"I need the name of a trusted counterpart in England we can contact about a portable flash drive handed off to someone by that escaped terrorist—the one that was captured trying to assassinate the American reporter last night in England. I'm with that reporter now, and we've encountered a questionable police detective here, so we don't dare take this to the police ourselves. Is there someone whose loyalty you trust explicitly?"

"Flynn, where are you?"

"Just outside of Bath, trailing a policeman who 'invited' a couple of my friends to go to headquarters for a little questioning. I think this officer may be looking for the flash drive, which we just found. Who can we talk to over here?" Flynn paused and looked at Maggie. He'd just had a new thought. "Who knows? This might have something to do with the terrorist bombings. I don't feel like sitting on this for any length of time, Gary."

"This could be big, Flynn. Maybe we should get MI5 involved right away."

"Who?"

"Military Intelligence, Section 5—the Security Service."

"I'm not sure we should start there. Put me in touch with someone you know personally that can take a look at this thing and see what kind of encryption we're talking about. If it's a simple encryption and your guy can decipher it, we won't have to get the higher-ups involved until we know what's on it. I'd hate to make this into a big deal if it's nothing more than directions to make a homemade bomb. After we determine what it contains, we can go from there. Who can we trust, Gary?"

"Actually, my best contact works closely with MI5. His name's Tad Collins. He's a detective chief inspector with Counterterrorism Command in London—with high enough rank to pull some strings if necessary. Just a minute and I'll get you his cell number."

Flynn signaled for Maggie to get a pencil and paper. He repeated the number as Sloane gave it to him, and Maggie wrote it down. "Thanks, Gary. I owe you one."

"Don't worry, I won't let you forget. Just be careful over there. You're playing pretty high stakes if this is what you think it is."

"I'll keep that in mind," Flynn said, disconnecting, then handing Maggie the phone. "Dial Tad Collins, then add him to the directory."

Maggie did, but Tad's office line went straight to voice mail, suggesting he was on another call. She tried again in a minute and it rang. She gave the phone to Flynn. Before Flynn could do anything more than speak his name, Collins said he'd just talked to Sloane in Chicago.

"Then you know I have something I need you to see right away. I'm near Bath. Where can we meet?" Flynn asked.

"You're in luck. I'm actually working out of the office in Bristol this week. If you head this way now, you can be here in about thirty minutes. I should be back in town in forty minutes myself and could meet you at the little café on the corner next to the station." Inspector Collins gave Flynn the address and hung up. Flynn repeated the address to Maggie, and she wrote it down.

"Are we going to see where they're taking Rolf and Alyssa or go to Bristol?" Maggie asked, a concerned look in her eyes.

"We'll follow Rolf and Alyssa, of course. Once we figure out what's happening there, we can proceed to Bristol. Hmm, I wouldn't have thought the police station was in the middle of downtown, but that looks like where we're headed."

\* \* \*

Heliport outside Bath
Friday, 1:30 P.M.

"Mr. Constantine, sir. My man in Bath just telephoned me. He has both Rolf Owen and the American reporter with him on their way to the station in Bath. How do you want this handled?"

"I've just landed at the heliport, Edward. Have your man bring them to the Crystal Palace Pub, and I'll meet them there. We don't want them to think they're under arrest, after all. We just need to find out if they have any further information on Mrs. Albright. I'll treat them to lunch, ply them with good food and wine, and see if that will loosen their memories as well as their tongues."

"No wonder you're such a success in government circles, Mr. Constantine. You certainly know how to get around someone. Let me know if there's anything else I can do for you."

"You know I will. Thank you, Edward. You're irreplaceable. As usual, you've done an excellent job."

Constantine exited the private helicopter and got into the car that had been waiting for him. "Crystal Palace, 11 Abbey Green," he told the driver. Then he sat back and relished what he was about to do, including relieving the American reporter of that blasted bag that Ulric hadn't been able to get his dirty hands on.

After his successful interview with the American reporter, in which he would conveniently plant some intriguing clues in the girl's memory that she had forgotten, he would retrieve the flash drive. Then Scotland Yard would announce to the world that the kidnapping had been solved because of clues given him by the American reporter, and Mrs. Albright and her children would be safely found and returned to her sister. And he could get on with his plan that had been damagingly delayed.

* * *

Bath
Friday, 1:40 P.M.

Flynn stayed two cars behind the dark sedan and parked halfway down the block when the sedan pulled up to the Crystal Palace Pub. Maggie and Flynn looked at each other. A pub? They watched Rolf and Alyssa get out of the car and go inside with the man who'd driven them there. Flynn reached into the back seat for the hat, jacket, and bow tie he'd used as a disguise in Wells.

"You stay out of sight while I go see what's happening," Flynn said, settling the hat low over his eyes. "We don't need anyone to see you."

"Not on your life. I'm with you all the way." Maggie had spotted a woman selling scarves near a book kiosk, and she took her wallet from her bag, left her big bag in the car, and bought a large, neutral-colored scarf to tie over her hair. She put on dark glasses and faced Flynn. "How's that?"

"A little more over your forehead so that shock of red hair doesn't show, and I think you're good."

"Auburn, not red," Maggie corrected. "Just make sure you lock the car. Everything I need is in that bag, and I feel absolutely lost without it hanging on my shoulder. Oh, wait. I need my camera."

"Don't you go anywhere without that?" Flynn asked when she returned.

Maggie smiled. "No. It's an extension of my arm."

Flynn waved the remote at the car, locking it, and they proceeded to the Crystal Palace Pub. As they approached the entrance, a tall, slender man, perhaps in his early thirties, stepped from a car which had stopped right in front of the door. They paused while he hobbled inside on crutches.

Maggie turned to Flynn. "For some reason, he looked familiar."

"He looks like he'd be comfortable among the rich and famous. Maybe you've seen his picture in the paper or on television," Flynn suggested as they followed a short distance behind the man.

They watched in surprise as the policeman who brought Rolf and Alyssa waved to the man on crutches and hurried to meet him. Maggie and Flynn slipped into a table near where they were standing, unaware that the events of the next thirty seconds would be the most surprising of all.

# SEVENTEEN

The policeman bobbed his head in a gesture of deference at the tall man before he pointed out the table where Rolf and Alyssa were seated in the far corner of the pub. A look of shock registered on the tall man's face. Just as quickly it was masked, and he turned abruptly as if to prevent Alyssa or Rolf from seeing his face.

"I can't stay," he said to the policeman. "I've just had an important call and have to return to London immediately. I wanted to see the young man and woman, but you're going to have to interrogate them for me. Please press for every detail the reporter might remember of her encounter with Mrs. Albright. Oh, and one other thing. Will you check her bag? Actually, I will check it for you if you will bring it out to me in my car. I'll wait. You can return it to her immediately."

Maggie and Flynn looked at each other and nodded slightly. Just as they expected—a case of mistaken identity, and Alyssa and Rolf must have been playing along all this time. The tall man thought Alyssa was Maggie. And he was definitely the man who wanted the flash drive. He seemed to be some high-ranking government official. But who was he, and what was his role in all this?

Maggie slipped her camera out of her pocket, turned off the flash, and as the man passed their table on his way outside, she snapped his picture, getting only a profile, then dropped the camera in her lap and bent her head, studying the menu.

* * *

Constantine whirled around upon hearing the clicking sound, but no cameras were in sight and no one even seemed to be looking at him. He was no stranger to cameras. Everywhere he went, people wanted his picture, but today especially he didn't want to be photographed, and not here. He decided it must have been some other sound. He was jittery. He'd just had a shock. That face had been too familiar!

He hurried to the car and waited for the officer to bring the bag to him, but when the officer appeared with a small clutch purse in his hand, Constantine was puzzled. Hadn't Ulric said something about a large bag that the girl carried everywhere on her shoulder?

He dumped the contents on the seat beside him and riffled through them. No memory stick. No secret compartments in which she could have stashed it. He looked at the ID of the girl. Alyssa Lawson, San Buenaventura, California. Wrong name, but right location for the reporter. *Hmm. California.*

Constantine scooped the few articles back into the little purse and returned it to the officer waiting at the open window.

"Treat them to lunch, whatever they want to eat and drink." Constantine stuffed several bills into the hand of the officer. "Give them a royal feast. Find out what you can, and report back to me. I'll discuss it with your superiors tonight when I return from London. When you are finished, you can deliver them back to Wells. Just keep an eye on them quietly, so they don't suspect they are being watched."

"Yes, sir."

"Thank you. You are a good officer. I trust this encounter will not be entered on any report nor spoken of to anyone but your superior, Edward Thompson. He is the only one who should ever have any knowledge of it. Understood?"

"Yes, sir."

"I will see that you receive a reward for this bit of detective work."

"Thank you, sir."

Constantine rolled up the window and tapped the glass between him and the driver. "Back to the heliport," he said, relaxing in his seat to ponder the face he had just seen in the pub.

* * *

Maggie studied the picture of the man she had just photographed. She needed her laptop to enlarge it enough to get a really good look. Where had she seen that face?

"Excuse me," Flynn said. He stood and headed straight for the table in the corner where Rolf and Alyssa were listening intently as the officer explained the behavior of the man who had taken her purse and sent it back again. He couldn't hear everything before he entered the restroom near their table, but enough to know they would be returned to Wells after lunch and their interview.

After a moment, Flynn nodded to Maggie, indicating that they could leave now. Maggie preceded Flynn out the door and waited for him on the sidewalk.

"What's happening?" she asked. "What did the officer say?"

"Apparently they'll be interviewed over lunch, but not by the man who was to conduct the interview, because he'd just had an important phone call from London. Instead, the officer will do the questioning. After lunch, they will be returned to Wells."

"Flynn, you saw the look on his face when he saw Rolf and Alyssa. It was more than surprise—it was total shock. He saw something he absolutely hadn't expected to see. He recovered nicely, but I think that's why he left so abruptly. Do you suppose he knows Rolf? Or Rolf knows him?"

"No idea, but we have an important appointment in Bristol we need to keep. We have to get this tiny package into the right hands as soon as possible and find out what it contains."

Maggie stayed focused on the puzzling behavior of the man in the restaurant. "I don't think either Rolf or Alyssa saw his face. They were looking at each other and not at the man as he came in the door. Thank heaven I got his picture. Maybe Rolf will recognize him."

They got in the car and removed their simple disguises. Flynn entered the address of the police station in Bristol into the GPS system, and they drove out of Bath.

They discussed what the flash drive might contain, who the mysterious man might be, what his relationship to Rolf might be, whether the kidnapping of Jennie Albright and her children had anything to do with the flash drive, and every other topic related to the present mystery, carefully avoiding any mention of their relationship—or lack of it.

They sat silently for a few miles before Maggie filled the void. "Now that we finally have time to talk, how have you been, Flynn? How's your book coming? Are you still immersed in your practice to the exclusion of all other things?"

"Actually, the book is nearly finished," Flynn said. "I've cut back some on my practice to spend more time with my family, which delights my sister and her kids and makes my mother unbelievably happy. I've read a best seller or two in the past few months, and I've walked on the beach. I've taken my nieces and nephews shopping for birthday and Christmas presents instead of buying them online and having them mailed to their house. I even took them bowling once, but they beat me so badly I've never done it again."

Maggie laughed. "Honestly?"

"Honestly," Flynn said. "Now that I've been honest with you—"

Maggie interrupted him. "I think I know where you're going with this, and that's not the way it works. I didn't leave you in order to find answers. You left me. And until you've found those answers, I can't put myself through this again." She turned and looked out the window. "Until I know what your decision is on those very important issues, I simply can't say any more than that I'm so glad to see you and I've missed you."

Maggie never learned where their conversation might have led, since they arrived in Bristol at that moment. They quickly located the address Tad Collins had given them and discovered what Tad had called a café—basically another pub. Maggie and Flynn stepped inside, saw no one they would have considered the agent they were to meet, and went back outside where there were shady tables under green umbrellas.

"He said he'd probably be back in town by time we arrived, but I think we should eat now and not wait for him," Flynn said.

"I second the motion," Maggie said, examining the menu posted on the door.

* * *

Ravenwood Estate
Friday, 2:30 P.M.

"Leonard, contact the cells in Paris, New York, and Los Angeles. Make sure everything is ready. With only twenty-six hours until our ultimatum expires, it's imperative that everything be in place soon, at the very least twelve hours before deadline."

"Will do, sir. The cell leaders in those cities have indicated they're ready, but I'll double check to make sure all the details have been worked out and notify you of any problems. What about London? When do we start moving the goods into the city? Did you recover the plans Ulric was bringing from Australia?"

"No," Constantine replied tersely. "We are going forward on the assumption that we'll not have that information in our hands in time to implement it. We have the targets. The goods will be loaded into delivery trucks, high-dollar cars, left in suitcases on buses and in taxis. The Daisy Cutter will destroy Trafalgar Square and National Gallery treasures and Buckingham Palace. The British Museum and St. Paul's Cathedral are too far apart, so they will each be the target of trucks full of munitions. Not as effective as if we had been able to plant the explosives according to plan, but it will, of course, accomplish our goal."

"What about Tower Bridge and the Tower of London?" Leonard asked. "Can we take out both of those with a single blast?"

"Not unless your expert can plant and detonate his explosives himself. We'll also need to give individual attention to Westminster Abbey and the House of Parliament. Since we don't have the original plans, I'm drafting some myself to make sure nothing precious to the British people is left standing. Of course, I'm sure when the London Eye goes down, there'll be no tears shed from those who hate that modern abomination as much as I do."

"When are you coming out to the conference room? You need to go over this with the crew. They're getting antsy with all the publicity about Ulric's arrest."

"Yes, that was most unfortunate," Constantine said, thinking that was too mild an expression. "I'll be out as soon as I can get away from here. I'll call before I arrive so you can have everyone assembled." He paused, then added, "When you contact the cell leaders, make sure they understand, they are not to act until they hear from me personally. If they do not get a direct command from me to activate the explosives, they are not to act. Is that understood?"

"Of course, sir."

"We don't need further destruction when they have complied with the instructions and we have their money."

Constantine hung up and dialed another number. Ulric would pay dearly for his foul-up. "Edward, I need something very special accomplished as soon as possible." He described the job and the timing.

"I understand, sir. I hope you realize how dangerous this will be for me, and how expensive for you. Ulric is being held in maximum security right now."

Mr. Constantine sighed wearily. "Yes, I know. I'm prepared to pay whatever it costs to have him silenced for good. And the quicker the better, before he spills everything he knows and compromises our plans."

* * *

Bristol
Friday, 2:30 p.m.

Maggie and Flynn were just finishing lunch when Detective Chief Inspector Tad Collins appeared. He walked quickly to their table and introduced himself, presenting his ID.

"How did you know we were the ones you were looking for?" Maggie asked. "You didn't even look inside. You came straight to us."

"I had your passport pictures faxed to me so I'd be sure to connect with the right people." He smiled. "I also had my secretary do a quick background check to make sure you weren't a couple of quacks." He settled in a chair and waved to the waitress.

"Okay, what do you have that only I get to see? And why didn't you just call Scotland Yard yourself?"

"I'm sure Gary told you we're not sure who to trust," Flynn said. "We've just observed a plainclothes detective and a government official searching for this very item—which I'm sure no one at Scotland Yard or MI5 even knows exists yet."

Maggie put her laptop on the table and inserted the flash drive. She turned the computer so the British agent could see the unintelligible mess of letters and numbers on the screen.

"Hmm. You're right." Collins nodded. "Definitely a job for our cryptographers."

"Can you get it deciphered without anyone else knowing about it?" Flynn asked. "It could be nothing more than recipes for home-made bombs, but if it actually has something to do with the world-wide terrorist bombings, and there is a higher-up in the government trying to get his hands on this for evil purposes, I really don't want him to succeed before anyone else has seen it."

"I agree. A friend in cryptology owes me a couple favors I can call in tonight. I'll leave for London right now. By the time I get there, everyone else in that department should have gone home."

Maggie handed the flash drive to Tad Collins. "I'm relieved to have it out of my hands—and I'll be even happier when everyone who wants it knows I no longer have it."

Collins nodded. "I'd be very careful where I went the next couple of days if I were you."

The waitress approached as Collins rose. "Did you want to order something?" she asked.

"I did, but I don't have time now." He pocketed the flash drive and hurried back to his car, dialing his cell phone as he went.

"What do you want to do now?" Flynn asked as Maggie folded up her laptop and restored it to her bag.

"I'd like to find out something about my older brother Llewellyn Rathford. He's such a mystery—no one seems to know anything about him since he left home. Damon wouldn't talk about him and forbade me to try to find him."

"And you're still willing to try?" Flynn asked, signing the credit card receipt.

"I've come too far now to not see this through." Maggie stood. "What if he would love to learn he has two sisters he didn't know about?"

"And conversely, what if he wants to be left alone?" Flynn asked, taking Maggie's arm to lead her back to the car.

"Then I'd be happy for *him* to tell me that."

"Fair enough," Flynn said. "Where do we start looking for this elusive brother?"

"Maybe by talking to his mother in Wells." Maggie settled into the car and waited for Flynn to get in the other side. "Of course, I do have to deal with the *ifs*—*if* she'll see me, and *if* she'll tell me where he is. Damon said Llewellyn had changed his name, so unless Mrs. Rathford wants to reveal that, I may be out of luck."

"Any reason she wouldn't want to talk to you about him?" Flynn asked.

"Damon said Llewellyn wasn't in contact with anyone in the family, even his mother. But I'm willing to bet Mrs. Rathford knows exactly where her son is. I just have to discover how to find her, and then I think I'll be able to find Llewellyn."

# EIGHTEEN

Wells
Friday, 4:00 P.M.

Rolf and Alyssa had just arrived from Bath when Maggie and Flynn reached the hotel. Flynn suspected the officer would still keep them under surveillance. And he was right—the man drove around the block, parked down the street, and sat in his car after he dropped them at the hotel.

Maggie and Flynn parked behind the hotel and entered by the back door so the twins would not be seen together. The fewer people who realized there were two, the better.

"Dr. Ford!" Alyssa exclaimed. "What are you doing here? I just talked to you in Chicago."

"Actually, he was here, trying to catch up to me," Maggie explained.

Flynn nodded. "I saw the officer approach you at the bench and called you to see what was happening. I didn't know whether I should call in the cavalry or just follow you and see where that officer was taking you."

"So we followed you," Maggie said. "How was your lunch?"

"Lunch was delicious. The shepherd's pie was incredible," Alyssa said. "You should try it sometime."

Flynn laughed. "I see your twin bond is still as strong as ever. That's what Maggie ordered for lunch."

"What did the officer really want from you?" Maggie asked, bringing the conversation back to the more urgent business of the day.

"That might still be a bit up in the air," Rolf said. "He asked all sorts of questions. I'd told Alyssa about your encounter with Jennie

Albright, and she played along, saying just about what you told me."
Rolf laughed. "She's a pretty good actress."

"A pretty good liar, you mean," Alyssa said.

"No, I meant actress," Rolf said. "You were pretending to be Maggie,
and you did a great job."

"Did either of you see the man who came in to interview you?"
Maggie asked.

"I didn't," Alyssa said. "Inspector Graham said someone was supposed
to have been there, but he was called back to London, so he had the pleasure of taking us to lunch and asking questions himself."

"Did you see him, Rolf? He was tall, slender, brown hair, fashion-
ably dressed—an impressive looking man, fairly young," Maggie said.

"No," Rolf said. "Did he actually come and then leave again?"

Then Maggie remembered the picture she'd taken. "Oh, wait.
Look at this and see if you've ever seen the man before." She handed
them her camera. "He walked in the door and talked to your Inspector
Graham, who pointed out your table. When he saw you, he looked
like he'd seen a ghost. He whipped around and left, telling the officer
he couldn't stay. Does he look familiar?"

"Can't really say from this profile," Alyssa said. "Maybe if I saw
his face full on—but no, I don't think I've ever seen him."

"Rolf?" Maggie asked.

Rolf shook his head slowly. "I don't think so."

"He might be an official in the government. Does that ring any
bells?" Maggie asked.

Rolf kept slowly shaking his head. "I can't place him—can't even
think of where I might have seen him, if I have."

"Oh, well. Maybe it will come to one of you. He did look familiar
to me, but I can't imagine where I could have seen him either," Maggie
said. "Now, I think we should go find Mrs. Rathford and ask about
her son Llewellyn."

Alyssa's eyes got big. "I thought you said he didn't want anything
to do with the family."

"That's what Damon told me. It may or may not be true. I think we
need to find out for ourselves. Who's going with me?" Maggie asked.

"Actually, I think you girls would have better luck with Mrs.
Rathford if you went by yourselves," Flynn said.

Maggie thought about it for a minute and then agreed. "You're probably right. Rolf, while Alyssa and I go upstairs and freshen up for a minute, will you find out where the Rathfords live? Mr. Rathford is supposed to be at home, but if he's still suffering, he may be in bed and we can talk to Mrs. Rathford alone."

When the girls returned to the lobby, Rolf had the address and directions written down for them.

"I'm going to check into the hotel, then wander over to the National Trust office and poke around a bit and get acquainted with your brother Damon," Flynn said.

"I'll do some inquiring about the family and their associations," Rolf said. "I don't think I'll be welcomed by Damon—our first encounter was anything but cordial."

Maggie and Alyssa left by the back door and drove Maggie's rental car through the back streets to the edge of Wells, carefully following Rolf's directions. A few hundred yards down a little lane, Maggie located the house and pulled into the driveway. Alyssa had barely moved or spoken since they got in the car.

"You are coming with me, aren't you?" Maggie asked.

"I don't like this, sis," she said, her voice little more than a whisper.

"I don't either," Maggie admitted, "but the sooner we get in and out of here, the more we'll know, one way or the other. Let's go."

Maggie knocked on the door and waited. Alyssa hung back, looking like she was ready to run the minute anyone showed up. Maggie knocked again. Finally the door opened a crack and a tired voice asked, "Who is it?"

"I'm Maggie McKenzie, and this is Alyssa. We are the other two children of Cleat Wiggins and his wife, Lily. I assume your husband told you about us. Could we come in and speak to you for a moment?"

The door opened a little more, just enough for the woman to see the girls and for them to see the pale face staring out at them. "Oh." A gasp of surprise escaped her thin lips, and she opened the door a little wider. She looked down the road before beckoning them inside.

"How ever did you find us?" she asked, staring at the girls who so closely resembled her two adopted sons.

"Didn't your husband tell you? The midwife who delivered Damon kept the envelope in which you mailed payment for delivering the baby. It had your address in Arundel. I tracked you from there. Mrs. Rathford, would you tell us the name Llewellyn has taken so we can find him? We'd like to meet him, if we can, before we return to America."

Mrs. Rathford seemed shocked beyond words. She simply stared at the twins in her entryway, her hand covering her mouth.

Maggie turned to her sister, who was standing beside the door, ready to escape. "Cleat told Lily that both of her other children had died at birth. We came to England to find out if Lily's sons had survived."

"What will happen when Lily wants to come and interrupt our lives?" The frail woman wrung her hands and backed away from Maggie, looking as if she would flee at any moment.

"If you don't want any contact with Lily, I promise that she will leave you alone. She will not try to contact the boys or you or your husband. But I would like to speak briefly with Llewellyn before we return to California. Damon said that Llewellyn wanted no contact from anyone in the family, not even you. I don't believe that. I believe that you're in touch with him. That's right, isn't it?" Maggie asked quietly.

Silent tears slid down Mrs. Rathford's thin cheeks. She neither denied nor affirmed Maggie's comment. "I don't know if he will want to see you. I don't know if I should . . ." Her words fell away into an awkward silence.

"I'm sure you have a phone number for him," Maggie said. "May I call on my cell phone and ask him if he'll see us? He may be as curious about us as we are about him."

The decision seemed agonizing for the woman. Finally she whispered a number. Maggie punched it in her cell phone as it fell from her aunt's lips.

"What name is he using?" Maggie asked as the phone rang.

"Richard," Mrs. Rathford said before she collapsed in the nearest chair, her shaking hands covering her ashen face. "Richard Constantine."

Someone picked up on the other end of the line, and Maggie began speaking. "Richard, my name is Maggie McKenzie. I'm your sister, Cleat Wiggins's daughter." Maggie almost gagged as she said the distasteful words. "My twin sister is with me. We'd like to speak briefly with you before we return to California. Could we please have an hour of your time, at your convenience?" Maggie held her breath, awaiting his answer.

There was total silence on the other end of the line.

"I'm sure this is a shock to you," Maggie continued quickly. "I had a similar shock seven months ago when I discovered I had an identical twin sister I never knew existed. We want nothing more than a few minutes of your time, and if you wish to have no more to do with us, we'll honor those wishes. Can we please come and see you briefly when it's convenient for you?"

"You've come from California just to spend a few minutes with me?" His voice, deep and pleasant, sounded doubtful.

"We came to see if we could locate Cleat Wiggins's sons. I was successful in finding your parents, met Damon, and discovered we had one more brother. May we come, please?" Maggie begged.

"I guess I'm as curious about you as you are about me," Llewellyn said. "Are you familiar with Wales?"

"I've never been there, but if you give me a town and an address, I can find it." Maggie pulled out her notebook and pen, nearly dancing with joy that he'd consented to see them.

"We'll meet in Usk. It's close to the border and where you are, and easy to find. Cross the bridge, drive through Caldicott, and go north on the A449. I'll meet you at the Cross Keys Pub. There's parking in back. Say, tomorrow at eleven o'clock?"

"We'll be there. I'm looking forward to meeting you." Maggie disconnected and knelt beside Mrs. Rathford. "Thank you for sharing his name with us. We'll protect his privacy and yours. I can't thank you enough." She kissed the pale cheek and as she started to her feet, her aunt clutched her arm.

"Wait."

Maggie returned to her knees and waited.

"I think . . ." Mrs. Rathford twisted her hands in what appeared to be an agony of indecision. She reached for a small writing tablet on the table next to the chair, then stopped and dropped her hand back into her lap. Finally her eyes met Maggie's, searched for something she apparently hoped to find there, and with a deep sigh, she covered her quivering mouth.

"Let me help you," Maggie whispered. "Whatever you need, please let me help you."

Tears welled in her aunt's eyes, and she shook her head. "I'm so afraid."

"Afraid of what?" Maggie asked, scarcely daring to speak, fearful she'd break the spell and the woman would send them away without finishing the conversation. Gently she took her aunt's frail, trembling hands in her own. "Tell me what I can do to help."

Mrs. Rathford stifled a sob as silent tears slid down her pale cheeks. "I've got to tell someone," she said, shaking her head back and forth as she spoke. "I don't dare tell my husband or Damon, and I can't go to the police. But I've *got* to tell someone." She pulled a tissue from her apron pocket and wiped her eyes.

Maggie held her breath as her aunt picked up the tablet, tore off the top page containing handwritten notes, folded it, and stuffed it in the envelope that lay beside the tablet. She licked the flap, sealed the envelope, and with an unsteady hand held it toward the stranger, a niece she hadn't known existed until today.

"Promise me you will do exactly as I ask if I give this to you."

"I promise, whatever you need," Maggie said, hoping Mrs. Rathford wouldn't change her mind and withhold the mysterious letter and the request.

"You must not open this until you are far away from here. Then you must type it and send it to the police, anonymously. No one can ever connect it to our family in any way. Promise me that you will not open it until you are on your way back to America. The police must never trace it to you or to us."

Stunned, Maggie nodded. "I promise I will do everything in my power to make sure you and your family will never be connected to the contents," she said to the frightened woman. Even as Maggie spoke that solemn promise, which she planned with all her heart to keep, she hoped she would be able to do so.

Mrs. Rathford grasped her arm with surprising strength. "Please don't let me down. Don't betray my trust. I don't know where else to turn."

"I won't let you down." Maggie tucked the letter in her pocket, leaned over and kissed her aunt, and Maggie and Alyssa quickly left, shutting the door quietly behind them.

"What secrets could she have written in that letter?" Alyssa asked as she buckled her seat belt. "She was so frightened, it scared me."

"Me, too. And all it did was raise more questions about our brothers." Maggie's mind went wild with possibilities, but it would accomplish nothing to ponder on a mystery she had no hope of unraveling today.

Lost in thoughts of what secrets might be contained in the letter, neither twin spoke on the return trip to the hotel.

# NINETEEN

Ravenwood Estate
Friday, 5:00 P.M.

"Terrence, do you still have your eye on the redhead and her friend you took to lunch?" Constantine barked into his cell phone.

"Yes, sir. They're in the hotel. I'm watching the door and will be on them the minute they leave," the officer said.

"I have reason to believe these two are not typical tourists, so your surveillance will have to be a little more sophisticated than just a casual observation. I want to know what they do and who they see and how many are in their party. They can't know they are being watched, so don't get caught."

"Yes, sir, Mr. Constantine."

Richard Constantine disconnected and leaned back in his chair, contemplating the conversation he'd had moments earlier with a sister he'd had no idea existed. He replayed the conversation in his mind. No, there were two sisters. Twins, she said. Just what he needed—more siblings.

So not only had the savvy reporter walked right into his hands, but she was also family. His own sister was the one who had his plans. Of course. Because family always tried to ruin everything. But this time they wouldn't. This time he was in control. If he could get his hands on those plans, it might not be too late to implement them, instead of the haphazard plot he was throwing together at the last minute for London. If Terrence could get her bag . . .

But if he couldn't; it wouldn't do to get too close, not at this stage of the game. Maybe he should postpone the meeting until after the deadline. That was only—he glanced at his watch—twenty-five hours. Twenty-five hours to wake up the world to a new balance of power—one in *his* favor.

\* \* \*

Wells
Friday, 6:00 P.M.

Damon entered the front lobby of the hotel as Maggie and Alyssa came in the rear door from the parking lot. He went straight to them and took their hands. "That was excellent timing. Are you up for a tour of my cathedral and then dinner?"

As Damon looked at Alyssa, Maggie caught Flynn's eye across the lobby in the business center. He nodded as if to say, *Yes, go with him.*

"I'd love to, Damon," Maggie said. "How about you, Alyssa?" Maggie held her breath, fearing Alyssa would look around for Rolf, but her sister had the foresight to simply accept the invitation.

"Great. I'll show you England's first completely Gothic cathedral, dating from about 1200." He linked arms with his look-alike sisters and led them back across the street, through the ornate gate called Penniless Porch, and onto the huge expanse of green in front of the cathedral.

\* \* \*

Ravenwood Estate
Friday, 6:02 P.M.

"Yes, Inspector Graham?"

"Mr. Constantine, sir, I'm seeing double. Actually, I'm seeing triple. The girl I picked up with that Rolf Owen character has a twin. And they are being escorted by a tall redheaded fellow that bears a striking resemblance to them. What do you want me to do?"

Constantine sat quietly pondering this revelation. The tall redhead was undoubtedly his brother, Damon Rathford. "Terrence, does one of the girls have a big bag?"

"Yes, Mr. Constantine. Oh," Inspector Graham declared, the light suddenly dawning. "The girl at lunch wasn't the reporter you were after. It was her twin!"

"That's exactly what I'm thinking. I need that bag. Do whatever it takes, but get it for me as soon as possible. We don't need to start another international incident—I think you can do it with class—but get it. Then bring it to me immediately."

"Do you want the whole bag, or is there something specific in there you need? Maybe I could just get whatever—"

Constantine interrupted him. "The whole bag, Terrence, and quickly." Constantine disconnected and paced the floor, then strode through the open French doors onto his terrace. His sisters' arrival on the scene must not interfere with his carefully laid plans. Once Terrence delivered the bag, Constantine would let the girls drive to Usk, but he wouldn't be there waiting. Their meeting could be postponed until after the deadline.

He gazed across his beautiful gardens without seeing them. One more thing to take place before six o'clock tomorrow night—Jennie Albright and her children would have to be released. That would bring the world's attention to something positive—before he popped their bubble and pulled the smug foundation right out from under them.

\* \* \*

Wells
Friday, 6:05 P.M.

As they approached the great golden cathedral, Damon became animated, pointing to the empty niches on the stone facade near the ground. "Cromwell's men stripped the statues from those. Fortunately, there were three hundred more they couldn't reach, so we have the largest gallery of medieval sculpture in the world on the facade of this cathedral."

Maggie took pictures while Damon gave a running dialogue of history and description. He was being totally charming, and she found she enjoyed his company immensely. The horror stories everyone had told her must have been exaggerated, or perhaps he'd changed as he grew older.

"Are you ready for this?" he asked with pride as he escorted them across the street and through an archway, into a narrow lane paved with ancient bricks. "I suppose I should say 'ta-da' or some such foolish introduction to this most marvelously preserved medieval street in all of Europe. It's the Vicar's Close."

Maggie laughed. "One of my guidebooks said something like 'perfectly pickled fourteenth-century houses.' It called this place the oldest continuously inhabited street in Europe."

"All true," Damon said, pointing out the forty-two chimneys standing sentinel in two flawless lines along the gray roofs.

"Who lives here?" Alyssa asked, staring wide-eyed at the amazing scene before her.

"Since the twelfth century, the gentlemen's choral has been housed here. The cathedral staff and some choir members inhabit these houses now."

They walked silently down the ancient narrow street, noting the individual gates to each tiny walled yard. Some were stone arches, some wrought iron, and some wood. The postage-stamp yards were also uniquely individual; some overflowed with flowers and shrubs, some displayed a well-kept line of rosebushes, and others had vines creeping over the stone walls.

"Imagine living in a house that was built over six hundred and fifty years ago," Maggie said. "Of course, they'd have to be modernized. I'd expect they now have electricity, running water, and telephones."

"And TV," Alyssa said.

"Nowhere is too sacred for TV, is it?" Damon laughed. "Now, let's return to the *pièce de résistance*."

This was only the second time Maggie had heard Damon laugh with pleasure; she thoroughly enjoyed this side of him.

"Tell me about your childhood, Alyssa," Damon said, linking his arm through hers while Maggie continued to take pictures.

"I felt I had a wonderful childhood," Alyssa said, "but looking back, it was quite strange. I assumed the Lawsons were my mother and father and that Lily was my nanny. In reality, Lily was my mother and the Lawsons my adoptive parents. Lily and I had a great relationship. Mother—Mrs. Lawson—was quite the social butterfly, and she was gone all the time until she became ill and died, but Lily was there for me constantly. My folks had money, so I had everything I wanted. I did well in school, I had great friends, and I had a horse that was my most favorite thing in the world. That was the good part. Then Cleat intervened."

She looked up at Damon as they left the medieval close and crossed the street back into the modern world. "Now you tell us about your childhood."

"I was a delight to my mother, an irritation to my older brother, and a puzzle to my father," Damon said. "I wanted to be everywhere I shouldn't have been, which my mother thought very cute, my brother hated, and my father did his best to ignore. My father tried to lead by example but rarely provided specific direction and wasn't consistent with discipline. My brother expected to be left alone instead of having a little shadow everywhere he went, attempting to do everything he did. My mother couldn't understand the rest of the family's exasperation with me."

"Sounds like a normal house with siblings," Maggie said, coming abreast of the two. "I followed my big brothers everywhere until they couldn't put up with me anymore, or until they were working and it became dangerous for me to be with them. Then they called for Mom to rescue them from the little pest and take me off their hands."

"I envy you two," Alyssa said. "I had Lily and my horse. They were often my only company."

"But now we all have each other!" Maggie said happily as Damon opened the massive door for them. "Now then, what's your favorite part of the cathedral?" she asked.

"You'll see as soon as you enter the nave."

When they walked through the huge front door, Maggie immediately knew the answer to her question. The symmetrical beauty and flow of the Gothic arches and pillars, uninterrupted from one end of the nave to the other, was breathtaking.

"It's exquisite," she exclaimed. It truly was. More light and airy than most medieval cathedrals, the high arches seemed to reach almost to the heavens. But the focal point, the dominant architectural feature of the cathedral, was the unusual arch at the point where the tower rose above it.

Damon stood close beside her. "You like it."

"'Like' is a gross understatement. It's incredible," Maggie said. "Tell me about that arch. It's almost like an hourglass. I've never seen anything like it."

"Nor will you. That's the famed scissors arch. In 1338, when the central tower was heightened, they discovered the foundations could not cope with the extra height and weight, and the tower began to crack. The architect devised a brilliant solution in this unique scissors arch under the tower. That solved the problems. Come, let me show you the rest."

Some of the beautiful stained glass windows had the usual biblical figures and designs, but some seemed to be simply a mosaic of colored glass. "Why aren't there pictures in those windows, like the others?" Alyssa asked.

"After Cromwell's men destroyed the originals, like they did in many other cathedrals," Damon explained, "craftsmen and townspeople painstakingly pieced the windows back together, sifting through piles and piles of broken glass to reconstruct them. Where they were unable to reassemble the original design, they used the broken pieces and formed a beautiful, colorful mosaic."

Maggie, busily photographing everything she saw, stayed close to hear Damon's knowledgeable explanations.

"This is an . . . uh . . . unusual tomb. It kind of gives me the creeps, really. How come there are two people here?" Alyssa pointed to the marble slab on which an elaborately clothed replica of a bishop lay in death; underneath, enclosed in glass, a human skeleton lay with only a layer of skin stretched tautly across his bones and a sheet draped around him.

"It's actually just one person. Bishop Bookington built his tomb before he died. The figure on top represents him in his priestly garments. His skeleton was placed underneath to show that no matter how high we rise in this life, we all end up the same after death."

"Do you believe that, Damon?" Maggie asked, curious as to what his beliefs actually were.

"Don't you?" he countered, turning slowly to face Maggie. He stared deeply into her eyes, as if he were trying to plumb the depths of her soul.

"No. I don't believe we'll all end up the same after death. God's grace is available to everyone, but I believe that if one person is more obedient to the commandments of God than another, that person will earn a better place in the hereafter. I believe that goodness and kindness and diligence are rewarded by a loving Father in Heaven."

Maggie took a deep breath and said more slowly, "And conversely, I believe there will be those who'll be quite devastated in the next life, because they disregarded the commandments and chose other roads in this life."

Damon's eyes never left Maggie's. His tone was icy cold. "Do you know anyone in that latter category?"

"Not personally," she said, not flinching. "I don't make it a habit to associate with people who would try to make me compromise my standards."

What Damon's reply would have been, Maggie never found out. At that moment, someone ran by her, jerked the bag from her shoulder, and fled toward the great door at the end of the cathedral. Maggie reacted immediately.

"Stop that man! He stole my bag," she screamed and sped after him. Damon and Alyssa were not far behind her, but when they reached the door outside, there was no sign of the thief. Maggie looked around and then sprinted for Penniless Porch and the exit of the cathedral green. How could he have gotten all the way across the green in those few seconds? But that had to be where he'd gone.

She couldn't lose that bag. It contained her life—photos, laptop, work, passport, ID, and wallet! As she flew through the gate and into the street in front of the National Trust office and the Crown Hotel, she spotted the man running down the street toward a dark sedan. She raced after him, hoping her daily morning run would pay off.

But the man made it to the car, got in, and headed straight for Maggie, who was still running toward him in the middle of the street. She barely jumped out of the way before he could run her down. As he passed, she got a good look at him—the same police officer that had interviewed Rolf and Alyssa over lunch. So he got the bag after all. At least he didn't get the flash drive.

When Damon and Alyssa caught up to her, Maggie, still clutching her camera in her hand, showed Damon the picture she had taken of the man in the pub. "Do you recognize this man?" she asked. "I'm pretty sure he's the guy behind the theft of my bag—and possibly something worse." As she stood next to Damon and looked up at his profile, she was startled to see a similarity to the profile in the picture.

She didn't have to wait for Damon's expression or words to tell her. "This is Llewellyn, isn't it? This is our brother." She tried to make sense of this. "I'm certain he ordered that man to steal my bag. Llewellyn's involved in something terrible."

"What do you mean?" Damon asked. "Why do you think it's Llewellyn in this photo?"

"Alyssa, look at that picture—that profile—and now look at Damon's profile. Tell me what you think."

"Hmm, I think they are very similar," Alyssa said. "Are you sure this isn't your brother, Damon?"

Damon's shoulders sagged, and he turned toward the Crown. "Come on. Let's have dinner, and I'll tell you about Llewellyn."

# TWENTY

Ravenwood Estate
Friday, 7:00 P.M.

Constantine prowled the halls and stairs of his rented estate like a caged animal, waiting for Terrence Graham in Wells to call him with news, any news. The absence of news agitated him, unnerved him. Even bad news was better than no news at all. At least it meant he had something to do, like devising a new plan—waiting was not his cup of tea. Suddenly the cell phone he held in his hand rang.

"Yes?" he barked.

"Mr. Constantine, sir! I've got it! I've got the bag."

"Good work, Terrence," Constantine said, adrenaline pulsing through him. "I'm leaving right now. I'll meet you at the heliport in Bath as soon as you can get there."

"I'm on my way as we speak, sir."

"Thank you, Terrence. I'll put your reward in the works right now. You deserve it."

As soon as Constantine was airborne, he called Edward Thompson. "Edward, your man in Bath who found Rolf Owen?"

"Yes, sir?"

"He's going to have a fatal accident on the way home from work tonight. He's on his way from Wells to Bath right now. We'll rendezvous in thirty minutes at the heliport. Unfortunately, the poor man will never see his wife again. See that she gets a small pension for his years of service, enough to keep her from complaining."

"Yes, sir. I'll get someone on it right away."

"Thank you, Edward. I know I can always rely on your discretion. There will be a deposit in your account to cover this expense."

"Thank you, sir."

Richard Constantine, a.k.a. Llewellyn Rathford, smiled all the way to his helicopter. Finally things were going his way. He'd deal with the matter of his sisters later. It was truly unfortunate they had to show up at this moment. Right now, he had to get his hands on those plans and get his explosives in place in London. That was the most important order of the day. Then he could think about dealing with siblings—if, indeed, he had any desire to see them. He might have to simply place another call to Edward. He would certainly be able to afford the few thousand pounds that would cost him.

Then his mind returned to his current problem. The United States and Britain wouldn't capitulate until Paris had been destroyed—that he was sure of. When Paris went, their resolve would crumble, as well as their hopes for some kind of compromise. But there would be no compromise. Either he received the whole billion in funds, or they could kiss their cities, treasures—and population—good-bye.

Constantine glanced at his watch as he took off. Twenty-three hours. A mere twenty-three hours until he became one of the most powerful men in the world; the billion dollars would just be a bonus for his cleverness and expertise. Then he could buy Ravenwood Estate and a dozen others that were even better.

\* \* \*

Wells, the Crown Hotel
Friday, 7:00 P.M.

When Damon entered the Crown with Maggie and Alyssa, he saw Rolf and Flynn across the lobby in the business center.

"Would you like Dr. Ford and your Welsh friend to join us?" he asked his sisters. Maggie and Alyssa looked at each other in surprise. Damon smiled at their reaction. "Dr. Ford introduced himself to me earlier today and told me about your relationship."

"If you don't mind, Damon, I think that would be very nice," Maggie said, catching Flynn's eye and beckoning him and Rolf to join them. Again she was confused by Damon's unpredictability. Earlier that day he'd practically growled at the possibility of an outsider joining them. Now he was perfectly gracious.

The hostess seated them in the dining room, and Damon suggested they order before he began his story. When that had been accomplished, with suggestions from both Damon and Rolf as to dishes they might enjoy, they sat back expectantly.

Damon reached for his water, avoiding the eyes of the others, and began meticulously wiping the condensation from the glass.

"You were going to tell us about Llewellyn," Maggie prompted quietly.

"Yes. Llewellyn the wonderful. Llewellyn the esteemed and popular government official." Damon's voice began rising. "Llewellyn the pyromaniac who will blow up the world sooner or later."

Maggie and Flynn glanced at each other.

Damon continued, his voice lower but tense. "Except no one will look at him—they'll all look at me. Do you know why?" Damon stared around the table at each member of the group. "Because he has blamed me for every misdeed he ever committed—and gotten away with it." He gave a short laugh. "And I'll probably get blamed for this, too."

"But why?" Maggie asked.

Damon shook his head and spread his hands in a hopeless gesture. "Apparently he's hated me from the day I came into this family. And he has set me up so many times, I can't even remember them all. Why do you think we had to move so often?" Without waiting for an answer, he went on, becoming angrier as he spoke. "Because he blew things up. He burned things down. He hurt people. And then he told them it was me. Since we looked so much alike, he could get away with impersonating me, saying things like 'You hurt Damon, Damon hurts you,' or 'You don't like Damon; Damon doesn't like you, either.' So they thought he was me. Even after he changed the color of his hair, he frequented the pubs wearing a red wig and dropped my name so everyone thought it was me drinking and partying and setting fires all over with his crazy experiments. Do you know what they called me? Demon. Demon! Can you imagine how I've felt?" He covered his face with his hands and released an anguished sigh.

Maggie reached out to touch his arm. "I'm so sorry, Damon."

"Do you know what your brother is up to now?" Flynn asked quietly.

Damon didn't respond for a minute, then he looked at Flynn and shook his head. "No. I think he may have made some undesirable connections when he was on assignment with the military. He was dealing with ordnance disposal at the time. My hunch is that his love of explosives found a new outlet and that he's been pursuing it ever since. So, what is he up to right now? I have no idea, but whatever it is, it isn't good and it isn't noble and it isn't worthy of the Rathford legacy."

Flynn's phone rang, and he stepped away from the table to answer it.

"Tad Collins here, Dr. Ford. Our cryptographer got right on that flash drive. It's beginning to look like your hunch was right. If so, this is no small potatoes. She's discovered enough to suspect it's a sort of map of bombs and explosives. She's still working on it, but that's her first guess with what she has. For the time being, we're supposing the city is London."

"What will you do with the information?" Flynn asked.

"Take it to the top, of course, but first I need to know the name of the bigwig you were afraid might get his hands on this."

"Collins, can you hold for one minute?" Flynn put his hand over the mouthpiece and moved back to the table to ask, "What name did you say Llewellyn goes by?"

"Richard Constantine," Damon answered.

"Richard Constantine," Flynn repeated in the phone, stepping away again. "I can't be sure, but we suspect he might also be behind the kidnapping of the American mother and her two children. He wanted to get his hands on that USB drive mighty bad. In fact, Maggie's bag was stolen a couple of hours ago by the police inspector who seems to be in league with Constantine. Fortunately, we had already given you the drive."

Tad Collins whistled softly into the phone. "Constantine and a police inspector—are you sure about this? If you're right, it will be the biggest scandal to rock the government in over a decade. Maybe two! Do you have any kind of proof? After all, this is pretty far fetched. Constantine's high up in the government and respected in those circles. He's made a huge name for himself the last few years. A young mover and shaker, as you say in the States."

"We have a picture of him in the Crystal Palace this afternoon. He'd mistakenly been having Maggie's twin sister watched, and even brought her and a friend in for questioning. Constantine even had the inspector take the sister's purse to his car to examine, thinking it was Maggie's. A case of mistaken identity. He didn't know there were two redheads in town today."

"Hmm, that's not much to go on, and as you say, you only suspect him. But maybe we can bypass him, as well as anyone working for him, and take preventative measures in secret. By the way, I'd like you and Maggie to meet with one of our guys at the Green Dragon Inn at nine o'clock tonight. It's not that far from where you are. We need to get some statements from you, and we'll also need that picture."

Flynn wrote down the directions and returned to the table. He looked around the group who sat anxiously awaiting his report.

"I guess you could say there's some good news and some bad news," he began, but before he could elaborate, Damon's phone rang.

He excused himself as Flynn had done, and when he came back to the table, he didn't sit down. "My father has taken a turn for the worse. I have to take him to the hospital. I'll be in touch." He turned and quickly left without another word.

They sat in uneasy silence until Maggie said, "I do hope Mr. Rathford is going to be okay." She looked at Flynn. "I guess you'd better give us the bad news first."

"Richard Constantine is a highly esteemed government official, and if he *is* behind any of this, it will be a huge scandal." Flynn paused before adding, "Because he is so respected, no one will want to believe the worst, so we'll have to have concrete evidence before anyone will even speculate about it."

Everyone groaned. "And the good news?" Alyssa asked.

"The good news is that Collins's cryptographer thinks she's broken the code. Collins called before she was finished, but the flash drive appears to contain the plans for placement of bombs and explosives. Until she finishes and they know for sure, they're assuming the city is London."

"No wonder someone wanted that flash drive so badly," Maggie said.

"Right. Bad enough to kill for it," Rolf noted.

Maggie shuddered. "You really were an angel unaware last night. Wow! Was that only last night?" She shook her head in amazement. "But anyway, thank you again, Rolf."

"Now what do we do?" Alyssa asked.

"Maggie and I are to meet with one of Tad Collins's associates at the Green Dragon Inn at nine o'clock tonight," Flynn said. "He assured me it wasn't far from here."

Dinner arrived at that moment. Conversation was suspended while the waitress placed their plates in front of them, administered black pepper from a foot-long pepper grinder, and refilled their water glasses.

Maggie happened to glance across the table at Flynn and caught him staring at her. She smiled when he winked, and butterflies went wild in her stomach. She knew they would not talk of their relationship until this was over, but she didn't know if she could possibly wait that long to find out what Flynn had on his mind.

* * *

Heliport at Bath
Friday, 7:30 P.M.

Terrence ran across the heliport to the small helicopter waiting on the pad, rotors still spinning. "Here it is, Mr. Constantine." He handed Maggie's bag through the open door.

"Thank you. I'm assuming you did not look inside," Constantine said, greedily grasping at the bag containing the information he had needed two days ago.

"No, sir, Mr. Constantine. I put it in my back seat and left it there until this minute."

"Good man. You'll be rewarded for your diligence. Thank you."

The helicopter took off for Constantine's estate as Terrence ran back to his car. The officer didn't see the battered gray van that pulled onto the street after him. He congratulated himself on being noticed by Mr. Constantine and couldn't wait to get home to tell his wife of his good fortune and the promised reward.

# TWENTY-ONE

Ravenwood Estate
Friday, 8:00 P.M.

Constantine raced into the house and dumped the large bag onto his desk in the library. He couldn't believe the contents. He was incredulous that anyone would carry this much stuff around. But as he frantically pawed through it, it soon became apparent the device he was looking for was simply not there.

Terrence! Had he taken it? Constantine dialed Edward Thompson.

"Yes, Mr. Constantine?"

"Has Terrence received his reward?" Maybe there was still time to search Terrence and his car.

Thompson looked at his watch. "Yes, sir. He should have been in the river for about fifteen minutes now. Tomorrow in the daylight someone will spot the car in the river, and they'll find poor Terrence there. He must have been driving too fast to make that sharp curve."

"Thank you, Edward." Constantine disconnected. He paced the floor. Maybe Terrence hadn't double-crossed him. Maybe that redheaded reporter—that newly discovered sister—had the device. Maybe that was why she wanted to meet.

He slammed his fist on the desk. He needed that information. There was barely time to move the goods into town and get them placed. He glanced at his watch. Twenty-two hours. They needed to be in place now!

He picked up his cell phone. Time to move the goods. Past time, in fact.

* * *

Wells, the Crown Hotel
Friday, 8:00 P.M.

"I'm so annoyed about my bag," Maggie said, pushing her empty plate toward the center of the table. "Thank heaven I had e-mailed Lily all the articles I'd written and had my camera in my hand." She sighed. "I can always buy a new computer, but there was so much on there I need, and so much in my bag I can't do without."

"If we're right about Richard Constantine—or Llewellyn Rathford—maybe you can get it back from him, since you're in on all this," Rolf suggested.

"Fat chance," Alyssa said. "If he is what we think he is, he'd probably just as soon kill us as meet us."

Flynn nodded. "Wish we had something more on him. I'm afraid we'd be laughed out of any court. In fact, we'd never even get that far with what pitiful evidence we have."

Maggie reached into her pocket for a tissue and touched an envelope. She drew it out and looked at it; it took a minute for her to remember what it was and where it had come from.

Alyssa sat up. "Maggie, isn't that the letter Mrs. Rathford gave you?"

Maggie nodded. "It is. I'd forgotten about it."

"Mrs. Rathford? Damon's mother?" Rolf asked. "You didn't say anything about getting a letter from her."

"I just got it this afternoon," Maggie said. "When Damon told me Llewellyn didn't want anything to do with family, and forbade me to contact him, it made me want to meet our eldest brother even more. I thought their mother might be able to help. When Alyssa and I went to see her, we got Llewellyn's phone number. Llewellyn, a.k.a. Richard Constantine, agreed to see us tomorrow at eleven o'clock in Usk, Wales. Damon would have been upset if he'd known we were meeting his brother, so we didn't tell him, and I forgot to mention it to the rest of you."

"Mrs. Rathford tore a sheet off a writing tablet and sealed it in an envelope," Alyssa said. "She made it sound very mysterious and made Maggie promise she would not read it until we were on the plane home.

I think under the circumstances, she can't be held to that promise. Can she?"

Maggie looked at Flynn and added, "Mrs. Rathford was extremely upset and almost didn't give this to me but finally said she had to give it to someone. She made me promise I'd keep any connection to their family secret from the police. No one could know where this information originated. I was to type it and send it to the police, making sure it couldn't be traced to me or to the Rathfords. She was terrified it would point back to her."

"I think you'd better open it and read it, Maggie," Flynn said. "It might be nothing, but then again, it might actually have some bearing on this."

"Oh!" Maggie gasped as she scanned the page. "Oh!"

"Out loud, Maggie," Flynn prompted.

"Richard Constantine is a member of a terrorist organization that for two years has been planning an attack on several important London locations. Last night the targets were identified for the first time. The attacks will take place the first Saturday in August as crowds . . .'"

Maggie turned the page over. The back was blank. She looked up at Flynn. "That's all. There's nothing else. She must have been interrupted—maybe Alyssa and I stopped her with our visit."

"Read it again," Flynn said.

Maggie repeated slowly the scant information contained in the unfinished note. She leaned back in the chair and rubbed her temples. "That's tomorrow—the same deadline as has been announced on television. No wonder Mrs. Rathford was a mess."

"But how did she find out?" Flynn asked. "I'm sure her son didn't tell her."

Maggie thought about that for a minute. "Damon said Llewellyn didn't want anything to do with family. I didn't believe that. When I asked Mrs. Rathford for her son's phone number, she gave it to me without looking it up, which points to her being in touch with him frequently."

"Actually, I did a little sleuthing while you were visiting Mrs. Rathford," Rolf said. "I spoke to some of their neighbors at the pub. They reported seeing a well-dressed man in a nice car visit Mrs. Rathford when no one else was home. That's what struck them. He never came when either Mr. Rathford or Damon were there. They thought that a bit strange."

"And your assumption is that it could have been Llewellyn?" Flynn asked.

Rolf nodded. "I think he and his mother kept their meetings and communication a secret. And if he happened to make a phone call while he was there, and she overheard it, that would explain how she came by her knowledge of her son's plan."

"Why would they have to keep their meetings a secret?" Flynn asked.

Maggie shrugged. "It sounds like Llewellyn was disowned for his pyromaniac habits, and Damon and Mr. Rathford wouldn't have approved of the visits. Also, he may have been trying to avoid a public connection between his old life and his new one."

"So how did he get where he is now?" Flynn asked.

"Damon said he'd gone to Wales, changed his name to Richard Constantine, done a short tour of duty in the military, set up a respectable business, and established a name and reputation in politics. Apparently he became powerful in his niche. That's all I know. Does that sound like a terrorist?" Maggie asked.

"In today's troubled world—yes," Flynn said. "Look at his background. What were his interests? Fireworks, bombs, blowing things up. And it sounds like he didn't much care what or who was hurt by what he did. That's fertile soil for a terrorist group to cultivate. It's possible that he's the ringleader, but it's also possible that he's acting out the designs of other terrorists. They could have quietly trained him and subtly influenced his thoughts and values, preparing him for an assignment someday in the future. He could have gone on with business as usual until they needed him. They might even have funded his rise in politics so he could be a powerful ally for them."

Flynn sat quietly thinking for a minute. "Maggie, I'd better tell Inspector Collins about this letter immediately. We can't withhold something like this from the Counterterrorism Command. Inspector Collins may want us to tell his detectives about it when we meet them."

"Is there time to do a little research on the Rathford family before we have to meet Tad Collins's people?" Maggie asked. "Maybe we'll be able to find something useful."

Flynn glanced at his watch and nodded. "We'll have to hurry though. He said we were about thirty minutes from the Green Dragon Inn. You go start. I'll call Inspector Collins and break this little piece of news and see what he wants us to do with it."

Maggie jumped up and hurried across the lobby to the business center and logged on to the Internet. The only sound in the center as the minutes ticked swiftly by was the clacking of computer keys. Suddenly Maggie gasped.

"What did you find?" Flynn asked, bending over her shoulder.

"Unbelievable," Maggie said quietly, never taking her eyes off the object of her astonishment. "Alyssa, come and look at this."

Rolf and Alyssa hurried across the small lobby. Everyone peered over Maggie's shoulder at the small computer screen.

"What is it?" Alyssa asked.

Rolf whistled. "That makes my parents' place look like a dollhouse."

# TWENTY-TWO

An elaborate Gothic mansion with countless turrets and battlements filled the monitor screen. It stood atop a hill with acres of well-manicured grounds flowing down to high wrought-iron gates.

"That is the Rathford family ancestral estate," Maggie announced, her voice filled with awe. "Dragonwyck."

"You're kidding." Alyssa's tone of disbelief expressed everyone's feelings.

Maggie shook her head. "Not kidding. This is for real. The blurb with the picture gives ancient family history, including names going back for generations. The firstborn son of each generation has been christened Llewellyn, and the second born, if there was one, named Damon."

"Coincidence?" Flynn asked. "What's the given name of Damon and Llewellyn's father?"

"Llewellyn," Alyssa said quietly, hardly breathing as she stared at the sight on the screen.

"Could this be another branch of the family that carried on the tradition of the family names? You know, a brother several generations back that decided he liked the idea?" Flynn probed, still not willing to accept without further proof that this was the twins' bloodline and family heritage.

"Anything's possible," Maggie said. "Something like that might have happened. We need to find birth dates to link them for certain. I don't know when Damon and Llewellyn were born, but if you add approximately two years to our birthday for Damon, and another four years for Llewellyn, I think we'll be in the ballpark."

"I'll call Lily," Alyssa said. "She ought to remember when she gave birth."

"Great idea," Maggie said, reaching for her oversized bag that was no longer there. "Oh! What am I going to do without my bag? My cell phone was in there, too." She turned to Alyssa. "While you're at it, ask for Cleat's birth date, and whether Lily knows anything at all about his family in England."

Alyssa glanced at her watch, figured the eight-hour time difference, decided Lily would be at work, and called. She kept the call brief, explaining they were searching records on the family and needed the boys' birth dates.

"Get this," Alyssa reported when she'd disconnected. "Cleat never talked about his background or his family. Mom suspected he might have been from England because of his accent, but she said he side-stepped her questions, refusing to say anything about his life before they met. He said nothing mattered before he met her. Don't you think that's strange that he never talked about his home?"

"Sounds like everything about this family is strange," Flynn said, turning again to the article on the computer.

"Do you suppose he was afraid Lily would want to meet his folks and she'd see where he came from—the estate, I mean?" Maggie said. "It's possible both Mr. Rathford and Cleat lived in the mansion as they were growing up, if this is the same Rathford family."

"Supposing this *is* the ancestral home, why aren't Mr. and Mrs. Rathford living there now?" Maggie asked. "The article doesn't say it's owned by anyone else, so apparently it's still in the family. Can't they afford to live there? Has it been turned into a fancy hotel? Or *does* the family still inhabit the place?" Maggie stopped short. "The family. That would be Damon's grandparents. Mr. Rathford's parents might still be living there." A strange thought occurred to her.

"*Our* grandparents," Alyssa said softly.

Maggie nodded. "That's exactly what I was thinking."

"So how do you find out?" Flynn asked. "Short of knocking on that huge door and asking them yourself."

"That might be a good idea," Maggie said, her mind racing.

"What else does the article say?" Rolf looked over Maggie's shoulder at the screen. "Any further enlightenment on the family? Coat of arms? Family motto? Those are big here, and they impact the family values and traditions for generations."

Maggie scrolled down through the text.

"I cannot, in any way, see Cleat Wiggins coming from that house," Alyssa said. "He was trash. Poor white trash. He didn't have a civilized bone in his body. No manners, no breeding, no compassion, no morals. He could barely be called a human being."

Flynn replied with a wry smile, "Just because someone comes from money doesn't mean a thing. All the money in the world can't give a person humanity. And you have to remember, just because this is a mansion, it doesn't mean the family has money."

"Right," Rolf agreed. "Taxes are high in Britain, and many of the landed gentry are forced to open their homes for tours, or turn them into bed-and-breakfasts just to pay the taxes so they don't lose the ancestral holdings."

"Mr. Rathford told me Cleat was kicked out of their home and apparently disowned from the family because he organized a theft ring and was caught stealing. That might indicate there wasn't a lot of available money for him," Maggie said thoughtfully.

"Or that he wanted what other people had, no matter how much he already had," Flynn suggested.

"True," Maggie agreed. "Here's something interesting. It says that the following quote has appeared in all literature having to do with the Rathford family since about 1790. It's an excerpt from Goethe's *Iphigenia*." Maggie read the poem aloud.

Flynn smiled at the stilted early English wording. "So, to put that in modern terms, a person is happy who can look back on his ancestors and talk about the good things they did, and consider himself an important part or link of that family by continuing those traditions. Families aren't created wonderful all at once, but step by step. Year by year, individuals in a family become good or evil, a joy or a horror to the world. So true."

"This could have deep meaning for the family and be the reason Cleat was given the boot," Maggie said slowly. "So much benefit comes from even one person's goodness. If the Rathfords stressed that down through the generations, it would have impressed upon them a sense of responsibility to do good for the family. In the current generation, if Llewellyn wasn't setting a good example, and he was doing things that would bring disgrace upon the family, they would have cut off the offending member. Kicked him out of the nest. Disinherited him."

"Remember what Damon said at dinner?" Alyssa reminded them. "That what Llewellyn was doing wasn't noble and wasn't worthy of the family legacy."

"That brings it back to this family motto. So what's our next step?" Maggie asked. "We still have some time before we need to leave for the Green Dragon Inn; where do we go from here?"

"Determine if this Rathford estate is actually the childhood home of Damon and Llewellyn's father," Flynn said.

"How do we do that?" Alyssa asked.

"Like I said, by knocking on that huge door and asking them yourself." Flynn placed his hands on Maggie's shoulders and asked, "Where is the estate? Does it give a location—an address?"

Maggie's heart did a flip at Flynn's touch as she turned her attention back to the computer screen, feeling momentarily light-headed.

"It says it's just outside of Gloucester. Wherever that is," Maggie said. "I relied on Rolf to know where everything was this morning and haven't spent much time studying the map since he came along." Maggie turned to Rolf and smiled. "He's better than a map—he also provides a history lesson and an informative running commentary."

"Gloucester is only about fifty miles from here," Rolf said. "And Usk, where you're supposed to meet Llewellyn tomorrow, is just across the River Severn. Both are very close to Wells."

"I'm going to see what the library in Gloucester might know about the Rathford estate," Maggie said. "Can I borrow your phone, Alyssa?"

Maggie dialed the number for the library listed at the end of the article, hoping it kept late hours. "Librarians can be repositories of a wealth of information," she said while she waited for someone to answer the phone. It rang several times, and Maggie was just about to hang up when a breathless voice answered.

"Gloucester Public Library. How may I help you?"

"Oh, I'm so glad you're still open," Maggie said. "I need some information."

"Actually, we close at eight o'clock. I was just at the door and had to run back to catch the phone. I thought my husband might want me to get something from the market on my way home."

"I hate to impose, but do you have one minute to answer a couple of questions? I'm in England searching for ancestors, and I've discovered a

Rathford family in Gloucester. Could you tell me about them? Do they still live on the estate, or has it been sold?"

"You must be speaking of Dragonwyck. Yes, the Rathford family still resides at the ancestral estate, and they're still active in community affairs. In fact, they are among the most generous supporters of the library foundation. Mrs. Rathford is head of the fundraising committee."

"Did the Rathfords have other children besides Llewellyn and his younger brother, Damon?" Maggie asked.

"No, there were just two sons," the librarian said. "Llewellyn was an upstanding young man, a credit to the family name, who now works for the National Trust. Damon disgraced the family and disappeared years ago. No one ever heard from him after his father disinherited him."

"Does Llewellyn still live at Dragonwyck with his parents?" Maggie asked, knowing the answer but curious how much the librarian knew.

"Oh, no," the newsy librarian said. "He married; he and Mrs. Rathford currently reside at Wells with their son Damon."

Maggie asked yet another question, hoping the talkative soul on the other end of the telephone wouldn't tire of her queries. "Do the Rathfords living in Wells have other children besides Damon?"

The woman hesitated. "I'm quite sure there is an older son, but I know nothing about him. Mrs. Rathford doesn't mention him."

"Just one more question. If I am related to this branch of the family, do you think they might welcome a visit at their home, or would that be an imposition? American and English customs are quite different, I understand."

The woman laughed. "Yes, our customs do differ, but I would think Mrs. Rathford would be happy to meet a relative. I should think you could call her now and make an appointment to visit tomorrow. Do you have the number?"

"No. I'd be delighted if you could give it to me." Maggie waited while the librarian looked up the number. She wrote the name *Dragonwyck* on the top of her pad and drew a dragon with fire blazing from his nostrils while she waited for the librarian to furnish the telephone number, and finally the address and directions. Maggie kept taking notes as the librarian remembered a few more tidbits about the family.

"Oh, I just thought of one more question," Maggie said as she was about to thank her benefactor for the information. "In my research, I've seen no mention of daughters. Do you know of any in preceding generations? I know years ago female children weren't valued much in society, so frequently they weren't even mentioned except as an entry in the family bible noting their birth, marriage, and death."

"Oh, yes, all too true." The librarian clucked her tongue. "If a daughter didn't marry, she quietly faded into the background. If there was anything in her demeanor that wasn't in keeping with family honor, she could be closeted away in an institution to spend her life."

"That's so sad. Did that happen in the Rathford family, or were there only sons born?" Maggie asked.

"To my knowledge, there were only sons. I've known the Rathford family since I was a young girl. I don't remember ever seeing girls about the place until the boys took wives. I believe there are at least three generations of Rathfords that had two sons, both named Llewellyn and Damon. I don't know much about the elder Mr. Rathford's younger brother Damon. He seemed to have been disinherited for something, disappeared years ago, and Mr. and Mrs. Rathford have had the estate to themselves ever since. I must say, it is all quite confusing, all these Llewellyns and Damons. I don't know how they keep them separate from generation to generation."

Maggie laughed. "You're right. It is very confusing. Thank you so much for this information. I can't tell you how helpful you've been. I'm sorry I kept you, but I hope you have a good evening."

"And good luck to you on finding your family."

Maggie whirled around in her chair. "This is the place in the article! Dragonwyck! Can you believe it? In three generations, there were only two sons born in each family, and until our generation, the younger son of each family, named Damon, apparently went bad. This generation seems to have broken with the tradition."

"We hope that's the case," Flynn said. "Because of Mrs. Rathford's note, we're supposing that this Llewellyn is the rotten apple."

"And his appearance at the Crystal Palace," Maggie added.

"And his interest in your bag," Alyssa said.

Flynn glanced at his watch. "Maggie, we've got to leave for the Green Dragon Inn now or we'll be late." He turned to Rolf and Alyssa.

"How about if you two keep digging on the Internet and wherever else you can think of, and see what you can find? We shouldn't be more than a couple of hours. We'll meet you back here about eleven."

Maggie reached again for the nonexistent bag and sighed. It was like part of her was missing. "Alyssa, maybe you and Rolf can find out how Mr. Rathford is doing while we're gone. After all, he is our uncle."

"And his parents are our grandparents," Alyssa said softly. "I've never had grandparents."

"Let's hope they'll welcome a couple of granddaughters to the family," Maggie said over her shoulder as Flynn took her hand and pulled her toward the door. "There doesn't seem to be much of a precedent of females in the recent history of the family."

# TWENTY-THREE

"As soon as we finish our meeting at the Green Dragon Inn with Tad Collins's counterterrorism agents, maybe we ought to go find your Dragonwyck and answers to some questions," Flynn said, opening the hotel door for Maggie.

Maggie looped her arm through Flynn's and walked close beside him, matching her strides to his long ones. She wanted a lot of answers. She pondered the worrisome question that had plagued her since she'd discovered her less-than-desirable bloodline. It kept going through her mind, over and over—which had the most influence on personality: heredity or environment? Was Cleat's sociopathic behavior inheritable? Or was character molded by daily associations?

"You're deep in thought," Flynn said to a very quiet Maggie.

"So much has been happening—there's a lot to think about," she said, looking up at Flynn. "I'm so glad you came. I don't know what I would have done if I'd had to face this alone."

"That's why I'm here. When I heard about the terrorist threat, I thought I'd come and quietly follow you around, doing my best to prevent anything from happening to you. I didn't plan on letting you know I was here. Of course, I didn't expect someone to be trying to kill you, either."

Flynn opened Maggie's door, and she settled into the seat while he went around to get in behind the wheel. Flynn fastened his seat belt, then reached for the GPS to enter the address of the Green Dragon Inn. Instead, he dropped his hand on Maggie's and squeezed it. "I've missed you." Their eyes met for an instant, then as quickly as it had happened, the moment was gone. Flynn removed his hand and programmed the address into the GPS system.

Maggie took a deep breath and a moment to recover. "That almost makes maps obsolete," she said, wanting to continue looking into Flynn's eyes, wanting to know what his feelings really were for her, and yet knowing it wasn't the right time to pursue these matters.

Flynn maneuvered out of the alley and onto the street, continued through the little town to the interchange with A-37, then accelerated into the stream of fast-moving traffic.

"Are we going to give this note to the men we're meeting, or do we save it to give to Tad Collins personally?" Maggie asked. "What did Collins say when you called him?"

"The police will need to have it." Flynn paused. "Maggie, I know you promised you wouldn't connect Mrs. Rathford to this note, but I see no way the Rathfords can be left out of the investigation. In order for the police to do their job, they have to have all the information available. We tie their hands by withholding anything that's pertinent to the case."

Maggie sighed. "Maybe they'll be very discreet and not . . ." She didn't finish her sentence. "I guess that's way too much to hope for. They really can't even start the investigation without interviewing Llewellyn's parents, can they? Mrs. Rathford will be so upset with me."

"Maybe not," Flynn said. "Maybe she'll be relieved to have it all out in the open so something can be done to stop her son from killing a lot of people."

"Let's hope she looks at it in that light," Maggie said softly. "I'm afraid she's going to see it as a betrayal of her trust."

"Maggie, when you promised you'd do what she asked, you had no idea what was at stake. There's no way you can keep an agreement that will endanger the lives of possibly hundreds, if not thousands. It's the same principle as Nephi being commanded to cut off Laban's head. One person had to suffer in order to save an entire people. Mrs. Rathford may have to suffer some humiliation and embarrassment in order to prevent her son from killing a lot of people in London tomorrow night."

Maggie looked up sharply at Flynn. He'd been reading the Book of Mormon. What exactly did that mean? That he'd been actively investigating the Church? Or that he'd just been reading the book? How far had he gone if he were investigating seriously?

Flynn kept talking, seemingly unaware that Maggie's mind had suddenly veered on a totally different tangent than the subject they'd been discussing. "I'd think she'd be relieved to have someone stop her son. Can you imagine how she'd feel the rest of her life being known as the mother of the monster who blew up London?"

That pulled Maggie back to the subject at hand. "You're right. I hope I don't have to point that out to her the next time I see her." Maggie stopped. "I probably never will see her again. As soon as this assignment is finished, I'm leaving England and may never get back."

"You said you believed the kidnapping of Jennie and her children was in some way tied in with the terrorists. That's something we need to explore with the CTC," Flynn said. "Tell me again your reasoning behind that thought."

"The television appeal to the American woman who helped Jennie and her children had to be a ploy for someone to get their hands on the flash drive the terrorist dropped in my bag at the airport. I certainly knew nothing that would help them find her. I think I was followed from the airport—they may have been following Jennie, too, thinking we were together. Llewellyn probably had her kidnapped so he could get to me and the gadget containing his plans."

"That makes sense to me," Flynn said, slowing for the exit. "Hope it makes sense to the Counterterrorist Command."

"Are we here already?" Maggie asked, peering into the darkness.

"Close. We have to get off the main road onto a little lane. It's another few miles."

"The Green Dragon Inn sounds intriguing." Maggie glanced at the clock. "What's the plan after we finish with the detectives? It might be too late to find Dragonwyck."

"It's about a thirty-minute drive either back to Wells or on to Dragonwyck. We'll see how long this takes. I don't know about you, but I'm too keyed up to be sleepy. Maybe a drive up there just to see where it is will be relaxing enough to induce a good night's sleep when we finally get back to the hotel."

"I probably couldn't shut my mind off enough to get to sleep either," Maggie said. "It just keeps going in circles with all this information we've discovered. Connecting Llewellyn to something as big as this current terrorist situation is so mind-boggling I can't process it. If it were just a plot to destroy London, this all might seem more believable, but to have an agenda that includes destroying the world's greatest cities—it's too overwhelming. Within about a ten-year time frame, could Llewellyn really have gotten into something of this magnitude?"

"We don't know it's only been ten years," Flynn reminded her. "And with financing available from an established terrorist group, yes, he could easily be involved in something this big. Today's technology makes anything possible."

The road turned into a lane with trees and bushes obscuring whatever lay behind them. Flynn followed the little red arrow on the GPS and turned down still another lane. The headlights illuminated a gravel parking lot in front of a large, two-story rock building. Two cars were parked in the circular parking lot, and several bicycles stood in a rack next to a hedge. Flynn drove around the circle and parked facing out, following the lead of the other two vehicles.

Fresh green shutters framed the windows on both floors, updating what appeared to be an ancient structure. Lace curtains adorned the windows and England's ever-present flower baskets hung between the windows, and on either side of the front door. The wooden sign hanging above the weathered door sported a green, fire-breathing dragon.

As they stepped inside, Maggie immediately fell in love with the ambiance of the old inn. A carved, highly polished bar stood at the center of the large room. Round tables and chairs clustered in front of and surrounded the bar, and they flowed into the back portions of the huge room behind it.

Fireplaces warmed the room on either side, and well-worn leather chairs surrounded round, low coffee tables where patrons sipped their ale and chatted in comfort.

From a table beyond the bar, almost hidden in the shadows, a young man watched them enter. He rose, signaled to Flynn, and made his way toward the back of the room. Flynn and Maggie followed him into a small, windowless room directly behind the bar, apparently a private meeting room.

The furnishings in the room consisted of one large, circular table surrounded by eight wooden captain's chairs. The silvery gray paneling, as in the other room, looked like it had been stripped from an old weathered barn.

A mature man with black horn-rimmed glasses stood as they entered the room. "I'm Detective Chief Inspector Alistair McConklin," he said, extending his hand to Maggie, then Flynn. "Sit, please. Can we get you something? Ale, Coke, coffee, tea?"

Maggie shook her head. "Nothing for me, thanks." Flynn also declined.

Inspector McConklin pointed to the man who had led them into the room. "This is Detective Sergeant Tim Murphy. Tim, I'll have another cup. This may be a long night." He handed his cup and saucer to the younger man, settled back into his chair, and got immediately to the point. "May I see the note?"

Maggie glanced at Flynn and reluctantly produced the note and envelope from her pocket and handed it across the table to the inspector.

He examined the note and the envelope, and then turned his eyes on Maggie. "Tell me why you are here and everything that has happened since you arrived, culminating in the receipt of this piece of paper."

Sergeant Murphy returned with a steaming cup for the inspector and pulled out a notebook and pencil to take notes.

Maggie tried to organize her thoughts so her story would sound coherent instead of fragmented and totally scatterbrained, which was how she felt at the moment. "As the travel editor for a small Southern California newspaper, I came here to write a series of articles on how to see England on one hundred dollars a day for a new glossy Sunday magazine we're publishing. Just as I was leaving, my boss gave me an additional, more personal assignment, which entailed searching for my sibling who was adopted at birth and brought to England by his aunt and uncle to raise. I was able to locate the family and discovered that both of my brothers are still living. My biological twin sister, Alyssa, has joined me to meet them."

Inspector McConklin interrupted her narrative. "Be precise, please. I want to know when you arrived, where you stayed, where you traveled and with whom."

Maggie began again, filling in the details she'd skipped over. She hesitated ever so slightly while she wondered if she should tell the inspector everything. Exactly how much did he need to know?

"Everything, Miss McKenzie. I want every detail, every move-ment, every person you talked to, every impression you've had since you arrived in England. I also want every plan you made, and if you changed it, why you changed it."

"Do you read minds, inspector?" Maggie asked with a nervous smile.

He nodded, leaned back in his seat, and sipped his coffee. "Yes, Miss McKenzie. Sometimes I can read minds. It comes from thirty years of listening to testimony and sorting through clues. It comes from a close, continual study of people and their gestures, their nervous habits, their hesitancy as they speak. So give me the entire story, not just what you think I need to know, because, in fact, I need to know it all."

So Maggie gave it all to him. Every detail she could think of, right up to the time Flynn arrived on the scene, including the foiled attempt on her life at the Manor, Rolf's intervention with the terrorist, and the subsequent announcement on television asking her to call Scotland Yard regarding her brief acquaintance with the kidnapped American woman and her children. The only thing she left out was the real reason the terrorist had followed her, citing instead her old revenge theory. She wasn't sure why—it just seemed like the right way to present the information.

"Now, Dr. Ford, will you pick up where Miss McKenzie left off?" Inspector McConklin directed.

Flynn concentrated on events, on how he came to be in England, and how he'd observed the tailing and questioning of Maggie's identical twin sister and Rolf. He spoke of their pursuit of Inspector Terrence Graham to the Crystal Palace and keeping an eye on Alyssa and Rolf; he told how they had observed Richard Constantine as he approached Alyssa and Rolf to interrogate them. He recounted Constantine's shocked expression when he saw the couple, his quick retreat to his car, and his instructions to obtain the purse belonging to Alyssa and bring it to him in the car for his examination.

"And what would he have been looking for in the purse?" McConklin asked.

Tim Murphy snorted, then quickly swallowed his smirk at a glare from the inspector.

Maggie involuntarily glanced at Flynn, sensing that he was reluctant to reveal this information as well. She didn't want anyone to know about that flash drive except those who absolutely had a need to know. Could they trust these men? That question loomed large in her mind.

Flynn calmly looked McConklin in the eye and said, "I've discussed this with Tad Collins. If he feels you should know, I'd rather you get that information from him. I don't think we should discuss it without his approval."

Detective Chief Inspector Alistair McConklin sat back in his chair, sipped his coffee, and looked from Flynn to Maggie.

"And why not?" Tim Murphy demanded, his voice harsh with indignation.

"I'm just not at liberty to discuss that aspect of this case," Flynn said with a slight smile. "Is there something else you'd like to know?" *Sorry, Murphy,* Flynn thought. *There's something about you that rubs me wrong.*

# TWENTY-FOUR

"Now, Miss McKenzie, I want opinions and impressions. I want gossip and hearsay. I want every thought that has come into your head concerning this note and the abduction of Mrs. Albright. I need to know everything you know—or have been told about your brothers."

Maggie recounted her first impressions of Damon, which stemmed from her conversations with the woman at the information center in Arundel, the old woman at St. Nicholas church, and the vicar, Father Richards. She recited the reaction of the girls in the pubs to her remarkable resemblance to Damon, and the additional piece of information each gave about Damon's activities and personality. Then Maggie relayed Damon's revelation at dinner that he had been blamed all his life for his brother's indiscretions. Maggie told the inspector that she had felt Damon was being totally truthful as he professed his innocence.

Maggie's description of her first meeting with Mr. Rathford and Damon at the National Trust office in Wells and the questions Mr. Rathford asked were of great interest to the inspector. He seemed to read much more into that meeting than Maggie had.

Inspector McConklin pushed aside his empty cup. "And this young man, Rolf. Tell me as much as you can remember about his conversations with the locals he spoke with in Wells."

Sergeant Murphy never stopped scribbling notes as Maggie and Flynn spoke, filling page after page in his small notebook.

"Tell me about your meeting with Mrs. Rathford, Miss McKenzie. I want your intuitive analysis of her as mother, wife, and individual; and your analysis of Mr. Rathford as well," Inspector McConklin directed.

Maggie leaned forward and folded her hands on the table. "I thought Mr. Rathford seemed worn down and very tired. I suspect he's a timid individual who never knew how to handle his adopted sons. Mrs. Rathford is a frightened woman, but I believe she truly cares about her husband and both her sons. Having never seen Mr. and Mrs. Rathford together, I can offer no opinion on their relationship."

She paused to picture in her mind the scene at the Rathford home. "Mrs. Rathford is a good housekeeper—their home seemed spotless. She's very pale, so apparently she doesn't get outdoors much. I felt she was ill or tired or both, but fear can manifest itself in different ways in different people. Maybe she's just afraid of what's happening in her sons' lives."

"Thank you, Miss McKenzie. You appear to be a very observant young woman. Now what can you tell me about Llewellyn, a.k.a. Richard Constantine?"

She described Damon's report about Llewellyn's rejection of his brother, as both child and adult. "Damon said Llewellyn worked in ordnance disposal when he was in the military, and he suspected Llewellyn's never given up his passion for explosives to this day. I haven't spoken to Llewellyn in person, but I have an appointment to meet with him in the morning."

"Do you plan on keeping that appointment?" the inspector asked.

Maggie looked puzzled for a minute. "Do you want me to? If he's involved in this plot to blow up London . . ."

Sergeant Murphy shook his head. "What an imagination," he mumbled. Inspector McConklin glared at him, and the younger man shut up.

Maggie glanced at Flynn. Did he have the same impression of this arrogant man Maggie did? Sergeant Murphy apparently didn't believe a word of Maggie's story.

"But we aren't sure of that, are we?" the inspector reminded her. "Yes, I think we would like very much for you to keep that appointment, just in case he does show up. Of course, we'll be there with you. I understand, Miss McKenzie, that you promised Mrs. Rathford you would not read the contents of the envelope until you were on your way back to America. What else did she ask of you?"

Maggie told Inspector McConklin Mrs. Rathford's conditions.

"But you read the note before you left England."

"When I realized that Mrs. Rathford's son might be involved in a terrorist plot, I decided I couldn't keep that promise if there was the slightest possibility the envelope contained a clue about it."

"Any ideas on what the rest of the note might have contained?" the inspector asked. "What any of the targets might be?"

"Absolutely none. However, if I were in your shoes, which I'm very glad I'm not, I'd probably pick the busiest, most populated rail and underground stations, or those closest to your national treasures—Westminster Abbey, the Tower of London, St. James Palace, London Bridge, and anything else closely identified with London. I'd protect them however I could."

"Anything else?" The inspector relaxed in his chair and watched Maggie's face.

Maggie leaned forward and looked Inspector McConklin in the eye. "If I were a terrorist, I'd want to destroy the things that would demoralize the English people. I'd try to disrupt the transportation as much as possible so that it couldn't be repaired quickly. Bring chaos and confusion and death and suffering to as many as possible. But you already know all of that, so why are you asking me?"

"I thought it might be interesting to have your thoughts." He glanced at Sergeant Murphy.

Sergeant Murphy snorted. "Sounds like a nutcase to me. You can't actually believe all that malarkey?"

"He has a point. You could have written that note, Miss McKenzie," the inspector said, pointing his finger at Maggie. His voice was no longer friendly. He stood, leaned over the table toward Maggie, and in icy tones accused her. "You could have staged this whole thing in order to write some sensational story for your paper."

Flynn knocked his chair over as he stood in Maggie's defense. Inspector McConklin waved Flynn to silence as Sergeant Murphy took an offensive stance. Maggie simply sat there, her mouth open, unable to say anything.

*He's testing you,* her mind told her. *Don't panic. Don't cry. Don't get mad. Just stay calm. He knows better. He's just trying to judge your reaction.*

Finally she found her voice. "Sorry, Inspector. If I were writing an exclusive, it wouldn't be for the little paper I work for. I'm only the travel editor on a small paper no one has ever heard of unless they live on the coast near San Buenaventura. And as for making this whole thing up, you're a better judge of character than that. With thirty years of experience, your intuition should tell you that I'm innocent of all your accusations. I simply want to prevent thousands of people from being killed and your beautiful city from being destroyed. We didn't have to tell you about this at all, you know. I could have just flown back to California and let London be blown to smithereens."

DCI Alistair McConklin suddenly turned his attention to Flynn. "What are your plans for tonight, Dr. Ford?"

"We'd planned to go to Dragonwyck and visit the Rathford grandparents. But since it's too late, we'll be returning to Wells."

"Change of plans. You are not to leave the premises without my permission. You'll get a room here for the night. Sergeant Murphy, I want a man posted outside their door and outside on the grounds to make sure they don't leave."

"You'll need two men outside the doors unless our rooms are close together," Flynn said. "We don't share a room."

Both Englishmen looked surprised, but neither said anything. "Very well, I'll see if you can have rooms next to each other so we can cut down on the officers needed here. Consider yourselves under house arrest. You need my permission to even go outside for a smoke."

"Neither of us smoke, Inspector," Maggie said getting to her feet. "I thought you were taking this seriously, but apparently I was mistaken. My judgment is as impaired as yours." She turned and headed for the door.

Sergeant Murphy made a move to stop her, but she sidestepped him, marched to the door, and threw it open. "I hope you're the one who gets to stay up all night watching to see if I'm going to slip away and bomb your precious city, Sergeant."

Flynn and Maggie reserved rooms under the watchful eyes of the two policemen that Maggie now considered the enemy instead of the allies she'd thought them to be. The girl at the desk handed them keys to rooms on the second floor, which Murphy confiscated immediately so he could check out the rooms first.

Maggie silently followed the sergeant upstairs. She had nothing more to say to him. When he'd made sure that the windows couldn't be used for an easy escape and that both their doors could be seen from a single point in the hall, he gave Maggie her key and retreated downstairs to give Flynn the key to his room.

"Sleep tight, Dr. Ford," Detective Chief Inspector McConklin said. "After we've checked you out with the US authorities, you may be free to go, but until we get a green light on you and Miss McKenzie, you'll remain in my custody. If you try to escape, it will no longer be house arrest in a comfortable room, but a jail cell. Will you pass that along to Miss McKenzie?"

"Yes, sir. I'll do that." Flynn leveled a look at Murphy. "I think you should know that Maggie is in the habit of running early every morning. I plan to join her. I assume you or your man outside will accompany us." Flynn smirked as he took the stairs two at a time to find his room.

Maggie discovered their adjoining rooms shared a single bathroom. When Flynn came upstairs, they walked to the end of the hall, away from Murphy, and sat in the alcoved window seat.

"If I need to talk to you tonight, can I knock quietly and open the door?" she asked.

Flynn nodded. "Of course. Maggie, don't worry. I don't foresee this house arrest as being any kind of problem. Neither of us have anything in our records that would convince Inspector McConklin he needs to hold us tomorrow. We'll have a clean slate, and we can leave as soon as we want in the morning." He reached for her hand and smiled. "Unless, of course, you've stepped out of character and have been racking up arrests and citations."

"Don't try to cheer me up. I'm mad." She waved her hand when Flynn tried to interrupt. "I know. I know he's just doing his job. Why couldn't he just have said he was going to check on us instead of being such a jerk about it? And I could have gladly punched Sergeant Murphy's lights out. What a moron!"

"They're testing the water, Maggie girl." Flynn gently ran his finger down the side of Maggie's cheek. "I know this is cliché, but you really are beautiful even when you're angry. How I've missed you. I have a dozen questions that would take all night to answer. How's your job? Do you like living in California? What do you do in your spare time? How's your family?" He stopped. "Have you missed me?"

He held his hand up. "Sorry. Don't answer that. I have no right to ask until we have time to sort everything out."

Maggie's heart ached. She wanted to throw her arms around Flynn and tell him there was no need to wait. They could discuss it right now. But what if Flynn needed time to find a way to tell her that he still cared about her but had found someone else? Or that he couldn't embrace her religion? Or that he had grown comfortable with his single lifestyle and simply wasn't interested in pursuing a serious relationship and just wanted to remain good friends?

Maggie rose. She didn't need to punish herself with these terrible thoughts or the emotional roller coaster such close proximity to him caused. "Good night, Flynn. Thank you for coming. This would have been unbearable without your support."

Flynn stood, looked into Maggie's sapphire blue eyes, and pushed back a stray curl from her face. Finally he leaned down and softly kissed her cheek. "Good night. Please wake me if you need to talk— or anything."

Maggie turned quickly and returned to her room. She locked the hall door and leaned against it, finally surrendering to the tears that had been close so many times tonight.

"Oh, Flynn. What are you feeling?" she whispered.

# TWENTY-FIVE

Maggie's next thought was of Alyssa. She swiped at the tears on her checks, hurried into the joint bathroom, and rapped on Flynn's door.

"I do need something," she said when he opened the door. "I need to call Alyssa and tell her what's happened."

Flynn surrendered his phone without comment. As Maggie punched in Alyssa's cell phone number, Flynn folded his arms and leaned against the door, watching her. *Always thinking of someone else,* he thought. *She's the most thoughtful, unselfish person I've ever known.* Then as Maggie waited for Alyssa to answer, Flynn had another thought. A dark thought.

"Maggie," he said, "tell Alyssa and Rolf to disappear for the night. Tell them to get away from the hotel as quick as they can and check into another or just go into hiding. On the off chance that these two policemen aren't as trustworthy as Tad Collins thinks they are, they need to be safely out of the hands of anyone who would do them harm or put them under house arrest."

Maggie nodded as Alyssa said hello. "Lyssa, listen carefully. We've been placed under house arrest by the officers Tad Collins sent us to meet. Flynn says you two should leave the hotel immediately and go into hiding—either at another hotel away from there, or somewhere where no one will see you. There's an extra key to my rental car in the outer pocket of my suitcase. I remember thinking it was odd they gave me two keys, but now I think the agent was inspired. Anyway, let Rolf drive you some-where, and you two stay out of sight until I call you tomorrow."

"Maggie, what happened? Are these men dangerous?" Alyssa sounded frightened.

"Flynn assured me it's nothing to worry about. Inspector McConklin says they have to check us out with the American authorities since this is a pretty big deal—accusing a high government official of planning to blow up London, which would include treason and espionage, in addition to kidnapping. They said as soon as they get our clearance in the morning, they'll let us go. You and Rolf just stay out of sight until then."

"We're out of here now," Alyssa assured her. "Should we actually check out of the Crown?"

"No. You might want to take your toothbrush with you, though," Maggie said with a smile. "Wish I had my bag with me. I'd have everything I need." She said goodnight and disconnected, handing Flynn's phone back to him. "Thanks. I've got to get my bag back. I don't think I can survive without all my stuff."

Flynn refrained from taking her in his arms, though he wanted to do so more than anything else. He simply nodded and said, "Yes, you can, Maggie girl. You can do anything—anything you have to do."

* * *

Maggie looked up at Flynn. She could do anything but live without him. She mumbled goodnight and quickly shut the door, but she couldn't sleep. She couldn't even convince her wound-up body to lie down on the bed. She scribbled her journal on paper from the desk drawer and finally got in the shower to relax. She flipped through a local tourist magazine on the desk and located the Green Dragon Inn and its proximity to Dragonwyck.

For some reason she kept thinking about Jennie and Tara and the baby. Where were they? Maggie hoped they were comfortable and that Tara and the baby weren't upset and crying. Poor Jennie. Could anyone actually be cruel enough to do something so horrible? She only had to think of Cleat Wiggins to realize the answer was a resounding yes.

Not only was Maggie convinced that Llewellyn Rathford/Richard Constantine had arranged the kidnapping of the Albrights, she was sure the terrorist who had trailed her from Los Angeles to get the flash drive would have killed her if he'd had the chance, on orders from her corrupt brother.

She certainly hoped Tad Collins had a tail on Richard Constantine despite his important position in the government. If Llewellyn had everything in place for the destruction of London, what made anyone think he would stick around and watch it happen? He'd probably be long gone by morning. He'd hide out somewhere, collect his billion dollars, and live high the rest of his life in some remote Shangri-la. Their meeting tomorrow was simply a way of putting her off—of that she was convinced.

At midnight she finally was able to turn off her busy mind, pray for Jennie's safety, and fall asleep.

At four A.M. she sat straight up in bed. If Llewellyn had kidnapped Jennie, where would he have taken them? Somewhere out of the city where no one would happen upon a crying baby. How about Dragonwyck? It was isolated. It looked huge. Llewellyn would have been very familiar with his grandparents' home. Surely there might be somewhere there to hide Jennie's little family.

Maggie jumped out of bed and threw on her clothes. She checked the window to see if she could climb out without being seen by the sergeant watching the outside of the inn. He was probably in front by the cars.

She silently slid the window open and surveyed the area back of the Green Dragon. It was a straight drop two stories to the ground. A single bulb hung over the back door, barely illuminating the ground beneath the window. A vine grew up the back of the house, but Maggie wasn't sure it would hold her. Maybe the pipe that ran from the ground to the roof was sturdier.

She thought of Flynn in the adjoining room. He wouldn't be happy if she left him, and she'd certainly rather have him by her side than try anything on her own. She quietly opened the bathroom doors between their rooms, crept into Flynn's room, and lightly touched his arm. He grabbed her hand and sat up in bed.

"Shh," Maggie said. "Don't make any noise. Sergeant Murphy may be right outside."

"What are you doing?" Flynn whispered, noting she was fully dressed.

Maggie sat on the edge of the bed and spoke softy. "What if Llewellyn stashed Jennie and her children at Dragonwyck? I'm going to find them. Do you want to come along?"

"What about our friend Detective Chief Inspector Alistair McConklin?"

Maggie smiled. "In this case, I think it's better to ask forgiveness than permission. I know the inspector is just going by the book, but I can't let him keep me from locating Jennie if she's actually this close. Tara will be frightened out of her mind, and I can't imagine how Jennie is coping trying to take care of two little ones—wherever they might be. Are you with me or not?"

"With you," Flynn assured her. "But before we leave the safety and comfort of our rooms, what's your plan?"

"Dragonwyck is only about thirty miles down the road, remember? My instincts say that if Llewellyn snatched them, there's a strong possibility he's taken them to Dragonwyck. It looks big enough to hide an army in there for a week without anyone noticing. I thought we might storm the castle and see if we could find them. And if they are there, that just might give Tad Collins the concrete evidence he needs to implicate Llewellyn/Richard in all of this."

"Give me two minutes. And let's figure out how we're going to get our car—I'm not up for walking thirty miles this morning."

Maggie returned to her room and shut the bathroom door. She'd figured out how to get out of the inn but hadn't gotten as far as getting out of the parking lot. There had been bikes in the rack last night, but they were probably gone this morning; besides, she didn't think DCI McConklin would be very forgiving if they stole transportation to escape house arrest.

She reached out of the window and gripped the pipe, testing it. The masonry screws that held it in place pulled right out of the rock. New plan. Maggie tried the vine, but it, too, tore easily away from the house.

Flynn silently appeared at her side. "It always works in the movies," she said, "but it's not going to work for us."

"Not a problem." He whipped the sheets from the bed and tied them together, then tied one corner to the steam radiator next to the window.

Maggie looked down. "That works in the movies, too, but these aren't long enough. We'll make too much noise when we drop to the ground."

"I'll get my sheets too." He was back in a flash. With four sheets tied together, they climbed down and silently stepped into the grass.

Maggie leaned up and whispered, "Let's see if the officer is sleeping in his car, or if he spent the night more comfortably in the inn. I didn't come up with transportation. Did you?"

Flynn nodded. They stayed close to the house until they were near the front. Maggie stifled a scream when a friendly cat rubbed against her leg. The police car out front appeared empty. Flynn peeked through the window of the inn.

"There he is, comfy as can be in that nice leather chair by the fire," Flynn whispered. "If we can get to the car and put it in neutral, we can push it out of the parking lot and start it when we're down the road."

Maggie and Flynn crept through the semidarkness to the driveway, trying to make as little noise as possible on the gravel.

After a couple steps, Flynn shook his head. "This isn't good. This will make enough racket to wake the dead."

"At least it's not cinders. They crunch when you step on them. I think we're okay," Maggie whispered back.

Flynn silently opened the car with the key instead of the beeping remote, moved the gear into neutral, and signaled Maggie to open the door on the passenger side and push.

The hard part was getting the car moving; after that it took little effort to keep it moving down the lane. Maggie kept looking back, sure that any minute they were going to be caught, but finally Flynn said, "Get in."

She hopped in, Flynn started the car, and they held the doors ajar until they were well down the lane so slamming them wouldn't wake the sergeant.

Maggie threw back her head and laughed. "We did it!"

"Now what?" Flynn asked.

"Now you can program your magic genie with Dragonwyck's address and sit back and enjoy the sunrise." Maggie found the address in her pocket, and Flynn pulled off the lane into a driveway to enter the address in the Global Positioning System.

"Twenty-five miles. Thirty-five minutes," Flynn read before he reentered the lane and made a quick escape from the area. "The sun should be up by that time, so we won't be stumbling around in the dark. Wonder if they have armed sentries on the estate."

"More likely guard dogs, if anything," Maggie said and suddenly fell silent.

Flynn glanced at Maggie, her pensive face illuminated by the dash lights. "Worried?"

Maggie bit her lip. She turned to Flynn. "I'm so afraid. What if he harms them, or moves them? And what if it wasn't Llewellyn at all? What if it was someone else with a totally different motive in mind and we never find them? I don't even know why I'm so certain they're here. I just woke up in the middle of the night with this feeling, this certainty that they were being held at Dragonwyck. I have no basis for that feeling at all, except that if Llewellyn is involved, it makes sense."

Flynn reached for Maggie's hand. She put her cold hand in his big warm one and drew immediate comfort. "Remember the old adage, 'It's always darkest just before the dawn'? It's now just before dawn, so you're entitled to feel pessimistic for a minute. But we've got to figure out where Jennie is—and if she is at Dragonwyck, how to get to her. For all we know, the whole family is in on it."

"You mean old Mr. and Mrs. Rathford?" Maggie paused. "That would actually be Grandmother and Grandfather Rathford, wouldn't it?" The thought that they might be involved hadn't entered her mind. She shook her head. "I'm having a hard time adjusting to all these new family members. All I can do is pray that they'll accept us and that we'll have help in finding Jennie and her children. I can't imagine the older generation being in on something like this, but then again, I had a hard time imagining someone wanting to murder me."

Flynn glanced at Maggie. "Have you considered that since you and Alyssa are the children of Cleat and Lily, just as Damon and Llewellyn are, you might each stand to inherit a fourth of the estate?"

Maggie stared at him. "No. I'd never even thought about it. I don't want a fourth, or any part of it. I just want to finish my work here, then go home and get back to my normal life." She knew even as she said it that it wasn't entirely true. No, she didn't just want to go back to normal life. She wanted Flynn in every aspect of her life from now on. She looked away from him, trying to distract herself.

"There it is!" Maggie said, her voice filled with awe. "Dragonwyck!"

Set back from the road, high wrought-iron gates were connected in the middle by a huge gold crest containing a large winged dragon with a forked tongue—the same symbol of the dragon she recalled seeing engraved on Damon's unusual ring.

"How do we get in?" Maggie asked.

"Maybe the gate's unlocked." Flynn jumped out and examined the gateposts, unlatched the gates, and swung one open. Flynn drove through, and Maggie got out and closed the gate.

Neither spoke a word as they wound up a narrow lane, heavily wooded on one side and lined with gardens and a lawn on the other. It was clear that the grounds had once been beautifully manicured, but now the grass grew high and unkempt, roses and ivy spread out of control obscuring statuary, and the hedges and shrubbery were badly in need of trimming.

"A very creepy place," Maggie whispered.

With no house in sight yet as they neared the top of the hill, Maggie wondered if it still existed. Suddenly they crested the hill and there it was, in Gothic splendor, far more elaborate and magnificent than the picture portrayed on the Internet. Bay windows and balconies, towers and turrets, chimneys and castlelike walls sprouted everywhere, as if each succeeding generation had added its own section to the sprawling house.

"Oh—my—gosh." Maggie exhaled the words as Flynn stopped the car.

They sat gaping as the rising sun illuminated the stark beauty before them. Stonemasons had crafted intricate designs above and below each of the dozens of mullioned windows, and the delicate lacy look of the stone balconies rivaled anything Maggie had seen in the splendid cathedrals.

Beautiful roses flourished under the front windows, and two huge stone urns near the driveway overflowed with brilliantly colored blooms. The cultivated flowers seemed out of place compared with the neglected grounds they'd just driven through.

Maggie automatically reached for her camera and snapped a couple of pictures before Flynn proceeded slowly around the curved driveway, stopping just beyond the immense front door. Guarding the door sat two winged dragons with forked tongues and long tails curving around their clawed front feet.

"Are you coming with me?" Maggie asked, trying to summon the courage to get out of the car and walk up to that forbidding door. "There's a light on, so someone must be up."

"Of course," Flynn said, hopping out and opening Maggie's door for her. "I wouldn't miss this for the world. It's not every day I get to travel back in time a couple of centuries."

They paused momentarily, staring up at the huge menacing dragon sculpted above the arched entry. Maggie moved slowly toward the massive carved wooden door with heavy wrought-iron hardware holding it in place.

It seemed to say, *Stay out, Maggie McKenzie. You don't belong here.*

Maggie instantly thought, *What makes you think I want to belong here?*

She didn't wait for Flynn. Defiantly she strode to the front door and grabbed the imposing door knocker, banging the tail of a dragon against a worn, ancient-looking metal plate. She waited, counting, giving them one minute before she knocked again. Then Maggie whanged the dragon's tail for all she was worth.

Flynn stood beside her, but she no longer needed his moral support. This house had angered Maggie—had defied her to enter, to belong. She didn't want to belong to this place that had produced Cleat Wiggins and how many other sons like him! What did living in a place like this do to those who inhabited it?

Her first order of business was to find Jennie. But then she had to know, had to find out—was there a biological family curse, handed down through the ages, that contaminated one of each set of siblings? That was the question Maggie burned to ask—the question she knew she must answer before leaving this forbidding place.

She reached for the knocker again, and as her hand closed around the dragon's tail, the golden dragon's eye moved. In its place, a very human eye appeared.

# TWENTY-SIX

Dragonwyck
Saturday, 5:00 A.M.

Maggie stumbled back, her heart pounding like thunder in her ears. The door slowly creaked open, and a tall, robust-looking elderly gentleman with ice-blue eyes, white hair, a red mustache, and bushy red eyebrows stared at her.

"What kind of apparition appears on my doorstep in the wee hours of the morning?" The old man squinted to see her more clearly. "Where do you come from, you who could be twin to my grandsons?"

Maggie stared right back at him. She imagined that this was what Damon and Llewellyn would look like forty years from now. She finally found her voice. "You must be Llewellyn Rathford, my grandfather." Maggie stepped forward and offered her hand.

The old man descended from the doorstep and peered down at her. "I don't believe it." His voice sounded breathless, and he touched her face, looked up at Flynn, then back at Maggie. "Can it be?"

"Cleat Wiggins sired me—and an identical twin as well." Suddenly Maggie remembered the reason for this sunrise visit and blurted out, "We think there might be a young woman and her two children hidden somewhere here at Dragonwyck." *Whoa, slow down,* she thought. *You can't surprise a man with your existence like this and accuse his grandson of kidnapping all in the same breath.*

Just then, Maggie saw a young man leading a saddled horse down the driveway. Grandfather Rathford signaled him to wait.

He turned back to Maggie. "It sounds as if you have an interesting tale. I'd like to hear it in order rather than receive it in bits and pieces that I won't be able to put together, so please start at the beginning."

Maggie took a deep breath. "My name is Maggie McKenzie. This is Dr. Flynn Ford, a friend of mine."

She repeated the story she'd told so many times about Lily and this man's son, Cleat Wiggins. She told about Cleat selling the children, and Lily running away from her abusive husband with Alyssa, the only child she thought remained alive. She didn't even spare details about Cleat kidnapping Alyssa, her seven years of terror, and how Maggie and Flynn had met and then searched for and found Alyssa last December.

Maggie brought her grandfather quickly up to date on her search for the two sons Cleat had said he buried, how she had found Damon, and her appointment with Llewellyn later today.

"Then you've never met Llewellyn?" Grandfather Rathford asked.

"I have an appointment to meet him at eleven o'clock this morning. But last night," Maggie stumbled for the right words, "I suddenly had a notion the woman I befriended on the plane might be here. She was kidnapped from London with her two small children earlier in the week. Their picture has been on the news since Thursday morning. I can't really explain it, and I had planned to come here anyway to meet you, so . . ." At this point Maggie was at a loss as to how to approach the subject of a search of Dragonwyck.

As she paused, trying to formulate her plea for help, Grandfather Rathford swept her into his arms in a bear hug that left her breathless. "A granddaughter," he said with amazement. "Never thought I'd live to see the day. And there are two of you? Just alike?"

Maggie laughed as he set her back on her feet. "Yes, two of us so alike you wouldn't be able to tell us apart. In fact, if you like, I'll call her and have her come so you can meet her."

"I'd like that very much," the old man said, scarcely taking his eyes from Maggie's face. "Now, why do you believe a young American woman and her children may be hidden somewhere on my estate?"

While Flynn called Alyssa's cell phone, Maggie explained how she had been asked via TV to tell the police everything she knew about the American Jennie Albright, how she had felt it was a ruse to get her to come forward, and how she had discovered that a terrorist had accidentally slipped a computer flash drive into her bag.

"Slow down," Grandfather Rathford said kindly. "You're not making much sense."

So Maggie told the whole story, or at least as much of it as she could, so that it did make sense. She avoided implicating Llewellyn, saying simply that after researching the Rathford family, she had awakened out of a dead sleep convinced that Jennie was here.

"Does Dragonwyck have a cellar or dungeon or unused wing where they might be hidden?" Maggie asked.

The delight had disappeared from Grandfather Rathford's face. It seemed he believed her story. "We would know if someone was in the house, but we do have a cellar, a dungeon of sorts." He motioned to Flynn and Maggie to follow him around the corner of the house.

"Alyssa is very disappointed that you came to Dragonwyck without her but is willing to forgive you if you wait for her and Rolf to get here before you do anything else," Flynn reported after ending his phone call. "They're are on their way and should arrive within about thirty minutes. She doesn't want to miss anything else exciting."

As they walked, Grandfather Rathford told them about the dungeon. "It's never used, hasn't been for decades, but I think my boys, and then my grandsons, used to play there when they were little. I'd find evidence that someone had moved the stones I blocked the entrance with. We'll have a look."

They followed a stone path through a garden and around a wing of the house. Beyond the stables was uncultivated natural terrain—scattered trees, bushes, and knee-high golden grass still wet from morning dew. When they reached a high wall with tall windows near the top, the old gentleman stopped and pointed at the stones mounded around the base of the wall.

"I think you can see, no one's been here for a while. The grasses aren't trampled, and the stones are still in place, so it must not be our dungeon in which they're held."

Maggie thought for a minute, remembering all the gothic novels she'd ever read. "Is there another entrance to the house somewhere, an escape tunnel? I remember reading once that the residents of a mansion had a tunnel leading from the chapel to a place in the woods some distance away in case they had to escape the king's soldiers, or some other enemy. Do you have one of those?"

Grandfather Rathford turned to the stable boy who had followed them, took the reins of his big strawberry roan, and said, "Bring two horses, quickly." The stable boy took off on a dead run, and the old man turned to look at Maggie, his eyes resting on her hair. He motioned to his horse. "Just the right shade of red. A good match, don't you think?"

Maggie laughed. "My brothers always said I was a strawberry roan."

"In answer to your question, yes, we do have a tunnel, though I'm not sure I'll be able to find the entrance quickly. I'd forgotten about it. It's another part of the estate that is never used—no need for it anymore. The boys loved playing there, as did my grandsons. The forbidden and the mysterious, you know. Unfortunately, I have an appointment with some of my tenants this morning, and I mustn't keep them from their work while they're waiting for me, so our search will be hurried." He stopped and reached out to touch Maggie's red hair. He shook his head in disbelief. "What a miracle to find you now, or rather, for you to find us."

"Grandfather, you asked if I had met Llewellyn. Why?"

Mr. Rathford sighed. "I'm worried about that boy. I'm afraid he's into something rather deep and can't get out." He looked across the rolling hills behind the estate. "Though I'm not sure he wants to get out at this point. I don't know what he's up to right now, but I fear it is no good."

Maggie decided to take the plunge. "Would Llewellyn have any reason to kidnap anyone?"

Mr. Rathford turned sharply to her. "Are you suggesting that Llewellyn is the kidnapper?"

Maggie rolled a pebble around with her toe, hardly daring to look into her grandfather's face. Finally she looked up into indignant blue eyes. "I don't know. I don't know anything, except that someone stole my bag, and Llewellyn was the one who asked them to do it."

The stable boy returned then with two saddled horses.

"Tell Arthur there will be at least two more for breakfast, and perhaps others," Mr. Rathford instructed the boy, who ran off to do his bidding. Maggie and Flynn mounted, and Grandfather Rathford started off at a fast clip. He turned and shouted over his shoulder, "I should have asked if you ride, but I see you do."

No one spoke as they galloped through high golden grass toward a copse of trees about half a mile down the hill. "I think it's somewhere near here, but I'm not sure where," he called over his shoulder again.

Suddenly he wheeled his horse and examined the ground. Maggie saw what he was looking at—car tracks had flattened the dry grass. Riding at a full gait, they followed the tracks, which led directly to a large mound of rocks surrounded by dense brush and trees.

"Someone has been here recently, and I suspect you may have guessed right," Grandfather Rathford said, dismounting. "This is the entrance to the tunnel, though I couldn't have found it so easily without the tracks." He led them around the rocks to the other side, stood back and examined the scene, then removed a bush that appeared wilted. It came up in his hand.

They moved several more bushes that had been torn up by their roots or cut off, uncovering a crevice in the rocks. Fresh footprints in the dirt led inside the dark slit. Grandfather Rathford pulled a small flashlight from his saddlebag and started for the entry, then offered the light to Flynn.

"I'm not as young as I used to be. Perhaps you wouldn't mind leading the way?"

Flynn accepted the light then shined it inside the crevice before disappearing into the darkness. Maggie followed right on his heels, and Grandfather Rathford squeezed through the narrow entrance behind her.

Not knowing what they might find, the three crept along the tunnel as quietly as possible until they came to a wider area. Flynn flashed the light around the walls and saw two cribs, a small folding table, and a cot against one wall.

Maggie hurried forward. "Jennie? Is that you?" she whispered.

There was movement from the cot. Flynn shined the light on the cribs, revealing two sleeping children. Jennie sat up. "Who is it?"

"It's Maggie McKenzie. I met you on the plane. Are you okay?"

"How did you ever find me? Can you get this chain off of me and get us out of here?" Jennie sounded close to tears.

Flynn focused the light on her. She had a chain around her ankle, anchored into the rock wall behind her. It was eight or ten feet long, just long enough so that she could take care of her children. Not long enough that she had any freedom of movement beyond the cribs and the table.

"I've got some wire cutters in my saddlebag," Grandfather Rathford said, looking at the scene in shock. "I'll get them."

"Jennie, do you know who did this?" Maggie asked. "And why?"

Jennie shook her head. "I've no idea. I couldn't believe there could be such inhumane monsters in the world until they brought me here to this horrible place with my babies. Who would do such a thing? I've wracked my brain to think why—or who—but I can't come up with a single name or reason. Why me? My family doesn't have enough money to pay any kind of ransom."

Maggie bit her lip, not knowing how to tell Jennie that it was probably her fault that Jennie had been kidnapped. However, Grandfather Rathford returned at that moment and saved her from having to confess.

While he worked on the chain, Maggie asked, "Do your captors stay here? Is there anyone else around?"

Jennie rubbed her ankle and thanked Grandfather Rathford when she was released. "No, I think we must be so far from anyone that they just left us. They said we could scream all we wanted but no one could hear a thing. They left food, lights, diapers, and books for Tara, and haven't been back." She picked up her sleeping baby from one crib and grabbed the diaper bag.

Flynn stuffed the books into a duffel bag that lay at the foot of Jennie's cot, then scooped the snacks from the table into the bag while Maggie picked up Tara. The little girl opened her eyes and began to whimper, but Maggie shushed her and held her close. "Tara, do you want to ride a horse?" she asked quietly. That woke the child in a flash.

"A horse? A real horse? Not just a merry-go-round?"

"Yes, a real horse. Have you ever ridden a real horse before?" Maggie asked, pleased the child was excited and not scared.

"No," Tara said, hiding her eyes in Maggie's shoulder as they exited the cave into the now bright sunlight.

After Maggie climbed into the saddle of her horse, Flynn boosted Tara in front of her and gave Maggie the diaper bag, which she slung over her shoulder. Grandfather Rathford held the baby while Flynn boosted Jennie into the saddle of his horse, and then Grandfather handed the baby up to her. Flynn mounted behind Jennie with the second bag on his shoulder.

Grandfather Rathford quickly mounted his own horse. "If you'll return to the house, Arthur will have breakfast ready for you. I'd be pleased if you'd stay until I return. I do want to get to know you, but I have people waiting on me right now, so I can't come back with you. Your grandmother will have been informed you're here, and she'll greet you." He turned his horse and rode off down the hill.

Jennie turned to Maggie. "I can't believe it. How did you find us clear out here?"

"It's a very long, very complicated story," Maggie said. "By the way, this is my friend Dr. Flynn Ford, and that man was my newly discovered grandfather. Jennie, what happened? How long have you been here?"

Aware that Tara was listening, Jennie carefully formed her answer. "The night before last, a man and a woman knocked on the door and took us from my sister's house. It was a long drive here, so I'd guess we arrived around midnight."

Maggie waited to ask further questions until they were out of earshot of the impressionable four-year-old.

"We'll probably have company waiting for us when we get back to Dragonwyck," Flynn said, turning his horse toward the mansion perched on the hill opposite.

"Do you think Alyssa and Rolf could have gotten here this fast?" Maggie said in surprise.

"I was thinking of other company," Flynn said, with a sly wink at Maggie.

"Oh! Detective Chief Inspector McConklin. I'd totally forgotten about the police!" Maggie exclaimed. "What do you think they'll do to us when they find us?"

# TWENTY-SEVEN

"Are they coming to take us back to London?" Jennie asked.

"Unfortunately, they may have a warrant for our arrest. Not you, of course," Maggie added hastily as she saw Jennie's confusion and alarm. "Just me and Flynn. When we met last night to give them some information on the terrorist attack on London, they placed us under house arrest until they could check out our story. But I woke up this morning with the idea that you were being held here, so we left," Maggie explained.

"You mean you just walked away?" Jennie exclaimed, her voice full of disbelief.

"Not exactly." Maggie laughed. "We climbed out of the second-story window. The two officers who were supposed to watch us were sleeping on the job."

They'd been following the crushed grass track and had reached the point where the car must have veered off. Flynn reined in the horse.

"Do you want to see where this goes, or do you want to just go back to the house?" he asked.

"I'd like to follow it, if you don't mind a short delay, Jennie," Maggie said. "I want to take a look at the other entrance to the estate, since Grandfather didn't see whoever brought you here."

"No, I don't mind," Jennie said. "I guess I'm still in shock. I'm not thinking about anything beyond the moment right now."

"Before you return to London, Jennie, you should spend a little time with Dr. Ford. He's an expert in the psychological effects of kidnapping and the aftermath." Maggie turned to Flynn. "I assume you're as good with children as you are with adults?"

Flynn smiled at Tara. "I think we'll get along just fine. Tara can tell me about the great adventure she's just been on."

They walked along the trail, not wanting to frighten the children by going faster with the horses. The baby was awake now and seemed to enjoy the jostling ride. They soon found a gate almost hidden in the trees next to the river.

"This is definitely not a seldom-used road," Flynn said. "Look how compacted the dirt is here at the entrance. If the kidnapper had used this road only a couple of times, you could see his tire tracks in the soft dirt, but this is a well-traveled access to the estate. We need to find out if it's used by the tenants or if the Rathfords have machinery that comes through this gate frequently."

Maggie was thinking. "Or, could this have been the meeting place for Llewellyn's group? Maybe we need to investigate that tunnel more thoroughly. We might find something rather interesting down there."

"Hmm. Good thought," Flynn said. "But first, let's get back to the house and see if Inspector McConklin has put two and two together and located Dragonwyck yet."

"I'd rather not," Maggie said, "but I guess we don't have a choice, do we?"

"Nope. Time to face the music," Flynn said, turning the horse back toward the big house.

As they approached the mansion, they saw Rolf and Alyssa pulling into the driveway, and were greeted by Detective Chief Inspector Alistair McConklin, who waited impatiently with his arms folded, leaning against one of the dragons.

The stable boy hurried to take the horses while Flynn and Maggie prepared to face the inspector, who hotfooted toward them, followed by an angry-looking Detective Sergeant Tim Murphy.

Rolf and Alyssa trailed behind, not wanting to miss what looked like it would be a major confrontation.

"Before you say a word, Inspector, I'd like to introduce the missing Jennie Albright and her baby, and this beautiful child is Tara. Right behind you is my twin sister, Alyssa, and our friend Rolf Owen. Alyssa, would you like to boost Tara down?"

The little girl looked down at Alyssa, then turned in the saddle to look up at Maggie. "You're just alike," she said.

"That's right, Tara. Alyssa is my twin sister." Maggie handed the child down to Alyssa, then turned back to the inspector. "Our secret mission during the night was successful, as you can obviously see."

Inspector McConklin pointed a finger at Flynn and Maggie. "I'd put you two fugitives behind bars for that little stunt, except that your records are clean."

Maggie flashed a smile. "May we go in and meet our grandmother? And I'm sure Jennie would love a hot shower and an opportunity to change the baby."

He hesitated. "Yes, you can go on in. I'll keep Dr. Ford here to get his story. Then I'll want to talk to the rest of you."

Jennie approached Inspector McConklin. "Sir, may I call my sister? I know she's worried sick. She can call my family back home."

Inspector McConklin nodded absently. "Just tell your sister not to let anyone know you've been found. If the press gets hold of this news, we may miss our chance to capture your kidnappers."

Flynn handed Jennie his cell phone. "I'm sorry, Jennie. I should have thought of that as soon as we got you out of the cave." Inspector McConklin pulled Flynn aside and began questioning him as they walked away from the house. The stable boy led the horses away, much to Tara's chagrin.

Maggie took Tara by one hand and grabbed Alyssa by the other. Rolf shouldered Jennie's bags, and they approached the entrance to Dragonwyck. As Maggie rapped the golden dragon's tail against the brass plate, she remembered her feelings when she approached this forbidding door an hour ago. Once again trepidation gripped her heart. Grandfather Rathford had been excited to meet them. But what kind of welcome would they get from the rest of the household?

Jennie connected with her sister while they waited at the door. Suddenly she removed the phone from her ear. "What about my parents? Can't she call and tell them I'm okay?"

Maggie looked at McConklin and Flynn conversing down the driveway. She thought of how her own mother would feel. "Tell your sister to swear them to secrecy. No one can know that you've been found until they catch the kidnappers. In fact, could your sister come here without the press following her? If you show up at her home, it will blow everything."

"Here, to this place?" Jennie asked, looking up at the ancient turrets towering above her.

"If she can get here to Dragonwyck, it's only a short drive to my parents' home in Wales. No one should think of looking for you two there," Rolf said.

"Except that your picture has been plastered all over the news since you saved my life the other night," Maggie said. "Have you spoken to your parents since then? I'll bet they've been hounded by the media ever since it happened."

"Actually, Alyssa and I spent the night with my parents last night, and they said no one has said a word. Nobody mentioned in the article the fact that I was from Wales, so apparently the press hasn't discovered that yet. I'm sure we can manage to keep Jennie and her family hidden away until they can safely emerge back into the spotlight."

"How does that sound, Jennie?" Maggie asked, not wanting to make decisions for the young mother.

Jennie nodded her head. "I'll do whatever you think is best." She finished her conversation with her sister, who agreed to slip away from London and come to Dragonwyck. Rolf got on the phone and gave directions to Jennie's sister.

The heavy door creaked open, and an ancient, tall, emaciated man stood before them, a shock of white hair falling onto his forehead. He was dressed in formal black, the quintessential butler's uniform. The old man hesitated, looked at Maggie, then Alyssa, and back again.

Maggie stepped forward. "We'd like to speak to Mrs. Rathford, please."

The butler, who Maggie estimated had to be at least eighty years old, moved slowly toward them, pulled a small pair of glasses from his pocket, and put them on. His astonished expression, though he immediately suppressed it, communicated to Maggie they would be admitted. She relaxed just a bit.

He backed out of the way and motioned to the interior of the house, inviting them to enter the dark foyer. They moved silently into the great hall, awed by the antiquity they felt and the immensity of what they saw before them.

The old man pointed to a room to the right of the foyer. "You may wait in the drawing room," he said quietly, then shuffled slowly down the great hall to where Maggie could see a light shining under a door. Instead of entering the drawing room, the guests lingered in the hall to discover for themselves what a genuine Gothic manor looked like.

Along the left side of the great hall, a wide, carpeted staircase led to a second-story landing with stained-glass windows. The center sections contained the Rathford dragon, colorfully constructed in small diamond-shaped panes. The thought flashed through Maggie's mind that if a small pane was broken, at least the entire window didn't have to be replaced like those in the cathedrals. She wondered how many times the small panes had been replaced as a result of raising boys in the house.

"Look, Tara. Can you see that beautiful dragon up there?" Maggie said, still holding the child's hand.

"Maggie, there are dragons everywhere," Tara exclaimed, dancing with excitement. "Look, the sun is shining through them, and there are even some on the floor."

Maggie looked to where the little girl pointed. Dark wood banisters gleamed in the light from the high windows, and that light shone through the dragon-shaped cutouts of the heavy balcony railing, leaving little light splotches on the worn stones and carpet of the hall floor. The stairs continued spiraling up at least two more floors that Maggie could see.

"Where else can you find dragons, Tara?" Maggie asked, hoping to keep the wiggly child happy and occupied.

Tara pulled at Maggie's hand and led her across the hall. "I see some! I see some!" Maggie, Tara, and Alyssa entered a huge rectangular room with a monumental fireplace on one wall. Above it hung a silk banner with a six-foot red dragon, and embroidered underneath was the name *Dragonwyck*.

"See, Maggie. Isn't it pretty?" Tara said, so excited she jumped up and down.

A dining table at least thirty feet long and six feet wide stood in the center of the room, surrounded by chairs with backs taller than Maggie. The emblem of the dragon was carved into each of the chairs. On the far wall opposite the hall, long banners hung from poles, each containing a crest of some sort.

Maggie boosted Tara up to feel the dragon carved into the wood. When Maggie put her down, the excited little girl let go of Maggie's hand and ran around the table, counting dragons. Alyssa followed her, helping her count.

The fact that Maggie couldn't see a single cobweb impressed her. Someone cared for this massive place that resembled a museum more than a home. On the wall opposite the fireplace, tall windows overlooked the driveway. Maggie stepped closer. The glass was clean. No dust on the frames of the small panes.

"Is this a dining room?" Alyssa asked. "It's enormous."

"This would be the banquet room," Rolf explained quietly. "The banners probably denote the crests of various English lords the Rathford family served in different wars or campaigns. As a member of the family rises to any political significance, he can commission a banner to signify that occasion—so these banners would be the history of the Rathford family."

"I wonder if our brother Llewellyn has one up there," Alyssa said.

At that moment, the old butler silently appeared and motioned for them to follow him. Just as they started down the long hall, Inspector McConklin came in the front door and asked Jennie if she would come into the drawing room and speak with him. Tara took her mother's hand and waved good-bye to Maggie.

Maggie and Alyssa followed the tall, slender fellow shuffling down the hall. Rolf hesitated, staying behind, but when Maggie realized he wasn't with them, she turned and beckoned him with her hand. He'd come this far. He needed to share the climax of this family drama.

"Do you feel like you've come home?" Alyssa whispered.

Maggie shook her head. "No, I feel like I'm in a museum. But it's strange—I want these people to like us. I want to be accepted by Grandmother and Grandfather Rathford."

"Why do you think it's strange you want them to like you?" Alyssa asked quietly.

"Because I have two sets of very loving grandparents at home, and I don't need any more. How do you feel about them?"

"I guess I'm like you. I'd really like them to welcome us and be kind. Most of all, I'd like them to be good people. I'd like to think there's good blood back there somewhere. I'm a little nervous having a father like Cleat Wiggins and a terrorist for a brother. I don't like being related to killers."

Maggie nodded. She couldn't agree with her sister more. But beyond that, she didn't want to think some evil psychosis lay dormant within her, some abnormality of birth, just waiting for the opportunity to break loose.

# TWENTY-EIGHT

The old butler finally reached the door at the end of the great hall, which was set back under the second-story balcony. Everything he did seemed to be in slow motion, or was it just Maggie's anxiety and anticipation that made it seem that way? He reached for the ornate brass handle and turned it, slowly pushing the door open to reveal a light, airy, modern-looking room.

A petite, silver-haired woman gracefully arose from her chintz-covered rocker by the fireplace. She came toward the visitors, then stopped, her eyes widening in disbelief. One frail, thin hand flew to her heart as she reached with the other for the nearby table to steady herself.

Maggie rushed forward, afraid she'd fall. She took the woman by her arm and led her back to the rocking chair, helped her sit down, then stepped back and apologized. "I'm sorry to give you such a start."

The woman's long, slender fingers fluttered as if to brush away the apology. "No, Arthur warned me there were two young women asking to see me who carried a striking resemblance to our grandsons, but I had no idea just how striking that resemblance would be."

She stared from Maggie to Alyssa. Finally she said, "Oh, forgive me. Please sit down." She motioned to the love seat next to her, and waved Rolf to the chair opposite her on the other side of the fireplace.

"Thank you for seeing us. This is Rolf Owen, a friend who's been helping us. I'm Maggie McKenzie and this is Alyssa Lawson. We believe we are your granddaughters."

"If you are my granddaughters—and your appearance certainly points in that direction—" the old woman said with a smile and nod of her head, "who is your father?"

Maggie took a deep breath, looked at Alyssa, and said, "You had two sons: Llewellyn and Damon, I believe. Your eldest, Llewellyn, lives in Wells with his adopted son Damon. I understand your second son disgraced the family and went to America. That man sired us."

Mrs. Rathford looked deep into Maggie's blue eyes, so much like the eyes of her grandsons. "You say 'sired' you, instead of stating he was your father." She paused before adding, "And your tone sounds mildly distasteful."

Maggie looked at her hands, ashamed she'd not concealed her emotions more carefully.

"Look at me, child," Mrs. Rathford said. Her tone was not harsh, nor unkindly, but it left no doubt it was a gentle command to be obeyed.

Maggie's eyes met those of her grandmother. "I'm sorry I revealed that. I didn't mean to. But he was not a father in any sense of the word. You know, of course, that he sold his first two children to his brother."

Mrs. Rathford nodded slightly. "We were grateful to have the boys back in the family, especially since our own Llewellyn wasn't able to produce heirs. Go on, my dear."

Maggie repeated the story yet again of Cleat selling the babies.

When Maggie paused, Grandmother Rathford said, "I would appreciate it if you would tell me the whole story, please, withholding nothing. At my age, there is nothing left than can shock me." She stopped and smiled. "Nothing short of seeing the two of you, of course. You don't need to couch your feelings in polite terms. Your expressive eyes tell much of the story for you." She glanced at Alyssa. "So you feel the same way about this Cleat Wiggins?"

Alyssa shook her head and looked at Maggie for support. "No, ma'am. I don't just dislike him, I loathe him. Forgive my saying it, but he was a beast."

Grandmother Rathford raised her eyebrows and looked at Maggie again.

"I guess the best way to answer your questions is just to tell the story," Maggie said. "Then you'll understand. When Lily became pregnant a third time, she insisted on going to a hospital so she wouldn't lose this baby, too. During her difficult delivery they administered general anesthesia, so she didn't know she'd delivered twins. Another woman in delivery at the same time had previously lost two little girls, and the baby she delivered that day also died at birth. Her husband was afraid for her sanity once she discovered her loss. Cleat Wiggins sold one of the twins to this man and his wife. They took me home with them, so Alyssa and I were separated at birth, and we had no idea we had a sister somewhere in the world."

"An identical twin sister," Mrs. Rathford said quietly, looking from one girl to the other. "Go on."

"Alyssa, this is your part of the story," Maggie said, grasping her sister's hand. "You tell it."

Alyssa's story poured forth, telling how her mother, Lily, had escaped from the brutality of her husband and raised her daughter in the home of the childless, wealthy couple who had adopted the little girl but kept Lily on as the nanny.

"I had a wonderful childhood, thinking Lily was just my wonderful nanny. But when I was sixteen, the night of my big coming-out party, Cleat Wiggins kidnapped me and made me his slave for seven years." Tears welled in Alyssa's eyes and spilled over as she retold her horror story. "He was a brute and a murderer. I wish I could say I'm sorry he's dead, but I can't."

Mrs. Rathford leaned back in her chair and closed her eyes for a minute. The twins suddenly realized this was the first she had heard of Cleat's death. Neither knew what to say. Should they—could they—offer condolences?

Then Mrs. Rathford opened her eyes and nodded matter-of-factly, as if she heard her son described in this way every day and received such unusual news hourly. She abruptly changed the subject. "How did you discover there were two of you?"

Maggie picked up the story. "I was hired as a reporter for a newspaper by the owner, and when I showed up at his San Buenaventura paper my first day, Lily nearly fainted when she saw me. She eventually told me I looked very much like the editor's daughter, who'd been kidnapped. From the moment I heard about this story, I felt drawn to the missing girl who supposedly looked just like me. I felt a connection to her—and in many ways, it was that connection that led me to Alyssa."

Maggie stopped and looked at her grandmother. "That might sound a little strange, but the connection I feel with Alyssa couldn't be more real. I've heard it's not uncommon with twins."

Grandmother Rathford stared at the two girls. "No," she said slowly. "It doesn't seem strange at all. It is well documented that this sort of thing happens with identical twins." The room was quiet except for the ticking of a clock and the crackling of the fire.

"Now then," the old woman said, "tell me how you came to England and why."

"I came on assignment from my paper, but with an additional errand to perform. Alyssa's adoptive father hired a detective to discover whether there had been a midwife with Lily who might remember something, since Lily had not gone to the hospital with her first two births. That search produced an envelope with your son's name— Llewellyn Rathford—as well as his address in Arundel. Llewellyn sent money to the midwife to pay for the delivery. I traced them from the address in Arundel to Wells, where I met your son and Damon."

"And what did you think of Damon?" Grandmother Rathford asked, her eyes narrowing in interest. She noted Maggie's hesitation.

"The truth, child," she said. "We are only after the truth here."

"I thought he was perfectly charming, except he has a temper that frightens me a little," Maggie admitted.

"Have you met his brother, Llewellyn?" As she asked that question, the older woman leaned forward, seeming anxious for Maggie's answer.

"Llewellyn!" Maggie exclaimed looking at her watch. "I'm supposed to meet him at eleven o'clock this morning."

"Are you going to keep that appointment now that you have found Dragonwyck?"

Maggie hesitated. How could she tell her grandmother the police wanted her to keep the appointment so they could capture the man they suspected of kidnapping and being involved in a horrendous terrorist plot?

"I'm waiting for your answer, Maggie," Grandmother Rathford said. She concentrated on folding her lace-trimmed, white handkerchief for a moment, then leaned back in her chair and added with a weary note in her voice, "I doubt there is much you could tell me that I don't already know."

Maggie looked at Alyssa, then down at her hands. How could she know of the murderous designs of one of her grandsons? Unless Flynn had actually guessed the truth—that their grandparents were somehow involved.

# TWENTY-NINE

"Why are you so undecided about keeping your appointment to meet Llewellyn?" Grandmother Rathford asked.

Maggie and Alyssa looked away from the penetrating stare of the woman. What could they say that wouldn't be an absolute insult to the woman? Maggie tried to mumble some excuse, but her grandmother waved her handkerchief at her as if to shoo away any excuses.

"Who told you about this place if my grandsons did not?" Mrs. Rathford asked, changing the subject.

Alyssa spoke, finally hearing a question she was comfortable answering. "We did some research, found the information on the Internet, and decided to see if our grandparents were still living."

Mrs. Rathford nodded. "Very clever. And what do you intend to do now that you know about Dragonwyck?"

*That's the second time she's asked that question,* Maggie thought. What did she expect them to do? Move in?

"I'm hoping to find answers to some questions that have haunted me since I discovered I had a twin sister and our birth father was not a nice man," Maggie said simply. "Then I'll work on my writing assignment and return to California."

"That's all? You're not planning to pursue a relationship with your family here now that you've found us? You're not interested in Dragonwyck?" The older woman studied the girls closely.

"Of course we'd love to get to know you and learn more about your beautiful home." Maggie and Alyssa looked at each other. "Do you mean you think we only came to claim some part of this place?" Maggie asked, aghast at the idea.

"Didn't you?" Grandmother Rathford asked icily. "Would you have come here if we'd lived in a rundown cottage by a little stream?"

"Of course," Alyssa said. "We wanted to discover family we didn't know existed until now."

Then Maggie remembered that Flynn had mentioned they might be entitled to a portion of the inheritance of Cleat Wiggins.

"Mrs. Rathford, would you like us to sign some sort of document stating that we have no intention of pursuing any interest in Dragonwyck?"

Before Grandmother Rathford could reply, the butler opened the door. "Breakfast is ready, madam."

"We'll be right there. Thank you, Arthur."

The butler nodded and shut the door.

Maggie knew she had to break the news of Jennie and her children before her grandfather returned. "There is one other thing I need to tell you. When we came this morning and met Grandfather Rathford, he led us to the end of the old tunnel, and we found the Albright family, who were kidnapped the night before last. You may have seen them on the news. My investigation led me to Dragonwyck, and Grandfather led us to them."

Grandmother Rathford nodded and looked as though she had just seen through Maggie's hesitation. "And you suspected Llewellyn had something to do with the kidnapping, so you came here."

"Yes," Maggie said simply. What else was there to say?

"I see. Well, let's not keep our guests waiting. Dragonwyck is known for warm hospitality." She turned to Rolf. "Young man, would you see me to the garden room?"

Rolf took her arm and led her toward the door. Maggie hurried to open the door—and came face-to-face with eyes as blue as her own and Alyssa's.

"Hello, Maggie. Fancy meeting you here."

Maggie stared at the man who had to be her other brother. "Llewellyn, I presume," she said, hoping her voice didn't quiver, since her knees were doing so at the moment.

"Very good," he said with a smile. His voice was rich and deep, the voice of an accomplished speaker.

"This has to be my other sister, Alyssa," he said, nodding at Alyssa. "And this is your helpful friend from Wales. How do you do, Rolf?" He nodded in Rolf's direction, then took Maggie's elbow in a painfully firm grip and steered her into the great hall.

Grandmother spoke from the doorway. "She doesn't need help, Llewellyn. You can release her arm." Her grandson obeyed and stepped aside, waiting for his grandmother and Rolf to enter the hall. One withering glance from Llewellyn, and the young Welshman wisely abandoned his duty as chaperone, relinquishing it to the eldest grandson.

At that moment, Damon came in the front door. "Well, I haven't seen a crowd like this for years." He nodded to Jennie and the children still in the drawing room with Inspector McConklin. When he spotted Llewellyn, his smiling countenance changed to a scowl. Waiting for Llewellyn to take his grandmother down the hall and out of earshot, Damon advanced slowly until he stood next to Maggie and Alyssa.

"Damon, how is your father?" Maggie asked.

His expression softened at her concern. "He's resting well. Thank you for asking. They gave him some new medication that will help temporarily, but they're going to have to move him up on the surgery schedule, or I'm afraid he may not survive another attack." Damon smiled down at his sisters. "I see you had a busy night. Flynn told me—"

Maggie hurried to stop Damon from saying any more. "Speaking of Flynn, can I get him? I'd like him to join us and meet Grandmother." Llewellyn and his grandmother might be far enough down the hall not to hear Damon, but if Llewellyn hadn't already seen Jennie, Maggie didn't want him to know she was here.

But how could Llewellyn have come in the front door and not seen her? By the same token, how could he have come in the front door without Inspector McConklin seeing him?

"I'll send Arthur for Flynn." Damon turned to the butler and repeated Maggie's request. Arthur tottered back down the great hall to the front door.

She wanted to shout after him, *Hurry up! We have a man here who's planning to blow up London.* Maggie didn't dare let on that she was afraid of Llewellyn or that she distrusted him, and she hoped Alyssa would play it very cool, too. They just needed the inspector and his men to come right now, while Llewellyn was still relaxed and unsuspecting.

Then Maggie thought, *Unsuspecting?* Hadn't Llewellyn passed the police coming in—or had he been in the house all the time? Was he even aware the police were here? How could he not know? How could he have missed that? Unless he thought they had not connected him to Richard Constantine and felt quite safe just being Llewellyn Rathford at the moment.

The entourage followed Damon to a sunny room where green plants and flowers flourished in the light from large windows on three sides. The white wicker furnishings set this room a world apart from the Gothic appearance of the front of the house.

Where were the police? Llewellyn needed to be apprehended. Maggie was too anxious to appreciate beautiful statues of nymphs peeking out from the greenery and the fountain in the center of the room bubbling merrily. She paid no attention to the bright orange koi swimming lazily over cobalt blue rocks in the pool at the bottom of the fountain. Her only concern was Llewellyn's apprehension.

Breakfast steamed on an elaborate old sideboard, and near it were two large, round wicker tables, each with six place settings. Damon held Maggie's chair for her while Rolf assisted Alyssa, and Llewellyn escorted his grandmother to her seat. He leaned over and kissed her cheek, whispered something in her ear, and swiftly left the room

Maggie jumped to her feet and rushed to follow him, but he'd disappeared and was nowhere to be seen. There wasn't even the sound of footsteps to follow. She ran to the front door just as Flynn and Sergeant Murphy flew through it.

"He's gone," Maggie blurted. "He vanished into thin air fifteen seconds ago!"

# THIRTY

Damon hurried from the garden room with Rolf right behind him. "Maggie, where did you go? Breakfast is ready and Grandmother is waiting."

"Damon, Llewellyn just disappeared. Where did he go?" Maggie asked. "He walked out of that room and vanished. I was right behind him, but he's gone. How could he do that?"

Damon glanced at the police, at Flynn, then back to Maggie. "Over here." He led them a few steps to a panel beneath the stairs and pressed a section of the woodwork. The panel swung into a dark recess.

"Where does this lead?" Inspector McConklin asked.

"To the old escape tunnel, but I don't know if it's still open. I haven't been in it for years," Damon said.

"Someone has," Maggie said. "That's where we found Jennie and her children this morning."

"Dr. Ford, you've been to the other end of the tunnel. Take Sergeant Murphy there. I'll go through this way," the inspector said, fishing a small LED light from his jacket pocket and plunging into the darkness.

Flynn stopped long enough to prevent Maggie from following them. "You stay here with Alyssa and make sure Llewellyn doesn't come back into the house. Rolf, you stay with the girls and don't let either of them out of your sight."

Then he sprinted out the front door with Sergeant Murphy on his heels. Maggie heard car doors slam and knew they'd take the river gate, following the car tracks to the entrance. She could get the horse and meet them there.

Alyssa had joined them in time to hear Flynn's instructions. She took one look at Maggie's face and grabbed her arm. "Oh, no you don't. Flynn said to stay here, and we're going to do just that. You're not leaving me. What if there's a place in that tunnel where Llewellyn could hide while the inspector passes, then he doubles back and comes out here?"

Maggie looked up at Damon, who seemed dazed by what had just happened. "Could he do that? Is it just a straight tunnel, or are there places where he could hide?"

Damon shook his head slowly as if clearing the mist from his mind. "Yes, there are places where he could easily hide. There are even a couple of dead end tunnels to throw off someone following you."

"But if he goes in, he has to come out either here or in the woods, right?" Maggie asked.

"Yes. What's this all about? Why are the police after Llewellyn?" Then Damon stopped. "I guess I should say, what did he get caught doing? They should have been after him a long time ago."

Grandmother Rathford appeared in the doorway of the garden room, leaning on her cane. "Are you going to take breakfast or not? Your food is getting cold. It will not be worth eating if you stand there in the hall talking all morning."

Maggie was torn. She didn't want to sit down and endure shallow small talk while Flynn chased the man she was sure had ordered that terrorist to follow her—the same man she felt positive had ordered Jennie and her children kidnapped in order to get Maggie's bag with the flash drive. If they cornered him, she had no doubt he'd lash out to do bodily harm to anyone nearby. She couldn't stand the thought of Flynn being hurt.

Alyssa took Maggie's arm and pulled her toward their grandmother. "Let's give Grandmother an opportunity to get to know us," she whispered. Reluctantly Maggie allowed herself to be drawn along with Rolf and Damon back to the garden room with their grandmother, but she made sure the door to the hall was left standing open.

A pleasant young woman in a black dress with a white apron and cap appeared, leading Jennie and her children to breakfast, then stood at Grandmother Rathford's elbow to do her bidding while everyone filled their plates. Maggie had no appetite. Rolf and Alyssa ate enough for the entire company. Damon sipped a cup of coffee and toyed with a cheese Danish that he never got around to eating.

Tara chattered all through breakfast about the goldfish in the pond and the trees in the house. She gave names to each of the statues and delighted Grandmother Rathford with her bright babble and sunny disposition. Maggie was glad Tara hadn't realized the danger she'd been in—it had all been made to seem like an unusual adventure.

The conversation was amiable, and everyone avoided the topic of the strange occurrence in the hall minutes ago or the implication that the girls were fortune hunters, which Maggie felt Grandmother Rathford truly believed. The petite woman was a gracious hostess and put Jennie at ease immediately.

Maggie stayed focused on the hall, hoping that if anyone entered from any direction, she'd hear them. She barely heard the conversation, participating only when someone asked her a direct question. Her entire focus was on the spot where Llewellyn had disappeared just steps from where she sat.

They talked of the house, of the heavy responsibility of preserving the treasured heritage that had been passed down through so many generations, as well as the expense of keeping it up. Rolf kept Damon busy answering questions on the classic Gothic architectural features of the ancient structure, and even Alyssa hung on every word. It seemed that Damon was becoming more friendly toward Rolf, and the two men seemed to be establishing a rapport.

"I'm sure you were appalled at the gardens in front," Grandmother Rathford said. "They've been dreadfully neglected, but our old gardener died two months ago and we can't find another. I tend the roses in the front and in the rear garden, but the rest of the property is too much for me."

"I keep telling Grandfather he needs to just invest in one of those lawn tractors so he can ride around and cut it himself," Damon said, "but he'd rather ride his horse."

It would have been interesting to see the two brothers together, Maggie thought, watching Damon. If Llewellyn hadn't changed his hair color to brown, they'd look very much alike, though Llewellyn had a more muscular build.

Where was Llewellyn—had they caught him? Why were they taking so long getting back to the house? Had something gone wrong? Maggie was tied in knots waiting for answers.

With breakfast finally completed, Maggie and Alyssa thanked Grandmother Rathford for her gracious hospitality. Rolf complimented her on her excellent cook, then rose from his chair, bent low in front of her, and kissed her hand, endearing himself to her forever.

*How nice some of the old customs are,* Maggie thought, wishing this type of chivalry and etiquette hadn't gone out of style.

Jennie asked if there was somewhere she could take her children and relax for a bit. "Just a corner anywhere will do," she said.

Grandmother Rathford directed the maid to take them upstairs to the nursery. "There are toys for Tara and a crib for the baby, as well as a bed for you. Please make yourself at home, and if you need anything, just ring for Grace and she'll come running."

Grace took Tara by the hand and led the little family toward the stairs. Tara waved good-bye to Maggie and Alyssa and skipped happily beside Grace.

"What a pleasant child she is," Grandmother Rathford said, then turned to her other visitors. "Would you like a tour of this monstrous house, my dears? I'm sure you're curious about it. I rather imagine that at one time you read many Gothic novels and wondered what it would be like to live in a place like this."

Maggie stared at her. "Why do you think that?" How could she know that Maggie had loved Gothic novels in high school and had read everything that Mary Stuart, Victoria Holt, and other authors had written?

"Why, I thought all young women indulged in the genre." Grandmother Rathford smiled. "When I visit the bookstores in town, the shelves are full of them. We can't keep them stocked at the library."

"Of course." Maggie nodded. "Yes, I loved reading them and getting lost in that world that was so foreign to me."

Grandmother Rathford turned to Alyssa. "And you? Did you enjoy them?"

Alyssa shook her head. "No. Growing up, I spent all my spare time with my horse. When Cleat kidnapped me, I wasn't allowed to read anything. He cheated me out of so many happy years."

Grandmother Rathford placed her tiny hand over Alyssa's and squeezed it. "I understand your bitterness, my dear, but please don't let his betrayal canker your soul. You have your whole life ahead of you, so just let it go. It's over now. Put the past behind you." She paused and looked at the four young people. "And speaking of that, why don't you go immerse yourselves for a while in some of your family's history? Would you do the honors, Damon?"

Damon stood and helped Maggie with her chair while Rolf assisted Alyssa with hers. "Come and let me show you this wonderful old place," Damon said and helped his grandmother to her feet, then looped her arm through his and took her back into her sitting room.

Maggie followed them out of the garden room, but hovered near the panel in the hall. She noted the close proximity to the sitting room, where French doors would have provided a quick escape. Had Llewellyn escaped using this route? Maggie had been so close behind Llewellyn, she was sure she would have seen him if he'd gone that direction, or at least heard the doors, but she'd heard nothing.

"There you are, old dear," Damon said affectionately, kissing his grandmother's forehead. "You can rest for an hour while we do the grand tour, then we'll come back to say good-bye."

She settled into her chair by the fire. "Then I'll answer Maggie's questions before she leaves." Her fluttering fingers shooed them from the room. "Put everything back where you found it, Damon," she called.

"Of course, Grandmother." He shut the door and turned to the trio waiting in the hall. "I suggest we begin upstairs and work our way down," he said, leading them to the wide staircase. "I suppose you want to know about the dragons you see everywhere."

"Oh, yes!" Alyssa said.

"Begin by telling us about the dragon on your ring," Maggie said. "I notice you and your father have one, but Llewellyn wasn't wearing one. Is there some special significance to the ring?"

"Only legitimate heirs of Dragonwyck are allowed to wear them. The rings are a replica of the seal our ancestors used to seal their documents."

"The dragon is similar to the one associated with King Arthur Pendragon. Is there a reason for that?" Maggie asked.

Damon smiled. "Family legend has it that we are descended from the mythical King Arthur." He started up the stairs. "Are you ready for the tour?" he asked.

"You'll have to go without me," Maggie said. "I'm not budging from this panel for one minute." She looked at Damon thoughtfully. "Are you sure there's no other exit from this passage? If he entered the tunnel here, there would be absolutely no other place he could come out besides exiting out on the hill in the rocks and trees?"

Damon shook his head. "No, Maggie. I'm not sure. Let me qualify— there didn't used to be any other exit. I can't promise that Llewellyn hasn't gone in and carved out another one. He's full of mysterious surprises, most of which are not pleasant."

"So there's a possibility he's been working on the tunnel and forged another exit somewhere that you don't know about?" she asked.

Damon thought for a minute. "It's entirely possible."

"Where would that exit most likely be?" Maggie pressed.

"One of the dead end tunnels used as a decoy heads toward the river. I guess he could have extended that and built an entrance, but I'm sure grandfather would have seen signs of construction. He's all over the estate every week, covering some part every day. I ride with him at least once a week. I can't think Llewellyn, or anyone, could do something like that without him or me or one of the groundskeepers knowing about it."

Suddenly Maggie heard noises in the tunnel. She motioned to Rolf and Damon to be ready, and threw open the panel door.

# THIRTY-ONE

Inspector McConklin stepped into the hall, brushing cobwebs from his jacket.

"Did you find him?" Maggie asked, assisting the inspector in the cleaning process. She shivered at the thought of all the spiders that had spun these webs sticking to his jacket.

"No. Dr. Ford and I met at the center. Llewellyn wasn't there." The inspector turned to Damon. "There has to be another exit. I'd like you to come with me and show me where he could be hiding or where he could have escaped."

Inspector McConklin pointed to Rolf. "I'd like you to stay here at this entrance until backup arrives, just in case he's been hiding in a niche I didn't see and I passed him. My officers should be here any minute." The two men disappeared into the dark interior of the passage.

"Hmm. Near the river," Maggie mused, thinking about what Damon had said. "If the work was done at night, no one would be out and about to see what was happening. They could toss the material into the river and it would wash away, thus there would be no residue from the dig. If this plot on London has been in the planning for two years, they would have had ample time to build another entrance to the tunnel. They could actually have been having their meetings right here at Dragonwyck."

"That nearly hidden gate would be to their advantage," Rolf said. "They wouldn't have to come anywhere near the house, so the servants would probably never see them."

"I saw a movie where people who lived in the city carried their bicycles on their cars to places with bike paths, parked, and rode bikes on country lanes where there wasn't a lot of traffic," Alyssa added. "They could have parked in different spots, then two by two or three quietly ridden bikes onto the property by the hidden gate near the river. Who would ever consider people bicycling as dangerous or criminal?"

"You're perfectly right, both of you," Maggie said. "I need to search by the river and find that exit, if it's there. I can't stay here and twiddle my thumbs while Llewellyn may be escaping. You two watch this end of the tunnel. I'll grab the stable boy, get a horse, and ride down to the river."

Maggie headed for the front door before Rolf and Alyssa could stop her, but as she grabbed the handle of the heavy door, it swung open, nearly knocking her off her feet.

Flynn looked as surprised as Maggie. "You seem to be going somewhere in a hurry. Where would that be?"

"To the river by that gate we found this morning. There's a possibility Llewellyn may have built another exit to the tunnel that leads there. Damon said one of the decoy tunnels headed in that direction, so we thought it logical that that's the new exit, if there is one. What are you doing back—did you find him?"

"No. Let's go." Flynn whirled around, and they raced for the car he had just parked in the driveway.

"What made you think of another entrance?" he asked as they sped out of the circular drive and down to the wrought-iron gates.

"The inspector came back and asked Damon about the possibility, and Damon remembered that one of the decoy tunnels headed toward the river. They're looking at that possibility now. But I'm afraid Llewellyn has already gotten away. He's had plenty of time while everyone was searching the old tunnel."

"If, in fact, there is a new tunnel," Flynn reminded her. "There hasn't been any sign of construction, remember. We would have seen it when we were there."

"What if they dumped all the dirt and rocks in the river?" Maggie speculated. "No one would be able to see any change in the area—no piles of dirt to attract attention or prove someone had been digging."

"But when you build a tunnel, there's more to it than just digging dirt out of a hole. You have to shore it up, which requires some rather large timbers. Surely someone would have seen that sort of activity," Flynn argued.

"It all could have been done at night. That's a pretty deserted area. The trees almost hide the gate. They would screen most everything from the road." Maggie stopped. "I wonder if that's natural growth, or if some of those bushes were planted to conceal activity there. That's pretty dense stuff along the fence line and by the river."

She looked out the window to see how the bushes were planted inside the tall wrought-iron fence that ran alongside the road. The bushes were fairly thick, but only a double row grew just inside the property line, and there were many places where the neglected gardens and outbuildings were visible. Suddenly, as they approached the river, the bushes and foliage were so thick you couldn't see through them at all.

"You may have a point," Flynn said. He pulled off the road, parked in front of the gate and locked the car, and they climbed over the fence. "If he's still here, I don't want him slipping through our fingers. My car may slow him for a minute or two."

Maggie shook her head. "He's gone, Flynn; I'm sure. You went through this gate to the exit where we found Alyssa and Rolf, and he came out of the new exit as soon as you passed. I'm betting he was gone before you met Inspector McConklin in the middle of the tunnel."

Flynn flashed a smile. "You're being pessimistic, Maggie girl. That's not like you." He began searching along the dense tree line for anything that looked like an entrance, quickly disappearing into the brush.

Maggie walked straight to the river, hoping to find the place where dirt and gravel might have been dumped to wash away as someone dug it out of the tunnel. On this bank, for a hundred feet in either direction of where she stood, the river bottom was covered with pebbles and gravel.

On the other side of the narrow channel, the bottom of the sparkling water was all dirt—a mud bottom. There were no pebbles along the entire side that she could see. She walked upstream and found soft mud midstream, and on the other side there very few stones in the bottom of the river.

She retraced her footsteps downstream and found the same thing. This convinced Maggie that her hypothesis was right. She pulled her camera from her pocket and photographed the riverbed.

In the next instant, Flynn proved her correct. "Here, Maggie. I found it."

She raced into the brush where Flynn disappeared. There was no obvious path to follow, but it was easy to wind through the bushes. At the side of a small hill, Flynn stared at an area similar to the one they'd ridden to out on the hill that morning.

"Does this look familiar?" he asked.

"Sure does. It's the very same setup as the exit to the tunnel in the trees where we found Jennie. It looks like we should be able to squeeze through just fine next to that big tree."

But Flynn made no move to enter the tunnel.

"Aren't we going in?" Maggie said, wondering why they were standing outside talking when they could be exploring the tunnel.

Flynn shook his head. "Not on your life. If he's in there, we don't want to meet him in the dark. We'll wait right here for Damon and Inspector McConklin to come through."

Maggie perched on one of the rocks. "What a day this has been! Or days, I should say. Never in my wildest imagination could I have dreamed up what's happened in the last thirty-six hours."

Flynn settled on the rock next to her. "Are we going to make it a career to rescue people from kidnappers?"

Maggie laughed. She turned to Flynn, but his face was so dangerously close to hers it took her breath away. She looked up into eyes that burned into hers, that erased any sane thought in her mind. She froze in place, wanting to lean forward just the tiniest bit, knowing Flynn would kiss her if she did. But he would have to make the first move.

Time stood still while she sat breathlessly waiting for something to happen. And it did. But not what she hoped for or expected.

# THIRTY-TWO

Llewellyn burst from the tunnel, cell phone in one hand, a gun in the other. As he swung the gun at Flynn's head, it connected with a sickening thud. Flynn crumpled over on top of Maggie, and they fell to the ground in a heap.

Llewellyn dodged nimbly through the trees and leaped the gate. Maggie heard the sound of brakes squealing to a stop, a car door slam, and the motor rev as the car sped away. As she tried to extract herself from under Flynn's dead weight, Inspector McConklin and Damon raced through the opening. They stopped and stared at Maggie struggling to roll Flynn over.

"Llewellyn's gone," Maggie cried. "He called someone as he ran out of the tunnel, and they were right there to pick him up. He struck Flynn's head with his gun."

Inspector McConklin raced to the gate while Damon hurried to lift Flynn so Maggie could get to her feet. They stretched him out on the ground, and Maggie knelt to check the damage. Flynn tried to open his eyes, but other than a slight flutter of his eyelids, he wasn't moving.

"Wake up, Flynn, wake up." Maggie touched his cheek, rubbed his arm, and silently prayed for him. "Please be okay," she whispered. She pulled a tissue from her pocket and pressed it against the wound.

"What were you two doing here?" the inspector asked.

Maggie leaned back on her heels. "Damon said there was a possibility Llewellyn had extended the tunnel near the river. We came to see if he had, hoping to catch Llewellyn if he was still here, but I was so positive he'd already escaped that we were just waiting for the two of you to come through."

"At least you determined that he was there and that he'd been using the tunnel. Excuse me." Inspector McConklin stepped away to use his cell phone. As he waited for an answer, he turned back to Maggie. "I don't suppose you happened to see the make of automobile he's in?"

"Sorry, I didn't," Maggie said, busily attending to Flynn, who finally opened his eyes. With Damon's assistance, Maggie helped him sit up and lean against the rock.

"You have a talent for being in the wrong place at the wrong time, Maggie," Flynn said, "and unfortunately, I seem to be there with you."

"I'm sorry, Flynn; you'll probably have a doozy of a headache," Maggie said, still pressing her tissue against the wound. "But look at the bright side. You're not bleeding too badly and won't even need stitches, even if it was a mean blow."

The inspector finished his call. "Let's get you back to the house, Dr. Ford. I'll have my men search the tunnel. If the terrorists were using it, they may have stored explosives here."

Maggie sat in the back seat, keeping pressure on the cut in Flynn's head while Inspector McConklin drove Flynn's car back to the mansion. When they arrived, Damon opened the back door and helped Flynn out.

Rolf and Alyssa hurried out the front door when Flynn's car drove up. "Did you catch him? Was there really a new tunnel?" Alyssa asked.

"No, we didn't catch him, and yes, there is a new tunnel," Maggie said, explaining what had happened at the river.

Flynn insisted he could help with another search, but Inspector McConklin rather forcefully suggested that he take it easy for a while and leave the chasing of bad guys to the professionals.

"And the rest of you—" he waved to Damon, Alyssa, Rolf, and Maggie—"If you would remain here for the time being, I'd appreciate it. Please don't leave until I return. I'm sending some men to search the tunnels and grounds for anything that will connect the terrorists to Dragonwyck. Sergeant Murphy will show them where to go." He turned to his car, then before he got in, stopped and said, "And Murphy will also make sure you stay put." He slammed the car door and sped down the circular drive.

Damon led them into the house. "The library is very comfortable, Dr. Ford. You can settle down with a good book or just close your eyes and relax." He turned to the other three. "Since we don't seem to have anything else to do, and since our tour was sidetracked, would you like to see the house now?"

Maggie started to follow Flynn into the library, but he waved her away. "Shoo. Go on. I won't get any rest if you're here, and this may be your last opportunity to have a guided tour of your ancestral home."

Reluctantly, Maggie followed Damon to the stairs. Alyssa and Rolf were excited about the tour, and as they progressed through the house, their enthusiasm became contagious and Maggie found herself enjoying Damon's narrative immensely.

There had to have been miles and miles of hallways and a maze of corridors that led from one area to the next. Damon showed them secret passageways built to hide the family from the king's soldiers or the current enemy, and one that led down a spiral staircase all the way to the basement, then out through a musty tunnel to the woods where family members could escape without being seen.

"Does this connect with the tunnel Llewellyn escaped into and the one Jennie and her children were in?" Maggie asked.

"Yes," Damon admitted.

"Then Llewellyn could actually have gone into the upstairs of the house instead of out the panel into the tunnel?" Maggie asked.

Damon nodded. "I'd totally forgotten about this upstairs portion. As I said, I haven't been in any of them for years—in fact, since I was a boy."

Maggie thought it strange that Damon would forget something like this—or had he just conveniently not mentioned it to the inspector?

As they toured the guest bedrooms in the towers, Maggie noted the heavy wooden doors with massive locks and wondered if these had held voluntary guests or those who had not chosen to be here at all.

Damon turned to her and laughed. "There have probably been times when the guests were not happy to be here."

Maggie stared at him. Had he read her thoughts? She shook her head. Not possible, but his comments certainly could be unnerving.

"But you can see that the accommodations are the finest around," Damon said, hastening to add, "and no one ever starved to death here." He laughed at what probably was an old family joke. Maggie's sense of humor wasn't the best right now, and all she could muster was a faint smile, thinking that one of the brothers might actually want to lock them here and throw away the key.

She knew which brother clearly wanted her dead, but suddenly she wasn't sure about this second brother. Had Damon delayed Inspector McConklin in the tunnel so Llewellyn could escape? Had he purposely not revealed any number of things that might have aided in Llewellyn's capture? Was he, in fact, a party to the terrorist plot? What did she really know about this man, anyway?

"The tapestries are beautiful," Alyssa said, running her hands over the colorful silken threads. "Is it true they were used to keep the cold from seeping through the stone walls?"

"The tapestries helped, and they beautified the stone, but you'll notice every room has a fireplace," Damon said. "In the main parts of the house, Grandmother and Grandfather did some modernizations, so many of the rooms now have gas heating."

"Speaking of Grandfather, where is he?" Maggie asked. "He said he'd be back shortly."

"This morning he had an important meeting with his tenants. He spends his days riding the estate, directing the laborers who work the farmlands, and keeping the tenants happy. Dragonwyck comprises a lot of property to manage." Damon paused. "I think the day he retires, he'll probably die. Being busy keeps him alive."

"Is he in good health?" Maggie asked, noting Rolf and Alyssa had begun their own conversation. "He certainly appeared to be this morning."

Damon smiled and nodded. "He's a robust old soul, just the opposite of Grandmother. Physically—and temperamentally—they're poles apart. She rules this family with an iron fist and keeps the estate financially sound. Grandfather is just like my father—a gentle soul, content to let someone else tell him what to do, let someone else make all the decisions—especially the hard ones."

"Does he make the decisions for the property?" Maggie asked.

"Everyone believes he does, and for the minutiae, that's probably true. But every evening my grandparents discuss what went on during the day, and Grandmother suggests what might need to happen tomorrow. Then he makes it happen." Damon shrugged. "Apparently it's a successful system, as they've been working this way for over fifty years."

Maggie moved down the hall with Damon. "What will happen if—when Grandmother dies?"

"Grandmother is training me to take her place. I come once a week, sit in on their evening discussions, and go with Grandfather all the next day. She is determined that I know everything there is to know about running the estate."

"I'm glad, Damon," Maggie said. "It would be such a shame to have it fall into disrepair and lose it after having it in your family all these centuries."

"Our family, Maggie," Damon corrected.

Maggie laughed. "No, your family, Damon. This is your family home. My family home is on a little ranch in the middle of the Idaho sagebrush."

Damon glanced at his watch. "I'm afraid we're going to have to step it up a bit if we're going to see the rest of Dragonwyck." He motioned to Rolf and Alyssa, still deep in conversation. "Come, let me show you the rogues' gallery."

"Let me guess," Maggie said aloud. "That would be the portrait hall."

"Ah, you've been reading Gothic novels," Damon responded with a knowing smile. "But you must see these paintings to appreciate how the species has improved over the centuries."

They wandered through another maze of halls, up more staircases, and finally came to a long gallery literally covered with paintings along one wall. The opposite wall held a balcony overlooking a large room with a grand piano.

Alyssa peered over the edge. "What's down there?"

"The small ballroom and music room. This gallery was designed for a dual purpose. When adults entertained, children were allowed to watch the party from up here as long as they were very quiet and didn't let their presence be known. And they were expected to be able to identify each of their ancestors and know something about them, so it functioned as a classroom at other times."

"How many generations of your ancestors have lived in this house, Damon?" Rolf asked.

Damon laughed. "I'm afraid I was a bad student. I don't remember. But the house was begun in the early 1700s and has been built and improved upon almost continually since then, so approximately three hundred years' worth of Rathfords have been born and bred at Dragonwyck."

"Damon, why are there so few pictures of women?" Maggie asked. "Surely, all these men had to have wives to propagate the line. Where are their pictures?"

"We do have a women's gallery somewhere in the house," Damon said. "I think we had a feminist great-great-grandmother. She rounded up all the pictures of the females and turned a couple of the rooms into galleries."

"How many generations of males have been born with no sisters?" Maggie asked. "Did your father have any sisters?"

Damon shook his head. "No."

"Did Grandfather have sisters?" Alyssa asked.

"I don't believe so," Damon said. "No one has ever mentioned them."

"How about your great-grandfather?" Maggie asked.

Again Damon shook his head. "I love history, but I'm not the greatest genealogist in the world. I'm afraid I was just never interested enough to inquire. Why do you ask?"

Maggie shrugged. "It seems strange that there are so few females in the family, that's all."

"May I say that my two sisters more than make up for that lack." Damon said it with a charming smile, but Maggie wondered how he really felt.

"One more family question," Maggie said. "You mentioned Llewellyn wanted nothing to do with the family, yet he turned up today as if it were a normal occurrence to breakfast with his grandmother."

Damon smiled. "Breakfast or luncheon with Grandmother when she summons is not like having anything to do with the rest of the family. None of Llewellyn's public ever see him in this setting, and they know him by his assumed name, not the Rathford name, so this is safe, anonymous territory for him."

"Your grandmother summoned you both for breakfast today?" Maggie asked, not quite understanding what he meant.

Damon shook his head. "Not today. This is my normal day at Dragonwyck. I was enormously surprised to see Llewellyn here. That was unusual."

"Could he have left Jennie and her children in the tunnel yesterday and spent the night here without anyone knowing?" Maggie asked.

"Oh, yes," Damon said. "There are so many rooms, that wouldn't have been an issue at all."

"Do you think he did? Do you think he was here in the house all morning and watched us with Grandfather—and knew we were going to the tunnel to look for Jennie and her children?"

Damon's expression turned dark. "I'm not able to follow the warped thought processes of my brother. I've long since stopped trying to second-guess anything he will do."

# THIRTY-THREE

Damon turned to include Alyssa and Rolf, smiling politely. "I think you must be tired of all this antiquity." He pointed to still another staircase and led the group down it. "Once you're cleared by the police to go, what are your plans in England?"

"Well, we've found you and even discovered other family members, so now I just need to finish my assignment for the paper." Maggie said. "I don't know what Alyssa's plans are."

"I'm not sure yet, but I'm glad I came," Alyssa said, smiling at Rolf. Then she turned to her brother. "Thank you for the tour, Damon. I can't imagine having to keep this huge house clean. How do they do it?"

"Once a month grandmother has a task force of cleaning ladies from the village give it a thorough cleaning—wipe down cobwebs, move the dust around, hoover or beat the carpets, shake out the linen on all the beds and remake them, wash the windows if they need it. And she keeps a couple of good mousers on the payroll. All you can eat, you know." He smiled at his little joke.

Maggie had noticed a couple of cats snoozing in a sunny window and nodded.

"She has a staff of a dozen or so servants, some who have lived here all their lives and whose children also live and work here. Some have been with the family for generations. They live in one entire wing of the house and get meals, uniforms, and a stipend."

Damon led the way back to Grandmother Rathford's sitting room and opened the door to find her pulling a sweater around her shoulders. "You're going out, Grandmother?" he asked.

"Maggie and I have some unfinished business. I must convince her I'm not unsympathetic and harsh." She smiled. "I know you have things to do, Damon, and I'm sure Alyssa and her Rolf won't mind sitting by the fire for a few minutes while we talk."

Damon gave his grandmother a hug and strode from the room. Maggie waited for the older woman to lead the way. Grandmother Rathford selected a cane from a holder by the door, opened the French doors, and led Maggie outside to an intimate garden just off the sitting room.

As they strolled through the fragrant roses she'd lovingly tended and trimmed, Grandmother Rathford pulled a dead leaf from one, a spent blossom from another. She turned and looked at Maggie with a gaze that seemed to bore right into her granddaughter's heart. "Maggie, forgive me for seeming so cold earlier. I've heard one too many stories of fortune hunters running scams. I just wanted to make sure your story rang true. I believe it does. Now, ask me those burning questions that brought you all the way to England."

"As I believe you know, Cleat Wiggins was not a good man," Maggie said quietly, jumping immediately to the core of the matter. "I carry his genes in me, his blood in my veins. I suspect he had serious psychological problems—psychotic tendencies. I worry that I'll take after him instead of Lily. Would I ever dare to have children, knowing what their grandfather was like, and apparently what some of the men were like in generations before and after him? I guess my burning question is simply, what is the history of insanity in the family? Is there any likelihood that this could still manifest itself in me or my children? What inherited characteristics can I expect to find?"

The delicate, diminutive lady led the way to a marble bench beneath a small blossoming tree. She sat down and patted the seat next to her. Maggie settled beside her.

"What kind of woman is this Lily?" Grandmother Rathford asked, facing her granddaughter to watch her eyes, her expressions, her reactions.

"She's a good woman—a tender, loving mother. I don't know how she ever got tangled up with the likes of Cleat Wiggins." Suddenly Maggie remembered she was talking about this woman's son. She looked at her grandmother, aghast at what she had been saying.

"My son died many years ago, Maggie," the older woman said quietly, patting Maggie's knee gently. "When he grew up, he changed and was not the same child who was born to me."

"How can two brothers be so different? Your other son, Llewellyn, isn't like that. And didn't Grandfather Rathford have a brother who was disinherited? I understand the same situation may exist with my brothers. When your son mentioned questionable family traits, I assumed he meant one with good tendencies and one with not so noble ideas. Is that true? Is it real?"

"You're worried that tendency is inherited, and that you and Alyssa may suffer from it." Grandmother Rathford took Maggie's hand and held it in her two small ones.

Maggie nodded. "That is my greatest fear. Before I go home, I need answers so I can plan my future—I must know if I dare to have children or not."

"Set your mind at rest, my dear. There is no history of genetic disorders, just poor choices. I cannot speak for my grandson Llewellyn, as I do not know what troubles him, but I do know my husband's brother was a man who let his lusts dictate his actions. He was not insane or 'born bad'—he simply made one bad choice after another." Grandmother Rathford spoke quietly, but with a conviction that bore into Maggie's fearful heart. "*You'll* choose what you'll be, Maggie. If you want to be good, you will be. If you want evil, then that is the course you'll choose. Every decision you make—every day—leads you down one road or the other. Each decision, for good or evil, determines how you'll live your life and how you respond to influences around you."

She paused reflectively before resuming. "My son Damon—your birth father—allowed drugs to take over his body. Eventually he bore little or no resemblance to the Damon I loved. He was consumed by greed, paranoia, and a desire to control others, perhaps to compensate for his inability to control himself.

"My son—Cleat, as you call him—chose evil. I rather imagine that you will continue to choose the good. You radiate a light that will draw others to you. You can be an influence for good on your sister. I suspect that she is not as strong as you are, so she'll need your guidance. Without your help, she might easily be led astray and make wrong decisions. You're a good girl, Maggie."

Maggie looked into the clear gray eyes of her grandmother. "Thank you," she whispered.

Grandmother Rathford squeezed Maggie's hand reassuringly. "Don't dwell another minute on this problem of undesirable inherited characteristics, child, but if you must, remember that you also inherited Lily's genes, and she is a good woman." She gazed across the patio for a minute, then said quietly, "Remember this day. We may not share much time together, but remember that you are *my* granddaughter. I believe you have special gifts. Use them wisely."

"Gifts?" Maggie questioned. "What do you mean?"

"From your story this morning, I perceive you have an ability to make the most of a bad situation, a willingness to forgive, and a curiosity that will lead you into interesting and exciting adventures. You've shown a spark of independence that is quite refreshing, and courage in the face of adversity that you will need throughout your life."

Grandmother Rathford smiled and continued. "You'll need it because I think your curiosity will certainly get you into places from which you will need courage—and common sense—to extract yourself. These are gifts to be developed to a greater degree and which you should use to help those not as gifted as yourself. Forgive and forget Cleat Wiggins. He has nothing to do with you anymore."

Impulsively, Maggie hugged her grandmother. "Thank you. I can't tell you how much better that makes me feel. I'm so glad I've been able to meet you. I would love to stay here longer, but I have work responsibilities I can't ignore. I'll have to be on my way as soon as Inspector McConklin says we can leave."

Grandmother Rathford's brow wrinkled. "You're not staying even another day or two?"

"I've discovered Damon and Llewellyn, plus the bonus of you and Grandfather, so I have to finish my assignment for my paper and then get back to California."

The older woman sat quietly for a long moment before speaking slowly. "Do you believe in miracles, Maggie?"

Maggie thought about all the priesthood blessings she had received in her life, blessings of comfort, of healing, and the special blessings she had received from her father for guidance. She thought of all the answers to prayers she'd received and the many critical times she'd realized her guardian angels had been on duty, or when the Holy Ghost had quietly whispered instruction. Of course she believed in miracles.

Weren't these all modern-day miracles bestowed by a loving Father in Heaven to His children as they faced daily challenges of one magnitude or another?

"Yes, I do believe in miracles," Maggie said emphatically. "I've been the recipient of many in my lifetime."

"Continue to believe, Maggie. Never stop believing, especially as you face the unknown. Fear has a way of making belief waver. Keep your faith in miracles strong, Maggie McKenzie, because you will surely need it." As she spoke, her voice quivered and a tear slipped down the wrinkled cheek.

"Grandmother, what's the matter?" Maggie asked, alarmed at her grandmother's sudden change of countenance and demeanor.

"Go, my child. Send Alyssa to me. I want to speak to her." She released Maggie's hand and gently pushed her toward the house. "You have a good heart, Maggie. Follow it."

Maggie hurried through the French doors. "Alyssa, Grandmother wants to speak to you." Maggie wiped her eyes. The words her grandmother had spoken were strangely familiar to her. Then she realized with a start that they were very similar to gospel teachings. Her grandmother had repeated Church doctrine that Maggie had been taught all her life. It would be wise counsel from any source, but it was surprising coming from this octogenarian who Maggie didn't think knew anything about the gospel.

"Are you okay, Maggie?" Rolf asked as Alyssa hurried to join her grandmother in the garden.

Maggie nodded. "I'm sorry we put you through this torturous time, Rolf. I had no idea what we'd find here, and certainly no inkling of the tension and emotions this visit would evoke from all quarters."

Rolf walked to the French doors and looked into the garden, watching Grandmother Rathford's expressions as she spoke to her granddaughter. "No need to apologize. It's been interesting. The tour of this extraordinary house made any discomfort worth it. The English are usually a private people, and you don't just knock on their doors and ask to see their home, no matter what an exceptional example of architecture it might be. As I told you, some have resorted to opening their homes to tours or paying guests, but the price is quite out of my reach, so this is a rare treat for me."

"I'm glad we met, Rolf. You've been such an incredible help. I just hope we haven't jeopardized your tutoring job by keeping you away from the university." She gasped. "Oh no! You were supposed to meet someone there this morning!"

"It's okay. I phoned a friend to fill in for me. There was no way I was going to bail out on you now. Things were just getting interesting." Rolf moved to the fireplace and leaned against the mantel, looking at the photographs there, his playful expression turning serious. "Being with you has made me realize—again—that life is precious and that there is so much to be explored in relationships and family. We become complacent and take for granted those people who make such a difference in our lives. How horribly different and difficult Alyssa's life would be if you hadn't found her."

"And how different my life is with her now," Maggie said.

"Look at these pictures," Rolf continued. "If there was a good feeling between those two sons, what great joy there could be in this family. But because, for whatever reason, they hardly tolerate each other, it has created a tension in the family that makes being with them very uncomfortable—not just for them, but also for outsiders."

Maggie joined him at the fireplace to look at the pictures.

"They look so happy here when they're little," he said. "But in this next one, when they're a bit older, your brothers look like they could happily throttle each other. And it continues, with each of the pictures. Look, these at the end are solos—either they couldn't get the brothers together on the same day, or they refused to have their picture taken together."

"Damon said he'd been blamed for Llewellyn's indiscretions all his life. That would certainly be enough to drive a wedge between them," Maggie said.

"I wonder if Damon will stay in touch with you once you leave England," Rolf said, "or if life will go on as it has for all those generations before. If I found some long-lost siblings, I think I'd want to spend time with them, to establish family bonds, to get to know them."

"Unless, of course, one of them wanted to kill you," Maggie reminded him. "That may be reason enough for me to not maintain any connection with the family when we go home."

"Um, righto. That small detail had momentarily slipped my mind," Rolf admitted.

Alyssa and her grandmother entered the sitting room, interrupting their conversation. Rolf and Maggie turned to the French doors to see Alyssa wiping tears from her cheeks. "I wish I had known you all my life," she said wistfully, kissing her grandmother on the cheek. "You've healed so much of my hurt. I've needed you."

"Then you should come back and visit me again—very soon." Maggie noted the cautionary note in her voice, almost as if the woman knew her time left in this life was short. "Please bring Lily," Grandmother Rathford directed. "I'd like to meet her. She must be an extraordinary woman to have overcome her challenges as she apparently has done."

Alyssa nodded. "She is."

The woman leaned on her cane, seeming to become weary before their very eyes. "Thank you for coming. Arthur will see you out. If you do happen to stay longer in England, please come back and visit me. You'll always be welcome at Dragonwyck. Good-bye, my dears."

There seemed to be nothing left to say. Maggie kissed her grandmother's cheek and went quickly to the door. The others followed, closing it softly behind them, and hurried through the great hall to the library to find Flynn. The library was empty.

Arthur appeared. "Dr. Ford is in the nursery visiting with Mrs. Albright and her children. He said to tell you he would be down shortly."

"Thank you, Arthur," Maggie said. She motioned to Alyssa and Rolf. "Let's go in the drawing room and wait for Flynn and for Inspector McConklin to give us the green light to leave."

"I wonder where Damon disappeared to so fast," Alyssa said, pulling back the red damask drapes and curling up in the window seat.

"He said today was his day to ride the estate with his grandfather. I imagine he went to do just that." Maggie stopped. "Unless he's in this conspiracy with Llewellyn and just made his escape . . ."

# THIRTY-FOUR

Alyssa sat up. "Maggie! You can't mean that . . . can you?"

Maggie shook her head. "No. I'm just being paranoid. I asked him why Grandfather was gone so long. Maybe he hurried away to find out." Maggie paced the room, unable to relax. Something nagged at the back of her mind, something that wasn't quite right, but she couldn't figure out what it was. She shrugged it off, hoping it would come to her soon.

"What did Grandmother tell you, Alyssa?" Maggie asked, turning her mind to another subject.

"She repeated what she'd said earlier—that I need to let go of all my angry, hateful feelings toward Cleat. I must completely forget about him and pretend that it was all a bad story I'd read once, like a bad dream that had nothing to do with me." Alyssa paused. "I need to totally disassociate him with my life, like you've done, Maggie. I asked her why we had to be born to such a horrible person so that we felt dirty and ashamed when we thought of him as our father."

"What was her answer to that?" Maggie asked, very much wanting that answer herself.

"She said she didn't believe it made a great deal of difference who our parents were—that didn't have to be the determining factor in our lives. What matters most is what we make of ourselves after we get old enough to make our own decisions. Who or what our parents were isn't as important as the decisions we make every day to determine who we will be. That made me feel a lot better."

"That makes sense. Why should we let him have any say in what we become?" Maggie agreed, then slipped out into the hall and listened for activity in the house, especially for Flynn's return from the nursery. She was sure Jennie would appreciate his counsel, but she was anxious to check his injury and to have his companionship again.

Rolf joined Alyssa on the window seat. "Not that I mind just sitting around with you two, but how long do you suppose we'll have to stay?"

"No idea," Maggie said, "but I could make much better use of my time than I'm doing." She pulled her camera from her pocket to photograph Dragonwyck, not just for an article, but to show her family back home. She slipped outside, where her camera lens captured the carved dragon above the front door and the two sitting beside the entry. Was this symbolic of the nature of the Rathford family—this fearsome, intriguing beast?

Next she pointed her camera at the beautiful roses reflected in the mullioned windows, then turned and took a picture down the forsaken-looking lawn—extreme examples of nurture and neglect. Roses, like families, thrived on nurturing. What had happened to this family?

Maggie returned to the house to photograph the elegant front drawing room, including some shots with Rolf and Alyssa. They followed her into the great hall to watch her at work, then tiring of that, Rolf and Alyssa wandered into the garden room to watch the koi swim in the fountain's pond.

The stained-glass dragon in the second-story window called to Maggie's artistic nature, and she captured several intriguing shots, one through a dragon keyhole on the banister. This became fun, and Maggie snapped pictures of everything in sight. She especially liked the pictures she composed of the banquet room with its colorful banners and Dragonwyck's emblem.

Deciding the secret panel would be an interesting addition to her photo collection, she photographed the closed panel door beneath the staircase, then opened it. Out of curiosity, she decided to go a few steps into the tunnel to see what this end looked like. Having never been in a secret tunnel until today, she hardly knew what to expect. Mice and rats and spiders, she assumed, but probably no skeletons.

Before entering the tunnel, Maggie found Arthur and asked for a flashlight. She decided to leave the panel door open so that if someone came looking for her, they'd know where to find her.

Cautiously she descended the steep, ancient stone steps. Two dozen steps down, where the stairs ended and the passage leveled off, the flashlight caught some scratches in the stone wall, and as she took a picture, the flash illuminated the dark passage.

Without the flash, she'd have completely missed the offshoot tunnel here that veered sharply left, hidden by a jutting rock that seemed a natural part of the wall as it curved. Maggie supposed the tunnel she was in led out to the exit in the trees, but this offshoot branch must be the decoy tunnel that Llewellyn had turned into another exit, the one Damon had showed Inspector McConklin.

Excited, she headed down that passage, anxious to see where the old tunnel ended and how Llewellyn had constructed the new portion. She'd only gone a few steps when she heard her name echo through the tunnel. She almost ignored it, wanting to get on with the exploration, but thinking it might be Flynn, she turned back.

As she did, the hair on her neck stood up. She thought she heard footsteps. Was someone else in the tunnel with her? Hurriedly she retraced her steps and fairly flew up the steep stone stairs to the welcome light and Rolf and Alyssa waiting in the doorway.

"You look like someone's been chasing you," Alyssa said. "What did you find down there?"

Maggie's laugh sounded nervous instead of humorous. "When you called me, I turned around to come back and swore I heard someone in the tunnel behind me. It was probably the men Inspector McConklin sent to explore the tunnel. What's up?"

"Nothing," Alyssa said. "We just wanted to know where you'd disappeared to. We thought you'd found something exciting to do instead of waiting for Inspector McConklin to tell us we can finally go sightseeing."

"Is Flynn finished with Jennie?" Maggie asked.

"Did I hear my name?" Flynn said, descending the stairs.

"You did. We were wondering if you were through counseling Jennie." Maggie turned him around to examine his head. "Not too serious. No lingering effects from Llewellyn's gun connecting with your head?"

Flynn shook his head. "None," he said. "I have a pretty thick skull." Then he noticed the open panel. "Have they finished exploring the tunnels?"

"We haven't heard from or seen anyone since Damon left," Maggie said. "Grandfather hasn't returned yet, either. I thought Inspector McConklin would be back by now or that someone would have reported on the results of the tunnel search. In fact I was just down there and thought I heard someone. Shall we go see what's going on?"

Flynn frowned. "That may be a crime scene. They may not want us in there."

"There have already been people everywhere—you, Sergeant Murphy, Inspector McConklin, Damon. And I think the inspector's men must have entered from the other end, because I'm pretty sure I heard someone there."

Alyssa laughed. "You should have seen her shoot out of that passage. I thought someone was chasing her."

Flynn shrugged. "Okay. I'm game for a little exploring. The police have probably finished their search by now. Is everyone going?"

Alyssa shook her head. "Sorry. Count me out. I've had enough of dark, scary places to last a lifetime."

"I'll keep Alyssa company," Rolf volunteered. "Actually, someone is still supposed to be watching this passage, so we'll take that duty."

The door to the sitting room opened, and Arthur came out carrying a bottle of water, with Grandmother Rathford right on his heels. "Did the police delay your departure?" she asked, seeing the four standing in the hall.

Alyssa hurried to her grandmother's side. "Well, they haven't come back to tell us we're free to go. Do you have time to tell us some history of the family and Dragonwyck?"

"Certainly, but come to my room where it's cozy. The rest of the house is more like an old museum with cold stone walls." As she returned to her room, Alyssa waved to Maggie, held out her hand for Rolf, and the two joined Grandmother Rathford by the fireplace, leaving the door open behind them so the entrance to the passage was visible.

"Good," Maggie whispered to Flynn. "I'm glad Grandmother is willing to share her stories and her time, especially with Alyssa. She needs that connection."

Arthur handed Flynn the bottle of water. "Madam asked that I give you this with the instruction to drink it all. That's her antidote for bumps on the head." He smiled faintly before he turned and tottered away.

Flynn waved at the entrance to the passage. "Ready to see if the police discovered anything?"

Maggie flashed the light on the stairs. "I wish they'd put lights down here, or that I had a flashlight that really illuminated the place."

"I've got a bigger one in the car. Wait, I'll get it." Flynn hurried down the great hall and retrieved his flashlight from the car while Maggie waited.

"Since you've got the better light, you go first," Maggie said, stepping aside so Flynn could enter the passage under the staircase in front of her. They silently descended the steps, examining the ancient stones that had been so carefully placed centuries ago.

"I've been thinking," Maggie said. "There's got to be a meeting room down here. Otherwise, why would anyone want to extend the tunnel? If these passages weren't used anymore, what would be the purpose of going to all that trouble? This could be where they planned their terrorist activities, or whatever it is Llewellyn does. The other end of the tunnel would be a perfect location—far enough from the house but still on private property where the general public couldn't stumble across it. It seemed apparent someone had planted a lot of bushes and trees around the gate, as well as put up that section of the fence to keep it secluded from the road."

"That's true," Flynn said, shining the light on the section of the wall where Maggie had found the second passage.

"Shh." Maggie stopped and listened. "Did you hear anything?" she whispered.

Flynn listened. He shook his head, but before he stepped into the tunnel that they guessed led to the gate by the river, he leaned down to whisper in Maggie's ear. "We'll assume it's the police, but on the off chance it isn't, we'll sneak up on them."

Maggie nodded, and they slipped quietly into the new passage she'd discovered a few minutes earlier. They'd only gone a few steps when goose bumps shivered down her arms and she moved a little closer to Flynn. This time they both heard the sound.

Flynn clicked off the high-beam flashlight, and they stood frozen in absolute blackness for what seemed an interminable length of time, but the noise wasn't repeated. Flynn whispered, "Let me have your little light. It won't be seen as far."

Maggie traded him lights. They crept silently forward while Flynn played the smaller beam on the walls as they passed, watching for the end of the old passage and the beginning of the new section. They hadn't gone much further when Flynn stopped again. Someone *was* in the tunnel—not far ahead. They could clearly hear voices. Flynn switched off the light, and they stood totally still, barely breathing so they wouldn't be heard.

"Hurry up and finish smearing mud on that door. Police will be crawling all over this place any minute, and they can't find this stuff. We don't have time to move the rest of it until everybody vacates the premises today. Come on. Move out."

Maggie moved closer to Flynn. They remained in that position until they couldn't hear any more sounds ahead. Then they proceeded quietly, cautiously, deeper into the tunnel without lights. Finally satisfied the men had gone, Flynn turned on the little light and began playing it over the walls.

In another fifty feet, they found the end of the old stone tunnel and the beginning of the new section that had been carved out of the hard-packed earth and shored up with timber.

A few feet further, Maggie stopped. "I smell wet dirt," she whispered.

Flynn shone the light on the walls. Nothing unusual was readily apparent, so Maggie turned on Flynn's brighter light. In that stronger beam, wet mud glistened on the tunnel wall.

"Look how well they've smeared that to blend into the dirt," Flynn said. "No one would ever see that after it dried." He took out his pocket knife and began scraping at the mud, quickly uncovering a seam outlining a door.

"Clever people," Maggie said. "They've covered the door with dirt so you can't tell it from the walls unless you know it's here."

Flynn felt around the door for some kind of a latch and finally slid the knife blade into the slit and pried the door open. It swung open easily—and silently. Maggie shined the light around the room.

"Unbelievable," she gasped.

# THIRTY-FIVE

Stacks of boxes lined the walls on all four sides of the large room. Some were marked EXPLOSIVE, and on some of the boxes, the symbol for hazardous materials glowed in fluorescent paint when the light struck it. These were stockpiles of dangerous chemicals. This wouldn't be just another terrorist bombing—these people were planning biological warfare as well.

Flynn murmured something under his breath, but Maggie remained speechless, trying to take in the import of the hundreds of boxes along the walls and papers and notebooks covering a small table in the center of the room. Flynn dropped his water bottle on the table to pick up a handful of papers, and as he scanned each one, he became more astounded.

"We've got to get McConklin down here fast before they come to get this stuff," Flynn said. "Come on. Let's go find him."

Maggie shook her head. "No, you go. They said they won't be back until tonight. I'm going to take pictures of all of this stuff and examine these things on the table. Maybe they've left behind some clues about the targets and times. If McConklin isn't back yet, find Sergeant Murphy. He should still be around somewhere. It's funny—I haven't seen him or any of the police that were supposed to be coming."

Flynn stopped to argue with Maggie, but she turned him around and pushed him toward the door. "Go, for heaven's sake. I'll be just fine. They've all gone."

While Flynn raced back through the tunnel, Maggie shut the door and began snapping pictures of everything in the room, then turned her camera on the table and its contents—maps of London marked with X's and circles; railroad timetables with stations and times under-lined; and codes, symbols, and names from mythology, all tossed in disarray on the table.

Maggie first photographed the tabletop, then each page individu-ally before putting them all back where they had been originally, referring to her first picture a couple of times to make sure she'd put them in the right place.

She stood in the center of the room marveling at the horrendous destructive capability that surrounded her. Her next thoughts terrified her. What if the police weren't coming back? Damon had said that Llewellyn held some high political office—what if, as Richard Constantine, he had influenced the police or bought them off? Or what if he managed to come back through some other way?

Maggie didn't panic, but she did the closest thing to it. She looked frantically for someplace to hide in case someone did return while she was there. Unless she moved boxes and climbed behind them, there wasn't a single area where she could conceal herself.

She grabbed Flynn's bottle of water, checked quickly to make sure everything was exactly as they had found it, and left the room. She set the flashlight on the floor, and mixing the water with the dirt Flynn had scraped from the seam, she covered the door seam again so it looked just like the men had left it. She scraped the lip of the empty bottle against the opposite wall near the floor to mark the location of the door, gashing a long, deep line in the dirt.

Then she had a decision to make. Which end of the tunnel was closest? Should she go back the way she and Flynn had come and meet him and whoever he'd found to bring with him? Something told her no.

Then she remembered Sergeant Murphy. That's what had been both-ering her! McConklin had instructed the sergeant to remain in the house and keep an eye on everyone until the men came to explore the tunnels. Instead, Murphy had disappeared immediately, and no other officers had ever arrived. That made Maggie very suspicious and extremely uncomfort-able, especially since it was obvious the police hadn't been here exploring the tunnel after all.

With a prayer in her heart for guidance, she turned toward the river. Flynn might be unhappy that she'd left the room with all the explosives, but she didn't feel safe staying there. She thought she'd be closer to the new end of the tunnel, and from there she could return to the house through the trees.

As she crept quietly toward the river, she kept shining the light on the walls to see if there were more offshoots or passages or doors. Suddenly she smelled wet dirt again. Maggie stopped and played the light up and down the walls. The walls didn't shine like the last area, so she began running her hands over them. Two feet from where she'd stopped, she found more damp dirt. Another room—or another passage?

She almost paused to scrape the mud off and open the door, but she felt impressed not to stop. She needed to get out of this tunnel before Llewellyn or any of his men, or Sergeant Murphy, or even Damon came. She still didn't completely trust Damon. She absolutely didn't trust their eldest brother or Murphy. And at this point, she wasn't even sure about DCI Alistair McConklin.

With her empty water bottle, Maggie repeated the marking of the wall opposite the newly mudded door. If necessary, she wanted to be able to locate this door quickly. Then she resumed her silent flight toward the entrance, still shining the light over the walls. If she'd found two doors, might there more?

Maggie reached the end of the tunnel without discovering anything else, but she realized that didn't mean there wasn't something more to find. She listened, then poked her head out of the tunnel. She couldn't see anyone, so she emerged into the trees surrounding the entrance. She ran through the brush and trees, staying out of open areas until she came to the stable.

When she rounded the corner of the house from the garden, Maggie found Flynn pacing the driveway in a high state of agitation. She could almost see smoke coming from his ears he was so mad. When he saw Maggie, he raced toward her and grabbed her by the arms.

"What happened?"

"Is Sergeant Murphy here?" Maggie asked, ignoring his question.

"Yes. He wouldn't let me go back in the tunnel."

"What did you tell him?"

Flynn let go of her arms and relaxed a bit. "As I came from the tunnel, Alyssa and Rolf met me. Murphy came in the front door just then and wanted to know why the panel to the tunnel was open. I told him we'd thought about exploring it. I asked if the officers had finished their investigation of the tunnels. He said no, they hadn't arrived yet, but that they would be here soon, and no one was to go into the tunnels until they were finished. I decided I'd better not tell him we'd been there—or that you were still there."

"Good thinking," Maggie said, much relieved. "Didn't he ask where I was?"

"No, and I managed to stop Alyssa before she blurted out that we'd gone down there. He told us to take a walk and get some fresh air—that Inspector McConklin would soon be here and we'd be free to leave, and in the meantime, we weren't to go near the tunnels."

"Where are Rolf and Alyssa?" Maggie asked.

Flynn pointed across the driveway. "They're down wandering through the front garden, examining the mess. They thought they might pull a few weeds or something constructive to keep busy. Why did you come out the other exit?"

"I just got this creepy feeling and thought if anyone came back, I'd be trapped with nowhere to hide. I decided I'd better get out fast. I resealed the door with some water left in your bottle. Thanks for leaving it, by the way. I explored the tunnel to the river exit and found one other door, but I didn't stop to investigate the contents."

Sergeant Murphy strolled out of the wide open front door and leaned on one of the dragons, watching Flynn and Maggie.

"Where's Jennie and the kids?" Maggie asked.

"They were going to rest until Jennie's sister arrives," Flynn checked his watch, "which should be in the next hour or so. She said she had about a three-hour drive from London. Then they'll leave immediately for Rolf's parents' home in Blaenavon."

"Let's join Rolf and Alyssa pulling weeds," Maggie said, taking Flynn's arm and glancing at Murphy. "I don't trust that man. It wouldn't surprise me one bit if he delayed the officers' arrival until he was sure everyone had hidden their tracks and left the tunnel."

"That's quite a reach, don't you think?" Flynn said as they crossed the cobblestone drive and entered the sad-looking garden. Flynn opened his pocket knife and began trimming dead roses from a large bush.

"Inspector McConklin said his officers would be here right away, but he had told Sergeant Murphy to call them. All Murphy had to do was tell the additional officers to arrive in an hour or two instead of rushing to get here." Maggie bent to pull weeds from around a graceful statue of a Greek goddess. "And where on earth is the inspector? I'm not sure I trust him either, but I want to get these pictures into someone's hands, and he's the most logical choice, unless I went over his head to Tad Collins."

"What did you find on the table?" Flynn asked, adding to his growing pile of faded roses.

"I photographed enough information to pinpoint a huge number of targets in the city. If the inspector can confiscate all those explosives and have all these places watched, that would probably prevent the entire attack from happening." Maggie stood up abruptly. "What if they have another stash somewhere else? What if this is only part of the plans and explosives?"

"Hmm." Flynn thought for a minute. "You have a point. Terrorists always seem to have a backup plan for any big operation. In case one team can't get through, there are several backups."

"You don't happen to travel with a laptop computer, do you?" Maggie asked.

"Actually, I do. I work on my book whenever the opportunity arises, and later tonight I was planning to enter today's discussion with Jennie."

"Is it in your car? Do you have it here?" Maggie asked.

"It is. What do you want with it?" Flynn asked.

"I need to download these pictures to your hard drive," Maggie said. "If terrorists always have a backup plan, the good guys need one, too. Can you bring it here?"

"Sure." Flynn ambled back to his car, casually retrieved his laptop, and wandered back to where Maggie waited, absently trimming dead roses from the bushes with Flynn's knife.

She sat on a marble bench beneath the goddess statue, hidden from the watchful eyes of Sergeant Murphy, and downloaded the pictures to the hard drive. She hid the file, then slipped the memory stick back into her camera.

"Okay, I'm ready for the inspector," Maggie said, feeling a rush of relief when she finished. "Did he give you his number last night? Can we call him before he gets back here and Murphy grabs him?"

Flynn opened his wallet. "Tad Collins gave it to me along with McConklin's e-mail address."

"Can I use your phone again?" Maggie asked. She checked on Murphy, then dialed the number and waited. It rang so long she thought he'd never answer. She was just about to hang up when she heard, "McConklin."

"Chief Inspector, this is Maggie McKenzie. Are you on your way back to Dragonwyck?"

"Shortly. I've been with Mr. and Mrs. Rathford in Wells all morning, taking their statements. Why?"

"Listen very carefully and hear me out before you scoff at my hypothesis. First, a question: Are your officers supposed to be here investigating the tunnels?"

"Of course. They should have that completed by now. Why?"

"This is the tricky part, Inspector. Please weigh carefully what I'm about to present, and please, don't dismiss me as a paranoid amateur detective before you've thoughtfully considered it."

"Miss McKenzie, will you just get on with it?"

Maggie plunged in. "First, your men have not arrived. Second, I believe Sergeant Murphy is in cahoots with Llewellyn Rathford/Richard Constantine, and I believe he purposely delayed the arrival of your men. Murphy just returned, after being gone for well over two hours. While he was gone, Flynn and I explored the new tunnel and found a room filled with explosives and crates containing biological materials. I photographed it all, including maps, train schedules, and codes that are probably the plans for the attack on London. Someone was down there with us as we approached. They sealed the door with mud to look like the passage walls and left, saying they'd be back later to transport the materials to another place."

Maggie stopped for a breath. "I'd like to personally put these pictures in your hands without Murphy being aware of it. I've downloaded them to Flynn's laptop. If we were somewhere you could look at them, you wouldn't have to wait to have them printed before you saw them."

Silence.

"Inspector, are you still there?" Maggie asked, checking again on Murphy.

"You certainly don't let the grass grow under your feet, do you, Miss McKenzie?"

"No, sir. Can we meet with you without Murphy? I'd like to get this material into your hands immediately."

"Very well. I'll not accept your conclusions of Murphy just yet, but I want to see that material without delay. I'm going to call Sergeant Murphy and instruct him to send the four of you to the station. Then I'm going to give him an assignment that will keep him away from the station and Dragonwyck for an hour. I'll send one of my most trusted officers to watch the house."

"Thank you, Inspector. Might I suggest you send three trusted officers—one at each end of the tunnel, and one in the front hall by the panel. But they need to stay well hidden. I'm sure some of Richard Constantine's men are watching the tunnels. If I were the terrorists, I certainly wouldn't leave that kind of cache unattended with so many new people poking about the place."

"Yes, Miss McKenzie. I had already thought of that, but thank you for making sure I'm covering all bases and doing my job."

Maggie cringed at the sarcasm in his voice.

"I'm going to call Murphy now." Detective Chief Inspector Alistair McConklin disconnected without saying good-bye.

"Ouch," Maggie said, hanging up the cell phone.

"What did the inspector say?" Flynn asked, watching Murphy answer his phone.

"It's not so much what he said, but how he said it. He's certain I'm a meddling, foolish amateur detective who thinks I know better than CTC and MI5." Maggie sat down hard on the stone bench. "Flynn, Damon took Inspector McConklin through that new tunnel to the river. Granted, they didn't spend a lot of time looking, and the mudded door would have been hard to find if the mud had dried, but McConklin wasn't given a chance to explore."

"On the other hand, they were hurrying to catch Llewellyn, hoping he was still in the tunnel. And in fact, he was," Flynn said. "So they didn't stop to search anything."

"You're right." Maggie shook her head. "I'm seeing bad guys everywhere. I don't want Damon to be involved in this, but half the time I can't help but suspect him."

Flynn glanced toward the house. "It seems Sergeant Murphy has received his assignment," he said. "And he doesn't look happy about it."

"Neither am I," Maggie said. "I'd rather not be in the same car with the jerk."

"Dr. Ford, Miss McKenzie. Would you bring the other two and come here?" Sergeant Murphy called.

Flynn called to Alyssa and Rolf, who were wandering halfway down the garden, holding hands. They started back to the house immediately.

Before Maggie could consider the implications of the hand-holding, she had a horrible thought. She grabbed Flynn's arm. "What if he doesn't take us to the station? What if he takes us somewhere else and keeps us hostage until this is all over? Or worse," she added as an afterthought.

# THIRTY-SIX

Detective Sergeant Murphy explained the request from DCI McConklin that they report to the station to give their statements. He motioned them toward his car.

"What about our car?" Maggie asked. "Can we follow you, so we'll have our own transportation? We don't plan on returning here, and that would save you from having to bring us back when we're through at the station."

Murphy thought for a minute. "Actually, McConklin said to send you, so I guess that would be okay."

Maggie and Flynn got in his car, and Rolf and Alyssa hurried to Maggie's rental car. Murphy climbed into his own automobile and headed down the driveway with the others following closely behind.

Flynn's phone rang before they were even out the gate. He handed it to Maggie. "I'm sure it's Alyssa."

It was. "Maggie, what's going on? What did you find in the tunnel?"

Maggie explained all that had happened, with Flynn interjecting points Maggie neglected to mention. "Now we're on our way to the station, where Murphy's going to be given some assignment to get him out of the way while I show McConklin the pictures I took. If they turn out to be what I think they are, we may have just foiled Richard Constantine's plan."

When they arrived at the police station, Murphy waited for them to park and escorted them into Inspector McConklin's office. The inspector motioned for everyone to sit before handing a sheet of paper to Murphy. "Take care of this personally, Murphy, then come back here directly when you've finished," the inspector said.

Murphy glanced at the paper, frowned, and left the office scowling. McConklin pointed at the door. Rolf jumped up and closed it.

"All right, Miss McKenzie, let's see what you think you've discovered."

Maggie already had Flynn's laptop turned on. She placed the computer on the inspector's desk and called up the file.

"How do I know you haven't just staged this whole thing, Miss McKenzie?" he said as he started the second time through the file, examining the revealing photos.

Maggie groaned. "Don't start that again, Inspector. I haven't staged anything. We lucked out and got there in time to hear them talk about sealing the door with mud, or we'd never have found it. If we'd been ten minutes later, the mud would have dried and I wouldn't have smelled it."

"You smelled the mud?" Inspector McConklin finally took his eyes off the screen and looked up at Maggie.

"Of course. It was a totally different odor than the rest of the tunnel. When we shined the light around, the mud was still wet and shiny. Five minutes later when I started out of the tunnel, I could still smell the fresh mud on the second door I found, but it had started drying and I had to feel with my hands to find it. I couldn't see it, even with the bright flashlight."

"And how are we going to find these doors if they are so well patched with mud?" the inspector asked dryly.

"I scraped a line near the floor exactly opposite the doors. If you enter the tunnel from the house, the doors are on the right side of the passage and the marks on the left. I could show you. I think I have a pretty accurate feel for how far into the tunnel they are."

"Thank you, Miss McKenzie, but you have been quite enough help already." He inserted a USB drive into the computer and copied the file, then started printing the pictures. "I'm grateful for your assistance, but I think CTC can handle it from here. Is there anything else we need to know?" He closed the laptop computer and handed it back to Flynn.

Maggie felt her jaw drop. He was dismissing them. He was going to send them away before they caught Richard Constantine—before they caught any of the terrorists. Before they even knew the extent of what she'd given them.

"I can't think of anything," Flynn said, filling the awkward silence. "Can you, Maggie?"

Maggie was still in shock. She couldn't formulate any kind of answer.

Flynn turned to Alyssa and Rolf. "Anything you'd like to add?"

They shook their heads.

Inspector McConklin stood. "Thank you. I'd appreciate it if you would stay in touch. In close touch," he emphasized. "Please don't leave the country before I give my permission. I'd like to know where you're staying and where you're going so I can get ahold of you quickly if I need you."

Flynn handed him his card. "My cell phone is listed." He looked at Alyssa, who quickly recited her number. "Unfortunately, Llewellyn had Maggie's bag stolen, so she doesn't have her cell phone," Alyssa explained.

Rolf gave his number, and Flynn took Maggie's elbow and escorted her from the room. When they got outside, Maggie finally exploded. "He just kicked us out. Dismissed us without the blink of an eye. I can't believe he'd do that."

Alyssa looked at Flynn. "She's like a dog with a bone. She's not going to let go of this that easy."

"Bone?" Flynn repeated.

"Maggie doesn't leave loose ends," Alyssa explained. "If she thinks this isn't all wrapped up, she's going to find some way to stay in England until the case has been solved and the guilty parties are locked up."

Flynn glanced at Maggie. "Is that true?"

Maggie blushed. "Only a little."

"A little?" Flynn pressed. "What does that mean?"

"It means she has to follow everything through to the end. If my father gives her an assignment on the paper and she's almost through with it, and he gives her a second assignment and tries to get someone else to finish up the first one, she won't let go of it. Even if she has to stay up night and day for a week, she'll finish them both herself. Like a dog, she just won't give up that bone."

Flynn laughed. "I knew you were tenacious, but I didn't realize to what extent that characteristic controlled you."

Maggie objected. "It doesn't control me. I just don't like leaving things unfinished."

"And if Inspector McConklin feels this will wrap it up, does that mean you'll be returning to America soon?" Rolf asked Maggie, but his gaze was on Alyssa.

"I'm not sure," Alyssa said quietly.

Maggie turned to Rolf. "I do need to get back as soon as I've finished my assignment for my Sunday travel supplement, but that may take me another week."

"But you won't leave until you're sure the case really is solved," Alyssa said.

"Actually, Inspector McConklin may not be willing to let any of us leave the country any sooner than that," Flynn said.

"Apparently we have this afternoon off. What do you want to do?" Alyssa asked.

Maggie shook her head. "I haven't the foggiest idea. I've been so focused on all the immediate crises I haven't thought beyond them, but I do need to keep working on articles for the supplement."

"I know what we can do," Rolf said, a smile lighting his face. "We can go to Blaenavon. Whatever else you get to see, I promise this will be one of the highlights of your trip. And you can photograph it and be working on your assignment at the same time, Maggie."

Maggie looked at Flynn and Alyssa. "I can't think of anything better, if that's what everyone would like to do. But what about Jennie and the kids? I hate to run off and leave them while we're having fun."

"Not to worry," Alyssa said. "Grandmother promised that when they were through resting, she'd have Grace bring them down so they could get better acquainted. She was entranced by little Tara, so if Jennie's sister doesn't get there right away, Grandmother will entertain them."

Alyssa's expression changed, and she fell silent, staring off into the distance.

Maggie looked at her suddenly subdued sister. "Where are you? You're somewhere else entirely, Lyssa."

Alyssa chewed on her fingernail. "I've been thinking," she said slowly. "Maybe I don't want to go home right away. Maybe I should call Mom and tell her to come now. She could meet Grandmother and Grandfather Rathford, Damon, and Rolf. We could spend some time sightseeing, and you could come with us and write about everything we saw. What would you think about that?"

Maggie was so surprised she couldn't even reply. Finally she said, "I guess I'd think you'd lost your mind. I thought you just wanted to track down our brother, then get back to your home and your classes. Now you want to have Lily come and stay a couple of weeks? What brought about that complete change of heart and mind?"

Alyssa didn't answer for a minute. Then she said quietly, "Grandmother Rathford."

"Why?" Maggie asked. "What happened that reversed your opinion so dramatically?"

"I think she needs me. I think she wants me here. I don't know, maybe I'm imagining it, but I felt a bond to her. And she said I must come back again and bring Lily, but I shouldn't wait too long."

Maggie nodded. "I had the feeling she didn't think she had a lot of time left on this earth, but my experience with her was entirely different. She said she expected we wouldn't meet again, and when she told you to come back soon, that really threw me. Very puzzling, indeed."

"Not so puzzling," Flynn said. "Many older people feel the end nearing and realize they don't have a lot of time left. If Grandmother Rathford thought you were returning home to your job, Maggie, she would realize she might not see you again. But with Alyssa wanting to bring Lily to meet her—and the friendship between Rolf and Alyssa—that would explain why she expected to see one of you and not the other."

"We're wasting a lot of time standing here talking," Rolf reminded them. "I'm off the hook for today's tutoring, so how about some good seafood for a late lunch before our tour of Blaenavon?"

Everyone got in Flynn's car, and Rolf directed them to the road out of town. Rolf entertained them with the history of the area as they drove, and suddenly they were in Wales. Maggie began to feel a certain excitement, anticipation, a quickening of the senses. Wales had long intrigued her, this country of legends and lore, and of strong Celtic culture filled with ancient castles and ruined abbeys.

"'To be born Welsh is to be born privileged,'" Rolf quoted quietly. "'Not with a silver spoon in your mouth, but with music in your blood and poetry in your soul.'" He leaned forward. Softly, almost in a reverent whisper, he asked, "Can you feel it, Maggie? Can you feel the magic, the undercurrent, the aura that is present here? It's what you wanted to write about."

Maggie nodded silently. She could feel it. Or was it the anticipation that something would be happening that night to culminate in some kind of climax? She looked at her watch. Six hours before the powers that be either agreed to pay Richard Constantine his outrageous ransom demand, or cities began to be destroyed, one by one. Unless by some miracle, the terrorists could be stopped.

# THIRTY-SEVEN

"Flynn, will you pull over as soon as you can?" Maggie asked quietly. "We're getting further and further away from Dragonwyck with each mile, and I'm starting to get uneasy. Can we brainstorm for a few minutes?"

"Sure," Flynn said, looking for a spot where he could safely leave the road.

"Up the road about a mile is an overlook above the River Severn," Rolf said. "You could pull off there, and we can enjoy the view while we're brainstorming."

"What's the subject of this discussion?" Alyssa asked.

"There are only six hours until the world will be changed forever. Either the world's governments will capitulate to terrorists' demands and cities will temporarily be saved from destruction, or they'll stand firm and not give in to the demands for exorbitant amounts of money, and we'll have massive destruction very soon."

"You say 'temporarily' because as soon as they give in this time, another group of terrorists will try the same thing," Flynn said.

"Exactly," Maggie said.

Everyone agreed with that.

"What are you proposing?" Flynn asked. "What do you think *we* can do?"

"Probably nothing," Maggie acknowledged, "but we are a little closer to the situation than most, you'll have to admit."

"Whether we wanted to be or not," Alyssa said.

"We're pretty sure Llewellyn, a.k.a. Richard Constantine, hasn't been taken into custody yet, so where would he go?" Maggie asked. "Where would he hide to watch the destruction on TV? Where would he feel safe?" Maggie reached out and touched Flynn's arm. "Dr. Ford, you're the psychologist here. What do you think?"

Flynn thought about it for a minute. "Two avenues of thought: first, he might return to where he feels safest and most in control. Second, he might stay as far away from loved ones as possible to prevent them from being hurt. It depends on the personality of the person in question."

"And since we don't know a lot about Llewellyn's real personality, we're back to the original question," Maggie observed.

"Certainly not back to where he's been living," Rolf said. "By the way, does anyone know where that is?"

"Who do we ask, Inspector McConklin or Tad Collins?" Maggie looked at Flynn. "Any ideas?"

Flynn handed Maggie his cell phone. "Call Collins and find out. He'd surely know. See if they've searched the place, and ask if they've ever had a tail on him or if they thought he was too high up in government to touch until they had some proof he was involved."

"What if none of this matters?" Alyssa asked. "I watched a movie the other night where the explosives were set to go off at a certain time no matter what happened. The only way they could stop the ship from blowing up was to find the bomb and cut the wires, which, of course they did with only two seconds to go."

"True," Maggie said. "Maybe it won't make a difference, but what if it does? What if Llewellyn wants to be in control right up to the final countdown and give the order himself to press the button? Maybe if we could find him, we could prevent a catastrophe tonight."

Flynn pulled off the road and parked at the scenic overlook. Maggie handed the phone back to him. "You can do it, now that your hands are free."

"Do I know what I'm supposed to ask him?" Flynn asked, checking the directory for Tad's number.

"You'll think of something," Maggie said with a smile.

"Collins, this is Flynn Ford. I'm inquiring about Richard Constantine. Did you ever put a man on him to see where he went and what he did, or was he too big a fish to touch?"

"I did put a tail on him, and I'm embarrassed to say that he slipped away unnoticed. I understand that he showed up at the family estate and vanished from there as well," Collins said.

"Unfortunately, that's true. Any possibility you were able to search his home?" Flynn asked.

"Officially, no. We couldn't get a warrant—insufficient evidence to issue one. But unofficially, we heard rumors there was a break-in while he was away. The investigating officer was very surprised to find a woman's bag on his desk. The contents were dumped and strewn about." Collins's voice took on a teasing tone. "I believe it belongs to an American reporter, one Mary Margaret McKenzie. If you happen to run into her, you can tell her I have it in my possession."

Flynn laughed. "That will be about the best news she's had all week. I'll pass it along, but I have another question. What's the status of the world right now? We've been out of touch with the TV and newspapers. Have government leaders given in to the terrorists' demands, or are we still on a countdown to meltdown?"

"Everyone is holding their collective breaths for the next five hours plus. No news yet." Then Tad chuckled. "I heard about your escapade last night, giving Murphy the slip from the Green Dragon Inn. Good work locating the Albright woman and her kids. How did you find out they were there?"

"Miss McKenzie is an investigative reporter. I think she keeps her sources confidential." Flynn smiled at Maggie, who was dying to hear the rest of the conversation.

"Tell her if she doesn't reveal her source this time, we might investigate her for the kidnapping." There was a weighty pause before he added, "I'm kidding, Ford. McConklin told me she figured Llewellyn did it and that he might have taken them to his old stomping grounds, so she went there herself to find them."

Flynn laughed. "Miss McKenzie is a free spirit and thinks better when she's not locked up. In fact, she's thinking right now about where Llewellyn might be. We'll keep in touch in case we find him. Oh, any word on the encryption?"

"She's working on it," Collins said. "I'll let you know when she's through."

"Thanks, Tad. Keep us informed, if you can, on what's happening on all fronts."

Flynn disconnected and reported the conversation.

Maggie was pleased that her bag had been found but couldn't be distracted for long from her current puzzle. "So no one has any idea where he is." Maggie leaned her head back on the seat and pondered the problem.

"They know where he isn't," Alyssa said. "Isn't that helpful?"

Maggie turned around and looked at Alyssa with an *aha* expression. "Yes, it is. Where else do we know that he isn't?"

"Apparently not at his parents' home in Wells," Rolf volunteered. "Inspector McConklin spent most of the morning there."

"Good," said Maggie. "Where else? Keep the ideas coming."

"I'm sure he has an office in London, being in the government, but I think we can be certain he isn't there. The police should be watching that quite closely," Rolf said.

"We don't know that he isn't back at Dragonwyck," Flynn said.

"Right. So if he couldn't go to his home, wherever that is, and he couldn't go to his parents' home, why am I thinking he would go back to Dragonwyck?" Maggie asked. "Convince me that he wouldn't go there now. He even took—or had taken—his kidnap victims there. It's probably been his headquarters for his terrorist cell for at least two years. There are a million—well, a dozen—places he could hide. Tell me why he wouldn't go back there."

"Because the police are all over the place now that you found the tunnels with the munitions in them?" Alyssa asked.

"Because he flew out right after he left Dragonwyck this morning, and he's on his way to Timbuktu where no one will ever think to look for him," Flynn ventured.

"Because his grandmother would be all over him for being such a bad boy," Rolf said.

Everyone laughed, even Maggie. Flynn started the car and turned it around.

Maggie looked at him in surprise. "Where are we going?"

"Back to Dragonwyck, of course," Flynn said with a smile. "That's where this discussion is heading, so we might as well get a head start so we can keep up with that investigative mind of yours."

"So if we really believe that he somehow returned, where is he now?" Maggie mused.

"Hiding in those secret passages Damon showed us this morning?" Alyssa said.

"Did you hear Damon tell me about a couple more that he'd forgotten?" Maggie asked. "I wondered at the time if he'd really forgotten them or if he thought Llewellyn might be using them and didn't want his scoundrel brother to be found."

"Maggie, I can't believe you can think such a thing!" Alyssa exclaimed.

"I don't want to, Lyssa, but I can't rule anything out just yet. You'll have to admit that he never once volunteered any information until he was pressed to do it, and he couldn't very well refuse to help."

"Well, I won't believe that he could be involved with any of this," Alyssa said stubbornly.

Maggie shook her head "I'm not accusing him of being involved. I'm just saying he's not helping a lot when I think he actually could. It's more like he's protecting Llewellyn whenever possible. It's clear Damon has some bad feelings towards him, but Damon also seems to have a strong sense of family."

"So how did Llewellyn get back to Dragonwyck, supposing that's where he's hiding?" Flynn asked. "Inspector McConklin had his men searching the place after we left."

"He *said* he was going to have men there. Actually, he said one. Then I said three, and he agreed. That's way too much acreage and house for three men to cover. It would take a platoon to search and secure." Maggie stopped. "And here again, we're supposing that McConklin is a straight cop and not a crooked one like Murphy. We seem to be running into more than our fair share of the latter this trip."

"I was thinking maybe we should call Inspector McConklin and tell him what you think about Llewellyn returning to Dragonwyck, but after what he said to you at his office, I guess you wouldn't want to do that, would you?" Alyssa said.

"Absolutely not." Maggie looked at Flynn. "Oh, what if he isn't a straight cop and we gave him all that information instead of taking it to Tad Collins? What if he's just burned it and is going to let London be destroyed?"

# THIRTY-EIGHT

Constantine's hideaway
Saturday, 12:30 P.M.

"Edward, do you have the communication lines ready to connect with the heads of state when they call to tell us they're acquiescing to our demands and that the money will be paid?"

"Yes, Mr. Constantine. Everything is ready."

"Are any rumors circulating from Number Ten Downing Street about the prime minister's current state of mind on the situation?"

"No, sir. Every head of state is being very quiet, and none of their offices are issuing statements at this time."

"I think we have them running scared, Edward. Do you have the press releases ready to send out on my untimely demise tomorrow morning? Of course, if we don't get paid, it will get lost in the head-lines screaming how many billions of dollars of damage was done and how many lives were lost in the explosions. Even if the officials hold out until midnight, eventually they'll pay up to make the destruction cease. In the meantime, with our new identities, we'll get lost in our new location and live happily ever after."

"Yes, sir. The press releases are finished. You died in a fiery heli-copter crash just off the coast of England, and eyewitnesses said there were no survivors. Your longtime associate from Scotland Yard was with you. Richard Constantine had no surviving family, and Edward Thompson is survived by an ex-wife or two who will share his estate."

"Nice touch, Edward. Don't forget to leave everything behind. Take nothing with you that you would not have taken on an overnighter into the country. You do have a tendency toward the sentimental at times. Resist it."

"Yes, sir."

"Everything is in place in Paris, New York, and Los Angeles? The cells are all ready?"

"Yes, sir. I've checked with them all within the hour, right down the list. Everything is a go. London has been our only problem."

"Good work. Call me if anything happens."

"Of course, Mr. Constantine."

Llewellyn rang off and paced the small room. He hated small spaces. He kept telling himself it was very temporary, only a few more hours and he'd be a free man. He did have one more thing to do, but he'd have to be very careful doing it. He wondered if the police had tapped his parents' phone when they interrogated them.

If he hadn't been so hasty getting rid of Terrence, this would have been a perfect job for him. No matter. A man with a brain like Richard Constantine wouldn't have a problem with something as simple a finding a safe meeting place to tell his mother good-bye.

* * *

On the road to Dragonwyck
Saturday, 12:35 P.M.

"Maggie, you don't think Llewellyn planted explosives in those tunnels to blow up Dragonwyck, do you?" Rolf asked.

"Oh," Maggie groaned. "I don't want to go there. I can't even think about such a horrible thing." She looked at Flynn. "You don't suppose he would do something like that, do you?

"Sorry. My brain doesn't work like his. I couldn't possibly predict what he would or wouldn't do," Flynn said.

"I hate to mention it," Alyssa said, "but remember when Damon explained about his ring? He said only legitimate heirs of Dragonwyck were allowed to have them. Llewellyn has been disinherited by his grandmother. Maybe he thinks if *he* can't have the estate, no one will."

"Oh, Lyssa. I didn't need to hear that." Maggie leaned back in her seat and closed her eyes. "But you're right. That's always a possibility."

She turned around and looked at her sister. "Do you think we could get our grandparents away from the house this afternoon, just in case?"

"What pretext could we use?" Alyssa asked.

"Why don't you just tell Grandmother Rathford right up front what you're thinking?" Flynn suggested. "You could even ask her for places in the house where Llewellyn could be hiding."

"Do you think she'd tell us?" Maggie looked out the window and watched the scenery speed by for a minute. "Somehow I can't see her taking us through the house and saying, 'He might be in here, or he might be in there.'"

"You could be right," Flynn acknowledged. "Then again, have you thought of how you'll manage to wander unnoticed through the house and look for hidden rooms and passages?"

"Actually, I thought I might take Tara sightseeing to find more dragons and see how many rooms she can count. That would give me an excuse to be in places I might not otherwise manage to get in. I could turn her loose and say she ran ahead of me, which would be the truth, because as soon as you let go of her hand, she runs wherever she's going."

"Speaking of the Albrights—Rolf, what time did Jennie's sister say she'd arrive to get Jennie?" Alyssa asked.

"She estimated about three hours, if she could easily slip away. If not, she wasn't sure when she'd arrive," Rolf said, looking at his watch. "I guess there's a remote possibility she has already come and collected her sister and they're on their way to my house in Blaenavon. I'm sure she wouldn't stick around unnecessarily."

"Let's hope Jennie's sister got hung up somewhere along the way and Tara is still there to be my accomplice," Maggie said.

"On the other hand, if you happened to discover Richard Constantine while you had Tara with you, that might not be the best thing for the child," Flynn pointed out.

"Hmm. You're right," acknowledged Maggie. "I hadn't thought of that. Back to square one. By the way, Flynn, how did your session with Jennie go? Did she have you talk to Tara, too?"

"Tara and I played a couple of games on the floor, and I asked her about what happened. Apparently—and Jennie confirmed this—the couple who took them from Jennie's sister's home was very courteous and kind, very gentle with the children and Jennie. Tara had no idea they were 'bad guys,' and Jennie played along so the child wouldn't be traumatized. Tara thought it was some kind of game they played in England, a version of blindman's buff. The kidnappers even fixed a candlelight dinner in the cave and made sure they were comfortable before they left them there," Flynn explained.

"What kind of game is it when you chain someone to the wall?" Maggie asked indignantly.

"Jennie asked them to not let Tara see the chains, and apparently in the dim candlelight Tara didn't see them. When I asked Tara how to play the game, the child never mentioned chains. It was at night, and the windows were darkened on the car, so they couldn't see where they were going. The kidnappers gave Tara goodies to eat in the car, and a flashlight to read her storybooks. Tara fell asleep on the drive there, so apparently it was relatively painless for her. She fell right back to sleep when they got to the cave, and because of jet lag she slept most of the day yesterday as well."

"Llewellyn, a.k.a. Richard, gets a point for that. He just came up a notch in my estimation. But it wouldn't have been painless for Jennie. Not for a minute. She was a nervous wreck in the airport trying to take care of her children in a different environment from home. I can't imagine what she must have been going through, not knowing why they'd been taken or what was going to happen to her babies and her." Maggie slammed the door with her fist. "He's no better than his evil father. We've got to find him and put a stop to his madness."

"Did you forget about the dungeon?" Flynn asked. "Maybe he's holed up in there."

"Brilliant, Dr. Ford. Yes, I had completely forgotten about it, and Damon didn't even mention it during our tour. There has to be an entrance from inside the house. I wonder where it is," Maggie mused.

Alyssa leaned forward. "Dungeon? How do you know about a dungeon at Dragonwyck?"

Maggie explained their early morning meeting with Grandfather Rathford and how he had taken them around the house to the sealed exterior entrance to the dungeon. "Obviously, no one had been using that entrance."

"You're thinking there's a connection between the tunnel and the dungeon?" Rolf asked.

"Oh, speaking of connections," Maggie said, twisting in her seat to face Rolf and Alyssa. "Damon told me while we were on the tour this morning that there was a spiral staircase that connected the third floor with the tunnel. If it connected with the tunnel, might there also be a connection to the dungeon, or at least access to it from the staircase?"

"It sounds like we have a lot of exploring to do. And not a lot of time to do it," Flynn said, looking at his watch. "Just over five hours."

"Do you suppose any of the explosives have been located in the target cities?" Rolf asked. "If the local police and whatever other agencies are involved could capture the explosives, their cities might be saved without having to pay the ransom."

"Unfortunately, if you'll remember, Daisy Cutter bombs were used in the first four instances, which were all delivered from the air. Even if every country's air force were involved, flying protection over those target cities, at least one—or more—planes are likely to get through. If the planes took off from small private air fields near the city, they could fly in under radar and drop their bombs, even if all legal air traffic had been grounded." Flynn shook his head. "As much as we hope these cities are able to protect themselves and stop the explosions, I don't see it happening, and certainly not in every case."

No one spoke for several miles. As they approached the border between England and Wales, Rolf smiled. "For those not of Welsh extraction, I should let you know that being English is a step down, although being English is definitely a step above other nationalities. Such is Welsh national pride." He laughed. "That was my grandfather's philosophy. He told me once that to be a coal miner in Wales was better than being a king in England."

"Did he tell you why?" Flynn asked.

"If you were a coal miner in Wales, you were a free man. If you were a king in England, everyone wanted your throne, and you needed sons to replace you instead of happily enjoying your daughters."

"Sound like a good philosophy to me." Flynn laughed. "Actually, my heritage is Scots-Irish, so maybe I'm a step above some of those other nationalities, but unfortunately not Welsh."

"King Arthur was born in Wales, wasn't he?" Maggie asked. "Down in Tintagel?"

"Legend says that's where he was conceived," Rolf said. "Legend also says that when the British Isles are in the most danger, Arthur will return to save them. Everyone thought he'd appear during World War II during the Nazi bombing, but no one ever saw him."

"And you survived without him," Flynn commented.

"Maybe this is the catastrophe that will bring him back," Rolf said, clearly only half kidding.

Flynn looked at Maggie. "You're awfully quiet. What are you plotting now?"

# THIRTY-NINE

"What do we do if we get back to Dragonwyck and McConklin's men won't let us in the house?" Maggie asked. "Assuming, of course, that McConklin actually did send them there."

"They couldn't keep us out, could they?" Alyssa asked. "We're simply visiting our grandparents before we return to California."

"Good girl," Maggie said. "That's the perfect excuse to get in the house."

"What's your plan once we're admitted?" Flynn asked. "Do we boldly announce to your grandparents that we're going to search the house for their wayward grandson and capture him before he can blow up the world?"

Maggie pondered that for a minute. "I've been thinking about that, and I can't come up with anything that sounds plausible. I considered telling Grandmother I wanted to do a photo layout of the house for my articles, or a future one, but when we were here before, she kept insisting on getting only the truth, so I think that may be our best angle."

"She did say there isn't much she doesn't know about her grandsons," Alyssa agreed. "But I don't think she knew that he was involved in kidnapping, attempted murder, and planning to destroy the world's beautiful cities."

"If you'll drop Alyssa and me at the police station, we'll bring Maggie's car back to Dragonwyck," Rolf said as they approached the street where the station was located.

"Good idea," Alyssa said. "Maggie, as you suggested, we didn't check out of the Crown, but we did bring all of our belongings, just in case we needed something. Our suitcases are in the trunk of your rental car."

"That was thoughtful of you. I guess I might as well call the Crown and check out, since I have no idea if or when we'll get back there. Did you get everything?"

"Every last item, sis," Alyssa said. "I was taking care of you for a change instead of you always taking care of me."

"Thanks," Maggie said, grateful for Alyssa's foresight. "Now at least I'll have a change of clothes, even if I don't have my bag. Wonder when I'm ever going to see my stuff again."

Rolf and Alyssa got the rental car and followed Flynn and Maggie the few miles to Dragonwyck. Maggie kept silent all the way and was grateful that Flynn seemed to sense her need to be alone with her thoughts.

Maggie was praying for the power of discernment at that moment. She needed to know whether or not she could trust Damon. Was he involved with Llewellyn, or did he actually have the best interests of Dragonwyck and his family at heart? Maggie had to know, and this was the only tried-and-true method she knew of finding out.

As Flynn approached the big wrought-iron gates with the Rathford dragon emblazoned across the front, Maggie got out and swung open one gate. Flynn drove through with Rolf right behind him. When Maggie had shut the gate and reentered the car, Flynn drove slowly up the curved driveway.

"Are you ready?" he asked, looking at Maggie.

She took a deep breath. "Ready," she said, squaring her shoulders. "I'll ask Grandmother first if she knows anyplace where Llewellyn could be hiding in the house. If she's cooperative, we'll have her show us. Then I'll ask if we can search the spiral staircase and the secret passageways Damon told us about this morning. If she's not going to cooperate, do you think a phone call to Tad Collins might work in our favor?"

"Possibly," Flynn said. "What if McConklin is here? Maybe he had the same idea and is searching right now."

"If he is, he left his car somewhere else. There are no cars in the driveway," Maggie noted with relief as they neared the front of the house. She didn't want to have to fight that battle again.

They approached the door, and Maggie grabbed the tail of the golden dragon, pounding it against the worn plate. Arthur appeared more quickly than Maggie had expected.

"We'd like to see Grandmother again, if we may, Arthur," Maggie said.

He swung the door open and moved aside so they could enter. "I believe Mr. and Mrs. Rathford have been expecting you. They're waiting in the library."

Maggie and Alyssa looked at each other and then at Flynn and Rolf. Wordlessly they followed Arthur to the library. When the butler opened the door, Maggie could see that not only her grandparents were here, but Damon and his parents were present also.

Damon jumped to his feet. "Inspector McConklin said you would probably return. We've been waiting for you."

Maggie felt wary. "And what did he say we would be coming back for?"

Grandmother Rathford spoke from her chair by the fire. "He said you would be looking for Llewellyn—that you probably thought he would be hiding here."

"Which means that the good inspector is sure that Llewellyn's not here, or he would never turn you loose on the estate to look for him," Flynn said quietly. Maggie nodded in agreement.

"We called our children home to have them close, no matter what happens tonight," Grandmother Rathford explained.

Feeling very awkward, Maggie crossed the room to Mrs. Rathford's chair. "I'm so sorry I had to break my promise and share the information in your note. When I discovered Llewellyn was involved in the kidnapping of Jennie Albright and possibly planning a bombing as well, we had to learn the contents of the letter."

Mrs. Rathford shook her head. "No, Maggie. It's all right. I should have had the courage to call the police myself when I overheard Llewellyn's conversation on the phone. I wasn't in the room, but he raised his voice and I heard him telling someone where the explosives were to be placed. He sounded angry that the person had called him, but I guess he had to make a decision at that moment." She sighed. "I knew Llewellyn had some problems, but I had convinced myself that he would grow out of them. Now I've realized it was only a matter of time before he self-destructed."

"I'm sure this is very hard for you, Mrs. Rathford. Hopefully we can find your son and get him the help he needs," Maggie said, then looked at the group. "So, do we think he may be here somewhere?"

"No," Damon said. "I can't imagine he would be so stupid as to return here with the police all over the place. They've barely left. But I'll help you search if you want. Father's not well enough, but Arthur could go with one of you, and we could split up to cover more ground."

"Thank you, Damon." Maggie turned to her grandfather. "Do you feel up to another ride this afternoon? I wonder if you and Alyssa would like to take Flynn and ride the perimeter of the estate. Check places that you have not been recently. See if you can find out how Llewellyn can come and go so invisibly. Is there a road at the back of the estate he could use? A trail he could take without being seen?"

Grandfather Rathford put his arms out to Alyssa. "I think Maggie forgot we haven't met." He wrapped Alyssa in a bear hug and kissed her forehead. "Welcome to Dragonwyck, my other redheaded grand-daughter. Do we have another young horsewoman here?"

Alyssa stood on her toes and kissed the old man's cheek. "Yes. I'd love to ride with you, Grandfather."

"You three have a cell phone in your group, and Rolf, you have one. Will you go with Arthur and have him show you the servants' wing and anything the two of you can think of that might become a hiding place? Arthur might remember places the boys hid as children, or places where other children have hidden. I would think he should know them all." Maggie glanced at Arthur standing near the door. He nodded.

"And you're going to the dungeon and the spiral staircase with Damon," Flynn said to Maggie.

She smiled, feeling a new confidence in Damon's allegiance since her prayer. "Yes, and any other place Damon forgot to show us this morning where . . . Richard Constantine might have hidden himself." She glanced at Llewellyn's mother and acknowledged the *thank you* the woman mouthed silently. It would be Constantine they pursued from now on. Everyone in the room caught the subtle suggestion.

"Damon, do you have your cell phone with you?" Maggie asked. "We need to be in contact if we find something." Maggie glanced at her watch, then up at the group. "It's one o'clock. If you can't be back here by three o'clock, call and let me know so I won't worry about you."

"I have my cell phone," Damon said and moved his hand to a bulge in his jacket pocket. Maggie looked at him in surprise—that wasn't just a cell phone. He nodded slightly. He was armed.

Arthur waited at the door for Rolf, and they started down the hall. Maggie and Damon followed. "Be careful," Damon cautioned. "Constantine's probably very dangerous at this point."

Arthur pulled a small pistol from his pocket and smiled at Maggie. "I'm a pretty fair shot. I keep grouse and quail on the table for dinner every week."

Maggie looked up at Damon and smiled. "Who'd have thought!"

Flynn and Alyssa accompanied Grandfather Rathford to the front door. "Please be very careful," Maggie said. "You'll be out in the open—sitting targets on those horses."

Flynn retraced his steps and took Maggie in his arms. "Just in case," he whispered and kissed her. He looked into her eyes and admonished, "You be careful yourself. I have something to say to you when this is over." He looked at Damon. "Don't let her do anything rash, okay?"

Grandfather Rathford stopped at the large, ornate hat rack that stood behind the door. He bent over and opened a small drawer in the bottom, moving aside brushes and shoe polish until he found what he was looking for. He pulled out a gun and handed it to Flynn. "Can you use this, son?" he asked.

Flynn nodded. "I can if I have to."

"I have one in my saddlebag," the older man said. "We won't be entirely at the mercy of . . ." He paused, unable to continue.

"At the mercy of Richard Constantine or his men," Alyssa finished for him.

Grandfather Rathford put his arm around his granddaughter and kissed her cheek. "Yes, of Richard Constantine." His voice cracked as he said it.

As Grandfather Rathford led the way through the front door to the stables, Maggie held up her finger. "Can you wait one minute, Damon? I'd like to ask your father one question."

Maggie hurried back into the library and knelt beside the chair of Mr. Rathford. "Sir, can you remember any place specifically you and your brother hid from each other, or places your sons loved to play or to hide from you when they visited here, someplace you haven't thought of for a long time—somewhere in the house where no one ever goes now?"

Mr. Rathford shook his head. "No, I'm sorry. But I'm sure Damon can show you all the places they used to go."

"Thank you," Maggie said quietly and hurried to join Damon, who had come to the door to watch Maggie and his father.

"He's dying, Maggie," Damon said so softly Maggie strained to hear. "He hasn't said as much, but I can see it in his eyes. He might have fought against it, if this thing with Llewellyn hadn't come up right now, but he's tired of fighting to protect the family against Llewellyn's bad judgment. He's tired of trying to preserve the Rathford name and reputation against all the insane things Llewellyn has done."

"There isn't anything you or the doctors can do?" Maggie asked as they climbed the stairs.

"The only thing that will save him is if Llewellyn quietly goes away and is never heard from again—if there's no scandal involving the Rathford name. But it doesn't look like that's going to happen, does it?" Damon fell silent, and Maggie could see tears glistening in his eyes.

"There's always the possibility that Richard Constantine can take the blame and that the Rathford name won't surface," Maggie said hopefully.

Damon shook his head. "Not with today's journalists—no offense. Even if British intelligence didn't release all the information, the paparazzi would never let it die until they'd drained the well dry and discovered every single tidbit of information on Constantine. Llewellyn could never have covered his tracks so carefully as to not have left any clue to his true origins."

"Where are we going first?" Maggie asked. She hadn't been paying attention to where Damon led her and didn't recognize the hallway they'd turned into.

"The nursery," Damon explained. "There was a secret passageway so the nurse could whisk the children away in case of danger. We used to play in it all the time."

"Speaking of the nursery, are Jennie and her children still here?" Maggie asked.

"No, her sister came about half an hour ago, and they left for Blaenavon," Damon said. "That was rather nice of Rolf to offer his parents' home as a sanctuary."

"Rolf's a rather nice guy," Maggie said.

"I'm ashamed I treated him the way I did when we met at the railway in Bath. I didn't want to share my newly discovered sisters with a stranger, but that's no excuse for my bad manners. Grandmother would have been appalled and reprimanded me severely."

"Your grandmother seems to be a driving force in your life," Maggie observed as they entered the nursery. She stopped short. It was exactly as she'd pictured it would be after reading all those British novels when she was younger.

A wooden rocking horse with faded paint stood in one corner. A set of building blocks tumbled nearby, and storybooks were scattered in front of a shelf filled with other colorful books. A small crib stood next to a twin-size bed covered with a handmade quilt. On the other side of the nanny's bed stood a toddler's bed with railings and rumpled covers, attesting to the recent occupation by Tara.

"Here, help me move the crib," Damon said. "It's behind that."

"I hope you remembered to bring a flashlight," Maggie said.

"I did. Needless to say, there are no lights in any of the passageways. Grandfather wanted to discourage us from using them. We usually just left flashlights inside each door so that one would be readily available if we ever dodged inside without a previous plan."

Maggie watched as Damon pressed a point in the paneling that was about shoulder height to her. He entered the opening and turned on his bright light. Maggie followed him through the door and stayed at his heels as he led her through the narrow, dark, musty passage.

"Damon," Maggie whispered. "If Llewellyn is here at Dragonwyck, where do you think he would hide?"

"I really don't think he'd come back here, Maggie," Damon said, keeping his voice low. "What would bring him back?"

"That's what we've got to figure out, because I really believe he's here, or will be, if he's not now. I know it sounds crazy, but I believe he'd want to be here tonight."

"Doing what?" Damon asked so quietly Maggie almost had to guess at what he said.

Maggie tugged on Damon's shirt, and he stopped. "I'll tell you how I envision him right now," she whispered. "He's in a little room somewhere filled with electronic equipment and telephones, and he's directing this terrorist plot from there. He has his finger on every city where explosives are set to go off tonight. He's calling the shots from Dragonwyck." Maggie shrugged. "At least that's how I imagine it."

Damon smiled. "Oh, little sister, you do have a great imagination. There is no such place here. First of all, it would require a great deal of electricity to do that, and I help Grandmother with the bills. There has been no increase in the electrical bill for years."

"I think Llewellyn has been using Dragonwyck as a headquarters for at least two years—maybe more."

"I'm sure I would have noticed a significant increase in electrical usage." Damon turned and continued to the end of the passageway. "There are entrances to this passageway from almost every room that backs on it. It leads to the spiral staircase and down to the basement, where it connects to the tunnel.

"Why didn't you tell me about it this morning, Damon?" Maggie asked as they reached the staircase. "We might have been able to catch him somewhere in the house hours ago."

Damon whirled from the top step and shined the light in Maggie's eyes. "I simply forgot about it," he snapped. "I was so stunned to find police at Dragonwyck, I didn't remember all the intricate little ways Llewellyn could have wound his way through the house."

He'd ceased whispering, and his voice carried down the staircase. Maggie retreated a couple of steps and for a minute considered turning and fleeing back where they'd just come from.

Damon reached out his hand to her. "Maggie, I'm sorry I frightened you. I didn't mean to. I'm just bewildered by the magnitude of this whole business. I'm afraid Father won't be able to stand it, and if he goes, I fear Grandmother will follow quickly. This will destroy the Rathfords."

"It's okay, Damon. I can't imagine how hard this must be for all of you." Maggie stepped toward the stairs and stopped.

"Did you hear that?" she whispered.

"What?"

"I heard something directly above us. Shine your light up there."

"Probably just a bird. This is the third floor—that's as high as it goes in this part of the house." But he shined the light up to show Maggie.

The spiral stairs continued up to the ceiling and dead-ended at a trapdoor. Maggie shivered. Was Damon trying to conceal something? Was he protecting Llewellyn?

# FORTY

"Where does that trapdoor lead?" Maggie whispered.

"To the roof. That's the access to make repairs so the roof doesn't leak."

"Can we go up there?" Maggie asked.

"No," Damon said, his tone quite definite. "You can see it is nailed shut. Even as older boys we were never allowed to go up there. The roof becomes quite steep, and over the years a couple of repairmen have fallen to their deaths. Do you want to see the dungeon?"

Maggie nodded and followed Damon as quietly as possible down the spiral staircase. It was tight and narrow, with each step barely wide enough for one foot. She wondered how Damon managed. Just putting his heel on the steps, she guessed. She silently berated herself for doubting her brother again. After all, the warm feeling she'd gotten after praying to know whether to trust him was from a source far more enlightened than herself.

As they reached each floor, Damon pointed out where in the house they currently were. Maggie was astonished at the narrow passageways on each floor that led to this tight little circle of escape. Wherever you were in the house, you wouldn't have been that far from an escape route, she thought. Was that how Llewellyn had eluded them today?

Again Maggie felt the certainty that Llewellyn was in this house. She could almost feel him laughing at her. She imagined the taunting echo as her footsteps descended lower and lower into the darkness. *You can't catch me! You can't catch me!*

When they finally reached the bottom of the stairs, Maggie was so relieved she could have cried out with joy. Her imagination was taking over her good sense. She pictured tiny security cameras and microphones following their movements through the monstrous house. She imagined Llewellyn plotting his revenge for her interference with his plans and bringing the police to Dragonwyck.

"Maggie, are you okay?" Damon whispered. "You're breathing funny."

"I'm probably hyperventilating," she whispered back. "Those stairs are killers. Where are we?"

Damon had led her down another narrow corridor. "We're just under the kitchen. There's a trapdoor that leads down here. Now we can take another little branch of passageway that probably hasn't been used since Llewellyn and I were little. I'm afraid it may be filled with spiderwebs and all kinds of creepy crawly things. Are you still game?"

"As long as you go first," Maggie said with a shudder. "It leads us to the dungeon?"

"Yes," Damon said. "There are three entrances. One from the outside—which I understand Grandfather showed you this morning—one from directly under the staircase in the grand hall, and this one."

"Why so many?"

"I take it the menfolk didn't want their dainty ladies to know who inhabited the nether regions of the castle, so they gave themselves the option of bringing prisoners in from the outside or in through the front door and directly down to the dungeon if no one was looking. I believe this way was for the cook to feed them."

They progressed slowly through the narrow passageway, but Maggie didn't see Damon swiping at any cobwebs. It looked pretty clean to her, meaning that someone had used this tunnel recently, maybe often. Maggie even envisioned Grace and her feather duster down here, sweeping away the cobwebs and dust.

Suddenly they came to a dead end in the passageway. Damon shined the light back and forth across the door and felt along its edges.

"Problem?" Maggie whispered.

"I've forgotten where the latch is," he said quietly.

The thought came unbidden to Maggie's mind. *Or you don't want to take me to the dungeon.*

Vanquishing the unwelcome thought, she whispered, "Maybe you just have to push it."

"They don't usually work that way," Damon said, but he gave the door a shove anyway. It slowly creaked open a couple of inches.

"Of course! The pressure where I was standing on the floorboards released the catch," he said quietly and led the way down the ancient stone stairs to a place that was damper and mustier than anywhere Maggie had ever been. Even the smell seemed primeval.

"How deep underground are we?" Maggie whispered. The tiny noise echoed off the metal doors in front of them.

"At least two stories. You can scream at the top of your lungs and no one in the house can ever hear you. I know. I screamed for help when Llewellyn locked me down here, and I'd have spent the night alone if Grandmother hadn't threatened him within an inch of his life if he didn't have me in front of her in five minutes."

"Thank heaven for your grandmother. I can't imagine being locked down here alone." *But you might be if Damon decides to leave you here.* Again an unbidden, unwelcome thought crept into her head, sending a shudder down her spine. She reminded herself that it wasn't Damon who had sent someone to stalk and possibly even kill her—it was Llewellyn.

Damon explored the room with the light, stopping in front of each of the half dozen stone cells with metal bars, just like she'd seen in the movies. But these cells were tiny, no more than six feet in any direction.

"Where's the entrance from the outside?" Maggie whispered.

"Over this way, I think," Damon said, taking a step away from Maggie. She quickly caught up to him, almost bumping into him when he stopped in front of two huge wooden doors. They had a beam spanning across them that was big enough to hold up a barn. No one would break through that to rescue prisoners held down here.

"As you can see, there's nothing here. No one has been here for probably twenty years. I think I was five or six years old when Llewellyn locked me in, and Grandmother made this place off limits from that time forward. Grandfather had the outside piled high with boulders too big to move, and I don't remember what they did to keep us out of the other two entrances, but I've never been back since that awful night."

"Then this can't be giving you happy feelings. Let's get out of here. It gives me the creeps. I'm beginning to imagine skeletons in every cell, and they're starting to move toward me."

Damon chuckled. "Maggie, you have the most fertile imagination of anyone I've ever met." But he didn't tarry. They quickly returned to the heavy wooden door, and Damon pulled at the huge iron ring in the center of it. The door didn't budge.

"Here, hold the light and let me get a little leverage," Damon said.

Maggie held the light and shined it on the rusted ring. When it didn't even creak at Damon's tugging, Maggie put down the light and tried to help him. When they'd expended all their effort without any progress, Maggie was near tears. *Don't panic,* she told herself. *Everyone knows we were going to the dungeon. When we don't return, they'll come looking for us.* But she wasn't going to sit around waiting to be rescued.

"Damon, where's the third entrance into the dungeon—the one from the grand hall?" She sounded more frantic than she'd intended.

"Right." He picked up the light and shined it around the stones, looking for another wooden door. "It's got to be here somewhere." His voice now carried a tinge of panic.

Maggie closed her eyes and said a prayer comprising only seven words: *Father, get us out of here quick.* She was so desperate, she forgot to say please. Both she and Damon couldn't panic—someone had to retain a level head. She breathed deeply, got herself under control, and went back to the big wooden door with the ring in the center.

"If this were a Chinese puzzle, force would only make it more secure," she said, more to herself than to Damon.

"What are you talking about, Maggie?" Damon came to watch her.

"If prisoners managed to get loose and were trying to get into the house, how would they do it?"

Damon shrugged. "Probably the same way we did—brute force."

"Exactly. And that didn't work. What if someone wanted to open the door, but didn't want any prisoners to see what they were doing—how would they accomplish that?"

"I'm not following your train of thought."

"Shine the light on the ring," Maggie said.

Damon moved to the bottom step and shined the light on the huge, rusted ring. Maggie moved up five steps so the ring was directly in front of her and, with both hands, turned the ring a quarter turn to the left. She gave a tug and the door opened an inch. Damon put his fingers in the crack and pulled it open wide enough for them to get through.

"Little sister, how did you do that?"

"I pictured the cook or a maid being sent down to feed the prisoners, or even one of the young boys who helped in the kitchen fetching wood. They wouldn't have had the strength to pull that door open. With a Chinese puzzle, the stronger you pull, the tighter the puzzle becomes. There had to be a trick to unlatch the door that a small person could handle."

"But you just walked up to it and opened it," Damon said. "You didn't even finagle it."

"Have you heard the saying, 'Right tight, left loose'?"

"Yes, I was raised with it. Oh, I see. If you had twisted the ring to the right, it would have remained locked, as in tight, but when you twisted left, it opened. How did you ever figure that out?"

Maggie laughed. "I read a lot of Gothic novels as a teenager. I put myself in the place of the heroine so often my mother was worried for my sanity. I was always imagining scenarios where I'd be trapped and have to escape because the hero was fighting the villain and couldn't get to me." Then she added softly, "I also had a little heavenly help."

"Hurrah for both your literary choices and your guardian angel. I'm more than happy to be out of there," Damon said, his voice filled with relief. "Can we go get some sunshine before we delve into any more of your searches?"

"By all means," Maggie said. "I'm definitely ready for some fresh air. I'll bet some of that air in the dungeon has been trapped there for centuries. Do we have to go all the way back up to the nursery, or is there a shorter route to the library?"

"We can intercept the tunnel in the great hall," Damon said, obviously equally ready for fresh air and a change of scenery that held happier memories for him.

He led the way back through the narrow passageway to the corner. As Maggie followed him, she remembered to silently say thank you for the quick answer to her prayer—another of those little miracles she'd thought about when Grandmother Rathford asked her if she believed in them. Most assuredly.

They stopped at the corner, but instead of turning left and continuing in the corridor, Damon ran his hands along the panel and the wall sprang open. "Be careful. This opens directly down into the tunnel. We have to descend a few steps, shut this door, then open the panel into the great hall."

"Damon, could Llewellyn have done that this morning when he disappeared?" Maggie asked.

"He could have, but I imagine he went directly down into the tunnel so he could get away. Here's the latch. Can you see how to open the panel?"

Maggie watched as Damon shined the light on what appeared to be a wooden plug, the kind used anciently in construction instead of nails. He pressed it, keeping well back on the fourth stair down so the door could swing open. They hastily exited from the darkness into the great hall, and Maggie went straight to the front door and threw it open.

She breathed deeply of the fresh air before noting with alarm how dark the sky had become. She glanced at her watch. It seemed they'd been down in the damp, musty dungeon for hours, but it was only two o'clock.

Two o'clock. She groaned inwardly. Only four hours left to find and stop Llewellyn. *Constantine,* she corrected. Alyssa's voice came into her mind. *Maybe the explosives have been set to go off at a certain time all by themselves.* Maggie prayed that wasn't so and that they would be able to stop the madness before it was too late.

# FORTY-ONE

Damon joined Maggie on the front step. "I just checked on Father. I'm worried. I'm afraid I may have to take him back to the hospital."

"Oh, Damon, I'm sorry," Maggie said, putting her hand on Damon's arm. "Is there anything I can do?"

"If he consents to going back to the hospital, will you just look in on Mother and Grandmother occasionally? This will be extremely hard on them."

"Just in case you have to leave, is there a television in the house so we can see what's happening in the world about six o'clock?"

"Of course." He smiled. "We really do live in the twenty-first century, in spite of dungeons and secret passageways and all our Gothic trappings. It's in the library in the tall cherry wood cabinet. I'm going to confer with Grandmother for a few minutes, and then I'll let you know what we're going to do."

"Damon, while you're doing that, can I borrow your cell phone? I want to contact Flynn and see if they've found anything."

As Damon removed the phone from his pocket, it rang. Damon glanced at it and handed it to Maggie. "It's Flynn. You two must be on the same wavelength."

Maggie grabbed the phone. "Flynn, where are you? Have you found anything?"

"I'm beginning to get on board with your hypothesis that Llewellyn may be here. We've discovered an area where someone has landed a helicopter and parked it. Either Llewellyn's an incredible pilot or he has one with him. He's using a deep ravine that looks just wide enough to set down a small chopper in the center of it. Then it appears that he rides a bicycle or scooter to the trees and enters the house through the tunnel."

"Good job," she praised. "Are you on your way back to the house?"

"Yes, we just spotted those black clouds moving in. We're racing to beat the rain. Looks like we're in for a Texas downpour."

"Um, you do realize we're in England, right?" Maggie joked.

Flynn laughed. "Sure, but all the same, I think it's going to rain buckets and barrels instead of little ol' raindrops. See you in a few minutes."

They disconnected and Maggie punched in Rolf's cell phone number and waited for him to answer.

"Rolf here."

"Have you found anything?" Maggie asked.

"I would never have thought searching for a terrorist could be so much fun," Rolf exclaimed. "Maggie, this place is wonderful."

"I know," agreed Maggie. "You should see the dungeon and spiral staircase. But have you found anything?"

"Nothing concrete, but I've learned enough about the house that I think we need to see a blueprint of the floor plan, if they have one. Otherwise, someone familiar with the house needs to draw a sketch. And you need to come to the third floor, to the hall where the servants' wing begins," Rolf said.

"I'm on my way as we speak." Maggie headed for the stairs and waved for Damon to follow. "What am I looking for?"

"I'll show you when you get here." Rolf clicked off.

"Where are we going?" Damon said, sprinting up the stairs after Maggie.

"Rolf said to come to the third floor corridor, where the servants' wing begins."

"Did Rolf and Arthur find something?" Damon said, catching up to Maggie at the second-floor landing.

"He didn't say. Damon, do you know if a complete set of floor plans exists for Dragonwyck?"

"Yes, they're in the library; well, actually in the library tower."

"Library tower? What's that?"

"Exactly what it sounds like," Damon explained. "Some ancestor a couple of centuries back had a fondness for turrets and towers and built four of them, two on each end of the house. One is off the library and contains an incredible collection of manuscripts and books. The second on that side of the house is just off Grandmother's sitting room. I believe that one was used primarily as guest quarters for visiting family when they had come from some distance and stayed for several months at a time."

"What's in the other towers?" Maggie asked, quite out of breath as they reached the third-floor landing.

"The front one—the third tower—connects to the conservatory off the ballroom. It was reserved for the entourage of visiting royalty. Apparently the particular ancestor that built this tower had an in with the current king, who spent a good deal of time here, so he had his own quarters, which were in the fourth tower. That one is the highest and has the fancy battlements."

"How many rooms do those towers contain?" Maggie asked. "Royalty could bring an entourage of a hundred people with them, according to the books I read."

"Oh yes, though not everyone would stay in the towers, then. If they put two people in a bedroom, the entire house could sleep about two hundred people. But they turned one whole wing into servants' quarters about a century ago, and some of the rooms have been remodeled to be bedrooms and sitting rooms, so I think Grandmother could only comfortably sleep seventy or eighty, supposing there were two people in a room."

"You mean there are forty bedrooms?" Maggie was incredulous.

"Don't hold me to that, but there are two floors with at least ten bedrooms each, plus the rooms in the towers. That should come close to forty, I'd think. I haven't counted them for years, if in fact I ever did."

They could see Rolf waiting at the end of the corridor, and they hurried toward him.

"I suppose when you're raised with something like this, it's rather easy to take it for granted and not pay particular attention to little details like how many rooms there are on each floor. At least, for a man—I'm sure a woman would know exactly how many."

Damon laughed. "You're right. Grandmother can tell you the number exactly, as well as which rooms are which color and whether a certain room would be better for a male guest or a female guest."

Rolf wasted no time with preliminaries. He pulled Maggie down the hall to the first window. It overlooked the stables and gardens. Part of the view was blocked by the massive tower that rose from the ground and continued at least two more stories higher than where they stood.

"Arthur said that's the king's tower," Rolf said. "Can we go in it, Damon? Arthur said the servants think it's haunted and no one will go near it."

Maggie unlatched the mullioned window, pushed it open, and stuck her head out to get a better look. The wind tore at her hair, and rain spattered her face. She quickly drew back and pulled the window closed.

"Oh, it's ugly out there. I hope Grandfather, Flynn, and Alyssa beat the storm." She wiped the rain from her face as thunder shook the house and lightning lit up the corridor where they stood. The lights flickered and went out.

Arthur tottered from a room down the hall with additional flashlights. "This looks like a major storm. Power may not be restored until morning."

Rolf laughed as he turned on his flashlight. "I imagine this is a scene right out of a novel, Maggie. But I still want to investigate that tower. Can we go in, Damon? Arthur said the doors are locked and it's not used anymore."

Damon hesitated. "I don't have keys. Grandmother would have to tell us where she keeps them. Do you think it's a good idea to start an endeavor like that in this storm? It would be much better with electrical power."

"Actually, Damon, I believe your grandmother had the power disconnected from the king's tower some years ago," Arthur said. "When the maids refused to go in there after that unfortunate accident, she decided to just close it up."

"Accident?" Maggie prompted.

Arthur suddenly seemed to discover that he had duties elsewhere and excused himself. Maggie turned to Damon.

"It was an accident I'd rather not talk about, Maggie. It brings back painful memories. Can we go back now? I need to talk to Grandmother about returning Father to the hospital," Damon said.

Maggie looked again at the tower, but with rain streaking the diamond-shaped windowpanes, she could see nothing. "We might as well go see whether the others got drenched or beat the storm."

\* \* \*

Constantine's hideaway
Saturday, 2:15 P.M.

"Edward, weather has compromised our plan. We'll need to devise a backup."

"Sir?"

"I don't know what the weather is doing in London, but we're experiencing a deluge here. We couldn't possibly land the helicopter in this wind and rain, and the ravine will be a raging torrent in a couple of hours—totally unusable for anything but an ark."

"What do you suggest, sir?"

"Commandeer a navy chopper, a big one. I've just received information that one of the terrorist cells involved in this holocaust is in Ireland. You're going to pick me up on the coast where my small helicopter has been grounded by the storm, and we'll proceed up the coast of Wales under cover of the storm to St. David's Head, then cross the St. George Channel to Loch Garman."

"Just a minute, Mr. Constantine. I'm getting all this down." Edward paused briefly. "Very good, sir. And what shall I tell them when they ask why you must accompany the squad of military they will want to send?"

"Tell them that my informant will take only me to his hideout, but we want the military to go with us to take over quietly when the hideout is revealed."

"Good, sir. I think they'll go for that. I'm sure just about everyone is looking for an excuse to get out of London tonight."

"We've experienced a power failure here, but with the backup generators, I believe I have enough power to get through until about nine o'clock. Paris goes at six o'clock, London at seven o'clock, and I'm sure the American president will submit to our demands before New York is scheduled to destruct at eight o'clock—definitely before they lose Los Angeles at nine o'clock."

"By then, the money will be in your Swiss bank account, Mr. Constantine, and we'll be safely away."

"Get on those arrangements immediately. It may take a few hours to get through channels to obtain the helicopter, after which the crew will have to be scrambled together. Don't take no for an answer if anyone refuses. You can be very creative, Edward. Use bribery or threats, promise favors—whatever it takes—but get that helicopter secured for a night sortie to Ireland. I'll be waiting at the dock in Cardiff at ten o'clock at the heliport. Be there."

"Yes, sir, Mr. Constantine. You know you can count on me."

They disconnected.

"Yes, I know I can always count on you, Edward," Richard Constantine said aloud. "That's why I'll miss you so much when you don't return from this sortie tonight—you and the unfortunate crew chosen to protect queen and country from those nasty terrorists."

# FORTY-TWO

Dragonwyck
Saturday, 2:20 P.M.

Maggie looked at her watch as she raced down the two flights of stairs with Rolf and Damon at her heels. Two twenty. The minutes were slipping away, and she didn't feel any closer to finding Llewellyn than she had two hours ago.

"Damon," she said over her shoulder, "is the library tower locked, or can we access it right now to see the floor plans of the house?"

"It's open. That's where Grandmother keeps the books—everything pertaining to Dragonwyck. She's in there at least once a day for something."

"Good. First I want to see the floor plans, then I'd like you to check the electrical bills for the last three years, or give them to Rolf so he can go over them."

"You really believe Llewellyn—"

Maggie cut him off. "I really believe Richard Constantine has been using Dragonwyck as a base for his terrorist activities for at least two years, possibly longer. He would need electricity. If he didn't tie into the house power, then he ran a line from somewhere else." Maggie stopped at the foot of the stairs and turned to him. "Do you know what we found in the tunnel?"

Damon shook his head.

"There was one room totally filled with explosives and detailed plans that pinpointed places to plant them all over London. I photographed them, page by page, and took them to the police a couple of hours ago.

This is not my wild imagination, Damon. Richard Constantine is the head of a cell of terrorists that for two years has planned this devastation of the world. It is documented."

"I'm sorry, Maggie. I know he's a miscreant, but—"

"Llewellyn is utterly reprehensible. However, Richard Constantine is a dangerous criminal who will stop at nothing to achieve his ends, including murder. Don't think for a minute that this is less serious than that." Maggie paused and looked up at her brother. "Damon, get this into your head: Richard Constantine will even destroy Dragonwyck if it becomes necessary, including *anyone* who happens to be in the house at the time."

Damon shook his head. "No, Maggie, you're wrong. He wouldn't. He couldn't."

Grandmother Rathford entered the great hall from the library at that moment. "I didn't mean to eavesdrop, children, but I was just coming to find some matches to light the candles." She approached her grandson. "Damon, she's right. Richard Constantine and Llewellyn must be disconnected in your mind. You must not think of them as one and the same. Richard Constantine is a murderer. He—"

The front door burst open, and Alyssa and Flynn flew into the shadowy great hall, laughing and dripping wet, preceding a tremendous clap of thunder by only seconds. Lightning illuminated the hall before it was plunged into gloomy shadows again.

"Look at us," Alyssa said, shaking the rain from her hair.

"It's a good thing I had Grace bring in your luggage when I saw the storm coming," Grandmother Rathford said. "I've put you in the rose room, Alyssa, at the top of the stairs on the second floor and down three doors on the right. Your suitcase is waiting for you with dry clothes," she added with a smile.

"Dr. Ford, you have the forest room, two doors on the left from Alyssa's. The door should be open, so you'll see your luggage." She turned to Maggie. "When you need your case, dear, it's in the blue room. But I'm sure you have other things on your mind right now. Master Owen, your knapsack is in the room next to Dr. Ford's. Now, I must find the matches and light the candles." She thumped her cane in front of her a couple of times, feeling her way along the dark hall to the sitting room.

"Grandmother thinks of everything," Damon said with a smile. "She can even anticipate the effects of a sudden storm."

"She's a remarkable woman," Maggie murmured.

Flynn and Alyssa were halfway up the stairs when Maggie called after them. "Where's Grandfather?"

Alyssa continued dripping up to her room, hurrying to make herself more presentable for Rolf, but Flynn turned on the stairs. "He stayed in the stable to help rub down the horses. He sent us in to get another assignment and said he'd stay there until the rain let up a little. He said he can't run as fast as we can, and that if the rain doesn't let up soon, Damon could bring out an umbrella and fetch him."

Damon laughed. "I'm sure Grandmother has sent at least one umbrella to the stable already. If he doesn't come in soon, I'll take another and 'fetch' him. In the meantime, Maggie, let's see if we can find what you're looking for in the library tower."

"Do you want me to go to the stable and bring him back?" Rolf asked.

"No. He probably wants to stay out there a bit to keep the horses company," Damon said, leading the way down the hall. "But thanks for offering."

They flashed their lights ahead of them into the library and to the double doors that Maggie had not even noticed when she'd been in the library before. An ornately carved teakwood screen inlaid with mother-of-pearl successfully prevented them from taking a casual glance around the room.

Damon opened the doors wide, and Maggie and Rolf followed him into a large, round room filled with cherry wood filing cabinets, shelves lined with books and folders, and two neat desks placed side by side. Opposite the desks, a reading area with four overstuffed chairs surrounded a substantial coffee table.

"I'll get the plans and you can spread them on that table," Damon said, pulling dowels draped in large papers from a rack beside one of the desks. "There are drawings of each floor and the entire estate, plot by plot."

"I think we can concentrate on the house for now. Let's see the ground floor first." Maggie looked again at her watch. Two thirty. *This had better work,* she thought. *If not, where do we go from here?*

Damon spread a paper three feet long and two feet wide on the table in front of Maggie and Rolf. "This is the library tower," Damon said, pointing to the rounded area midway between the front and back of the house. "You've been in the drawing room, which is on the ground floor in the front of the house."

Maggie ran her finger down the great hall, pinpointing the drawing room and banquet hall opposite the library, and the library tower where they were. On down the hall was Grandmother Rathford's sitting room with the French doors into the garden, as well as an entrance to the visiting families' quarters in the second tower.

"This is where the entrance to the tunnel is?" Maggie asked, pointing to a place that would be under the stairs about midway between the library and the sitting room.

Damon nodded, shining his beam on another room that jutted out from the sitting room. "This new addition is the garden room, with windows on three sides, where we had breakfast this morning. Continuing down this hall, past the garden room, is the kitchen, and beyond that on the left is the ballroom."

Maggie shined her light on a room marked *conservatory*, which was attached to the tower on the left side of the house. Behind it was another larger tower. "This is the king's tower?" Maggie asked.

Damon nodded.

"Which tower did you take us into this morning on our tour?" Maggie asked. "I was totally lost the whole time we were going through the house."

"You saw this smaller front tower that housed the king's entourage. We still use that third tower when it's needed, and it's kept ready for guests."

"Damon, I hate to ask it, but could you please tell me about the accident in the king's tower and why it was closed? I know you said it was a painful memory, but it might help us. It might give us some clue. We only have three and a half hours to stop the destruction of Paris."

Damon stood and walked to the desk. "I don't know why you seem to think you can stop anything, Maggie. Counterterrorist Command and MI5 can't seem to stop this, and neither can any of the other experts in the world—why do you think you're so much smarter than they are?"

"She doesn't think she's smarter. She just thinks she's got an inside track they haven't followed yet." Flynn walked in and sat down in the chair Damon had just abandoned. "What have you got, Maggie girl?"

"Besides a big brother who's reluctant to reveal family secrets, not much. But look at this. Rolf pointed out the king's tower, which is visible from the third floor servants' quarters. No one ever goes there anymore. The servants believe it's haunted. Damon won't divulge the details of the tragic accident that caused Grandmother to lock it up and turn off the power to it. Does that raise your curiosity, or what?"

Flynn raised his eyebrow and looked at Damon. "Absolutely. Can we investigate, Damon? See what's there?"

"I doubt Grandmother will give you the keys," Damon said.

"Then we'd better find out. Time's a-wastin', and if Constantine is here, there's no guarantee he'll stick around to see the results of his handiwork," Flynn said, getting to his feet.

"Wait one minute," Maggie said. "I want a quick look at the other floors in the house so I can get a feel for where everything is. Damon, can I have those layouts?"

Damon pulled a large map from another dowel on the rack and placed it over the first one. "Can you see where things are, or do you want me to point them out?"

Maggie examined the second floor, which was mostly bedrooms and sitting rooms. "Where is the spiral staircase we were on this morning?"

Damon pointed to a circle, which would have been in the vicinity of the kitchen and great hall on the ground floor. "There are two main hallways or corridors. A row of bedrooms in the front of the house has windows—the rooms opposite that hall do not. The little double line here is the narrow secret passage we were in this morning. On the other side of that passage is another row of bedrooms, then this hall, and a fourth row of bedrooms, which look out on the back of the estate."

"Got it," said Maggie. "Can I see the third floor?"

Damon spread that drawing on top of the other two. "Basically like the others."

"The servants' wing encompasses all three floors of this section?" Maggie asked, pointing to the L-shaped wing that ran perpendicular to the rest of the house.

"Right," Damon acknowledged.

"Are all the rooms in the servants' wing occupied?" Maggie asked.

Damon nodded. "For all intents and purposes. There are several families, and they all have nice, roomy quarters. That's their turf, and we don't interfere or poke into their private accommodations."

"Richard Constantine wouldn't go there, would he?" Maggie asked, looking up at Damon, who seemed more and more reluctant to help.

"No. There would really be no place he could hide. The children and grandchildren have free run of that wing, and I'm pretty sure there's no place they don't go."

"Then we're basically left with the family tower and the king's tower." Maggie looked at Flynn. "Ready?"

"Let's do it." Flynn stood and gave Maggie his hand to pull her to her feet.

"Maggie, no. Don't go there." Damon stepped to the door of the library tower, blocking her way back into the library.

# FORTY-THREE

"Damon, it's okay." Mrs. Rathford touched Damon's arm and he whirled around.

"Mother."

"You can't protect him forever—and protecting him won't make him love you. He'll just continue using you, as he's done all these years." Mrs. Rathford took her son by the arm, and they returned to the library. Maggie and Flynn followed. Rolf stayed behind to study the floor plans more carefully.

"The details of the accident aren't important," Mrs. Rathford said, sitting on the love seat and patting the cushion next to her. Damon settled beside his mother but kept his eyes trained on the floor. "Llewellyn conducted an experiment on a beloved pet of Damon's, and the results were tragic. He locked the tower to hide his deed, and no one discovered the results for several of months, at which time the horrible stench led us to close the tower for good."

"Will you give us the key so we may check for ourselves?" Maggie asked.

"I would," Mrs. Rathford said, "but you'll have to ask Grandmother Rathford. She is mistress of Dragonwyck. She must make that decision."

"Thank you." Maggie turned to leave, but turned back again. "How is your husband?"

"Resting quietly for the present. I would have had Damon take him back to the hospital but for the storm. The outcome of tonight . . ." Her voice caught, and she took a minute before she continued. "The outcome of tonight will probably determine whether he lives or dies. I'm afraid he doesn't have any fight left in him."

"I'm so sorry, Mrs. Rathford. We'll do what we can to help."

Maggie and Flynn left the library to find Grandmother Rathford, and Rolf raced after them. "Can Alyssa and I search the family tower while you explore the other one?"

"Please do. I've been so focused on the mysterious king's tower, I hadn't even thought there might be something in the family one," Maggie said.

Alyssa came down the stairs, shining her light in front of her, looking totally refreshed. "Okay, I'm ready for my next assignment."

Grandmother Rathford called to them from the door of her sitting room. "Will you children please come in here? I'm afraid to totter about in the half darkness for fear I'll fall."

The four entered the sitting room, warmly lit by the cheery fire and candles on the mantel and table.

"I know you need to do what must be done. Please forgive a senti-mental old fool, Maggie. No woman wants to believe she has conceived a monster—much less produced two in two generations. I truly didn't know the extent of Llewellyn's wickedness until you came and discov-ered that poor young mother and her children in the tunnel. Then when you found those horrible things in the new tunnel, I had to face the truth."

She pointed at the small polished chest on the mantel. "The keys to the king's tower are there. I believe Llewellyn has, for some time, been using the tower for something. I never wanted to know what. I felt that if he were here, at Dragonwyck, he would be grounded in love and turn from his other pursuits. Apparently I was wrong."

Maggie hurried to the little wooden chest and lifted the lid. "It's empty. There's nothing here."

Grandmother Rathford's hand went to her heart. "Are you sure, child?" she asked, her voice barely a breath.

Maggie picked up the ebony chest and turned it upside down. "There's nothing here."

"Then go quickly to the tower, Maggie, but be very careful. Someone has taken those keys this very day."

"Grandmother, Rolf says there's a tower connected to this room," Alyssa said. "We'd like to search it if we may."

"Go ahead, my dear, but I fear you will find nothing but spider-webs and dust." She pointed to an intricately carved Oriental screen. "The door is behind there. It's not locked."

Maggie and Flynn raced out into the great hall just as Grandfather Rathford blew in the front door with the rain pelting the ancient tiles a full yard into the hall. It was coming down horizontally in sheets, and the wind howled through the house, sending chandeliers rocking on their brass chains.

"'Tis a night fit for neither man nor beast," he said, shaking the rain from the umbrella and struggling to close the door behind him.

"Grandfather, which is the best way to get into the king's tower? From the conservatory or from the third floor?" Maggie called down the hall as she hurried toward him.

His eyes widened then narrowed as he searched Maggie's face. "And what will you be doing in the king's tower?"

"Searching for clues," Maggie explained, then quickly added, "Grandmother is in her sitting room. I think she needs you."

Maggie had turned to look for the conservatory entrance when Grandfather Rathford spoke quietly. "The stairs are better from the third floor. What you seek is probably at the very top of the tower." He suddenly sounded extremely tired, as though the storm had sucked all energy from him. Maggie knew that wasn't it at all.

Flynn had already started up the stairs, and Maggie raced up behind him. "Are you ready to call Inspector McConklin yet?" Flynn asked as they took two stairs at a time.

"No. He'd laugh all the way to London if there wasn't anything up here. I don't need to be the cause of any more jokes. I wonder what he's doing right now. I'm surprised we haven't heard from him since we left him with all that information. Maybe he's just riding out the storm in his nice, cozy, dry office."

"What do you expect to find in the tower, Maggie? Have you thought about it? Have you thought about what you'll do if you open a door and Richard Constantine is sitting there holding a gun on you?"

Maggie stopped at the top of the landing. "No, I haven't thought about what I might find. But I do think he's up there—and we have to stop him."

"How, Maggie?" Flynn persisted. "How are you going to stop a terrorist?"

Damon bounded up the stairs after them. "She won't have to. I will." He held a gun in one hand, which hung at his side. "Let's go. We only have three hours to stop this."

"If we can stop it. Alyssa suggested the bombs may have timers and will explode by themselves at the prescribed time," Maggie said, continuing up the stairs to the third floor.

"You did get the keys from Grandmother, didn't you?" Damon asked. "We can't get in without them."

"We tried, but they were gone," Maggie said.

Damon stopped midstride. "Gone? Where did they go?"

"She didn't know—it may be that Richard Constantine took them," Maggie said, hurrying down the main corridor toward the servant's quarters and the king's tower.

"He's stealthy enough to do it, but I would have supposed that long ago he made his own set of keys so he could come and go at his leisure." Damon remained silent as he kept pace with Flynn and Maggie. "It doesn't make sense. Who would take the keys?"

"Are they always kept in that same little chest on the mantel in the sitting room?" Maggie asked.

"As long as I can remember," Damon said. "We were forbidden to touch them unless Grandmother herself gave them to us to use."

"So you were obedient and didn't touch them," Flynn said, "and Llewellyn flouted authority and had his own set made."

Damon's silence bespoke his agreement.

"Well, if that's the case," Flynn said, "then either Llewellyn has taken them again to prevent our pursuing him, or someone else has beaten us to him."

They reached the end of the corridor and Maggie stopped. There was no door. Damon stepped forward and pulled open the heavy velvet drapes that covered the wall. A gush of moist air assailed them.

"That's why I didn't see a door here when I came up before," Maggie said. "I guess I thought those drapes covered a window."

"No!" Damon exclaimed, sounding like he'd just taken a blow to the midsection and had the air knocked out of him. He flew up the wide circular stone steps, two at a time. Maggie and Flynn raced behind him, confused at Damon's outburst and sudden rush of energy. The door at the top of the stairs stood open, but Damon didn't stop there. He continued through that room to another set of circular steps that led still higher.

Maggie only glanced at the attractive room with modern furnishings, staying as close behind Damon as she could. When they reached the top of the flight of stairs, everyone stopped. The round stone room at the top of the tower was filled with electronic equipment and a bank of phones. A door on the opposite side of the room led outside to a wide terrace surrounded by battlements. The door banged open and shut with the wind. Up here, the full fury of the storm was evident.

Damon ran out into the storm. Maggie and Flynn followed, only to be drenched in an instant. Rain plastered Maggie's hair against her face as the wind tore at her clothes. She brushed the hair from her eyes and gasped at the dreadful scene before her.

Silhouetted against the stormy sky, Llewellyn balanced on the three-foot-high wall of the battlements brandishing a gun in his hand. Mr. Rathford held a gun on him, softly and repeatedly telling him to put down the weapon or he'd be forced to shoot.

When Flynn flashed the light on him, Llewellyn whirled to Maggie. "You! You're the meddler," he shouted, pointing his gun at her. "You caused all this. You should have stayed in America where you belong." As he launched himself to attack Maggie, Damon tackled him. They struggled on the floor, rolling over and over, until Llewellyn flung his brother aside and jumped back on the ledge.

"Llewellyn, come down from there," Mr. Rathford said quietly. "Let's discuss this in a civilized manner."

Alyssa and Rolf crept up the stairs and watched as Llewellyn whirled to face his father. "That was always your answer, Father. 'Let's discuss it,'" he mimicked in a falsetto voice. "There's nothing further to discuss. Grandmother disinherited me, so unless my three siblings suffer an unexpected fatality, I have no chance of inheriting Dragonwyck." Llewellyn stood silent and motionless atop the wall for a moment, fighting to keep his balance in the strong winds.

Maggie held her breath. Flynn moved closer to her side, and Damon inched toward Llewellyn from his position on the floor near the battlement. Mr. Rathford raised his hand as if to help his son down from the ledge, but Llewellyn threw both arms in the air, waving his gun, and shouting, "Dragonwyck is mine. I'm the eldest. It's my birthright. I should be the favored son, not Damon." He snorted in derision and chanted, "Damon the demon! Damon the demon! That's how he's known."

"Thanks to you," Damon said, getting cautiously to his knees. "From the time I could walk, I got blamed for everything you did, for every vicious, malicious, dirty trick you ever played. You spread rumors everywhere we went about your deranged little brother, when you were the deranged one."

"But they still loved you more than me," Llewellyn wailed, sounding like a spoiled child. "Why did they love you more than me?"

Maggie couldn't believe the transformation in Llewellyn from one moment to the next. This side of the polished politician had never appeared in public, she suspected.

"On top of everything else, I think he's got dissociative identity disorder—multiple personalities," Flynn whispered to Maggie.

Mr. Rathford moved slowly toward his eldest adopted son. "You were never loved any less, Llewellyn. You were just so jealous that someone else had come into our family, you couldn't see the truth. Your perception was always wrong—from believing you weren't loved to thinking you could get favorable attention by doing wicked things."

"I didn't do wicked things," Llewellyn whined. "It was Damon. He made it all up." Llewellyn swayed on the wall, shaking his head. "He tried to make you think I did them. I'm a good boy. Mother knows I'm her good boy. Ask Mother. She'll tell you it wasn't me."

Mr. Rathford inched closer, speaking softly to the whimpering man on the wall. "Come down, son, and we'll go talk to your mother."

"Mother always loved me." Abruptly Llewellyn's tone changed to petulant. "Why doesn't Grandmother love me that way? Why can't she see I'm the one who should have Dragonwyck? It's not fair."

"Life isn't fair, or people would have seen through your facade to the real you, not the public face you put on," Damon said. "They wouldn't have endlessly persecuted me for your crimes."

Llewellyn laughed, a horrible, insane sound that sent a shudder through Maggie. "That was so beautiful to see. Poor little demon

Damon. Kicked out of every town we've lived in. Village mothers wouldn't allow their innocent children to play with the village bad boy. Serves you right for all the unhappiness you caused me."

His tone changed again to one that was dark and threatening. "Well, little brother, if I can't have Dragonwyck, no one will get it. I'm leaving here tonight after I watch Paris go up in smoke, and London crumble to the ground, and New York collapse into the East River. By that time, every government in the world will be on their knees, begging me not to destroy their beautiful cities—begging me to take their money."

Mr. Rathford had finally moved close enough to reach out for Llewellyn. Damon, seeing what his father had in mind, crept forward to grab his brother's other leg. Llewellyn, realizing he was about to be snatched from his perch, leaped over them and landed near Maggie and Alyssa, who were watching the volatile man in amazement.

"You thought you could come here with your blue eyes and red hair and take what was mine, my meddling little sisters. I'll have the last laugh. Minutes after I leave here, Dragonwyck will crumble to the ground, and no one can stop it."

"He's absolutely loony," Alyssa whispered. "Totally wacko."

Maggie suddenly had an idea. This man was a polished politician, used to being in the spotlight and having microphones shoved in his face and cameras flashing around him.

"Mr. Constantine, sir," Maggie said, pulling her camera from her pocket and holding it in her hand like a digital recorder. "The press would like a statement from the distinguished gentleman who has so strenuously sought out the kidnappers of Jennie Albright and her children. Can you tell us, sir, how you were able to locate Mrs. Albright and rescue her children from the clutches of those ruthless people?"

The crazed man stopped, confused for a minute about what was happening; then he slicked back his hair and smiled. "Of course. I felt a tremendous sense of compassion for the poor woman and her children, and I put every man on it we could find. We spared no expense in the search and were rewarded by the heroic efforts of our detectives, who relentlessly tracked down the despicable people who perpetrated the crime. We must make our streets and cities safe for our own people, as well as those who come to visit."

Mr. Rathford and Damon slowly moved up behind Richard Constantine and were about to seize him when the cell phone in Llewellyn's pocket rang. "Excuse me, miss. That will be Edward ringing to tell me my helicopter is ready to go rout out the terrorists who have plotted this terrible world situation." He moved with surprising agility, whirling away from his father and brother, and jumped back atop the wall.

At the same instant, the deafening whir of a helicopter drowned out the sound of the storm. Blinding lights illuminated the terrace as the helicopter swooped low over the battlements. Richard grabbed onto the ladder extending from the helicopter and disappeared into the darkness of the storm before anyone could move to stop him.

# FORTY-FOUR

Everyone rushed to the battlements just as a gust of wind caught the chopper, plunging it toward the earth. The pilot recovered control, gained altitude, and brought the chopper around to hover over a car that flashed its lights off and on in quick succession. The rope dropped again and a lone man grabbed hold and climbed into the helicopter.

But the pilot was struggling with the raging wind. He seemed to finally gain control and begin to attain the necessary altitude when another gust of wind slammed it back toward the ground again. Inspector McConklin joined them at the battlements to watch the drama, shaking his head.

"He'll never make it," he predicted. "He can't get over the trees." No sooner were the words out of his mouth than the chopper banked steeply to one side and plunged into the ground. The fiery explosion lit up the night.

McConklin watched with the speechless group until it was apparent there could have been no survivors, then spoke into his phone to his men on the ground. "I think Murphy just got on board that chopper. Check out that car and let me know. And stay with the chopper in case there were any survivors."

Flynn led Maggie back inside the control room right behind Damon and Mr. Rathford. What could she say to them at such a time? What consolation could she offer? She stood helpless as they looked around the room filled with electronics they hadn't known were there.

"I'm so sorry it had to end this way," Maggie said softly, reaching out to touch their arms as they stood. Damon simply nodded. No one spoke for what seemed an eternity, then Damon took his father by the arm and led him toward the circular stairs. Rolf and Alyssa silently joined them, and McConklin brought up the rear, shutting the door to keep out the storm.

"And so ends the illustrious career of the honorable Richard Constantine," Inspector McConklin said as they reached the door. "That's the information the press will be given. That's what my report will say. Dragonwyck's name will never be mentioned, nor Llewellyn Rathford's. I believe he died some time ago, didn't he?"

Mr. Rathford paused at the door and glanced back over his shoulder, nodded slightly, acknowledging the inspector's comment, and allowed Damon to lead him down the stairs.

Only then did Constantine's last words penetrate Maggie's preoccupied mind. She whirled around. "Inspector, what about his threat to blow up Dragonwyck?"

"We've been busy in the tunnel since you gave me those photos. We've determined there are no explosives set to detonate—everything we've discovered was designated for London. At least, that's what my men have found so far. They're still searching with a dog trained to sniff out explosives, just in case we missed another room off the tunnel."

One of McConklin's men entered the control room. "You needed me up here, Inspector?"

"Yes, Abernathy. These helpful people are just leaving, and you're going to disconnect everything in here that's connected to anything else. Be on the lookout for booby traps. Constantine seemed to have a backup for everything, so be sure there are no remote-controlled devices. Oh, and bring the dog up to sniff the room. We don't want the place blown up while we're searching it." Inspector McConklin turned and flashed a smile at Maggie. "Nor afterward, either. Right, Miss McKenzie?"

Inspector McConklin's light comment relieved the uncomfortable tension in the room, and everyone relaxed a bit.

Maggie laughed. "Right, Inspector. We really would like to preserve Dragonwyck, and everyone here. And we can take the hint. We're leaving it all in your very able hands now, and we'll get out of your way."

As they left, Flynn looked at Maggie. "What was that crazy stunt you pulled with the mock microphone?"

"I suddenly remembered this man had another life—one where he was constantly before microphones and in front of cameras—like a split personality. I decided I needed to see if I could reach the distinguished government official and get him away from the outraged child he was acting like. You said he had multiple personalities, and that gave me the idea."

"Good thinking," Flynn praised. "It worked."

"And now we know what happened to the key," Maggie said. "Mr. Rathford took it and opened the door to come up here and deal with his wayward son himself, so no one else would have to do it. When Damon saw the door open, he must have guessed what had happened. That's why he raced up the stairs so fast—to help his father."

Alyssa grabbed Maggie's arm. "Let's get out of these dripping clothes. You can answer questions later. I'm soaked to the skin again."

Maggie allowed Alyssa to lead her out of the control room and down the stairs, though she would have preferred to stay and see what Abernathy found—or didn't find.

"I thought you two were in the other tower," Maggie said to Rolf as they descended several steps behind Damon and Mr. Rathford.

Rolf laughed. "We were, but about halfway up those cobweb-filled, dusty, tiresome stairs, Alyssa got a 'twin impression,' and we hurried over to see what you'd found."

When they reached the foot of that flight of circular stairs, they stopped to examine the incredible tower room. "Wow," Alyssa said. "How did he get all this stuff up here without anyone knowing?"

Very tastefully decorated, it was the ultimate gentleman's sitting room/bedroom. Decorated in tones of gray to black with touches of red, it was not only stylish but afforded every comfort from a wide-screen TV to a king-sized bed and reading area next to the fireplace.

"Well, he certainly didn't bring it up the circular staircase," Maggie said.

"I'm betting he lowered it all from a helicopter," Inspector McConklin offered from the stairs. "I think if you'll inquire, you'll learn that on many festival days everyone in the household went to the village or to town to celebrate, and on Sunday everyone would be in church. That would give him ample opportunity to drop a piece of furniture on that nice wide ledge where you all were getting soaked by the storm a few minutes ago."

"So this is where he hid out when he wanted solitude," Rolf said, checking out the wide-screen TV. "Very nice."

Flynn nodded. "All he had to do was helicopter to his little ravine, hop on his bike or scooter, travel across the field to the tunnel, and go through it to the secret passageway. He could come and go as he wished and stay as long as he pleased."

"It was a bike," Inspector McConklin said, descending the rest of the stairs and joining them in the modern room. "We found it in the tunnel in a niche he had carved out especially for the bike. It was on an angle with the passageway, so it wasn't easily visible."

"Like the decoy tunnel that Llewellyn extended to the river," Maggie said. "If I hadn't been taking a picture of something on the wall, I never would have seen it."

"Richard Constantine," corrected Alyssa. "Not Llewellyn."

"Right," Maggie said. "We'd better go to Grandmother and Grandfather Rathford and our aunt and uncle. I imagine this is going to be pretty traumatic for them."

"Hopefully not as much as you're thinking," Inspector McConklin said. "If you'll come with me down to talk to the family, I'll explain it to everyone at once."

Everyone hurried down the ancient circular stone stairs, following Inspector McConklin into the third-floor corridor and down to the library. Damon was just escorting his stricken father slowly into the library as they reached the first floor.

Mrs. Rathford rushed to help Damon seat Mr. Rathford on the sofa, and they settled on either side of him. Grandfather and Grandmother Rathford were huddled close together on the love seat, looking weary and worried.

Maggie and Flynn stood on one side of the door, and Rolf and Alyssa huddled on the other side, reluctant to intrude further on this private family moment. Inspector McConklin quietly offered his condolences for the loss of a son, grandson, and brother.

"I understand your son Llewellyn has been dead for some time, but I was only made aware of it today. I'm also sorry to tell you that some terrorists have been killed in a helicopter crash on your estate. I'll have my men remove the bodies as soon as possible."

Maggie watched the expressions of the family as they received the news. As the full import of McConklin's words registered, relief replaced the fear in their faces, though Maggie knew the anguish could not be assuaged so easily.

Inspector McConklin continued. "Since this terrorist business is a matter of national security, today's events will go into a file for the prime minister's eyes only, and then the report will be filed in the most secure location—possibly even destroyed. No mention of Llewellyn Rathford or Dragonwyck will ever be made in connection with this matter."

"Can you do that?" Maggie asked, both pleased and a little shocked at the notion.

"Of course," the inspector said, smiling at Maggie's expression. "In matters of national security, I have that prerogative. I will direct that it happens that way."

"What about all the men who've been searching the tunnels?" Maggie asked. "How can you guarantee they won't let slip what they've seen and done here today?"

"Sergeant Murphy was the only person who actually knew that Llewellyn Rathford and Richard Constantine were one and the same man. I believe he was the last man to board that helicopter. The rest of my men will be placed under oath to not speak of any of the activities of this case, because it is an ongoing investigation into terrorism against the British government. Of course, there cannot be a one-hundred-percent guarantee that the name Dragonwyck will not be breathed in confidence sometime, somewhere, but the family integrity and honor should be safe from public taint of any kind."

Inspector McConklin directed his attention to Grandfather Rathford. "I assume you have a family cemetery on the estate."

Grandfather nodded. "Yes, it's just beyond the fence near that copse of trees." He pointed to the opposite side of the house from the stables and garden, an area Maggie had not seen. She guessed it was probably visible from the family tower off Grandmother Rathford's sitting room.

"You have a decision to make right now. You can have a private ceremony and bury an empty coffin in your family plot, and we'll take

Richard Constantine's body away—or what's left of it—or you can have a very quick, very private ceremony with just the people in this room with whatever remains we recover from the helicopter."

A heavy silence fell on the room. Everyone seemed to be waiting for someone else to make the decision. Maggie expected Grandmother Rathford to take charge and speak for the family, but it was Mrs. Rathford who broke the silence.

"My heart is torn. Of course I would prefer Llewellyn be interred with the rest of the family, but somewhere through the past few years, our eldest son disappeared and someone else appeared in his place." She looked around the room at the family. "If you all approve, I would like a simple stone erected with his name and nothing more—not even dates. I think it would be appropriate to have it placed at a time when no servants are on the premises—we don't need to call attention to it, but he should not be totally forgotten."

A quiet murmur of approval swept the library, and Grandmother Rathford looked at Inspector McConklin. "You may dispose of the body of Richard Constantine as you see fit, Inspector. We will grieve for Llewellyn privately. Thank you for being so considerate."

"Just to tie up all the loose ends for the press and other inanely curious souls, an announcement will be made that a helicopter crash occurred in the storm tonight. Richard Constantine, Detective Sergeant Murphy, and Edward Thompson were killed in Constantine's private helicopter while following a lead in the current terrorist threat against Great Britain. I think it is fitting that Constantine and Thompson's plan was carried out. The only three people in the world outside of this room with the knowledge of Constantine's former identity have taken that knowledge to their graves."

He looked back at Maggie. "Have I covered everything to your satisfaction, Miss McKenzie?"

Maggie blushed and laughed. "If I think of anything else, I'll let you know, Inspector."

"I'm sure you'll do that, Miss McKenzie, and our thanks to you for your vivid, overactive imagination and your tenacity that helped bring this to a satisfactory conclusion. If you ever want to change careers, let me know." DCI Alistair McConklin winked at Maggie.

He turned back to the three generations of Rathfords, who seemed overwhelmed by the day's events. "I'll be in the tunnels for a while securing that area, and I have a man in the tower finishing up there. We should be gone within a few hours, but I hope you'll bear with us while we make sure we've discovered everything." He nodded at the four standing near the door and turned to return to the tunnel.

Maggie grasped his arm. "Inspector, how can you be sure there will be no explosions in the other cities he talked about? What if they keep to the schedule he announced, even after his death, and blow up all those beautiful places?"

"Good question, Miss McKenzie, but our profiler has suggested that he was a very controlling, hands-on type personality, and from what we saw upstairs, with a phone to each of the cities, and a specially designated line to reach each of the world leaders in question, we're pretty sure he planned to give the go ahead personally. We are tracing each of those numbers and anticipate apprehending those on the other end within the hour. Anything else?"

Maggie shook her head. "Thanks. I think that covers it." She suddenly realized she was shivering with cold. "I guess it's time to get changed out of these wet clothes."

"That can wait for just a minute." Flynn grabbed Maggie's hand and pulled her out of the library and down the hall to the drawing room.

* * *

Alyssa and Rolf looked at each other and quietly followed them down the hall. "You aren't going to spy on them, are you?" Rolf whispered.

"Absolutely," Alyssa whispered back with an impish smile.

# FORTY-FIVE

Flynn stepped into the drawing room and stopped, taking both of Maggie's hands in his. "Maggie, I was terrified I was going to lose you up on that tower ledge when that madman came at you. I couldn't live with . . ." He stopped, took a deep breath, and backtracked.

"I guess I need to ask you a question before I go any further. Have you found someone you want to spend the rest of your life with?" He held his breath, waiting for her reply.

Maggie looked into Flynn's eyes and answered softly with a single word. "Yes."

Flynn visibly flinched. He didn't know what to say—didn't know how to continue.

Maggie filled the void. "Have you found someone you'd like to spend—" Maggie paused before she finished her question—"*eternity* with?"

Flynn looked puzzled for a minute, then he laughed. "You were teasing me, Maggie McKenzie." His voice became soft and apologetic. "I'm sorry. It wasn't fair of me to keep you in the dark this way. I know I said I'd give you my answer at Christmastime and that we could take this year to make sure of our feelings for each other, but then I showed up early, and the time never seemed right." He reached up and caressed her cheek. "I'm sure of my feelings now." He laughed softly. "Am I ever sure!"

\* \* \*

Maggie's heart stood still, and she held her breath, waiting for him to speak the words she'd hoped to hear for seven long months.

"I don't have to wait another four months," Flynn continued. "I love you—I want to spend all eternity with you. I've had all my questions answered, I've been studying, and I've already been baptized, so if you'll have me, we can be married on Valentine's Day next year, or whatever day you choose—in the temple of your choice."

Maggie stared at him. "You were baptized last February? And you never told me?" She wanted to hit him. No, she wanted to kiss him.

"I needed to give you time to see if you'd find someone else. I didn't want you to think you had to marry me just because I joined the Church." He shook his head. "I didn't do it for you. I did it for me. I finally discovered what I'd needed all those years, and I've found peace with myself."

They stood, just looking at each other, until Maggie reached out and touched Flynn's cheek. "I'm glad. And, yes, I want to marry you! That's all I've wanted for the last seven months!"

Flynn wrapped Maggie in his arms and kissed her. "And that, Maggie girl, is what I've wanted to do for the last seven months."

Alyssa squealed in delight and ran into the drawing room to throw her arms around Flynn and Maggie. Rolf followed close on her heels with a big grin on his face.

"It's about time," Alyssa said. "I'm so happy for you both." She released them from her hug, and Maggie and Flynn stepped apart. "Can I just call you Flynn now that you're going to be my brother-in-law?" she asked.

Flynn assured her that would be appropriate.

"Good," Alyssa said. "Dr. Ford is way too formal. And by the way, I can't think of anyone I'd rather have for a brother-in-law."

"That's a good thing," Maggie said, "because he's the only one you're ever going to get."

"So when will this take place?" Rolf said, kissing Maggie's cheek and reaching to shake Flynn's hand.

Flynn grinned. "Maggie hasn't chosen the date yet, because, as you know, she's only known for a minute herself. It can be anytime after next Valentine's Day."

Damon entered the drawing room to see what the commotion was about and caught the gist of the conversation. He offered his hand to Flynn and kissed Maggie on the cheek. "My congratulations and best wishes to you both. Is there a possibility you'll come back and see us on your honeymoon?"

Maggie laughed. "We haven't had time to discuss anything other than that we are definitely getting married. When, where, and everything else is yet to be decided. Maybe you can come to the States for the reception and meet your birth mother and my family."

"That would be strange for me, seeing my birth mother," Damon said quietly.

Maggie put her hand on her brother's arm. "I can totally empathize with you. I have a mother I've known all my life, so I can only call Lily by her given name. I can't call her mother. I'm sure she won't expect you to, either." She stopped. "Are you okay, Damon? It must have been really traumatic for you up in the tower tonight."

"I'm fine," Damon said. "Of course, I have mixed emotions—relief that the nightmare is finally over and that I'll no longer be blamed for Llewellyn's evil actions, but he was my brother, after all—my only brother."

"Not that we could substitute, but you do have two sisters now," Alyssa reminded him.

Damon smiled. "Yes, I do, and I'm more than a little happy about that, Alyssa."

"How is your father?" Maggie asked. "Will he be okay?"

"Surprisingly, he seems a little stronger than this morning," Damon said. "Knowing that MI5 will do everything in their power to keep Dragonwyck and the Rathford family name free from scandal was like a dose of strong medicine to him."

"What about your mother?" Flynn asked. "It's very traumatic to lose a son."

"As Mother said earlier, she had lost him a long time ago. The fear that he was going to harm so many people was destroying her. Like Father, she had mourned for him before. This is an anticlimax to his previous death—the death of the person they had known and loved."

"A very wise way to look at it," Flynn acknowledged.

"What about Grandmother and Grandfather Rathford?" Alyssa asked. "How are they doing?"

"Shaken, of course," Damon said. "Grandmother knew he was doing unethical things, probably even illegal things, but she had no idea of the scope of his activities. This has been more of a shock for them than for Mother and Father. And speaking of Grandmother, she asked me to bring you back into the library when you were through with your conversation. I think she may have guessed the topic you were discussing."

Damon led the four back into the library. Grandmother Rathford fluttered her long, slender fingers, motioning for Maggie and Alyssa to come to her. "I have something for you girls." She brought a lace-edged handkerchief from her pocket and spread it on her lap. Two rings sparkled in the light from a dozen candles.

"Here, Maggie. I think this one suits you," the old woman said. "Let me see it on your hand."

Maggie knelt in front of her grandmother and gasped when she saw the large blue star sapphire surrounded by sparkling white diamonds. Grandmother Rathford slipped it on her finger. It fit perfectly.

"This belonged to your great-great-great-grandmother. It was a gift from her fiancé on their engagement, so I thought it fitting that you should receive it today, as I could tell that there would be an announcement of an impending wedding before long. This ring has been in the Rathford family for generations."

Maggie kissed her cheek. "Thank you so much. I'll treasure this forever." She looked up into the woman's smiling eyes. "How did you know?"

She patted Maggie's hand. "You and Dr. Ford were probably the only ones who weren't completely aware of one another's feelings."

She turned to Alyssa. "For you, dear, I thought this pink diamond might be of special significance. Diamonds are forged under great pressure and heat, in the furnace of affliction, so to speak. You have been there and survived, much like this very precious stone. This was the wedding ring of my great-great-grandmother. I'm sure your young man will want to choose one for you himself someday, but I hope you treasure this as much as the newer one."

Alyssa bent down to her grandmother on the love seat and hugged her. "Thank you. It will be one of my greatest treasures."

Grandmother continued. "Now, my granddaughters, you have a part of Dragonwyck to take with you, and you must remember that you will always be a part of Dragonwyck. I'm sure this whole family will be happy to have you come and stay as long and as often as you can."

While the girls thanked their grandmother for her wonderful generosity, Damon observed, "I believe that means that she is expecting to see you on your honeymoon, Maggie." He turned to Alyssa. "And do I understand that you may be planning to stay with us for a while?"

Alyssa stood next to Grandmother Rathford, holding her hand. "Yes, I'm going to send for Mother to come, too. Grandmother has indicated she wants to meet Lily, and I'm sure Lily would love to meet you all, though if you're not ready, Damon, I'm sure she'll understand. But I won't be going anywhere for a little while, at least."

Rolf cleared his throat. "If I have anything to say about it, she won't be going back to California for a very long time."

Alyssa blushed and reached for Rolf's hand. "We'll see, won't we?"

# ABOUT THE AUTHOR

Lynn Gardner is an avid storyteller who does careful research to back up the high-adventure, fast-paced romantic thrillers that have made her a popular writer in the LDS market. She loves weaving historical facts and authentic locations into exciting stories with intriguing fictional characters.

Born and raised in Idaho, Lynn has lived all over the United States, served a mission in Armenia with her husband, and now resides in Southern California. She enjoys golfing with her husband of fifty years, traveling, researching family history, and spoiling her grandchildren.